ONCE UPON A TIME

ONCE UPON A TIME
A TREASURY OF MODERN FAIRY TALES

EDITED BY LESTER DEL REY AND RISA KESSLER
ILLUSTRATED BY MICHAEL PANGRAZIO

A Del Rey Book

BALLANTINE BOOKS • NEW YORK

Once upon a time: a treasury of modern fairy tales / edited by Lester del Rey and Risa
Kessler; illustrated by Michael Pangrazio.
p. cm.
Summary: A collection of original fairy tales by ten science fiction and fantasy writers, in-
cluding Isaac Asimov, Lester del Rey, and Anne McCaffrey.
ISBN 0-345-36263-2
1. Fantastic fiction, American. 2. Fairy tales—United States.
[1. Fairy tales. 2. Fantasy. 3. Short stories.] I. Del Rey,
Lester, 1915- .
II. Kessler, Risa. III. Pangrazio, Michael, ill.
PS648.F3053 1991
813′.087608—dc20   91-91885
                                                                  CIP

Text design by Alex Jay/Studio J

Manufactured in the United States of America

First Edition: 1991

10 9 8 7 6 5 4 3 2 1

TABLE OF CONTENTS

CONTENTS

FOREWORD

O NCE UPON A TIME . . ."

Those words are engraved above the gate to a land where magic still works and where all the creatures from our ancient myths still abound: dragons with fiery breaths, unicorns, grandmother-eating wolves, elves, witches, dwarfs, princes who are always noble, and princesses who are invariably beautiful and good.

The tales from that land are the classic fairy tales, beloved of millions of young readers and listeners. Adults remember them fondly, but seem to feel that they should be put aside with the toys of childhood.

Yet the gate to fairyland should never be closed to anyone because of age and adulthood. So to open it wide in welcome, we have decided to assemble this book. In it we have collected stories by writers of highly sophisticated skill, but with the sense of wonder and the love of myths and magic that were found in the classic fairy stories—truly modern fairy tales meant for mature, adult readers.

So how do these stories differ from the childhood classics? Not in spirit, most certainly. But in the method and purpose of their creation, they do differ a great deal, aside from the intended age of their readers.

Modern fiction is *written* to be read, not *told*, as was the older form. The difference is a major one, as one of the editors of this book learned by experience. He is the author of numerous published stories and has also enjoyed telling many stories orally, including a series of annual Christmas stories on a New York City radio station.

A written story is expected to develop its characters in depth and surround the basic events with many details to give it color and make it seem real. But a story to be told has no time for such frills if it is to hold its audience. The characters must often be nothing more than names with little characterization, and the basic events must stand on their own. The story is the thing.

The classic fairy tale was never written down, at least not until much later. It was passed orally from one generation to the next. Such tales were told by grandmothers around the fireplaces of rude peasant huts in the evening when the work was over, or by servants to the children of the nobility.

Most of the tale spinners could not read. But like many illiterate people of old, they had excellent memories, and their minds were uncluttered by the fiction found in books, movies, and television. The stories evolved very slowly, but with little change from generation to generation.

The lives of those who told the stories and those who listened were usually hard, filled with endless toil and trouble. There were still wild forests, and some of those who ventured there were never seen again. Dangerous beasts prowled many areas of the land. And there was still a belief in such things as witches and evil spells. Electricity had not been thought of, and the nights were dark and fearsome. Few could afford much use of candles, so people huddled around the fireplaces after the short days of winter or hastened to bed after work during the longer days of summer.

It's small wonder that many of the stories dealt with peril and horror. The marvel is that a thread of hope and beauty still appear in some tales, perhaps reflecting the yearning of the tale spinners.

The characters in those old tales were usually stereotypes. Stepmothers were evil, witches kept ovens hot for young children, and princes and princesses were always too good for words. Well, why not? The tellers of the tales had very little experience to draw on to enrich the characters. Most had never been as much as five miles from their homes, except perhaps to visit some crude, small fair not much farther away. They could hardly get to know the royalty that squeezed the pittance of their taxes from them. To the peasant, such noble beings were hardly human.

But they clutched the wonder and delight of fairy tales to their hearts and never forgot them.

Later, the Brothers Grimm collected many of the tales from peasant women and wrote them down for future generations. Other writers (most notably Hans Christian Andersen) created their own, obviously strongly influenced by the older tales.

The tales are not forgotten. The love of magic and the old myths are still with us, deeply etched into the most modern languages.

Modern writers are still carrying on the ancient task of preserving the magic and myths, but their stories are now written to be read and done with skills unknown of old. And readers are still reading and buying their fantasy novels, sometimes hundreds of thousands of copies of such a novel.

When we decided to do this book, we called upon the best of these fantasy writers. We told them we wanted real fairy stories, written for sophisticated modern readers.

Almost unanimously, they jumped at the chance. (Isaac Asimov, not usually considered a fantasy writer—so far as we can remember, he only wrote one previous fantasy, and that not a fairy tale—almost drooled at the opportunity. His story is included here—a real fairy story, but with his own slant, of course.)

These are stories by successful writers of adult fiction. But the ancient magic of the old classic fairy tale still sounds loud and clear. The spirit of the ancient stories is still very much with us.

We enjoyed every one. And we hope and believe that others will enjoy them as much as we did.

LESTER DEL REY
RISA KESSLER

ix

PRINCE DELIGHTFUL
AND THE
FLAMELESS DRAGON

ISAAC ASIMOV

KING MARCUS AND HIS COMfortable consort, Queen Ermentrude, were going to have a baby. At least the Queen was, but the King was a very interested bystander. They were both in their late thirties and had more or less given up hope of having one, and had even discussed adoption, but had to give that up, too, when it turned out that no foundlings of royal birth were available. Of course, anything less than royal birth was unthinkable.

But then, as so often happens, just talking about adoption resulted in a physiological stirring and before you could count the taxes wrung out of ten peasants, the Queen was whispering the glad tidings to the King. His eyes opened wide and he said, "Now how on Earth did that happen?" and the Queen said, rather tartly, that if he didn't know, no one did.

As the time approached (and for some reason no one can understand, it takes a Queen just as long to have a baby once it gets started as it would a milkmaid) the problem of the christening arose.

The Queen, who was feeling very uncomfortable by now and was wishing it was all over, said, "I do hope it will be a boy and that he will have all the characteristics expected of a respectable prince, because, my dear, I really don't think I can go through this a second time."

"We will make sure, my royal love. We will invite every fairy in the kingdom to the christening and, of course, they will ensure that he will be brave, handsome and everything else that is good and wonderful."

"Are you sure?" said Queen Ermentrude. "I was speaking to the sorcerer yesterday and *he* said that actually it is all a matter of genes."

King Marcus frowned. "Do you mean a child of mine will have to wear barbarian pantaloons?"

"No, dear, not jeans. *Genes.* They're pronounced the same but if you listen closely you will hear that it isn't a 'j', but a soft 'g'."

"What are soft-g genes?"

"I don't know, but we all have them, you see."

"Well," said the King, quite irritated, "I don't believe in this superstitious nonsense of having something we don't know or understand. We know and understand these fairy godmothers and that's what it's going to be."

"Very well, my dear," said the Queen, "but I hope you don't leave one out."

The King laughed. "Do you think I'm crazy?"

Both Marcus and Ermentrude had heard many stories of fairy godmothers not being invited to christenings. Invariably, they turned out to be particularly malevolent and, of course, they would show up anyway and make life very hard for the poor infant. You would think royalty would know better than to omit a malevolent fairy, but it happened amazingly often.

This was not going to happen to King Marcus and Queen Ermentrude, however. They consulted the Fairy Directory and made certain that the royal scribe indited an invitation to each and every one.

And that was a mistake, for it meant that an invitation went out to the fairy, Misaprop, and if the royal couple had known just a little more about it, they would certainly have omitted her. To be sure, she was the nicest and sweetest fairy godmother anyone could imagine, so that leaving her out would not have disturbed her at all. And if she were invited, she was the life and soul of the party, always laughing, always telling jokes, always singing songs. You might wonder therefore what could possibly be wrong either way. Well, once she attended a christening, she *would* insist on giving the baby a present, and that's where the trouble came in.

She didn't mean to do it, you know, but she *always* managed to get the spell wrong.

And that's the way it was. Fairy after fairy approached the crib in which the new young prince was lying. (It was indeed a prince and after he was born, Queen Ermentrude said very plainly—once she managed to get her breath back—that there would be no more.) One after another bestowed gifts on him—charm, a stately carriage, a luminous intelligence, a sense of humor, and so on and so on.

And then along came the fairy, Misaprop, and waved her wand over him and said the mystic words that would make him the most graceful prince who ever lived.

— The only thing was that she dropped her wand just before she got to the crib, and she was so flustered (heaven only knows why, for she was always dropping her wand) that she picked it up by the wrong end, and you know what that means.

One of the other fairies stepped forward and said, "Misaprop, dear, you're holding your wand—" but it was too late. Misaprop had pronounced the spell, waving the butt of the wand over the baby prince's dear little head and, of course, a characteristic that was precisely the opposite of what Misaprop intended flowed out over that head like a drunken halo.

It didn't take the royal parents long to find out that something had gone wrong. The Prince was three years old before he could walk more than two cubits without falling down. He couldn't pick up anything at all without dropping it a few times first. And he was always in the way. The royal butler was forever tripping over him and always did so when he was carrying the best wine. The little Prince just never got it through his head that he ought to get out of the way of people.

No one ever lost their temper with him, though, because he had all the gifts that the other fairies had given him. He was of a sunny temperament, understood what everyone said to him, was obedient, clever, sweet and all that was delightful—except for his gracelessness.

It's not surprising, then, that he had been named Prince Delightful by his delighted parents, and that's what he was to everyone. Even while he was breaking every priceless piece of crockery that he could place his hands on, everyone found him delightful.

The fairy, Misaprop, was consulted, you may be sure, and the Queen asked very politely (one must always be polite to a fairy as some of them are dreadfully short-tempered) what had gone wrong.

Misaprop turned quite red and said, "There, now, I must have managed to get the wrong end of the wand in my hand."

"Well, then, dear," said Queen Ermentrude, coaxingly, "can't you put the right end of the wand in your hand and try again?"

"I'd love to," said Misaprop. "I would do it at once, but it is quite against the fairy rules to try to cancel one's own spell after it has been made in good faith."

"If you don't," said the Queen, "you will leave us in a dreadful position."

"If I do," said Misaprop, "I will be expelled from the Fairies Union," and of course there was no answer to that.

Things continued to get worse. When Prince Delightful was thirteen, he was placed in the hands of a dancing master, for one of the prime duties of a prince was to attend the royal balls. There he would be expected to dance with the ladies of the court and to be perfect at gavottes, minuets, and all the other latest steps.

It was just hopeless. Prince Delightful would have been better off dancing on his hands. Whenever he was expected to extend his right foot, he would extend his left and vice versa. Whenever he bowed, his head would hit that of his partner. When he whirled, he invariably staggered into someone else. And he simply could not keep time.

The dancing masters, fearing to offend a royal personage, invariably told the Prince's parents that he danced like an angel, but of course, they could see he danced precisely as if he were a tipsy sailor.

It was even worse when he had to learn to handle arms. At sword play, the cleverest footwork of an opponent could not prevent him from striking the Prince with his épée. At wrestling, even when his opponent tried manfully to hold him upright, Prince Delightful managed to step on his shoelaces and fall down.

King Marcus was quite in despair. "My dear," he said to Queen Ermentrude, "our beloved son, Prince Delightful, will be twenty tomorrow, but we can't give a ball to celebrate it, because he can't dance. We can't hold a tournament because he can't fight. Indeed, I don't even dare hold a procession for he is liable to fall down."

"He might ride a horse," said Queen Ermentrude, doubtfully.

"You do well to say that doubtfully, my dear, for you must have seen him on a horse."

"I have," admitted the Queen.

"You know that he jounces up and down, in no way keeping time with the horse's natural movements."

The Queen sighed. "What are we to do?"

"What can we do? We must send him out to seek his fortune."

"Oh, no," said the Queen. "Not our only son."

"What do you mean, not our only son. The usual practice, I've always understood, is for kings to have three sons, and to send out all three, one after the other. We'll be sending out only one—because you always refused to have any more."

The Queen burst into tears at once. "That's a cruel thing to say," she said. "You wouldn't say it if *you* had to have them. I'd like to see you have a baby, if you think it's so much fun. I'd like to see any man—"

King Marcus said, hastily, "Now don't weep, my dear. That was thoughtless of me and I didn't mean it. But just the same, we do have to send out Delightful. It's customary."

"He'll get hurt. He can't help it. He's just not graceful, because that stupid Misaprop—"

"Quiet," said the King, quickly, "she might be flying about, invisibly, and she might hear you. Besides even if Delightful is graceless, he has all the other virtues, and they may suffice. He may go out and slay a dragon and marry a beautiful princess; then defeat an enemy army for his father-in-law and gain that kingdom as well as ours. He'll become a great king and conqueror. If you read history, you'd see that it happens all the time."

"But where will all this take place? There are no dragons about here that I know of. There haven't been for years."

"Of course not. Princes have been very busy slaying them so that dragons are now an endangered species. In fact, there's some talk of having all the kingdoms get together and forbid any further killing of dragons."

"That will be a fine thing for virgins," said the Queen indignantly. "That's all they eat."

"I know. The Virgins' Union is fighting the movement vigorously. I understand they are sending out appeals for funds under the slogan, 'Would you rather have a dragon or a virgin at your beck and call?' I suppose princes can slay basilisks, chimeras and hydras instead, but those are all endangered species, too. We live in hard times—just the same there's hope. I've had the sorcerer check the want ads in the *Dragon-Slayers Gazette*. The kingdom of Poictesme has a dragon they want slain, and the advertisement includes a miniature of his daughter. She seems quite beautiful but the dragon is apparently a large brute and the princes are rather shying away from the task."

"If he's a large brute then I *certainly* won't think of allowing Delightful to risk his life—"

"But, my dear, I've already consulted Delightful. Graceless he may be but he is as brave as a lion—a large-sized one, too—and he was very impressed by the measurements of the young lady, something the King of Poictesme had thoughtfully included in his ad."

"I'll just never see him again," wailed the Queen. "And I'm sure that hussy of a princess has silicone implants."

Still, though queens may weep, princes must do their duty.

The Prince packed his saddlebags, took an ample supply of gold pieces, studied the route to Poictesme on the map that the sorcerer had supplied, one that showed all the major highways. He took a pair of twelve-foot lances with him, and his trusty sword, and a suit of armor that the sorcerer said was light and would not rust, since it was formed of a magic metal named aluminum.

He took off, and the King and Queen waved at him for as long as they could see him. There were quite a few bystanders along the road, too, to cheer their Prince and to make an occasional bet as to whether he would fall off his horse while he was still in eyeshot. —He did, once or twice.

It took Delightful the standard time to make the trip from his father's kingdom to Poictesme—a year and a day.

Actually that was the time it took to reach the palace of King Faraday of Poictesme. He had reached the border of the kingdom some weeks earlier.

He was met by an old chamberlain who studied his ID card most carefully, looked up the location of his kingdom in a well-thumbed atlas and called up the Prince's Register for a credit rating. It all seemed to go well for the chamberlain nodded sourly and said, "You seem to be okay."

"Fine," said Prince Delightful, stumbling over a small projection on the smooth floor. "Do I take a number?"

"A number? Why do you want a number, Highness?"

"So I'll know my turn—when I may ride out to slay the dragon."

"Oh, you may do that any time. You're the only foreign prince on the premises at the moment. We've had quite a shortage."

"A deadly dragon, eh?"

"Who can say? The poltroons barely come within sight when they turn and leave hastily. Not one has had the decency to get himself killed before leaving."

The Prince clicked his tongue. It always depressed him to be made aware of the decay of good manners. "It will be different with me. I shall pause only to meet the King and obtain his blessing and to take a gander at—to greet the gracious Princess. What's her name, by the way? It wasn't included in the advertisement."

"Laurelene, Highness."

"To greet the gracious Princess Laurelene. Is my future mother-in-law, the Queen, alive?"

"Yes, but she has retired to a nunnery."

"Ah, that's probably good all around, except perhaps for the nunnery."

"The nunnery has indeed been complaining, Highness."

King Faraday greeted Prince Delightful with the deepest skepticism, especially after the Prince had leaned on his spear, allowing it to slip out from under him.

"Are you sure you know how to kill a dragon?" asked the King.

"With this spear," said Prince Delightful, flourishing it a little over-enthusiastically, so that it flew out the window breaking a stained-glass panel.

"It goes by itself, I see," said King Faraday, with another dose of skepticism, and sent a menial out after it.

Princess Laurelene absorbed Prince Delightful's looks and muscles and smiled most fetchingly. "Just don't get killed yourself, Prince, while you're slaying the dragon," she said. "You'd be no good to me dead."

"You're the best reason I have ever met for staying alive," said Prince Delightful, flourishing his hat as he bowed and catching its feather in the King's eye.

The next morning, he received directions from King Faraday's sorcerer, who also had a map. He then set out, waving jauntily at the King and his daughter.

The King waved back and said, morosely, "He *may* kill the dragon with his self-flying spear, or with his even more deadly hat."

"Think, Father," said Laurelene, who was as beautiful as the day and who had long blond hair that she barely had to touch up, "if he slays the dragon, all the virgins in the kingdom will be safe once more."

"And you, in addition," said King Faraday.

Whereupon Laurelene, with a roguish smile, said, "Now Father, what would Prince Delightful think if he heard you say that?" and she stamped on the old man's foot.

Prince Delightful followed the indicated course for a week and a day and found himself in the depths of a dark forest.

He began to suspect he might be in the vicinity of the dragon, when his horse's ears began to prick upward and his horse's nostrils flared.

His own ears began to prick upward as he heard the sound of rusty snoring, precisely like the sound described in his *Dragon-Hunter's Handbook*. It had a deep sound, one that seemed to presage a large beast.

Furthermore, the Prince's own nostrils flared as he detected the unmistakable smell of dragon-musk. Not a pleasant odor.

Prince Delightful paused to consider strategy. From the snoring, it was obvious that the dragon was asleep, and according to the *Handbook*, its sleep was deep and it was difficult to disturb. That made sense since dragons had no natural enemies except princes and could usually sleep securely.

It seemed only fair to begin by pricking the beast with his spear until he woke it up. He could then fight it fair and square, wakefulness to wakefulness.

On the other hand, thought Prince Delightful, was that truly fair?

After all, the dragon was much larger and stronger than the Prince was even if the princely horse were counted in. And the dragon could fly. And it could breathe flame.

Was that fair? No, thought Prince Delightful.

Did the dragon worry about that? No, thought Prince Delightful.

Since the Prince had studied logic under the sorcerer, he concluded quite correctly, that the balance would be somewhat restored if the dragon were asleep. If it slept, it could not fly or breathe flame, but it would still be far larger and stronger than the Prince, so it would still have the advantage on its own side.

Prince Delightful urged his horse forward until it entered a clearing in which he could clearly see the sleeping dragon. It was large indeed. It was nearly a hundred feet long and was covered with tough scales that, the *Handbook* told him, could not be pierced by an ordinary spear. The thing to do was to aim at an eye which, fortunately, was closed.

Prince Delightful leveled his spear and slapped his spurs against his horse's flank. The loyal horse now charged forward, and the Prince kept his own eye firmly on the closed eye of the monster.

Unfortunately, though the Prince's eye remained firm and steady and true, his spear did not. The effort to keep both objects, eye and spear, aimed correctly was too great for the Prince's inherent clumsiness and the spear dipped. It struck against the ground and the Prince pole-vaulted high in the air.

The pole wrenched itself out of his hand and the Prince came down on something hard and scaly. Instinctively, he clutched it in a death grip and found himself hugging the dragon's neck just behind its head.

The shock woke the dragon and its head lifted twenty feet into the air. Prince Delightful shouted involuntarily, "Hey! Hey!"

The dragon struggled to its feet, and the head shot up another ten feet. The horse, noting that its master was gone, wisely decided to go home. It turned and fled, and Prince Delightful felt deserted.

The dragon turned its head, looking apparently for whatever it was that had made the sound, and was now resting as a small weight upon its neck, but, of course, it could see nothing. There was no way it could turn its head through an angle of a hundred eighty degrees.

Finally, it said, in a deep bass rumble, "Hey, is anybody dere?"

Prince Delightful's eyes opened wide. None of the vast literature on dragons that he had read in the course of his princely education had stated that dragons could speak—and in what was definitely a lower-class accent.

He said, "Why, it is I. It is Prince Delightful."

"Well, whatcha doin' up dere. Get off, will ya. Get out of my scales."

"I don't like to, if it means you're going to eat me."

"I ain't gonna eat you. In the foist place, I ain't hungry. In the second place, what makes ya think ya taste good. Get down and let's talk. Ya ain't got no spear, have ya?"

"I'm afraid it's lost."

"Aw right, den. Get down and tawk like a civilized dragon."

The great head and neck lowered slowly and when it was down against the ground, Prince Delightful cautiously slipped off. There was a small rip in his doublet where it had caught on the rough edge of a scale.

He backed off into the woods. "You're sure now you're not going to attack me?"

"Cawse not. I said I wouldn't. I give you my woid. A dragon's woid is his bond. Not like you lousy princes. Why do you come bothering us for? One of you guys killed my sister. Another killed my father. What do we do to you?"

"Well, you do eat virgins, you know."

"Dat's a lie. I wouldn't touch a voigin. They always smell from cheap poifume. When I was little I licked one in the face. Yech. Powder. Voigins ain't edible."

"But then, what do you eat?"

"Nuttin' much. I eat grass and fruit and nuts and roots, maybe once in a while a bunny rabbit or a kitty cat. And den you guys come after us with spears and swords and horses and we ain't done nothin'."

"But everyone says you eat virgins."

13

"Dat's just de voigins trying to make demselves important. Boy, dat makes me mad."

"Wait a minute," said Prince Delightful in alarm. "Don't start spouting flame."

"Who, me?" The dragon's lower lip thrust outward and a tear the size of a pint container glinted in its eye. "I can't spout flame. I'm prob'ly the only dragon that can't spout flame."

"Oh? Why not?"

The dragon heaved a large sigh and a somewhat fetid odor filled the air. Prince Delightful held his nose but the dragon didn't seem to notice.

It said, "Mine is a sad story."

"May I hear it, uh, sir? What's your name, by the way."

"My name? Boinard, but you can call me Boinie. That's when the trouble started. At my christening."

"At your christening?" said Prince Delightful, forcefully. "What an odd coincidence. That's when my trouble started, too."

"Yeah, but what's trouble to a prince? Now you listen to me. My old man and my old lady, dey wanted I should get a good start in life with Boinard, a lucky name in my family, so dey invited every fairy in dis kingdom to the christening. And what do yuh know, a foreign fairy from somewhere else came, also."

"A foreign fairy?"

"Yeah. A nice old dame, my folks told me, but not all dere, you know what I mean? A regular klutz."

"Was her name Misaprop?"

"Yeah, dat was huh name. Howja know?"

"That same fairy was at *my* christening."

"And did she mess yuh up?"

"Very much so."

"Gee, it makes us kind of pals. Shake pal."

The dragon's gigantic paw extended itself out to Prince Delightful and swallowed up his small hand.

The dragon said, "You know what she did to me?"

"No."

"After all de other fairies made me big and strong and good-looking with nice scales, she came along to give me a good strong flame-throwing mout' only she got it all bollixed up. No flames."

"But I don't understand. If you don't have any flames, Bernie, why don't any of the other knights want to attack you? I'm told they all go away quickly when they meet up with you."

"Dat's the sad part. Nobody wants to hang around me. Not even lady dragons. Looka me. I'm big and strong and beautiful, an' I ain't had a dame look at me for seventy-five years."

"Why not?"

"Well, when I get mad or when I get passionate, if you know what I mean, I don't shoot out flame, I shoot out somepin' else."

"What?"

"You wanna see?"

"It won't hurt me, will it?"

"Cawse not. Just lemme think about de situation, so I get mad."

The dragon brooded a bit, then said, "Now!" It opened its mouth and exhaled and Prince Delightful dropped to the ground immediately, his hands over his nose. What had come out was the worst, the foulest, the most noxious odor he had ever smelled. He rolled about choking.

The dragon said, "It won't last long. I just gave you a little dose. In a way, I suppose it's better. Yuh can dodge the flame; yuh can't dodge dis. All de knights leave quick, when I breathe out. So do all the lady dragons. Wotta life."

The dragon shook its head sadly.

Prince Delightful got shakily to his feet. The forest still smelled, but it was bearable.

He said, "Bernie, how would you like to come back to Poictesme with me and be introduced to King Faraday?"

"What? And have a million knights sticking their spears into me."

15

"No, believe me. You'll be treated like a king yourself. You'll have all the bunny rabbits you can eat, and grass, too."

"How come?"

"You'll see. Trust me. I have to ride you back, though. I haven't got a horse anymore."

Prince Delightful came back on Bernie, sitting just behind his head, and viewing the world from thirty feet in the air.

At first everyone fled screaming, but Prince Delightful kept calling out, "Friends, this is a tame dragon, a good dragon. Its name is Bernie. Speak to them, Bernie."

And the dragon called out, "Hi, guys. It's just me and my friend, duh Prince."

Eventually, some peasants and workmen and varlets of varying degree, braver than the rest, followed along as the dragon took his huge steps carefully, making sure it treaded on no one by accident. Its great head turned on its long neck from side to side and the Prince waved majestically first to the right and then to the left.

Then, as the news spread, the populace began to line the road and by the time Bernie moved into the capital city and up the main boulevard to the castle, the cheering populace had turned it all into a triumphant procession.

The dragon said, "Hey, de human people ain't so bad when yuh get to know dem, Prince."

"They're almost civilized," said Prince Delightful.

King Faraday came out to greet them and so did Laurelene, who shouted, "Greetings, my brave Prince Delightful."

The sorcerer came out, too, and rubbed his eyes and said, "Of all things, an apatosaurus." But he often spoke gibberish and no one paid attention.

Bernie was housed in a stable as far removed from the palace as possible and King Faraday, having overseen that, returned to his throne room and said to Prince Delightful, "I admit that bringing back the monster was quite a feat, but it was not what I engaged you to do. You were supposed to kill it."

"Ah, but a tame dragon is far better than a dead one, if you'll let me explain matters to your Majesty."

"I'm listening."

"To begin with, I assume that, as a respectable monarch, you have a neighbor who is an enemy of yours and whom you have been fighting for generations. You have laid his lands waste and he has laid your lands waste, and many people have died in agony on both sides."

"Well, of course. This is a civilized land, and we would not think of behaving in any other way. There is war between myself and the faithless, barbarous land of Lotharingia to our east."

"And at the moment, is your army attacking them, or is theirs attacking yours?"

King Faraday coughed. "At the moment, Lotharingia has contrived to attain a slight advantage over us and has advanced to within ten miles of our provincial town of Papeete."

"Would you like to destroy their forces and impose a peace of your choosing upon them?"

"Without doubt, but who would bring about such destruction?"

"Why, Bernie and I. Alone."

"The Lotharingian forces include a thousand brave knights, armed cap-a-pie. Your dragon might kill some but it will be killed itself and our people would be greatly cast down at our failure."

"There'll be no failure. Let there be a saddle designed for Bernie's neck, and a pair of reins so that I won't fall off. Ask the sorcerer to design something that I may place over my head that will purify air, and have a small force escort me to the Lotharingian army."

"A small force?"

"They may move off when Bernie and I reach the Lotharingians. Bernie and I will face the enemy alone. However, have an army waiting on the flanks, ready to move in behind the enemy forces to cut off their retreat."

King Faraday said, "It is mad, but I will do as you say. After all, you brought back the dragon, when all the others merely fled."

Saddle and reins were prepared. The sorcerer brought a device of peculiar shape that fitted over Prince Delightful's head.

The sorcerer said, "This will keep the air pure. It is a gas mask." But, as usual, no one was impressed with the words he used.

Prince Delightful and Bernard appeared before the lines of the Lothoringian Army. The Lotharingians were in brave array and they bristled with spear points.

There was a tremor, however, that shook the ranks at the first sight of the dragon, with its rider high in the air and with his face hidden by some device that made him seem more fearsome than the monster he bestrode.

After all, every Lotharingian had seen pictures of dragons, but none had ever seen a gas mask, either in books or in real life.

The Lotharingian general called out bravely, however, and said, "It is only one beast upon another, my brave Lotharingians. Stand firm, acquit yourself like men. Circle the dragon, avoid its flames and hack at its tail. The pain will cause it to run."

The Lotharingians took heart and made their stand, waiting for the dragon to advance. It did not, however, but kept its distance.

Prince Delightful said, "Did you hear them? They're going to hack at your beautiful tail."

"Dat's what I hoid," rumbled the dragon, "but dey ain't gonna, because what dey said went an' got me real mad."

He opened his gigantic maw and, with a roar of thunder, there emerged a vast cloud of turbid, putrid gas. It rolled down upon the Lotharingian forces and where it struck and spread out, the armed men broke and ran, throwing away their weapons as they did so, concerned only to get away from the incredibly foul odor.

Some miles back, the army, reduced to a disorderly mob, met the waiting forces of Poictesme and few escaped either death or capture.

"You may have my beautiful and virginal daughter, Prince Delightful," said King Faraday, "and since I have no son, you will inherit my kingdom when I die and the conquered land of Lotharingia as well and your own father's kingdom, too. As for your dragon, he will be a hero to us for as long as he wishes to remain here. He shall live on the finest hay and we shall catch small animals for him when he feels the need for some."

"He would like a lady dragon or two," said Prince Delightful, diffidently.

"Even that might be arranged," said the King, "if he learns to control his passions to some extent."

Prince Delightful tripped on his train only twice during the marriage ceremony, but, as he said to Bernie in his stable afterward, "It doesn't matter. Actually, the Fairy Misaprop, made it all possible. My clumsiness landed me on your neck and your noxious breath destroyed the enemy army. —And now I must go to my fair wife."

As it turned out, he was not unduly clumsy on his wedding night and he and the Princess Laurelene lived happily ever after.

IMAGINARY FRIENDS

TERRY BROOKS

JACK MCCALL WAS TEN DAYS SHY
of his thirteenth birthday when he decided that he was dying. He had
been having headaches for about six months without telling anyone, the
headaches being accompanied by a partial loss of vision that lasted anywhere from ten to twenty minutes. He hadn't thought much about it since
it only happened once in a while, believing that it was simply the result
of eyestrain. After all, there was a lot of homework assigned in the seventh
grade.

But ten days before his birthday he had an attack as he was about to
go out the door to school, and since he couldn't very well ride his bike in
that condition or stand around pretending that nothing was wrong he was
forced to admit the problem to his mother. His mother made an immediate appointment with Dr. Muller, the family pediatrician, for that afternoon, sat Jack down until his vision cleared, then drove him to school,
asking him all the way there if he was all right and calling him "Jackie"
until he thought he would scream.

She returned promptly when school let out to take him to his appointment. Dr. Muller was uncharacteristically cheerful as he checked Jack
over, even going so far as to ruffle his hair and remark on how quickly he
was growing. This was the same Dr. Muller who normally didn't have
two words for him. Jack began to worry.

When the doctor was finished, he sent Jack and his mother over to the
hospital for further tests. The tests included X rays, blood workups, an
EKG, and a barrage of other examinations, all of which were adminis-

tered by an uncomfortably youthful collection of nurses. Jack endured the application of cold metal implements to his body, let himself be stuck repeatedly with needles, breathed in and out, lay very still, jumped up and down, and mostly waited around in empty, sterile examination rooms. When the tests were all done, he was sent home knowing nothing more than he had when he arrived beyond the fact that he did not care ever to go through such an ordeal again.

That night, while he was upstairs in his room fiddling with his homework and listening to his stereo, Dr. Muller paid a visit to his house. His parents didn't call for him, but that didn't stop him from being curious. He slipped down the stairway to the landing and sat there in the dark on the other side of the half wall above the living room while Dr. Muller and his parents spoke in hushed tones. Dr. Muller did most of the talking. He said that the preliminary test results were back. He talked about the body and its cells and a bunch of other stuff, throwing in multisyllabic medical terms that Jack couldn't begin to understand.

Then he used the words "blood disorder" and "leukemia" and "cancer." Jack understood that part. He might only be in seventh grade, but he wasn't stupid.

He stayed on the stairway until he heard his mother start to cry, then crept back up to his room without waiting to hear any more. He sat there staring at his unfinished homework, trying to decide what he should be feeling. He couldn't seem to feel anything. He heard Dr. Muller leave, and then his parents came up to see him. Usually they visited him individually; when they both appeared it was serious business. They knocked on the door, came inside when invited, and stood there looking decidedly uncomfortable. Then his father told him that he was sick and would have to take it easy for a while, his mother started crying and calling him "Jackie" and hugging him, and all of a sudden he was scared out of his socks.

He didn't sleep much that night, letting the weight of what he had discovered sink in, trying to comprehend what his dying meant, trying to decide if he believed it was possible. Mostly, he thought about Uncle Frank. Uncle Frank had been his favorite uncle, a big man with strong hands and red hair who taught him how to throw a baseball. Uncle Frank used to take him to ballgames on Sunday afternoons. Then he got sick. It happened all at once. He went into the hospital and never came out. Jack's parents took him to see Uncle Frank a couple of times. There was not much left of Uncle Frank by then. His once-strong hands were so frail he could barely lift them. All his hair had fallen out. He looked like an old man.

Then he died. No one came right out and said it, but Jack knew what had killed him. And he had always suspected, deep down inside where you hid things like that, that it might some day kill him, too.

The next morning Jack dressed, wolfed down his breakfast as quickly as he could and got out of there. His parents were behaving like zombies. Only his little sister Abby was acting as if everything was all right, which was the way she always acted since she was only eight and never knew what was going on anyway.

It was Friday, always a slow-moving day at Roosevelt Junior High, but never more so than on this occasion. The morning seemed endless, and he didn't remember any of it when it was finally over. He trudged to the lunch room, found a seat off in a corner where he could talk privately, and told his best friend Waddy Wadsworth what he had discovered. Reynolds Lucius Wadsworth III was Waddy's real name, the result of a three-generation tradition of unparalleled cruelty in the naming of first-born boys. No one called Waddy by his real name, of course. But they didn't call him anything sensible either. It was discovered early on that Waddy lacked any semblance of athletic ability. He was the kid who couldn't climb the knotted rope or do chin-ups or high-jump when the bar was only two feet off the ground. Someone started calling him Waddy and the name stuck. It wasn't that Waddy was fat or anything; he was just earthbound.

He was also a good guy. Jack liked him because he never said anything about the fact that Jack was only a little taller than most fire hydrants and a lot shorter than most girls.

"You look okay to me," Waddy said after Jack had finished telling him he was supposed to be dying.

"I know I *look* okay." Jack frowned at his friend impatiently. "This isn't the kind of thing you can see, you know."

"You sound okay, too." Waddy took a bite of his jelly sandwich. "Does anything hurt?"

Jack shrugged. "Just when I have the headaches."

"Well, you don't have them more often now than you did six months ago, do you?"

"No."

"And they don't last any longer now than they did then, do they?"

"No."

Waddy shoved the rest of the sandwich into his mouth and chewed thoughtfully. "Well, then, who's to say you're really dying? This could be one of those conditions that just goes on indefinitely. Meantime, they might find a cure for it; they're always finding cures for this kind of stuff." He chewed some more. "Anyway, maybe the doctor made a mistake. That's possible, isn't it?"

Jack nodded doubtfully.

"The point is, you don't know for sure. Not for *sure*." Waddy cocked his head. "Here's something else to think about. They're always telling someone or other that they're going to die and then they don't. People get well all the time just because they believe they can do it. Sometimes believing is all it takes."

He gave Jack a lopsided grin. "Besides, no one dies in the seventh grade."

Jack wanted to believe that. He spent the afternoon trying to convince himself. After all, he didn't personally know anyone his age who had died. The only people he knew who had died were much older. Even Uncle Frank. He was just a kid. How could he die when he still didn't know anything about girls? How could he die without ever having driven a car? It just didn't seem possible.

Nevertheless, the feeling persisted that he was only fooling himself. It didn't make any difference what he believed, it didn't change the facts. If he really had cancer, believing he didn't wouldn't make it go away. He sat through his afternoon classes growing steadily more despondent, feeling helpless and wishing he could do something about it.

It wasn't until he was biking home that he suddenly found himself thinking about Pick.

The McCall house was a large white shingle-shake rambler that occupied almost an acre of timber bordering the north edge of Sinnissippi Park. The Sinnissippi Indians were native to the area, and several of their burial mounds occupied a fenced-off area situated in the southwest corner of the park under a cluster of giant maples. The park was more than forty acres end to end, most of it woods, the rest consisting of baseball diamonds and playgrounds. The park was bordered on the south by the Rock River, on the west by Riverside Cemetery, and on the north and east by the private residences of Woodlawn. It was a sprawling preserve, filled with narrow, serpentine trails, thick stands of scrub-choked pine, and shady groves of maple, elm and white oak. A massive bluff ran along the better part of its southern edge and overlooked the Rock River.

Jack was not allowed to go into the park alone until he was out of fourth grade, not even beyond the low maintenance bushes that grew where his backyard ended at the edge of the park. His father took him for walks sometimes, a bike ride now and then, and once in a while his mother even came along. She didn't come often, though, because she was busy with Abby, and his father worked at the printing company and was usually not home until after dark. So for a long time the park remained a vast, unexplored country that lay just out of reach and whispered enticingly in Jack's youthful mind of adventure and mystery.

Sometimes, when the lure was too strong, he would beg to be allowed to go into the park by himself, just for a little ways, just for a few, tiny minutes. He would pinch his thumb and index finger close together to emphasize the smallness of his request. But his mother's reply was always the same—his own backyard was park enough for him.

Things have a way of working out, though, and the summer before he entered second grade he ended up going into the park alone in spite of his parents. It all came about because of Pick. Jack was playing in the sandbox with his toy trucks on a hot July afternoon when he heard Sam whining and barking at something just beyond the bushes. Sam was the family dog, a sort of mongrel terrier with a barrel body. He was carrying on as if he had unearthed a mountain lion, and finally Jack lifted himself out of the maze of crisscrossing paths he was constructing and wandered down to the end of the yard to see what was happening. When he got there, he found that he still couldn't see anything because Sam was behind a pine tree on the other side of the bushes. Jack called, but the dog wouldn't come. After standing there for a few minutes, Jack glanced restlessly over his shoulder at the windows of his house. There was no sign of his mother. Biting his lower lip with stubborn determination, he stepped cautiously onto forbidden ground.

He was concentrating too hard on what lay behind him. As he passed through the bushes, he stumbled and struck his head sharply on a heavy limb. The blow stung, but Jack climbed back to his feet almost immediately and went on.

Sam was jumping around at the base of the pine, darting in and out playfully. There was a gathering of brambles growing there and a bit of cloth caught in them. When Jack got closer, he saw that the bit of cloth was actually a doll. When he got closer still, he saw that the doll was moving.

"Don't just stand there!" the doll yelled at him in a very tiny, but angry voice. "Call him off!"

Jack caught hold of Sam's collar. Sam struggled, twisting about in

28

Jack's grip, trying to get back to his newfound discovery. Finally Jack gave the dog a sharp slap on its hind end and sent it scurrying away through the bushes. Then he crouched down beneath the pine, staring at the talking doll. It was a little man with a reddish beard, green shirt and pants, black boots and belt, and a cap made out of fresh pine needles woven together.

Jack giggled. "Why are you so little?" he asked.

"Why am I so little?" the other echoed. He was struggling mightily to free himself. "Why are you so big? Don't you know anything?"

"Are you real?" Jack pressed.

"Of course I'm real! I'm an Elf!"

Jack cocked his head. "Like in the fairy tales?"

The Elf was flushed redder than his beard. "No, not like in the fairy tales! Since when do fairy tales tell the truth about Elves? I suppose you think Elves are just cute little woodfolk who spend their lives prancing about in the moonlight? Well, we don't! We work!"

Jack bent close so he could see better. "What do you work at?"

"Everything!" The Elf was apoplectic.

"You're funny," Jack said, rocking back on his heels. "What's your name?"

"Pick. My name is Pick," muttered the Elf. He twisted some more and finally gave up. "What's yours?"

"Jack. Jack Andrew McCall."

"Well, look, Jack Andrew McCall. Do you think you could help me get out of these brambles? It's your fault, after all, that I'm in them in the first place. That is your dog, isn't it? Well, your dog was sneaking around where I was working and I didn't hear him. He barked and frightened me so badly I got myself caught. Then he began sniffing and drooling all over me, and I got tangled up even worse!" He took a deep breath, calming himself. "So how about it? Will you help me?"

"Sure," Jack agreed at once.

He started to reach down, and Pick cried out, "Be careful with those big fingers of yours! You could crush me! You're not a clumsy boy, are you? You're not one of those boys that goes around stepping on ants?"

Jack was always pretty good with his hands, and he managed to free the Elf in a matter of seconds with little or no damage to either from the brambles. He put Pick on the ground in front of him and sat back. Pick brushed at his clothes, muttering inaudibly.

"Do you live in the park?" Jack asked.

Pick glanced up, sour-faced once more. His pine needle cap was askew. "Of course I live in the park! How else could I do my work if I didn't?" He jabbed out with one finger. "Do you know what I do, Jack Andrew? I look after this park! This whole park, all by myself! That is a terrible responsibility for a single Elf!"

Jack was impressed. "How do you look after it?"

Pick shoved the cap back into place. "Do you know what magic is?"

Jack scratched at a mosquito bite on his wrist. "It turned Cinderella into a fairy princess," he answered doubtfully.

"Good gosh golly, are they still telling that old saw? When are they ever going to get this fairy tale business right? They keep sticking to those ridiculous stories about wicked stepmothers, would-be princesses and glass slippers at a royal ball—as if a glass slipper would last five minutes on a dance floor!" He jumped up and down so hard that Jack started. "I could tell them a thing or two about *real* fairy tales!" he exploded. "I could tell them some stories that would raise the hair on the backs of their necks!"

He stopped, suddenly aware of Jack's consternation. "Oh, never mind!" he huffed. "This business of fairy tales just happens to be a sore subject with me. Now about what I do, Jack Andrew. I keep the magic in balance, is what I do. There's magic in everything, you know—from the biggest old oak to the smallest blade of grass, from ants to elephants. And it all has to be kept in balance or there's big trouble. That's what Elves really do. But there's not enough of us to be everywhere, so we concentrate on the places where the magic is strongest and most likely to cause trouble—like this park." He swept the air with his hand. "There's lots of troublesome magic in this park."

Jack followed the motion of his hand and then nodded. "It's a big place."

"Too big for most Elves, I'll have you know!" Pick announced. "Want to see how big?"

Jack nodded yes and shook his head no all in the same motion. He glanced hurriedly over his shoulder, remembering anew his mother. "I'm not supposed to go into the park," he explained. "I'm not even supposed to go out of the yard."

"Oh," said Pick quietly. He rubbed his red-bearded chin momentarily, then clapped his hands. "Well, a touch of magic will get the job done and keep you out of trouble at the same time. Here, pick me up, put me in your hand. Gently, boy! There! Now let me settle myself. Keep your hand open, palm up. Don't move. Now close your eyes. Go on, close them. This won't hurt. Close your eyes and think about the park. Can you see it? Now, watch . . ."

Something warm and syrupy drifted through Jack's body, starting at his eyes and working its way downward to his feet. He felt Pick stir.

And suddenly Jack was flying, soaring high above the trees and telephone poles across the broad, green expanse of Sinnissippi Park. He sat astride an owl, a great brown-and-white feathered bird with wings that seemed to stretch on forever. Pick sat behind him, and amazingly they were the same size. Jack blinked in disbelief, then yelled in delight. The owl swooped lazily earthward, banking this way and that to catch the wind, but the motion did not disturb Jack. Indeed, he felt as if nothing could dislodge him from his perch.

"This is how I get from place to place," he heard Pick say, the tiny voice unruffled by the wind. "Daniel takes me. He's a barn owl—a good one. We met sometime back. If I had to walk the park, it would take me weeks to get from one end to the other and I'd never get anything done!"

31

"I like this!" Jack cried out joyously, laughed, and Pick laughed with him.

They rode the wind on Daniel's back for what seemed like hours, passing from Riverside Cemetery along the bluff face east to the houses of Woodlawn and back again. Jack saw everything with eyes that were wide with wonder and delight. There were gray and brown squirrels, birds of all kinds and colors, tiny mice and voles, opossums and even a badger. There were a pair of deer in a thicket down along the riverbank, a fawn and its mother, slender and delicate, their stirrings barely visible against the trees. There were hoary old pines with their needled boughs interlaced like armor over secretive earthen floors, towering oaks and elms sticking out of the ground like massive spears, deep hollows and ravines that collected dried leaves and shadows, and inlets and streams filled with lily pads, frogs and darting, tiny fish.

But there was more than that for a boy who could imagine. There were castles and forts behind every old log. There were railroads with steam engines racing over ancient wooden bridges where the streams grew too wide to ford. There were pirate dens and caves of treasures. There were wild ponies that ran faster than the wind and mountain cats as sleek as silk. Everywhere there was a new story, a different tale, a dream of an adventure longing to be embraced.

And there were things of magic.

"Down there, Jack Andrew—do you see it?" Pick called as they swung left across the stone bridge that spanned a split in the bluff where it dropped sharply downward to the Rock. "Look closely, boy!"

Jack looked, seeing the crablike shadow that clung to the underside of the bridge, flattened almost out of sight against the stone.

"That's Wartag the Troll!" Pick announced. "Every bridge seems to have at least one Troll in these parts, but Wartag is more trouble than most. If there's a way to unbalance the magic, Wartag will find it. Much of my own work is spent in undoing his!"

Daniel took them down close to the bridgehead, and Jack saw Wartag

inch farther back into the shadows in an effort to hide. He was not entirely successful. Jack could still see the crooked body covered with patches
of black hair and the mean-looking red eyes that glittered like bicycle
reflectors.

Daniel screamed and Wartag shrank away.

"Wartag doesn't care much for owls!" Pick said to Jack, then shouted
something spiteful at the Troll before Daniel wheeled them away.

They flew on to a part of the park they had not visited yet, a deep
woods far back in the east central section where the sunlight seemed unable to penetrate and all was cloaked in shadow. Daniel took them down
into the darkness, a sort of gray mistiness that was filled with silence and
the smell of rotting wood. Pick pointed ahead, and Jack followed the line
of his finger warily. There stood the biggest, shaggiest tree that he had
ever seen, a monster with crooked limbs, splitting bark and craggy bolls
that seemed waiting to snare whatever came into its path. Nothing grew
about it. All the other trees, all the brush and the grasses were cleared
away.

"What is it?" he asked Pick.

Pick gave him a secretive look. "That, young Jack Andrew, is the
prison, now and forever more, of the Dragon Desperado. What do you
think of it?"

Jack stared. "A real Dragon?"

"As real as you and I. And very dangerous, I might add. Too dangerous to be let loose, but at the same time too powerful to destroy. Can't be
rid of everything that frightens or troubles us in this world. Some things
we simply have to put up with—Dragons and Trolls among them. Trolls
aren't half as bad as Dragons, of course. Trolls cause mischief when they're
on the loose, but Dragons really upset the apple cart. They are a powerful
force, Jack Andrew. Why just their breath alone can foul the air for miles!
And the imprint of a Dragon's paw will poison whole fields! Some Dragons
are worse than others, of course. Desperado is one of them."

He paused and his eyes twinkled as they found Jack's. "All Dragons are bothersome, but Desperado is the worst. Now and again he breaks free, and then there's the very Devil to pay. Fortunately, that doesn't happen too often. When it does, someone simply has to lock Desperado away again." He winked enigmatically. "And that takes a very special kind of magic."

Daniel lifted suddenly and bore them away, skying out of the shadows and the gray mistiness, breaking free of the gloom. The sun caught Jack in the eyes with a burst of light that momentarily blinded him.

"Jackie!"

He thought he heard his mother calling. He blinked.

"Jackie, where are you?"

It was his mother. He blinked again and found himself sitting alone beneath the pine, one hand held out before him, palm up. The hand was empty. Pick had disappeared.

He hesitated, heard his mother call again, then climbed hurriedly to his feet and scurried for the bushes at the end of his yard. He was too late getting there to avoid being caught. His mother was alarmed at first when she saw the knot on his forehead, then angry when she realized how it had happened. She bandaged him up, then sent him to his room.

He told his parents about Pick during dinner. They listened politely, glancing at each other from time to time, then told him everything was fine, it was a wonderful story, but that sometimes bumps on the head made us think things had happened that really hadn't. When he insisted that he had not made the story up, that it had really happened, they smiled some more and told him that they thought it was nice he had such a good imagination. Try as he might, he couldn't convince them that he was serious and finally, after a week of listening patiently to him, his mother sat down in the kitchen with cookies and milk one morning and told him she had heard enough.

"All little boys have imaginary friends, Jackie," his mother told him. "That's part of growing up. An imaginary friend is someone whom little boys can talk to about their troubles when no one else will listen, someone they can tell their secrets to when they don't want to tell anyone else. Sometimes they can help a little boy get through some difficult times. Pick is your imaginary friend, Jackie. But you have to understand something. A friend like Pick belongs just to you, not to anyone else, and that is the way you should keep it."

He looked for Pick all that summer and into the fall, but he never found him. When his father took him into the park, he looked for Wartag under the old stone bridge. He never found him either. He checked the skies for Daniel, but never saw anything bigger than a robin. When he finally persuaded his father to walk all the way back into the darkest part of the woods—an effort that had his father using words Jack had not often heard him use before—there was no sign of the tree that imprisoned Desperado.

Eventually, Jack gave up looking. School and his friends claimed his immediate attention, Thanksgiving rolled around, and then it was Christmas. He got a new bike that year, a two-wheeler without training wheels, and an electric train. He thought about Pick, Daniel, Wartag and Desperado from time to time, but the memory of what they looked like began to grow hazy. He forgot many of the particulars of his adventure that summer afternoon in the park, and the adventure itself took on the trappings of one of those fairy tales Pick detested so.

Soon, Jack pretty much quit thinking about the matter altogether.

He had not thought about it for months until today.

He wheeled his bike up the driveway of his house, surprised that he could suddenly remember all the details he had forgotten. They were sharp in his mind again, as sharp as they had been on the afternoon they had happened. If they had happened. If they had *really* happened. He hadn't been sure for a long time now. After all, he was only a little kid then. His parents might have been right; he might have imagined it all.

But then why was he remembering it so clearly now?

He went up to his room to think, came down long enough to have dinner, and quickly went back up again. His parents had looked at him strangely all during the meal—checking, he felt, to see if he was showing any early signs of expiring. It made him feel weird.

He found he couldn't concentrate on his homework, and anyway it was Friday night. He turned off the music on his tape player, closed his books and sat there. The clock on his nightstand ticked softly as he thought some more about what had happened almost seven years ago. What *might* have happened, he corrected—although the more he thought about it, the more he was beginning to believe it really had. His common sense told him that he was crazy, but when you're dying you don't have much time for common sense.

Finally he got up, went downstairs to the basement rec room, picked up the phone and called Waddy. His friend answered on the second ring, they talked about this and that for five minutes or so, and then Jack said, "Waddy, do you believe in magic?"

Waddy laughed. "Like in the song?"

"No, like in conjuring. You know, spells and such."

"What kind of magic?"

"What kind?"

"Yeah, what kind? There's different kinds, right? Black magic and white magic. Wizard magic. Witches brew. Horrible old New England curses. Fairies and Elves . . ."

"That kind. Fairies and Elves. Do you think there might be magic like that somewhere?"

"Are you asking me if I believe in Fairies and Elves?"

Jack hesitated. "Well, yeah."

"No."

"Not at all, huh?"

"Look, Jack, what's going on with you? You're not getting strange because of this dying business, are you? I told you not to worry about it."

"I'm not. I was just thinking . . ." He stopped, unable to tell Waddy exactly what he was thinking because it sounded so bizarre. After all, he'd never told anyone after his parents about Pick.

There was a thoughtful silence on the other end of the line. "If you're asking me whether I think there's some kind of magic out there that saves people from dying, then I say yes. There is."

That wasn't exactly what Jack was asking, but the answer made him feel good anyway. "Thanks, Waddy. Talk to you later."

He hung up and went back upstairs. His father intercepted him on the landing and called him down again. He told Jack he had been talking with Dr. Muller. The doctor wanted him to come into the hospital on Monday for additional tests. He might have to stay for a few days. Jack knew what that meant. He would end up like Uncle Frank. His hair would fall out. He would be sick all the time. He would waste away to nothing. He didn't want any part of it. He told his father so and without waiting for his response ran back up to his room, shut the door, undressed, turned off the lights and lay shivering in his bed in the darkness.

He fell asleep for a time, and it was after midnight when he came awake again. He had been dreaming, but he couldn't remember what the dreams were about. As he lay there, he thought he heard someone calling for him. He propped himself up on one arm and listened to the silence. He stayed that way for a long time, thinking.

Then he rose, dressed in jeans, pullover and sneakers, and crept downstairs, trying hard not to make any noise. He got as far as the back porch. Sam was asleep on the threshold, and Jack didn't see him. He tripped over the dog and went down hard, striking his head on the edge of a table. He blacked out momentarily, then his eyes blinked open. Sam was cowering in one corner, frightened half to death. Jack was surprised and grateful that the old dog wasn't barking like crazy. That would have brought his parents awake in a minute. He patted Sam's head reassuringly, pulled on his windbreaker, and slipped out through the screen door.

Silence enveloped him. Jack crossed the damp green carpet of the backyard on cat's feet, pushed through the bushes at its end, and went into the park. It was a warm, windless night, and the moon shone full and white out of a cloudless sky, its silver light streaming down through breaks in the leafy trees to chase the shadows. Jack breathed the air and smelled pine needles and lilacs. He didn't know what he would tell his parents if they found him out there. He just knew he had to find Pick. Something inside whispered that he must.

He reached the old pine and peered beneath its spiky boughs. There was no sign of Pick. He backed out and looked about the park. Crickets chirped in the distance. The baseball diamonds stretched away before him east to the wall of the trees where the deep woods began. He could see the edge of the river bluff south, a ragged tear across the night sky. The cemetery was invisible beyond the rise of the park west. Nothing moved anywhere.

Jack came forward to the edge of the nearest ball diamond, anxious now, vaguely uneasy. Maybe this was a mistake.

Then a screech shattered the silence, and Jack caught sight of a shadow wheeling across the moonlight overhead.

"Daniel!" he shouted.

Excitement coursed through him. He began to run. Daniel was circling ahead, somewhere over the edge of the bluff. Jack watched him dive and soar skyward again. Daniel was directly over the old stone bridge where Wartag lived.

As he came up to the bridge he slowed warily, remembering anew the Troll's mean-looking eyes. Then he heard his name called, and he charged recklessly ahead. He skidded down the dampened slope by the bridge's west support and peered into the shadows.

"Jack Andrew McCall, where have you been, boy?" he heard Pick demand without so much as a perfunctory hello. "I have been waiting for you for hours!"

Jack couldn't see him at first and groped his way through the blackness.

"Over here, boy!"

His eyes began to adjust, and he caught sight of something hanging from the underside of the bridge on a hook, close against the support. It was a cage made out of stone. He reached for it and tilted it slightly so he could look inside.

There was Pick. He looked exactly the same as he had those seven years past—a tiny man with a reddish beard, green trousers and shirt, black belt and boots and the peculiar hat of woven pine needles. It was too dark to be certain whether or not his face was flushed, but he was so excited that Jack was certain that it must be. He was dancing about on first one foot and then the other, hopping up and down as if his boots were on fire.

"What are you doing in there?" Jack asked him.

"What does it look like I'm doing in here—taking a bath?" Pick's temper hadn't improved any. "Now listen to me, Jack Andrew, and listen carefully because I haven't the time to say this more than once!" Pick was animated, his tiny voice shrill. "Wartag set a snare for me and I blundered into it. He sets such snares constantly, but I am usually too clever to get trapped in them. This time he caught me napping. He locked me in this cage earlier tonight and abandoned me to my fate. He has gone into the deep woods to unbalance the magic. He intends to set Desperado free!"

He jabbed at Jack with his finger. "You have to stop him!"

Jack started. "Me?"

"Yes, you! I don't have the means, locked away in here!"

"Well, I'll set you free then!"

Pick shook his head. "I'm afraid not. There's no locks or keys to a Troll cage. You just have to wait until it falls apart. Doesn't take long. Day or two at most. Wouldn't matter if you did free me, anyway. An Elf locked in a stone cage loses his magic for a moonrise. Everyone knows that!"

Jack gulped. "But, Pick, I can't . . ."

"Quit arguing with me!" the Elf stormed. "Take this!" He thrust something through the bars of the cage. It was a tiny silver pin. "Fasten it to your jacket. As long as you wear it, I can see what you see and tell you what to do. It will be the same as if I were with you. Now, hurry! Get after that confounded Troll!"

"But what about you?" Jack asked anxiously.

"Don't bother yourself about me! I'll be fine!"

"But . . ."

"Confound it, Jack! Get going!"

Jack did as he was told, spurred on by the urgency he heard in the other's voice. He forgot momentarily what had brought him to the park in the first place. Hurriedly, he stuck the silver pin through the collar of his jacket and wheeled away. He scrambled out of the ravine beneath the bridge, darted through the fringe of trees screening the ball diamonds and sprinted across the outfields toward the dark wall of the woods east. He looked skyward once or twice for Daniel, but the owl had disappeared. Jack could feel his heart pounding in his chest and hear the rasp of his breathing. Pick was chattering from somewhere inside his left ear, urging him on, warning that he must hurry. When he tried to ask something of the Elf, Pick cut him off with an admonition to concentrate on the task at hand.

He reached the woods at the east end of the park and disappeared into the trees. Moonlight fragmented into shards of light that scattered through the heavy canopy of limbs. Jack charged up and down hills, skittered through leaf-strewn gullies, and watched the timber begin to thicken steadily about him.

Finally, he tripped over a tree root and dropped wearily to his knees, gasping for breath. When he lifted his head again, he was aware of two things. First, the woods about him had gone completely silent. Second, there was a strange, greenish light that swirled like mist in the darkness ahead.

"We are too late, Jack Andrew," he heard Pick say softly. "That bubble-headed Troll has done his work! Desperado's free!"

Jack scrambled up quickly. "What do I do now, Pick?"

Pick's voice was calm. "Do, Jack? Why, you do what you must. You lock the Dragon away again!"

"Me?" Jack was aghast. "What am I supposed to do? I don't know anything about Dragons!"

"Stuff and nonsense! It's never too late to learn and there's not much to learn in any case. Let's have a look, boy. Go on! Now!"

Jack moved ahead, his feet operating independently of his brain, which was screaming at him to get the heck out of there. The misted green light began to close about him, enveloping him, filling the whole of the woods about him with a pungent smell like burning rubber. There was a deadness to the night air, and the whisper of something old and evil that echoed from far back in the woods. Jack swallowed hard against his fear.

Then he pushed through a mass of brush into a clearing ringed with pine and stopped. There was something moving aimlessly on the ground a dozen yards ahead, something small and black and hairy, something that steamed like breath exhaled on a winter's morning.

"Oh dear, oh dear," murmured an invisible Pick.

"What is it?" Jack demanded anxiously.

Pick clucked his tongue. "It would appear that Wartag has learned the hard way what happens when you fool around with Dragons."

"That's Wartag?"

"More or less. Keep moving, Jack. Don't worry about the Troll."

But Jack's brain had finally regained control of his feet. "Pick, I don't want anything more to do with this. I can't fight a Dragon! I only came because I . . . because I found out that . . ."

"You were dying."

Jack stared. "Yes, but how . . . ?"

"Did I know?" Pick finished. "Tut and posh, boy! Why do you think you're here? Now listen up. Time to face a rather unpleasant truth. You have to fight the Dragon whether you want to or not. He knows that you're here now, and he will come for you if you try to run. He needs to be locked away, Jack. You can do it. Believe me, you can."

Jack's heart was pounding. "How?"

"Oh, it's simple enough. You just push him from sight, back him into his cage and that's that! Now, let's see. There! To your left!"

Jack moved over a few steps and reached down. It was a battered old metal garbage can lid. "A shield!" declared Pick's voice in his ear. "And there!" Jack moved to his right and reached down again. It was a heavy stick that some hiker had discarded. "A sword!" Pick announced.

Jack stared at the garbage can lid and the stick in turn and then shook his head hopelessly. "This is ridiculous! I'm supposed to fight a Dragon with these?"

"These and what's inside you," Pick replied softly.

"But I can't . . ."

"Yes, you can."

"But . . ."

"Jack! You have to! You must!" Pick's words were harsh and clipped, the tiny voice insistent. "Don't you understand? Haven't you been listening to me? This fight isn't simply to save me or this park! This fight is to save you!"

Jack was confused. Why was this a fight to save him? It didn't make any sense. But something deep inside him whispered that the Elf was telling him the truth. He swallowed his fear, choked down his self-doubt, hefted his makeshift sword and shield and started forward. He went quickly, afraid that if he slowed he would give it up altogether. He knew somehow that he couldn't do that. He eased his way warily ahead through the trees, searching the greenish mist. Maybe the Dragon wasn't as scary as he imagined. Maybe it wasn't like the Dragons in the fairy tales. After all, would Pick send him into battle against something like that, something he wouldn't have a chance against?

There was movement ahead.

"Pick?" he whispered anxiously.

A shadow heaved upward suddenly out of the mist, huge and baleful, blocking out the light. Jack whirled and stumbled back.

There was Desperado. The Dragon rose against the night like a wall, weaving and swaying, a thing of scales and armor plates, a creature of limbs and claws, a being that was born of Jack's foulest nightmare. It had shape and no shape, formed of bits and pieces of fears and doubts that were drawn from a dozen memories best forgotten. It filled the pathway ahead with its bulk, as massive as the crooked, shaggy tree from which it had been freed.

Jack lurched to an unsteady halt, gasping. Eyes as hard as polished stone pinned him where he stood. He could feel the heat of the Dragon against his skin and at the same time an intense cold in the pit of his stomach. He was sweating and shivering all at once, and his breath threatened to seize up within his chest. He was no longer thinking; he was only reacting. Desperado's hiss sounded in the pit of his stomach. It told him he carried no shield, no sword. It told him he had no one to help him. It told him that he was going to die.

Fear spread quickly through Jack, filling him with its vile taste, leaving him momentarily helpless. He heard Pick's voice shriek wildly within his ear, "Quick, Jack Andrew, quick! Push the Dragon away!"

But Jack was already running. He bolted through the mist and trees as if catapulted, fleeing from Desperado. He was unable to help himself. He could no longer hear Pick; he could no longer reason. All he could think to do was to run as fast and as far from what confronted him as he could manage. He was only thirteen! He was only a boy! He didn't want to die!

He broke free of the dark woods and tore across the ball diamonds toward the bridge where Pick was caged. The sky was all funny, filled with swirling clouds and glints of greenish light. Everything was a mass of shadows and mist. He screamed for Pick to help him. But as he neared the bridge, its stone span seemed to yawn open like some giant's mouth, and the Dragon rose up before him, blocking his way. He turned and ran toward the Indian burial mounds, where the ghosts of the Sinnissippi danced through the shadows to a drumbeat only they could hear. But again the Dragon was waiting. It was waiting as well at the cemetery, slithering through the even rows of tombstones and markers like a snake. It was waiting amid the shrub-lined houses of Woodlawn, wherever Jack turned, wherever he fled. Jack ran from one end of the park to the other, and everywhere the Dragon Desperado was waiting.

"Pick!" he screamed over and over, but there was no answer. When he finally thought to look down for the silver pin, he discovered that he had lost it.

"Oh, Pick!" he sobbed.

Finally he quit running, too exhausted to go on. He found himself back within the deep woods, right where he had started. He had been running, yet he hadn't moved at all. Desperado was before him still, a monstrous, shapeless terror that he could not escape. He could feel the Dragon all around him, above and below, and even within. The Dragon was inside his head, crushing him, blinding him, stealing away his life. . . .

Like a sickness.

He gasped in sudden recognition.

Like the sickness that was killing him.

This fight is to save you, Pick had told him. The Elf's words came back to him, their purpose and meaning revealed with a clarity that was unmistakable.

Jack went a little bit crazy then. He cried out, overwhelmed by a rush of emotions he could not begin to define. He shed his fear as he would a burdensome coat and charged Desperado, heedless now of any danger to himself, blind to the Dragon's monstrous size. To his astonishment, the walking stick and the garbage can lid flared white with fire and turned into the sword and shield he had been promised. He could feel the fire spread from them into him, and it felt as if he had been turned to iron as well. He flung himself at Desperado, hammering into the Dragon with his weapons. *Push him back! Lock him away!*

The great, gnarled shapes of the Dragon and tree seemed to join. Night and mist closed about. He was swimming through a fog of jagged images. He heard sounds that might have come from anywhere, and there was within him a sense of something yielding. He thrust out, feeling Desperado give way before his attack. The feeling of heat, the smell of burning rubber, the scrape of scales and armor plates intensified and filled his senses.

Then Desperado simply disappeared. The sword and shield turned back into the walking stick and garbage can lid, the greenish mist dissipated into night, and Jack found himself clinging to the shaggy, bent trunk of the massive old tree that was the Dragon's prison.

He stumbled back, dumbstruck.

"Pick!" he shouted one final time, but there was no answer.

Then everything went black and he was falling.

He was in the hospital when he came awake. His head was wrapped with bandages and throbbed painfully. When he asked, one of the nurses on duty told him it was Saturday. He had suffered a bad fall off his back porch in the middle of the night, she said, and his parents hadn't found him until early this morning when they had brought him in. She added rather cryptically that he was a lucky boy.

His parents appeared shortly after, both of them visibly upset, alternately hugging him and scolding him for being so stupid. He was still rather groggy and not much of what they said registered. They left when the nurse interceded, and he went back to sleep.

The next day, Dr. Muller appeared. He examined Jack, grunted and muttered as he did so, drew blood, sent him down for X rays, brought him back up, grunted and muttered some more and left. Jack's parents came by to visit and told him they would be keeping him in the hospital for a few more days, just in case. Jack told them he didn't want any therapy while he was there and they promised there wouldn't be.

On Monday morning, his parents and Dr. Muller came to see him together. His mother cried and called him "Jackie" and his father grinned like the Cheshire Cat. Dr. Muller told him that the additional tests had been completed while he was asleep. The results were very encouraging. His blood disorder did not appear to be life-threatening. They had caught it early enough that it could be treated.

"You understand, Jack, you'll have to undergo some mild therapy," Dr. Muller cautioned. "But we can take care of that right here. There's nothing to worry about."

Jack smiled. He wasn't worried. He knew he was okay. He'd known it from the moment he'd pushed Desperado back into that tree. That was what the fight to lock away the Dragon had been all about. It had been to lock away Jack's sickness. Jack wasn't sure whether or not Pick had really lost his magic that night or simply let Jack think so. But he was sure about one thing—Pick had deliberately brought him back into the park and made him face the Dragon on his own. That was the special magic that his friend had once told him would be needed. It was the magic that had allowed him to live.

He went home at the end of the week and returned to school the next. When he informed Waddy Wadsworth that he wasn't dying after all, his friend just shrugged and said he'd told him so. Dr. Muller advised him to take it easy and brought him in for the promised therapy throughout the summer months. But his hair didn't fall out, he didn't lose weight, and the headaches and vision loss disappeared. Eventually Dr. Muller declared him cured, and the treatments came to an end.

He never saw Pick again. Once or twice he thought he saw Daniel, but he wasn't certain. He looked for the tree that imprisoned Desperado, but he couldn't find it. He didn't look for Wartag at all. When he was a few years older, he went to work for the park service during the summers.

It made him feel that he was giving something back to Pick. Sometimes when he was in the park, he could sense the other's presence. It didn't matter that he couldn't see his friend; it was enough just to know that he was there.

He never said anything to anyone about the Elf, of course. He wasn't going to make that mistake again.

It was like his mother had told him when he was little. A friend like Pick belonged only to him, and that was the way he should keep it.

GWYDION AND THE DRAGON

C. J. CHERRYH

ONCE UPON A TIME THERE WAS A
dragon, and once upon that time a prince who undertook to win the hand
of the elder and fairer of two princesses.

Not that this prince wanted either of Madog's daughters, although
rumors said that Eri was as wise and as gentle, as sweet and as fair as her
sister Glasog was cruel and ill-favored. The truth was that this prince
would marry either princess if it would save his father and his people; and
neither if he had had any choice in the matter. He was Gwydion ap Ogan,
and of princes in Dyfed he was the last.

Being a prince of Dyfed did not, understand, mean banners and trum-
pets and gilt armor and crowds of courtiers. King Ogan's palace was a
rambling stone house of dusty rafters hung with cooking pots and old
harnesses; King Ogan's wealth was mostly in pigs and pastures—the same
as all Ogan's subjects; Gwydion's war-horse was a black gelding with a
crooked blaze and shaggy feet, who had fought against the bandits from
the high hills. Gwydion's armor, serviceable in that perpetual warfare,
was scarred leather and plain mail, with new links bright among the old;
and lance or pennon he had none—the folk of Ogan's kingdom were not
lowland knights, heavily armored, but hunters in the hills and woods, and
for weapons this prince carried only a one-handed sword and a bow and
a quiver of gray-feathered arrows.

His companion, riding beside him on a bay pony, happened through
no choice of Gwydion's to be Owain ap Llodri, the houndmaster's son, his
good friend, by no means his squire: Owain had lain in wait along the

way, on a borrowed bay mare—Owain had simply assumed he was going, and that Gwydion had only hesitated, for friendship's sake, to ask him. So he saved Gwydion the necessity.

And the lop-eared old dog trotting by the horses' feet was Mili: Mili was fierce with bandits, and had respected neither Gwydion's entreaties nor Owain's commands thus far: stones might drive her off for a few minutes, but Mili came back again, that was the sort Mili was. That was the sort Owain was too, and Gwydion could refuse neither of them. So Mili panted along at the pace they kept, with big-footed Blaze and the bow-nosed bay, whose name might have been Swallow or maybe not—the poets forget—and as they rode Owain and Gwydion talked mostly about dogs and hunting.

That, as the same poets say, was the going of Prince Gwydion into King Madog's realm.

Now no one in Dyfed knew where Madog had come from. Some said he had been a king across the water. Some said he was born of a Roman and a Pict and had gotten sorcery through his mother's blood. Some said he had bargained with a dragon for his sorcery—certainly there was a dragon: devastation followed Madog's conquests, from one end of Dyfed to the other.

Reasonably reliable sources said Madog had applied first to King Bran, across the mountains, to settle at his court, and Bran having once laid eyes on Madog's elder daughter, had lusted after her beyond all good sense and begged Madog for her.

Give me your daughter, Bran had said to Madog, and I'll give you your heart's desire. But Madog had confessed that Eri was betrothed already, to a terrible dragon, who sometimes had the form of a man, and who had bespelled Madog and all his house: if Bran could overcome this dragon he might have Eri with his blessings, and his gratitude and the faithful help of his sorcery all his life; but if he died childless, Madog, by Bran's own oath, must be his heir.

That was the beginning of Madog's kingdom. So smitten was Bran that he swore to those terms, and died that very day, after which Madog ruled in his place.

After that Madog had made the same proposal to three of his neighbor kings, one after the other, proposing that each should ally with him and unite their kingdoms if the youngest son could win Eri from the dragon's spell and provide him an heir. But no prince ever came back from his quest. And the next youngest then went, until all the sons of the kings were gone, so that the kingdoms fell under Madog's rule.

After them, Madog sent to King Ban, and his sons died, last of all Prince Rhys, Gwydion's friend. Ban's heart broke, and Ban took to his bed and died.

Some whispered now that the dragon actually served Madog, that it had indeed brought Madog to power, under terms no one wanted to guess, and that this dragon did indeed have another form, which was the shape of a knight in strange armor, who would become Eri's husband if no other could win her. Some said (but none could prove the truth of it) that the dragon-knight had come from far over the sea, and that he devoured the sons and daughters of conquered kings, that being the tribute Madog gave him. But whatever the truth of that rumor, the dragon hunted far and wide in the lands Madog ruled and did not disdain to take the sons and daughters of farmers and shepherds too. Devastation went under his shadow, trees withered under his breath, and no one saw him outside his dragon shape and returned to tell of it, except only Madog and (rumor said) his younger daughter Glasog, who was a sorceress as cruel as her father.

Some said that Glasog could take the shape of a raven and fly over the land choosing whom the dragon might take. The people called her Madog's Crow, and feared the look of her eye. Some said she was the true daughter of Madog and that Madog had stolen Eri from Faerie, and given her mother to the dragon; but others said they were twins, and that Eri had gotten all that an ordinary person had of goodness, while her sister Glasog—

"Prince Gwydion," Glasog said to her father, "would have come on the quest last year with his friend Rhys, except his father's refusing him, and Prince Gwydion will not let his land go to war if he can find another course. He'll persuade his father."

"Good," Madog said. "That's very good." Madog smiled, but Glasog did not. Glasog was thinking of the dragon. Glasog harbored no illusions: the dragon had promised Madog that he would be king of all Wales if he could achieve this in seven years; and rule for seventy and seven more with the dragon's help.

But if he failed—failed by the seventh year to gain any one of the kingdoms of Dyfed, if one stubborn king withstood him and for one day beyond the seven allotted years, kept him from obtaining the least, last stronghold of the west, then all the bargain was void and Madog would have failed in everything.

And the dragon would claim a forfeit of his choosing.

That was what Glasog thought of, in her worst nightmares: that the dragon had always meant to have all the kingdoms of the west with very little effort—let her father win all but one and fail, on the smallest letter of the agreement. What was more, all the generals in all the armies they had taken agreed that the kingdom of Ogan could never be taken by force: there were mountains in which resistance could hide and not even dragon-fire could burn all of them; but most of all there was the fabled Luck of Ogan, which said that no force of arms could defeat the sons of Ogan.

Watch, Madog had said. And certainly her father was astute, and cunning, and knew how to snare a man by his pride. There's always a way, her father had said, to break a spell. This one has a weakness. The strongest spells most surely have their soft spots.

And Ogan had one son, and that was Prince Gwydion.

Now we will fetch him, Madog said to his daughter. Now we will see what his luck is worth.

The generals said, "If you would have a chance in war, first be rid of Gwydion."

But Madog said, and Glasog agreed, there are other uses for Gwydion.

54

* * *

"It doesn't *look* different," Owain said as they passed the border stone.

It was true. Nothing looked changed at all. There was no particular odor of evil, or of threat. It might have been last summer, when the two of them had hunted with Rhys. They had used to hunt together every summer, and last autumn they had tracked the bandit Llewellyn to his lair, and caught him with stolen sheep. But in the spring Ban's sons had gone to seek the hand of Madog's daughter, and one by one had died, last of them, in early summer, Rhys himself.

Gwydion would have gone, long since, and long before Rhys. A score of times Gwydion had approached his father King Ogan and his mother Queen Belys and begged to try his luck against Madog, from the first time Madog's messenger had appeared and challenged the kings of Dyfed to war or wedlock. But each time Ogan had refused him, arguing in the first place that other princes, accustomed to warfare on their borders, were better suited, and better armed, and that there were many princes in Dyfed, but he had only one son.

But when Rhys had gone and failed, the last kingdom save that of King Ogan passed into Madog's hands. And Gwydion, grief-stricken with the loss of his friend, said to his parents, "If we had stood together we might have defeated this Madog; if we had taken the field then, together, we might have had a chance; if you had let me go with Rhys one of us might have won and saved the other. But now Rhys is dead and we have Madog for a neighbor. Let me go when he sends to us. Let me try my luck at courting his daughter. A war with him now we may not lose, but we cannot hope to win."

Even so Ogan had resisted him, saying that they still had their mountains for a shield, difficult going for any army; and arguing that their luck had saved them this far and that it was rash to take matters into their own hands.

Now the nature of that luck was this: that of the kingdom in Dyfed,

Ogan's must always be poorest and plainest. But that luck meant that they could not fail in war nor fail in harvest: it had come down to them from Ogan's own great-grandfather Ogan ap Ogan of Llanfynnyd, who had sheltered one of the Faerie unaware; and only faithlessness could break it—so great-grandfather Ogan had said. So: "Our luck will be our defense," Ogan argued with his son. "Wait and let Madog come to us. We'll fight him in the mountains."

"Will we fight a dragon? Even if we defeat Madog himself, what of our herds, what of our farmers and our freeholders? Can we let the land go to waste and let our people feed this dragon, while we hide in the hills and wait for luck to save us? Is that faithfulness?" That was what Gwydion had asked his father, while Madog's herald was in the hall—a raven black as unrepented sin . . . or the intentions of a wizard.

"Madog bids you know," this raven had said, perched on a rafter of Ogan's hall, beside a moldering basket and a string of garlic, "that he has taken every kingdom of Dyfed but this. He offers you what he offered others: if King Ogan has a son worthy to win Madog's daughter and get an heir, then King Ogan may rule in peace over his kingdom so long as he lives, and that prince will have titles and the third of Madog's realm besides. . . .

"But if the prince will not or cannot win the princess, then Ogan must swear Madog is his lawful true heir. And if Ogan refuses this, then Ogan must face Madog's army, which now is the army of four kingdoms each greater than his own. Surely," the raven had added, fixing all present with a wicked, midnight eye, "it is no great endeavor Madog asks—simply to court his daughter. And will so many die, and so much burn? Or will Prince Gwydion win a realm wider than your own? A third of Madog's lands is no small dowry and inheritance of Madog's kingdom is no small prize."

So the raven had said. And Gwydion had said to his mother, "Give me your blessing," and to his father Ogan: "Swear the oath Madog asks.

If our Luck can save us it will save me and win me this bride; but if it fails me in this it would have failed us in any case."

Maybe, Gwydion thought as they passed the border, Owain was a necessary part of that luck. Maybe even Mili was. It seemed to him now that he dared reject nothing that loved him and favored him, even if it was foolish and even if it broke his heart: his luck seemed so perilous and stretched so thin already he dared not bargain with his fate.

"No sign of a dragon, either," Owain said, looking about them at the rolling hills.

Gwydion looked about him too, and at the sky, which showed only the lazy flight of a single bird.

Might it be a raven? It was too far to tell.

"I'd think," said Owain, "it would seem grimmer than it does."

Gwydion shivered as if a cold wind had blown. But Blaze plodded his heavy-footed way with no semblance of concern, and Mili trotted ahead, tongue lolling, occasionally sniffing along some trail that crossed theirs.

"Mili would smell a dragon," Owain said.

"Are you sure?" Gwydion asked. He was not. If Madog's younger daughter could be a raven at her whim he was not sure what a dragon might be at its pleasure.

That night they had a supper of brown bread and sausages that Gwydion's mother had sent, and ale that Owain had with him.

"My mother's brewing," Owain said. "My father's store." And Owain sighed and said: "By now they must surely guess I'm not off hunting."

"You didn't tell them?" Gwydion asked. "You got no blessing in this?"

Owain shrugged, and fed a bit of sausage to Mili, who gulped it down and sat looking at them worshipfully.

Owain's omission of duty worried Gwydion. He imagined how Owain's parents would first wonder where he had gone, then guess, and fear for Owain's life, for which he held himself entirely accountable. In the morning he said, "Owain, go back. This is far enough."

But Owain shrugged and said, "Not I. Not without you." Owain rubbed Mili's ears. "No more than Mili, without me."

Gwydion had no least idea now what was faithfulness and what was a young man's foolish pride. Everything seemed tangled. But Owain seemed not in the least distressed.

Owain said, "We'll be there by noon tomorrow."

Gwydion wondered, Where is this dragon? and distrusted the rocks around them and the sky over their heads. He felt a presence in the earth—or thought he felt it. But Blaze and Swallow grazed at their leisure. Only Mili looked worried—Mili pricked up her ears, such as those long ears could prick, wondering, perhaps, if they were going to get to bandits soon, and whether they were, after all, going to eat that last bit of breakfast sausage.

"He's on his way," Glasog said. "He's passed the border."

"Good," said Madog. And to his generals: "Didn't I tell you?"

The generals still looked worried.

But Glasog went and stood on the walk of the castle that had been Ban's, looking out over the countryside and wondering what the dragon was thinking tonight, whether the dragon had foreseen this as he had foreseen the rest, or whether he was even yet keeping some secret from them, scheming all along for their downfall.

She launched herself quite suddenly from the crest of the wall, swooped out over the yard and beyond, over the seared fields.

The dragon, one could imagine, knew about Ogan's Luck. The dragon was too canny to face it—and doubtless was chuckling in his den in the hills.

Glasog flew that way, but saw nothing from that cave but a little curl of smoke—there was almost always smoke. And Glasog leaned toward the west, following the ribbon of a road, curious, and wagering that the dragon this time would not bestir himself.

Her father wagered the same. And she knew very well what he

wagered, indeed she did: duplicity for duplicity—if not the old serpent's aid, then human guile; if treachery from the dragon, then put at risk the dragon's prize.

Gwydion and Owain came to a burned farmstead along the road. Mili sniffed about the blackened timbers and bristled at the shoulders, and came running back to Owain's whistle, not without mistrustful looks behind her.

There was nothing but a black ruin beside a charred, brittle orchard.

"I wonder," Owain said, "what became of the old man and his wife."

"I don't," said Gwydion, worrying for his own parents, and seeing in this example how they would fare in any retreat into the hills.

The burned farm was the first sign they had seen of the dragon, but it was not the last. There were many other ruins, and sad and terrible sights. One was a skull sitting on a fence row. And on it sat a raven.

"This was a brave man," it said, and pecked the skull, which rang hollowly, and inclined its head toward the field beyond. "That was his wife. And farther still his young daughter."

"Don't speak to it," Gwydion said to Owain. They rode past, at Blaze's plodding pace, and did not look back.

But the raven flitted ahead of them and waited for them on the stone fence. "If you die," the raven said, "then your father will no longer believe in his luck. Then it will leave him. It happened to all the others."

"There's always a first," said Gwydion.

Owain said, reaching for his bow: "Shall I shoot it?"

But Gwydion said: "Kill the messenger for the message? No. It's a foolish creature. Let it be."

It left them then. Gwydion saw it sometimes in the sky ahead of them. He said nothing to Owain, who had lost his cheerfulness, and Mili stayed close by them, sore of foot and suspicious of every breeze.

There were more skulls. They saw gibbets and stakes in the middle of a burned orchard. There was scorched grass, recent and powdery under the horses' hooves. Blaze, who loved to snatch a bite now and again as he went, moved uneasily, snorting with dislike of the smell, and Swallow started at shadows.

Then the turning of the road showed them a familiar brook, and around another hill and beyond, the walled holding that had been King Ban's, in what had once been a green valley. Now it was burned, black bare hillsides and the ruin of hedges and orchards.

So the trial they had come to find must be here, Gwydion thought, and uneasily took up his bow and picked several of his best arrows, which he held against his knee as he rode. Owain did the same.

But they reached the gate of the low-walled keep unchallenged, until they came on the raven sitting, whetting its beak on the stone. It looked at them solemnly, saying, "Welcome, Prince Gwydion. You've won your bride. Now how will you fare, I wonder."

Men were coming from the keep, running toward them, others, under arms, in slower advance.

"What now?" Owain asked, with his bow across his knee; and Gwydion lifted his bow and bent it, aiming at the foremost.

The crowd stopped, but a black-haired man in gray robes and a king's gold chain came alone, holding up his arms in a gesture of welcome and of peace. Madog himself? Gwydion wondered, while Gwydion's arm shook and the string trembled in his grip. "Is it Gwydion ap Ogan?" that man asked—surely no one else but Madog would wear that much gold. "My son-in-law to be! Welcome!"

Gwydion, with great misgivings, slacked the string and let down the bow, while fat Blaze, better trained than seemed, finally shifted feet. Owain lowered his bow too, as King Madog's men opened up the gate. Some of the crowd cheered as they rode in, and more took it up, as if they had only then gained the courage or understood it was expected. Blaze and Swallow snorted and threw their heads at the racket, as Gwydion and Owain put away their arrows, unstrung their bows and hung them on their saddles.

But Mili stayed close by Owain's legs as they dismounted, growling low in her throat, and barked one sharp warning when Madog came close. "Hush," Owain bade her, and knelt down more than for respect, keeping one hand on Mili's muzzle and the other in her collar, whispering to her, "Hush, hush, there's a good dog."

Gwydion made the bow a prince owed to a king and prospective father-in-law, all the while thinking that there had to be a trap in this place. He was entirely sorry to see grooms lead Blaze and Swallow away, and kept Owain and Mili constantly in the tail of his eye as Madog took him by the arms and hugged him. Then Madog said, catching all his attention, eye to eye with him for a moment, "What a well-favored young man you are. The last is always best. —So you've killed the dragon."

Gwydion thought, Somehow we've ridden right past the trial we should have met. If I say no, he will find cause to disallow me; and he'll kill me and Owain and all our kin.

But lies were not the kind of dealing his father had taught him; faithfulness was the rule of the house of Ogan; so Gwydion looked the king squarely in the eyes and said, "I met no dragon."

Madog's eyes showed surprise, and Madog said: "Met no dragon?"

"Not a shadow of a dragon."

Madog grinned and clapped him on the shoulder and showed him to the crowd, saying, "This is your true prince!"

Then the crowd cheered in earnest, and even Owain and Mili looked heartened. Owain rose with Mili's collar firmly in hand.

Madog said then to Gwydion, under his breath, "If you had lied you would have met the dragon here and now. Do you know you're the first one who's gotten this far?"

"I saw nothing," Gwydion said again, as if Madog had not understood him. "Only burned farms. Only skulls and bones."

Madog turned a wide smile toward him, showing teeth. "Then it was your destiny to win. Was it not?" And Madog faced him about toward the doors of the keep. "Daughter, daughter, come out!"

Gwydion hesitated a step, expecting he knew not what—the dragon itself, perhaps: his wits went scattering toward the gate, the horses being led away, Mili barking in alarm—and a slender figure standing in the doorway, all white and gold. "My elder daughter," Madog said. "Eri."

Gwydion went as he was led, telling himself it must be true, after so much dread of this journey and so many friends' lives lost—obstacles must have fallen down for him, Ogan's Luck must still be working. . . .

The young bride waiting for him was so beautiful, so young and so—kind—was the first word that came to him—Eri smiled and immediately it seemed to him she was innocent of all the grief around her, innocent and good as her sister was reputed cruel and foul.

He took her hand, and the folk of the keep all cheered, calling him their prince; and if any were Ban's people, those wishes might well come from the heart, with fervent hopes of rescue. Pipers began to play, gentle hands urged them both inside, and in this desolate land some woman found flowers to give Eri.

"Owain?" Gwydion cried, looking back, suddenly seeing no sign of him or of Mili: "Owain!"

He refused to go farther until Owain could part the crowd and reach his side, Mili firmly in hand. Owain looked breathless and frightened. Gwydion felt the same. But the crowd pushed and pulled at them, the pipers piped and dancers danced, and they brought them into a hall smelling of food and ale.

It can't be this simple, Gwydion still thought, and made up his mind that no one should part him from Owain, Mili, or their swords. He looked about him, bedazzled, at a wedding feast that must have taken days to prepare.

But how could they know I'd get here? he wondered. Did they do this for all the suitors who failed—and celebrate their funerals, then . . . with their wedding feast?

At which thought he felt cold through and through, and found Eri's hand on his arm disquieting; but Madog himself waited to receive them in the hall, and joined their hands and plighted them their vows, to make them man and wife, come what might—

"So long as you both shall live," Madog said, pressing their hands together. "And when there is an heir Prince Gwydion shall have the third of my lands, and his father shall rule in peace so long as he shall live."

Gwydion misliked the last—Gwydion thought in alarm: As long as he lives.

But Madog went on, saying, "—be you wed, be you wed, be you wed," three times, as if it were a spell—then: "Kiss your bride, son-in-law."

The well-wishes from the guests roared like the sea. The sea was in Eri's eyes, deep and blue and drowning. He heard Mili growl as he kissed Eri's lips once, twice, three times.

The pipers played, the people cheered, no few of whom indeed might have been King Ban's, or Lugh's, or Lughdan's. Perhaps, Gwydion dared think, perhaps it was hope he brought to them, perhaps he truly had won, after all, and the dreadful threat Madog posed was lifted, so that Madog would be their neighbor, no worse than the worst they had had, and perhaps, if well-disposed, better than one or two.

Perhaps, he thought, sitting at Madog's right hand with his bride at his right and with Owain just beyond, perhaps there truly was cause to hope, and he could ride away from here alive—though he feared he could find no cause to do so tonight, with so much prepared, with an anxious young bride and King Madog determined to indulge his beautiful daughter. Women hurried about with flowers and with torches, with linens and with brooms and platters and plates, tumblers ran riot, dancers leaped and cavorted—one of whom came to grief against an ale-server. Both went down, in Madog's very face, and the hall grew still and dangerous.

But Eri laughed and clapped her hands, a laughter so small and faint until her father laughed, and all the hall laughed; and Gwydion remembered then to breathe, while Eri hugged his arm and laughed up at him with those sea-blue eyes.

"More ale!" Madog called. "Less spillage, there!"

The dreadful wizard could joke, then. Gwydion drew two easier breaths, and someone filled their cups. He drank, but prudently: he caught Owain's eye, and Owain his—while Mili having found a bone to her liking, with a great deal of meat to it, worried it happily in the straw beneath the table.

There were healths drunk, there were blessings said, at each of which one had to drink—and Madog laughed and called Gwydion a fine son-in-law, asked him about his campaign against the bandits and swore he was glad to have his friends and his kin and anyone he cared to bring here: Madog got up and clapped Owain on the shoulder too, and asked was Owain wed, and, informed Owain was not, called out to the hall that here was another fine catch, and where were the young maids to keep Owain from chill on his master's wedding night?

Owain protested in some embarrassment, starting to his feet—

But drink overcame him, and he sat down again with a hand to his brow, Gwydion saw it with concern, while Madog touched Gwydion's arm on the other side and said, "The women are ready," slyly bidding him finish his ale beforehand.

Gwydion rose and handed his bride to her waiting women. "Owain!" Gwydion said then sharply, and Owain gained his feet, saying something Gwydion could not hear for with all the people cheering and the piper starting up, but he saw Owain was distressed. Gwydion resisted the women pulling at him, stood fast until Owain reached him, flushed with ale and embarrassment. The men surrounded him with bawdy cheers and more offered cups.

It was his turn then on the stairs, more cups thrust on him, Madog clapping him on the shoulder and hugging him and calling him the son he had always wanted, and saying there should be peace in Dyfed for a hundred years . . . unfailing friendship with his father and his kin—greater things, should he have ambitions. . . .

The room spun around. Voices buzzed. They pushed him up the stairs,

Owain and Mili notwithstanding, Mili barking all the while. They brought him down the upstairs hall, they opened the door to the bridal chamber.

On pitch dark.

Perhaps it was cowardly to balk. Gwydion thought so, in the instant the laughing men gave him a push between the shoulders. Shame kept him from calling Owain to his rescue. The door shut at his back.

He heard rustling in the dark and imagined coils and scales. Eri's soft voice said, "My lord?"

A faint starlight edged the shutters. His eyes made out the furnishings, now that the flare of torches had left his sight. It was the rustling of bedclothes he heard. He saw a woman's shoulder and arm faintly in the shadowed bed, in the scant starshine that the shutter let through.

He backed against the door, found the latch behind him, cracked it the least little bit outward and saw Owain leaning there against his arm, facing the lamplit wall outside, flushed of face and ashamed to meet his eyes at such close range.

"I'm here, m'lord," Owain breathed, on ale-fumes. Owain never called him lord, but Owain was greatly embarrassed tonight. "The lot's gone down the stairs now. I'll be here the night. I'll not leave this door, nor sleep, I swear to you."

Gwydion gave him a worried look, wishing the two of them dared escape this hall and Madog's well-wishes, running pell-mell back to his own house, his parents' advice, and childhood. But, "Good," he said, and carefully pulled the door to, making himself blind in the dark again. He let the latch fall and catch.

"My lord?" Eri said faintly.

He felt quite foolish, himself and Owain conspiring together like two boys at an orchard wall, when it was a young bride waiting for him, innocent and probably as anxious as he. He nerved himself, walked up by the bed and opened the shutters wide on a night sky brighter than the dark behind him.

But with the cool night wind blowing into the room he thought of dragons, wondered whether opening the window to the sky was wise at all, and wondered what was slipping out of bed with the whispering of the bedclothes. His bride forwardly clasped his arm, wound fingers into his and swayed against him, saying how beautiful the stars were.

Perhaps that invited courtly words. He murmured some such. He found the courage to take Madog's daughter in his arms and kiss her, and thereafter—

He waked abed with the faint dawn coming through the window, his sword tangled with his leg and his arm ensnared in a woman's unbound hair—

Hair raven black.

He leaped up trailing sheets, while a strange young woman sat up to snatch the bedclothes to her, with her black hair flowing about her shoulders, her eyes dark and cold and fathomless.

"Where's my wife?" he cried.

She smiled, thin-lipped, rose from the bed, drawing the sheets about her like royal robes. "Why, you see her, husband."

He rushed to the door and lifted the latch. The door did not budge, hardly rattled when he shoved it with all his strength. "Owain?" he cried, and pounded it with his fist. "Owain!"

No answer came. Gwydion turned slowly to face the woman, dreading what other shape she might take. But she sat down wrapped in the sheets with one knee on the rumpled bed, looking at him. Her hair spread about her like a web of shadows in the dawn. As much as Eri had been an innocent girl, this was a woman far past Eri's innocence or his own.

He asked, "Where's Owain? What's become of him?"

"Guesting elsewhere."

"Who are you?"

"Glasog," she said, and shrugged, the dawn wind carrying long strands of her hair about her shoulders. "Or Eri, if you like. My father's elder daughter and younger, all in one, since he has none but me."

"Why?" he asked. "Why this pretense if you were the bargain?"

66

"People trust Eri. She's so fair, so kind."

"What do you want? What does your father want?"

"A claim on your father's land. The last kingdom of Dyfed. And you've come to give it to us."

Gwydion remembered nothing of what might have happened last night. He remembered nothing of anything he should have heard or done last night, abed with Glasog the witch, Madog's raven-haired daughter. He felt cold and hollow and desperate, asking, "On your oath, *is* Owain safe?"

"And would you believe my oath?" Glasog asked.

"I'll see your father," Gwydion said shortly. "Trickery or not, he swore me the third of his kingdom for your dowry. Younger or elder, or both, you're my wife. Will he break his word?"

Glasog said, "An heir. Then he'll release you and your friend, and your father will reign in peace . . . so long as he lives."

Gwydion walked to the open window, gazing at a paling, still sunless sky. He feared he knew what that release would be—the release of himself and Owain from life, while the child he sired would become heir to his father's kingdom with Madog to enforce that right.

So long as his father lived . . . so long as that unfortunate *child* might live, for that matter, once the inheritance of Ogan's line and Ogan's Luck passed securely into Madog's line—his father's kingdom taken and for no battle, no war, only a paltry handful of lies and lives.

He looked across the scorched hills, toward a home he could not reach, a father who could not advise him. He dared not hope that Owain might have escaped to bring word to his father: I'll not leave this door, Owain had said—and they would have had to carry Owain away by force or sorcery. Mili with him.

It was sorcery that must have made him sleep and forget last night. It was sorcery he must have seen when he turned from the window and saw Eri sitting there, rosy-pale and golden, patting the place beside her and bidding him come back to bed.

He shuddered and turned and hit the window ledge, hurting his hand. He thought of flight, even of drawing the sword and killing Madog's daughter, before this princess could conceive and doom him and his parents. . . .

Glasog's voice said, slowly, from Eri's lips, "If you try anything so rash, my father won't need your friend any longer, will he? I certainly wouldn't be in his place then. I'd hardly be in it now."

"What have you done with Owain?"

Eri shrugged. Glasog's voice said, "Dear husband—"

"The marriage wasn't consummated," he said, "for all I remember."

It was Glasog who lifted a shoulder. Black hair parted. "To sorcery—does it matter?"

He looked desperately toward the window. He said, without looking at her: "I've something to say about that, don't you think?"

"No. You don't. If you wouldn't, or couldn't, the words are said, the vows are made, the oaths are taken. If not your child—anyone's will do, for all men know or care."

He looked at her to see if he had understood what he thought he had, and Glasog gathered a thick skein of her hair—and drew it over her shoulder.

"The oaths are made," Glasog said. "Any lie will do. Any child will do."

"There's my word against it," Gwydion said.

Glasog shook her head gravely. "A lie's nothing to my father. A life is nothing." She stood up, shook out her hair, and hugged the sheets about her. Dawn lent a sudden and unkind light to Glasog's face, showing hollow cheeks, a grim mouth, a dark and sullen eye that promised nothing of compromise.

Why? he asked himself. Why this much of truth? Why not Eri's face?

She said, "What will you, husband?"

"Ask tonight," he said, hoping only for time and better counsel.

She inclined her head, walked between him and the window, lifting her arms wide. For an instant the morning sun showed a woman's body against the sheets. Then—it might have been a trick of the eyes—black hair spread into the black wings, something flew to the window and the sheet drifted to the floor.

What about the dragon? he would have asked, but there was no one to ask.

He went to the door and tried it again, in case sorcery had ceased. But it gave not at all, not to cleverness, not to force. He only bruised his shoulder, and leaned dejectedly against the door, sure now that he had made a terrible mistake.

The window offered nothing but a sheer drop to the stones below, and when he tried that way, he could not force his shoulders through. There was no fire in the room, not so much as water to drink. He might fall on his sword, but he took Glasog at her word: it was the form of the marriage Madog had wanted, and they would only hide his death until it was convenient to reveal it. All the house had seen them wed and bedded, even Owain—who, being honest, could swear only what he had seen and what he had guessed—but never, never to the truth of what had happened and not happened last night.

Ogan's fabled Luck should have served him better, he thought, casting himself onto the bedside, head in hands. It should have served all of them better, this Luck his great-grandfather had said only faithlessness could break—

But was Glasog herself not faithlessness incarnate? Was not Madog?

If that was the barb in great-grandfather's blessing—it had done nothing but bring him and his family into Madog's hands. But it seemed to him that the fay were reputed for twists and turns in their gifts, and if they had made one such twist they might make another: all he knew was to hew to the course Ogan's sons had always followed.

So he had come here in good faith, been caught through abuse of that faith, and though he might perhaps seize the chance to come at Madog himself, that was treachery for treachery and if he had any last whisper of belief in his luck, that was what he most should not do.

"Is there a child?" Madog asked, and Glasog said, "Not yet. Not yet. Be patient."

"There's not," Madog said testily, "forever. Remember that."

"I remember," Glasog said.

"You wouldn't grow fond of him—or foolish?'"

"I?" quoth Glasog, with an arch of her brow. "I, fond? Not fond of the dragon, let us say. Not fond of poverty—or early dying."

"We'll not fail. If not him—"

"Truly, do you imagine the dragon will give you *anything* if the claim's not legitimate? I think not. I do think not. It must be Gwydion's child— and *that*, by nature, by Gwydion's own will. That *is* the difficulty, isn't it?"

"You vaunt your sorcery. Use it!"

Glasog said, coldly, "When needs be. If needs be. But it's myself he'll have, *not* Eri, and for myself, not Eri. That's my demand in this."

"Don't be a fool."

Glasog smiled with equal coldness. "This man has magical protections. His luck is no illusion and it's not to cross. I don't forget that. Don't you. *Trust* me, Father."

"I wonder how I got you."

Glasog still smiled. "Luck," she said. "You want to be rid of the dragon, don't you? Has my advice ever failed you? And isn't it the old god's bond that he'll barter for questions?"

Her father scowled. "It's *my* life you're bartering for, curse your cold heart. It's my life you're risking with your schemes—a life from each kingdom of Dyfed, *that's* the barter we've made. We've caught Gwydion. We can't stave the dragon off forever for your whims and your vapors, Daughter. Get me a grandson—by whatever sorcery—and forget this foolishness. Kill the dragon . . . do you think I've not tried that? All the princes in Dyfed have tried that."

Glasog said, with her grimmest look: "We've also Gwydion's friend, don't we? And isn't he of Ogan's kingdom?"

Gwydion endured the hours until sunset, hungry and thirsty and having nothing whatever to do but to stare out the slit of a window, over a black and desolate land.

He wondered if Owain was even alive, or what had become of Mili.

Once he saw a raven in flight, toward the south; and once, late, the sky growing dimly copper, he saw it return, it seemed more slowly, circling always to the right.

Glasog? he wondered—or merely a raven looking for its supper?

The sky went from copper to dusk. He felt the air grow chill. He thought of closing the shutters, but that was Glasog's access. So he paced the floor, or looked out the window or simply listened to the distant comings and goings below which alone told him that there was life in the place.

Perhaps, he thought, they only meant him to die of thirst and hunger, and perhaps he would never see or speak to a living soul again. He hoped Glasog would come by sunset, but she failed that; and by moonrise, but she did not come.

At last, when he had fallen asleep in his waiting, a shadow swept in the window with a snap and flutter of dark wings, and Glasog stood wrapped only in dark hair and limned in starlight.

He gathered himself up quickly, feeling still that he might be dreaming. "I expected you earlier," he said.

"I had inquiries to make," she said, and walked to the table where— he did not know how, a cup and a silver pitcher gleamed in reflected starlight. She lifted the pitcher and poured, and oh, he was thirsty. She offered it, and it might be poisoned for all he knew. At the very least it was enchanted, and perhaps only moondust and dreams. But she stood offering it; he drank, and it took both thirst and hunger away.

She said, "You may have one wish of me, Gwydion. One wish. And then I may have two from you. Do you agree?"

He wondered what to say. He put down the cup and walked away to the window, looking out on the night sky. There were a hundred things to ask: his parents' lives; Owain's; the safety of his land—and in each one there seemed some flaw.

Finally he chose the simplest. "Love me," he said.

For a long time Glasog said nothing. Then he heard her cross the room.

He turned. Her eyes flashed at him, sudden as a serpent's. She said, "Dare you? First drink from my cup."

"Is this your first wish?"

"It is."

He hesitated, looking at her, then walked away to the table and reached for the shadowy cup, but another appeared beside it, gleaming, crusted with jewels.

"Which will you have?" she asked.

He hoped then that he understood her question. And he picked up the cup of plain pewter and drank it all.

She said, from behind him, "You have your wish, Gwydion."

And wings brushed his face, the wind stirred his hair, the raven shape swooped out the window.

"Owain," a voice said—the raven's voice, and Owain leaped up from his prison bed, such as he could, though his head was spinning and he had to brace himself against the wall. It was not the raven's first visit. He asked it, "Where's my master? What's happened to him?"

And the raven, suddenly no raven, but a dark-haired woman: "Wed-lock," she said. "Death, if the dragon gets his due—as soon he may."

"Glasog," Owain said, chilled to the marrow. Since Madog's men had hauled him away from Gwydion's door he had had this dizziness, and it came on him now. He felt his knees going and he caught himself.

"You might save him," Glasog said.

"And should I trust you?" he asked.

The chains fell away from him with a ringing of iron, and the bolts fell from the door.

"Because I'm his wife," she said. Eri stood there. He rubbed his eyes and it was Glasog again. "And you're his friend. Isn't that what it means, friendship? Or marriage?"

A second time he rubbed his eyes. The door swung open.

"My father says," Glasog said, "the dragon's death will free Prince Gwydion. You may have your horse, your dog, your armor and your weapons—or whatever you will, Owain ap Llodri. But for that gift—you must give me one wish when I claim it."

In time—Gwydion was gazing out the window, he had no idea why, he heard the slow echo of hoofbeats off the wall.

He saw Owain ride out the gate; he saw the raven flying over him.

"Owain," he cried. "Owain!"

But Owain paid no heed. Only Mili stopped, and looked up at the tower where he stood.

He thought—Go with him, Mili, if it's home he's bound for. Warn my father. There's no hope here.

Owain never looked back. Gwydion saw him turn south at the gate, entirely away from home, and guessed where Owain was going.

"Come back," he cried. "Owain! No!"

It was the dragon they were going to. It was surely the dragon Owain was going to, and if Gwydion had despaired in his life, it was seeing Owain and Mili go off in company with his wife.

He tried again to force himself through the window slit. He tried the door, working with his sword to lift the bar he was sure was in place outside.

He found it and lifted it. But it stopped with the rattle of chain.

They found the brook again, beyond the hill, and the raven fluttered down clumsily to drink, spreading a wing to steady herself.

Owain reined Swallow in. He had no reason to trust the raven in any shape, less reason to believe it than anything else that he had seen in this place. But Mili came cautiously up to it, and suddenly it was Glasog kneeling there, wrapped only in her hair, with her back to him, and Mili whining at her in some distress.

Owain got down. He saw two fingers missing from Glasog's right hand, the wounds scarcely healed. She drank from her other hand, and bathed the wounded one in water. She looked at Owain and said, "You wished to save Gwydion. You said nothing of yourself."

Owain shrugged and settled with his arm around Mili's neck.

"Now you owe me my wish," Glasog said.

"That I do," he said, and feared what it might be.

She said, "There's a god near this place. The dragon overcame him. But he will still answer the right question. Most gods will, with proper sacrifice."

Owain said, "What shall I ask him?"

She said, "I've already asked."

Owain asked then, "And the answers, lady?"

"First that the dragon's life and soul lies in his right eye. And second that no man can kill him."

Owain understood the answer then. He scratched Mili's neck beneath the collar. He said, "Mili's a loyal dog. And if flying tires you, lady, I've got a shoulder you can ride on."

Glasog said, "Better you go straightaway back to your king. Only lend me your bow, your dog, and your horse. *That* is my wish, ap Llodri."

Owain shook his head, and got up, patting Mili on the head. "All that you'll have by your wish," Owain said, "but I go with them."

"Be warned," she said.

"I am that," said Owain, and held out his hand. "My lady?"

The raven fluttered up and settled on his arm, bating as he rose into the saddle. Owain set Swallow on her way, among the charred, cinder-black hills, to a cave the raven showed him.

Swallow had no liking for this place. Owain patted her neck, coaxed her forward. Mili bristled up and growled as they climbed. Owain took up his bow and drew out an arrow, yelled, "Mili! Look out!" as fire billowed out and Swallow shied.

A second gust followed. Mili yelped and ran from the roiling smoke, racing ahead of a great serpent shape that surged out of the cave; but Mili began to cross the hill then, leading it.

The raven launched itself from Owain's shoulder, straighter than Owain's arrow sped.

A clamor rose in the keep, somewhere deep in the halls. It was dawn above the hills, and a glow still lit the south, as Gwydion watched from the window.

He was watching when a strange rider came down the road, shining gold in the sun, in scaled armor.

"The dragon!" he heard shouted from the wall. Gwydion's heart sank. It sank further when the scale-armored rider reached the gate and Madog's men opened to it. It was Swallow the dragon-knight rode, Swallow with her mane all singed; and it was Mili who limped after, with her coat all soot-blackened and with great sores showing on her hide. Mili's head hung and her tail drooped and the dragon led her by a rope, while a raven sat perched on his shoulder.

Of Owain there was no sign.

There came a clattering in the hall. Chain rattled, the bar lifted and thumped and armed men were in the doorway.

"King Madog wants you," one said. And Gwydion—

"Madog will have to send twice," Gwydion said, with his sword in hand.

The dragon rode to the steps and the raven fluttered to the ground as waiting women rushed to it, to bring Princess Glasog her cloak—black as her hair and stitched with spells. The waiting women and the servants had seen this sight before—the same as the men at arms at the gate, who had had their orders should it have been Owain returning.

"Daughter," Madog said, descending those same steps as Glasog rose up, wrapped in black and silver. Mili growled and bristled, suddenly strained at her leash—

The dragon loosed it and Mili sprang for Madog's throat. Madog fell under the hound and Madog's blood was on the steps—but his neck was already broken.

Servants ran screaming. Men at arms stood confused, as if they had quite forgotten what they were doing or where they were or what had brought them there, the men of the fallen kingdoms all looking at one another and wondering what terrible thing had held them here.

And on all of this Glasog turned her back, walking up the steps.

"My lady!" Owain cried—for it was Owain wore the armor; but it was not Owain's voice she longed to hear.

Glasog let fall the cloak and leaped from the wall. The raven glided away, with one harsh cry against the wind.

In time after—often in that bitter winter, when snows lay deep and wind skirled drifts about the door—Owain told how Glasog had pierced the dragon's eye; and how they had found the armor, and how Glasog had told him the last secret, that with the dragon dead, Madog's sorcery would leave him.

That winter, too, Gwydion found a raven in the courtyard, a crippled bird, missing feathers on one wing. It seemed greatly confused, so far gone with hunger and with cold that no one thought it would live. But Gwydion tended it until spring and set it free again.

It turned up thereafter on the wall of Gwydion's keep—King Gwydion, he was now—lord of all Dyfed. "You've one wish left," he said to it. "One wish left of me."

"I give it to you," the raven said. "Whatever you wish, King Gwydion."

"Be what you wish to be," Gwydion said.

And thereafter men told of the wisdom of King Gwydion as often as of the beauty of his wife.

THE FAIRY GODMOTHER

LESTER DEL REY

THIS, SAMANTHA TOLD HERSELF
for the fiftieth time, was no way to treat a princess! No way at all! And she *was* a princess. Her father was a king; the kingdom might not be the largest—might even be the smallest. But he was still the king, and she was his only heir. Someday she'd be the reigning queen. You'd think they might show a little respect and consideration for a genuine royal princess who was twelve going on thirteen. But no, never that!

Her parents were off to some regional conference of kings. Surely she should be going along if she were ever to learn anything about governing a kingdom. Instead, she was being packed off to severe, grumpy old Aunt Hepzibah to spend a month in her mausoleum of a house.

She'd tried everything on her father—sweet requests, reason, even tears, but he wouldn't relent. Her mother had decided! Her mother always decided things the way she didn't want.

And where was her fairy godmother in all this? She was supposed to have one, though nobody told her anything beyond the fact that there was such a creature. The older servants just got a bemused expression when she questioned them. And her parents told her to wait until she was older—as they did about everything.

She'd tried to summon the stupid creature at least a dozen times, but nothing came of that. Nothing ever did. Some fairy godmother!

She stomped about her room, staring idly at the clothes scattered over her bed. She was supposed to pack them. But she would not touch the ugly things. They were hardly more than work clothes for peasants, for

81

pity's sake, even if they had just been sewn by her mother's ladies. Ugh. Just because Aunt Hepzibah claimed *little girls* shouldn't primp, they should be learning to do some useful things—like working in Aunt Hepzibah's flower garden in place of the gardeners the old fuddy-duddy was too cheap to hire.

She heard clumping sounds from the stairs. That meant bossy old Wanda, her governess-maid when she was very young, was coming. Then the door banged open. The maid stopped just inside and stared about the room.

"Sammie, I thought I told you to get this stuff packed. We don't have all day to waste mooning around!"

"Don't call me that ugly name," Samantha screamed at her. "My name's Samantha. And you're supposed to call me Highness."

It did no good. It never did. Wanda muttered to herself, then began lugging out a bag for clothing from the closet. "You just go sit in that chair and stay out of my way, Sammie. We're supposed to be downstairs waiting in ten minutes."

Watching Wanda pack, she had to admit that the old maid was better at some things than her new one—now preempted for the journey by her mother after the queen's regular maid got sick. It didn't really matter, though. Aunt Hepzibah would never let her bring a maid.

She moved over to the window, pulled back the drapes, and looked down at the carriage driveway. "The carriage isn't even here yet," she observed.

"Don't you worry, it'll be there by the time you're ready for it," Wanda said, closing the bag on the last ugly dress. "Well, let's get moving, Sammie." She picked up the bag and followed Samantha.

She saw her mother and father waiting in the entrance lobby, and went up to give her mother the expected kiss. But the queen pulled away. "Don't rumple me, Samantha," she said, and kissed her daughter on the forehead carefully. "Have a nice time while we're gone, dear."

A nice time indeed! Little her mother cared. Sometimes she thought

Aunt Hepzibah had been right about one thing, at least. She'd quizzed Samantha on her parents' doings, then had shaken her head. "Seems to me your mother's getting biggety notions, forgetting she was just a rich commoner's daughter till your father saw her at a flower show and decided to marry her. Wants people to think she's more than she is!"

But her father was there, taking the bag from Wanda in one hand and holding the other out to her. "Come on, Sammie—Samantha. Can't keep the horses standing."

Then they were at the door, and she could see her "carriage." "Oh, no!" she gasped, not quite believing it. It was the old carriage from which they'd torn the top, used by the cook to go food shopping. And drunken Old John was driving.

"I'm sorry, Sam-mantha. But it's all we have. The second carriage's wheel still isn't fixed, and the third's being taken by your mother's maid and hairdresser. This was the best I could do."

It wasn't his fault, she knew. "It's all right, Daddy," she lied as he lifted her to be kissed, then put her down in the worn old seat. She could see worry on his face and she tried to smile.

"Be good, punkin," he told her. "I'll send a good carriage for you as soon as I can get back."

"You folks done back there?" Old John grumbled. "Come on, giddy-ap!" And they were off, with the two horses still fresh and prancing a bit. They were better than Old John usually drove, and he was having some trouble controlling them.

They swung out of the driveway of the big old house people insisted on calling the palace onto the main road, still fairly smooth and showing where local labor had filled in the worst of the winter damage. Old John seemed to get better control and gentled the horses down to a pace the ill-sprung carriage could handle. The miles sped by, while Old John retrieved a bottle from under the seat and relieved the dryness in his throat. His throat was always dry.

There was almost no other traffic, thank the good God! Samantha huddled down in the back beside the bag, trying to hide from anyone they might meet. But she began to get aches and cramps from her position and was finally forced to sit up.

The thinned and cared-for woods around the palace was falling behind, and she was now looking at woods that seemed wild. When she was younger, the maids had told her shiveringly delicious tales of things that dwelled in such forest: wolves that swallowed children at a gulp, witches, goblins, and bogeys. Somehow, the tales seemed more real now as she gazed at the darkness in the tangles under the great trees. The ditch beside the road was dry now, long past the spring melt-off, and mats of weeds and bushes were growing in it.

Beyond the forest lay Aunt Hepzibah with lectures and back-breaking work in the garden or sweltering tasks in her steamy kitchen, then more lectures and rewards in the form of little books that held morals thick enough to break one's teeth on. Thinking of that, she wished the forest might go on forever.

Old John was looking more alert now, putting the bottle back under the seat. He seemed to be trying to stare ahead around each turn of the road, though there was nothing to see.

Then suddenly there was a shout and two men broke from cover beside the road, riding hard toward them and brandishing huge pistols. "Hold or we fire!" the older one yelled. John stood up, sawing at the reins to stop the horses. But the younger man raised his pistol. There was a shot, and the off-horse jumped against the harness. One ear was nothing but a bleeding stump.

Both horses were panicking, trying to go in separate directions. The carriage skidded, swung to the ditch, and began to turn over. Samantha grabbed for a railing, but there was no time. The carriage bounced, turned, and was on its side in the ditch, spilling her out and beyond, almost through a clump of brush on the farther bank. She pawed her way free and scrambled behind its little shelter.

The horses lay in the ditch on their sides, tangled in harness and the tongue of the carriage, pawing hopelessly and screaming horribly. And Old John—

She wanted to throw up as she saw where his head lay against a rock, with blood and brains oozing from it. But she controlled herself, looking desperately for better shelter. There was none.

"Damn, Peter, I told you not to fire that thing!" the older bandit was saying as the two men dismounted. "Cut the throats of those beasts and shut them up. Where's Old John? Never mind, I see him. Dead."

"Better for us. One less to split with," the young man answered, busy with the screaming horses. A few minutes later they quieted. "Where's the girl? She all right?"

"Damned if I know. I was looking right at her, but she just seemed to disappear."

"Must be covered by all that clothing that spilled out. Hey, that stuff don't look much like what a princess would have!"

"Stuff a maid might wear—but it's all like this. She looked to be dressed in the same stuff. Maybe Old John got it wrong. Maybe it was only the maid of the princess he was supposed to take. Old fool was half drunk, last we talked to him. A fat lot of money we'll get for a maid's ransom! But where'd she go? She's sure not in the wreck or this stuff."

He was looking right at her, too. Even in the shadow of a tree, she *couldn't* be concealed by the thin stalks of the bush. Maybe her fairy godmother? But that didn't make sense, either. It would take a pretty stupid fairy godmother to wait until after she was in such a situation before doing something!

"Let's get the hell outta here." The younger bandit was looking at the road nervously. "Let the maid go. She'll be too scared to describe us. And there's gonna be others coming along this highway."

"Yeah. I suppose you're right," the older man agreed. He pulled himself up reluctantly. "Damn! I just wish I knew how she got away. All right, though. Let's go!"

A minute later, they were mounted and galloping off.

Samantha stood there, staring at the retreating horsemen until they rode out of sight around a bend in the road. Her ugly dress was dirty and torn, but when she looked at the others that had spilled from the bag, they were worse—filthy from being walked over by the rough boots of the highwaymen. She sighed and retreated behind the big tree, trying to consider what she must do.

She'd have to walk—either to Aunt Hepzibah's or back to the palace. She guessed that they'd come about halfway between. The idea of confronting her aunt with her appearance and tale was too much. It would have to be home to the palace. And she couldn't go along the road; the bandits might decide to ride back along it and would see her. That left the forest.

Well, the road went about north and south, despite the curves it made. So, if she went a ways into the forest and headed north, she'd come to the well-kept woods around the palace and then could easily find her way home. She stared at the dark, forbidding forest, feeling panic begin to take her. But she forced it away and set off.

From the distance, the underbrush had seemed impenetrable, but as she got closer she began to see openings and spaces where she could go. Moving through it, she found she could make fairly good time, though she began to accumulate small scratches on her arms. Most of the time, the big trees cut off all sight of the sun, but she'd heard a forester once explain how he kept on his way by moonlight—he just set his sight on the farthest big tree he could see in the right direction and headed for that, sighting along it for another farther on as he went. Occasional glimpses of the sun indicated to Samantha that his method seemed to be working.

She began to get hungry and thirsty, but there was nothing she could do about that. She decided after much thought that she should probably reach her home sometime tomorrow afternoon, and she'd just have to endure until then. Her shoes began to hurt her feet. When she took them off, she found blisters on her heels. Going barefoot didn't work; stones and

thorny brambles soon showed her she needed the shoes. She should have found another pair of socks from the spilled bag. Wearing two pairs would have eased the chafing. But it was too late for second thoughts now.

She found a tiny brooklet eventually and was able to assuage her thirst. She rested there for perhaps fifteen minutes, trying to wash some of the filth from her hands, face, and dress. Then she drank again and went reluctantly on.

Dark clouds were gathering in the sky; before the daylight faded, rain began falling, gently at first. It was rapidly growing dark now, and she could go no farther. She began looking for shelter for the night as the rain became heavier. Caves and hollow trees abounded in the old tales, but she could find none. She finally found a place she might use under a massive old oak. Against its trunk, conditions were not too miserable. She cleared away the sticks and stones as best she could, lay down, and pulled a leaf-covered bough she'd found over her for concealment and further protection from the rain. By that time, she was so tired that she was shivering all over.

Sleep wouldn't come. There were strange sounds in the forest: owls hooted like forlorn ghosts; things scuttled through the underbrush; and once she heard laughter, which was probably the barking of a fox. She started at each for a time, but eventually exhaustion won, though she came awake several times to the memory of something near and disturbing.

It was morning when she finally woke, not really rested, but aware that she had to go on. Rain was still falling, though gently now, and the sky was still overcast. Her hunger was a sick ache inside her, but there were rain pools from which she quenched her thirst. Her legs were stiff and sore and her body seemed a mass of anguish from the hard, lumpy bed. But she started off, trying to establish her previous direction. Visibility was limited, and she was forced to fix her sights at less distance than she liked.

She limped along. The blisters broke, changing the nature of her pain, and her legs began to feel numb. But she stubbornly refused to give up, sit down, and cry—as she wanted to.

Eventually, she came on a small clearing where wild strawberries grew—what the peasants called earth-berries. They were deliciously sweet and aromatic, and she ate all she could find—though that was hardly enough.

As she started to leave, the clouds broke apart, and she was able to see the sky—and her shadow, pointing away from her and shortened, as it was at noon. She groaned when she saw the way it pointed.

She'd been heading almost due east, not north at all! The entire morning had been wasted, taking her farther away from her home.

Again, she forced back her tears. She had no time for them. She saw that the sky was clearing and that she'd be able to pick proper sighting targets—and perhaps even get an occasional glimpse of the sun. Carefully, she positioned herself by the shadow she cast, sighted on a big tree far ahead, and started out again, heading northwest. If she overshot her goal, she'd still come out in familiar territory—she hoped.

By nightfall, she could hardly move. She'd found water during the day, but nothing that she dared eat, and hunger was making her weak. She seemed to have a million aches and scratches.

She took the first place that offered a chance to bed down, scraped away the worst of the stones and twigs, and simply flopped down, not even taking off her worn-out shoes. This time, she was asleep almost at once.

Something wakened her, probably around midnight, judging by the direction of light from the nearly full moon. She sat up tensely, listening. There was a faint rustling from the brush at her left, then something broke through. It looked like a tiny, brown man with a snarling, bestial face.

He stepped farther into the clearing, stared about without apparently seeing her, then lifted his head and sniffed loudly, testing the faint wind for odors. Evidently, he was satisfied. Samantha waited to be discovered, girding herself to leap to her feet and run. But he seemed not to see her, though he glanced right and left as he passed within twenty feet of her. He crossed the clearing and disappeared into the underbrush.

She waited tensely until she could be sure he was really gone. Finally, she let herself feel safe again.

It was a fox, distorted by her imagination, she tried to tell herself. It *had* to be a fox! But she didn't believe it.

She moved to a somewhat more hidden spot before trying to sleep again. She was stiff and sore from the earlier place, in addition to all the aches from before that. But sleep finally overcame her again.

In the morning, she could barely move for the first half hour or so until the exercise gradually loosened her muscles. But she forced herself on. Unless she had gone totally wrong, she should reach home before another night. At least, she prayed she would. She found water, but no food, though she seemed to be growing weaker and feeling sicker from hunger.

After a couple more hours, she came to another clearing. And there, surrounded by a stone wall with a stile, was a house, also built of stone, and a garden!

She clambered clumsily over the stile. She meant to go and knock on the door of the house, but the sight of the tops of carrots in the garden drew her eyes. If she could just get a few baby carrots to eat . . .

A window in the house opened, and a woman's voice came out, commanding. "You! Little girl! You stay right there until I can come out. Don't you take another step!"

The woman who came from the back of the house seemed to be about forty-five, gray-haired, short, and a bit stout. She was dressed in simple working woman's garments, and there was a touch of anger on her face.

Then that vanished as she drew nearer and got a good look at Samantha. "Oh, you poor child. Whatever happened to you?"

Samantha had been putting together her story since she first heard the woman. It would never do to admit who she was. Her ransom would probably be large enough to make even fairly honest people consider holding her.

"I'm lost. My mother and father—they left," she answered, giving the truth, but also a euphemism for death that was so common among the poorer classes. "I was supposed to be sent to my aunt. But when I got there, she'd moved. Nobody knew where and nobody there wanted me to stay. They told me to go to the King's Hospice for Orphans. So I left. Then I got lost in the forest—two days and two nights. It was horrible!"

The shudder she gave was real, as were the tears in her eyes. The woman patted Samantha's shoulder sympathetically. "Poor child, indeed. You have anything to eat?"

"I found a few earth-berries yesterday."

"You must be starving. Well, you just come along with me. We'll find you something to eat and see about a good hot bath. That will make you feel better, I'll warrant." She took Samantha's arm and led the way toward the back of the house. "What do people call you, child?"

"My name is Samantha."

"The things people afflict their children with. Why'd they call you that?"

"It was the name of my mother's mother," Samantha said truthfully.

"All right, then. I'll bet people call you Sammie, which is what I'll do, if you don't mind. And you call me Bessy."

Samantha shook her head. She was in no position to object. "But I'm not supposed to use first names to older people." Except servants, she carefully did not add.

"Got some manners, then. All right, call me Aunt Bessy. The lord's children did, before he died and we came here."

They were entering the back door then, and an older man was extending a work-toughened hand with arthritis-swollen knuckles.

"This is my husband Jonathan," Aunt Bessy introduced him. "I think he'll be happy if you call him Uncle Jon, Sammie. And this is Samantha, Jonathan."

He bowed and smiled. Then Samantha followed them to the kitchen and was seated at the table. Uncle Jon, apparently well-versed in what his wife would want, brought in a bucket of water and filled a large kettle, then shoved it on its hook over the fire in the fireplace. He added wood, before dragging in an old wooden bathtub. Then he left quietly.

"We had breakfast hours ago," Aunt Bessy said. "But I think maybe a couple eggs, a little of that bacon slab, some of the bread I baked yesterday, and maybe coffee. You allowed coffee, Sammie?"

She nodded. She'd had coffee since she was ten. Her mouth was already salivating. And in less time than she'd thought possible, she was eating real food, taking the first few bites slowly, as Aunt Bessy warned her she must, with the warmth of coffee spreading through her body. And the hot bath that soaked away her aches and muscle fatigue was heavenly.

"Not much I can do with what's left of this dress, I'm afraid," Aunt Bessy decided. "Got rips all over, and the dirt's ground in. Pity you ain't a boy. Umm, still, you're about the same size. You mind wearing some boy's clothes, Sammie?"

"I don't know. I never tried before."

"Well, let's try now. Be months before the cloth-seller gets around to here, and I used up the last lot on the curtains. You wrap that towel around you and come upstairs with me."

Upstairs was a general storage area directly under the roof and a low-ceilinged bedroom in the back, with a single window. Aunt Bessy went to a chest on one wall and began dragging out some clean and neatly folded boy's clothes. She held them up against Samantha and nodded.

"They were Billy's—our son and only child. He was ten and large for his age when he died. Diphtheria. He caught it from a playmate who also died from it. We buried him in his favorite spot, out behind the old elm tree he was always climbing. If you look out you can see where we buried

91

him beneath the tree. Still upsets Jonathan a mite, though I've learned to accept it mostly. Now, you just set yourself down on the bed and let me look at those feet of yours."

With much head-shaking and tongue-clicking, the inspection was soon made. Aunt Bessy spread a thick ointment from a jar she brought out of her apron pocket, then very gently drew on some boy's thick socks over Samantha's feet. "That should feel better in a little while. I think Billy's shoes are going to be a little wide in the toes, but they should do. But not today. Those feet are too sore for that. Maybe Jonathan can do something about your shoes. He's clever about such things."

It took some instruction before Samantha was fully dressed as a boy, but the clothes really fitted better than had the ugly dress. It felt odd at first, but she soon began to feel normal.

"Maybe I should have been a boy," she said. "I'm flat enough up here." She put one hand on her chest.

"Don't you worry about them," Aunt Bessy assured her. "They'll come in due time. And something else not so pleasant."

"I know about that. I—someone explained it all to me." She had almost slipped by mentioning her governess. Better be careful.

Moving about and getting used to the different clothes, Samantha went to the little back window and looked out. Most of the area below was the garden. The outhouse was near the back, and the hand-pumped well was a bit up the hill and away, where the water would be clear and uncontaminated. She saw the old elm in a corner at the back, with a little fence around it.

"Never put up a monument," Aunt Bessy told her. "He carved his name on the tree when he was nine with his birthday knife. We figured that was monument enough."

Then she drew back from the window and indicated the bed. "Maybe you better lie down till I call you for supper, Sammie. There's nothing much to do, and a bit of real rest will do wonders for you. Sleep in your clothes till I can cut down one of my nightshirts. All right?"

"It sounds wonderful, Aunt Bessy."

And it was wonderful. The sheet was clean and there were no lumps in the thick straw-filled mattress on the bed. She woke hours later, feeling better and more cheerful than she had felt since she learned she was supposed to spend the best part of the spring and summer with old Aunt Hepzibah.

Aunt Bessy called her and she went downstairs in her stocking feet to the kitchen, where supper was plain but very good. Once the dishes were washed and put away, they all went into the parlor, furnished with home-made but comfortable furniture. Aunt Bessy had her sewing with her and began on that. Uncle Jon, who seldom said much, just sat.

"Did you always live here?" Samantha asked.

"No. I was born in a hut about a mile north; it's gone now, and good riddance. But Jonathan was the son of the lord's blacksmith-carpenter. First we met, we were both in service."

It seemed that Aunt Bessy had gone, seeking employment to the lord, when she was fourteen. There the housekeeper took a fancy to her. She was put in the kitchen, but one hour each day the old lady spent teaching her to use the language properly and how to serve. She graduated to chambermaid, then to parlor maid. It was there Uncle Jon met her. He was second butler by then, far above her, but he knew what he wanted when he saw it. When another maid had to leave, she was put in charge of the young children of the lord, who seemed to love her—and Uncle Jon, when he came to visit her. In time, the lord let them marry.

Samantha gathered that the lord was a kind and thoughtful master, quite unlike so many Samantha had heard about. When he was killed in a hunting accident, it was found that he'd left a small income for the two to live on as long as either lived.

"I remembered this place," Aunt Bessy said. "As a child, I'd seen it and dreamed of it ever since. So Jonathan and I came back here. The old couple who'd had the place were dead, and it was empty. The new lord gave it to us for a small rental, and we've been here eighteen years now. I reckon we'll die here."

By then, Uncle Jon had put a chessboard on the small table and was setting up the pieces. "You play chess, Samantha?" he asked. At her nod, he beamed. "Black or white? White of course, so you move first."

She shifted her chair to the table and began by moving king's pawn to king four. And the game was under way. She'd always been good at chess, but she had to extend herself now. The endgame almost defeated her. But at last, she called, "Checkmate!"

He nodded and rose to put the board and set away. "You play very well, Samantha," he said. "Thank you. First game I've had in years."

By then, it was bedtime, and Samantha took the cut-down nightdress Aunt Bessy had been working on and climbed to her little room. She could hardly keep her eyes open by the time she'd undressed and put on the nightgown. The bed felt wonderful.

The next day was general cleaning day, it seemed. The house that looked spotless to Samantha had to be gone over completely, and the wash was boiled clean in the kitchen and rinsed out under the pump, which Samantha found not too hard to operate. They hung the clothes on the lines together where the sun would bleach and dry them.

And then it was baking and cooking time. A meat wagon drove up in the morning, and Aunt Bessy carried on a long-established banter with the driver as she made her selections. Meat came once a week and wouldn't keep, so it had to be cooked before it was taken to the cold-cellar under the house.

The day following was gardening, and there Samantha could be of real help, once Aunt Bessy was sure she knew a weed when she saw it and how to use a hoe without slicing the good plants. It wasn't too different from tending old Aunt Hepzibah's flowers—but a lot more pleasant.

And every night there was a game or two with Uncle Jon, who seemed to win about twice to her once.

She seemed to lose track of the days. But finally, she had to consider what she must do. There'd been no mention of her leaving. But she couldn't go on forever. Sooner or later, her old world would catch up with her. She didn't think anyone would report the wrecked carriage. It had been pretty well shattered in turning over. Predators would soon reduce the horses and Old John to bone, and most of what was left would vanish in the muddy flood from the rains that would wash down the ditch. Nobody looked very closely at wrecks in the ditch along the highway.

She wondered what would have happened if she'd told Aunt Bessy the truth at once. The reason for her lie had been a mistake, she knew now. But confessing her lie was going to be hard. Still, she had to make a clean breast of it sooner or later, and sooner was better.

Two more days. Just give me two more, she begged her fairy godmother. Not that the creature would care, if there really was one.

After she told the truth, what would happen? They'd forgive her, she was sure. But how would they get news to the palace? They had no horse, and neither of them could make the journey to the palace with her. But somehow, they'd find a way. She was sure of that.

Next day was gardening again. She and Aunt Bessy finished the rows of carrots, turnips, and young cabbages before noon. They stopped to rest at the end of the row, letting the pleasant fatigue drain from their arms and backs.

Samantha saw that her hoe was beginning to accumulate dirt. She bent down to clean it with a small stick and saw something bright-colored there. She bent closer.

"*No*, Sammie, NO!" Aunt Bessy suddenly screamed. The older woman's arm came down to snatch Samantha's hand back.

Something moved suddenly, striking upward. It was a snake, and its fangs were buried in Aunt Bessy's hand! Samantha struck at it with her hoe, but it wouldn't come loose. Both she and Aunt Bessy were screaming.

Then Uncle Jon was there, moving faster than seemed possible for him. He cut the head from the body with a single stroke of a sickle and began prying the stubborn mouth open. It fell free at last, and he ground it under his heel.

Aunt Bessy seemed near fainting from shock, and Samantha and Uncle Jon had to help her back to the house. There Uncle Jon put her in a chair and gently began cutting a cross across the bites to let the blood flow out. Then he began making some kind of a poultice to place on the wound, using the hottest water she could stand.

"We better take her to our room and put her to bed," he told Samantha. "Best that she doesn't move around much with that in her."

Samantha was crying. "It was all my fault," she wailed. "I was reaching for it, and she tried to save me."

"Enough of that!" Uncle Jon broke in sternly. "It's nobody's fault that you didn't know about such snakes. Now be quiet and help me get her to bed."

All that day they watched over her, changing the poultice frequently. Uncle Jon made a broth which he fed her. She seemed to sleep for several hours, then began tossing about. Her whole arm was swollen and red and felt hot to Samantha's touch. She quieted after a while. The poison slowly spread, and her arm swelled until it seemed three times normal. By evening, Uncle Jon had to tie her down to keep her from tossing herself from the bed.

All night they watched together over her. Samantha sometimes found herself sleeping in the chair, but it wasn't restful sleep.

In the early morning hours, Uncle Jon sighed heavily and stood up. "It's no good, Samantha. Without more help than we can give, she'll die tomorrow." The bones of his face stood out against the clenched muscles, and he looked years older.

"I guessed that," Samantha whispered.

"Soon as it's light enough to follow the path, I'm going to Edona for the doctor. Not that he'll do much for her, maybe, but we have to try."

"Not you. Me," Samantha told him. "I can run a lot faster than you can. Tell me how to reach the doctor, and I'll go."

He stared at her, then nodded reluctantly, accepting the logic of her words. When the first hint of dawn was breaking, he took her out the back door and pointed out the path to her. "It goes on for several miles before it forks. Take the right fork. That will bring you to the village, and anyone can tell you how to find the doctor. Godspeed and God bless you, Samantha!"

She knew she couldn't run that far, even in boy's clothes. She ran for a little ways, then walked, and ran again. It seemed to take forever—and probably did take more than an hour—before she reached the fork. The early sun was already well above the horizon.

There was a man in a black cloak with a black hood pulled low over his face sitting on a rock by the crossroads. She started to run past him, but he reached out with a dark walking stick and stopped her.

"What are you running from in such a hurry, youngster? Trying to run away from your master?"

"I'm not running *from* anyone," she snapped at him with what breath she had left. "I'm running *to* the doctor to fetch him for Aunt Bessy."

"Commendable, if true. And since my ears tell me you're a girl, what's wrong with her, young lady?"

"It's none of your business, but if you must know, a snake bit her," she answered. "And her arm's all swollen to the shoulder and she's stopped tossing around and just lies gasping. Now let me go!"

"And what's your stake in all this?" the man asked. It began to sound like a ritual. "Do you lose your good home when she dies?"

"No such thing. I've got to leave soon, anyhow. But she's been awfully good to me, and I think, if she dies, Uncle Jon won't live much beyond her. They're not my real aunt and uncle, but I—I guess I love them. Now can I go?"

The dark man stood up, taking the stick away. "Certainly. But you won't find the doctor—he's out on another call. And from what you say of your aunt's condition, you don't need a doctor of physic. You need a doctor of metaphysics."

The part about the doctor fitted her own suspicion. But she'd never heard of the other calling. "Where can I find one?"

"As it happens, young lady, you're very fortunate today. I happen to be an excellent practitioner of that art. At your service, my dear."

He bowed gracefully to her, then took her hand. "We must hurry," he said. He didn't really seem to hurry, and she had no trouble keeping pace with him back toward Aunt Bessy's home. But the land around seemed to swim past at an alarming rate.

Then she glanced back and saw the sun setting—in the east! "What—what's happening?"

"Just a bit of applied metaphysics, my dear. Don't worry if strange things happen. You might say that the clock has been turned backward for us."

They went on along the path while the stars appeared and began hurrying eastward. Soon the sun was rising from the west and flying eastward through the sky. In almost no time, it had passed its noonday position, and they were standing before the stile over the wall to the garden.

"We couldn't have helped today, so this had to be yesterday," the dark man told her. "Don't worry about it. It will be today for you. Don't be surprised or panic at anything that I tell you to do. And don't ever mention it to anybody. Will you promise that to me?"

She nodded, and he went on. "Now you climb up on the stile. You'll see your Aunt Bessy in the garden, looking fine. Don't be surprised. And there'll be a child beside her. Don't look too closely at her. I'm going to stay here, but when I snap my fingers, I want you to run and grab the hoe from the other girl's hand. Can you remember that?"

"I guess so. Then what do I do?"

"Just do what you think you should. Now . . ." His fingers snapped.

She jumped from the stile and grabbed the hoe, to seize it from the other girl's grasp. But there was no resistance. There no longer was another girl. The hoe was in her hand and she was looking down at something bright-colored on the ground.

"Aunt Bessy, there's a snake," she said.

The older woman glanced down and pulled Samantha back, yelling for Jonathan. He took one look and ran back to the toolshed. In no time, the snake lay writhing on the ground in six pieces.

Samantha looked around for the dark man, but he was gone, not even waiting to present his bill. And everything looked normal, as if all the trouble had never happened. Uncle Jon showed no sign of strain, and there was nothing wrong with Aunt Bessy.

Magic! It had to be some kind of magic. She'd promised that she would never speak of it to anyone. But if she ever saw the dark man again— which seemed more unlikely than meeting him once—she'd try to tell him just how grateful she was to him.

They went back to the garden after lunch. Uncle Jon got rid of the pieces of the snake and searched thoroughly to be sure there were no others. Soon everything felt normal again, and she was almost able to forget what had happened.

But as she lay down that night on her bed, she determined that she'd tell them the truth about herself tomorrow at breakfast. It would be hard, but she couldn't keep putting it off any longer.

It didn't quite happen that way, however.

Aunt Bessy broke in on her before she was fully dressed in the morning. "Sammie, he's here! The king is here. And he's looking for you! He says you're his daughter, the princess!"

"I am," Samantha admitted guiltily.

It didn't make sense. He couldn't be back from the conference yet. And how could he ever have heard that she was in this place, even if he did get back early?

"And here I've been treating you like any little girl—like my own daughter, for heaven's sake," Aunt Bessy was saying. "Forgive me, your Highness, please. And don't blame Jonathan."

"Please. Please, Aunt Bessy." She finished putting her shoes on and stood up to kiss the worried face before her. "I want you to keep right on treating me that way. Please. You've made me very happy. I'd be hurt if you didn't. And I guess I should be apologizing for lying to you at first."

"Pooh. We've been happy with you here, Jonathan and I. And if it took a little lie for that to be, then bless the lie. You're a very special girl, Sammie. And we're going to miss you."

When they descended the stairs, her father was sitting at the old kitchen table, explaining something to Jonathan as he finished a syrup-covered pile of pancakes. He leaped to his feet as he saw her.

"Sammie!" He gathered her to him, then pushed her back for a good look at her. "It's good to see you again. You had us all worried sick! We were beginning to lose hope for you."

"How'd you get here, Daddy? And what happened to the conference?"

"Bother the conference! We were just leaving the halfway inn for the second day's journey when the messenger arrived from the palace. One of my men, riding on an errand I'd left for him, spotted the wreck and recognized what was left of the carriage and the body of Old John. He knew you were supposed to leave to visit your aunt. He made a hasty search, but saw no sign of you. So he reported back to the palace. Further search still found no trace of you. So everyone decided you'd been seized by highwaymen for ransom."

"Two bandits planned to do that," Samantha interrupted. "Old John told them about it for a part of the ransom."

"So we discovered," the king said. "They sent word to us and continued the search. The minute your mother heard it, she sent one of the footmen on a horse of the landlord's to cancel our attendance."

"Mother did that?"

"She certainly did. One daughter is worth fifty of such conferences."

By the time they got back to the palace, some smart work by the head of security had already captured the bandits, who confessed "under rigorous questioning." The king had them hanged, of course, and sent out men with her description to all parts of the kingdom. But, despite two false leads, they could find no trace of her.

"Then late last night, a man in black with a hood came to the back door of the palace and claimed to know where you were. He even had a map of how to reach the place. But by the time I got there he couldn't be found. That seemed odd, since there was a reward, but I decided to leave for here as soon as I could, anyway. And here I am. I brought along some of your nice clothes, chosen by your mother. As soon as you change, we'll leave. Your mother's very worried about you."

She took the clothes when the footman brought them in and went back upstairs to change. They felt odd now and not nearly as easy to wear as the boy's had been. But she paid little attention to that.

The dark man again! Who and what was he, anyhow? Suspicion lay in the back of her mind, but she couldn't really accept it. She'd never even told him who she was. It couldn't possibly be *him*. But how could anyone else know she was here?

She went downstairs again, almost tripping on the stairs in her dress. There she ran forward to kiss and hug the two people who had given her shelter and treated her like their own child. She'd miss them terribly. They were crying—even Uncle Jon—and she felt her own tears start.

The king smiled at them. "I don't think you need be that gloomy," he told them all. "You're not going to lose her for good, I promise. We usually give her two weeks vacation in the fall and a month in the spring. She usually goes to stay with an old harridan of an aunt, and she hates it. That's going to stop. Suppose I just send her here instead. Would you like that, Sammi—Samantha?"

"Oh, Daddy. More than anything! But what about Mother?"

"I think right now is a good time to propose it to her. And she's going to agree, I promise you that. From what I've seen, this has been the best thing that ever happened, and I want it to continue. How about you, Bessy, Jonathan? Will you have her?"

"God bless your Majesty," Aunt Bessy said, bowing to him, with Jonathan joining in the bow.

"Then it's all fixed. And as I told you before, none of that formal fol-de-rol. You're both in the family now, you know."

Samantha watched them through the little back window of the carriage—the best carriage, this time! They stood together outside the front door, waving to her. Then the narrow, rutted road swung behind the trees and she slid back to the seat beside her father.

"I think we're going to have to start treating you a bit differently from now on, Sam-mantha," her father said. "Anyone who can keep going for two days with no proper clothes and no provisions through that part of the forest isn't a child anymore. My best forester swore you couldn't last for a day in there."

"Different how?" she asked. She wasn't quite sure she was ready for another change just yet. Going to visit Aunt Bessy and Uncle Jon instead of her other aunt seemed glorious enough a change for one day.

"I think we'll have to start teaching you how to govern a kingdom. You're going to be queen some day, and you'd better learn how. Some-times it's pretty dull, but it's important. And boys. We should be taking you with us when we visit other kings or our nobles, to meet some of the other youngsters—girls and boys. Some day you'll be taking on a consort, and you'd better know enough to pick a good one."

It all sounded interesting, if a bit scary. But her mind was on other things.

"Daddy, am I old enough to know about my fairy godmother? And do I really have one?"

"Indeed you do. She's been in the family for at least seven generations, maybe more. She always shows up at the christening of any possible heir to the throne."

"Did you ever really see her? And what's she like?"

They were on a side road now, but much better than the way to the little stone house with the garden. He leaned back and seemed to think.

"I saw her only once, at your christening. Just after the ceremony was finished, there she was. Nobody knew how she got there, but she was right beside you. I always figured she must be a withered old hag after so many years, but she looked young and beautiful. Long golden hair, braided and coiled into a corona around her head. Some kind of a fancy deep blue dress. There was a kind of glow over her as she touched you on the forehead and pronounced your gifts."

The description certainly couldn't be that of the dark man, no matter what the disguise. But the little suspicion still remained.

Then she realized fully what she'd heard. "Gifts? What sort of gifts, Daddy?"

"Odd ones. They always were. Umm, one was the gift of necessitous imperceptibility. The other was the gift of nonindulgent summoning. You know what they mean?"

"I can figure them out, Daddy. Not being seen when it's absolutely necessary and calling something or someone up when it isn't just being self-indulgent."

He nodded. She thought over past events, seeing explanations for what had bothered her before. The gifts explained why the bandits and the tiny, brown man—or whatever it was—hadn't been able to see her. And could she really have summoned the dark man when her need hadn't been selfish or petty? It seemed to fit.

"And what happened then?"

"She just vanished. Not with any cloud of fire or smoke, as the old tales tell it. And she didn't fly away. She just spread her wings and wasn't there."

"Wings?"

"Oh, yes. She had wings, something like those of a butterfly, growing from her shoulder blades. They seemed iridescent, changing colors as she moved. Beautiful."

And with that, Samantha's suspicion collapsed completely. There were no wings under the black cloak of the dark man—no room for even folded wings.

They were drawing near the main road now, and she glanced at the forest to her right. It looked as forbidding as ever, she decided. Then, a little ahead of them, something stirred on the shoulder of the road. She stared harder, frowning. It was the dark man! She started to call her father's attention to him, but he put his finger to where his lips should be, shaking his head.

Then, as she watched in startled silence, he began to loosen the cloak about him. It folded back, and the hood opened and fell away. There was a head of golden hair coiled into a corona and a mesmerizingly beautiful face. She was still wearing the blue dress. And the folded cloak was turning to a pair of iridescent wings. She smiled, still with her finger to her lips, and made the motion of blowing a kiss toward Samantha.

Then she wasn't there anymore.

Samantha sat back on the seat, feeling suddenly completely at peace with the world as they swept around a corner and were on the main road back to the palace.

Her father looked down at her and smiled affectionately. "Glad to be going home, Sammie—Samantha?"

"Yes, Daddy. With you. And Daddy—"

"Yes, punkin?"

"You can call me Sammie. I sort of like it now."

He reached out an arm and drew her closer. She snuggled up against him, and there was only the sound of the wheels and the clopping of the horses' hooves as they rolled on.

THISTLEDOWN

SUSAN DEXTER

HIGH-SUMMER. THE LEAVES OF the forest trees spread their widest, and by night the shadows beneath them were absolute. No glimmer from full moon or scattered stars fetched down to dapple the forest floor. For those whose lives depended upon such, that darkness was promise of sanctuary. A field mouse, whiskers a-twitch, foraged busily among old leaves and new growth at the roots of an aged oak.

The mouse froze, as hounds bayed distantly. A league off, the mouse's ears judged—although it did not reckon distance by the league. No present danger, so it returned to feeding.

Mid-gnaw, it went still again, ceased even to breathe. A moonbeam flickered among the tree trunks, on silver, cloven hooves.

Again the hounds gave tongue. The unicorn doe paused, turning lovely head and graceful neck to gaze back the way she had come. Her nostrils flared, sifting the breeze that turned the oak leaves. A moment she held so, then was on the move once more, placing her steps with a care that had nothing to do with the disguising of her trail.

At the edge of the oak glade, she hesitated. Beyond lay a tiny meadow, its open space courtesy of an aged oak that had fallen. Moonlight flooded the grassy spot, so that the shadows just under the trees seemed blacker than pitch by contrast. The doe pawed the soil delicately with one cleft forefoot. A shudder passed along her flanks and swollen belly. Her silver horn dipping, she nosed the dead leaves till she located a deep drift on the leeward side of the fallen oak trunk.

Kneeling, she lowered her body carefully to the leaves. Her hindquarters showed the strain as her hocks bent, and a grunt escaped her nostrils when she collapsed the final inches into the leaves.

The birth followed almost at once. After a few more ripples of the belly, two tiny hooves appeared. Then the forelegs, a slender muzzle lying along them. Between one breath and the next the entire fawn slipped out onto the leaves, wet and silvery—glistening as a fresh-caught fish.

The doe turned her head toward her fawn, which struggled to raise its muzzle to hers. Its nostrils opened, tasting air. The ears, plastered flat to its long skull, lifted and flopped about. The doe's tongue cleansed its face and would have tasted its scent—but unicorns are odorless at birth, that they may lie safe-hidden from the world's dangers until they are able to flee them.

A hound bayed—nearer now.

Stretching her forelegs out, pushing mightily, the doe sprang to her feet. The fawn's still-folded legs struggled to copy her. Gently, the doe's muzzle thrust it back into the leaves, and with a touch of her silvery horn she bade it remain still. Hound-song came more frequently—they were on the scent now.

The doe lingered a dangerous instant more, nuzzling the fawn. Then, whirling, she vanished into the forest, stirring no leaf, making no sound.

The fawn remained, and in the meadow dandelion puffs opened in defiance of dew and darkness, till the grass was thick-studded with silver globes. Among the trees, white trillium and bloodroot blossomed out of season to welcome the newborn creature—which took no notice of them, but laid down its head and fell asleep.

In a cot with walls of wicker, mud and smooth river stones, mostly supported by a hillside it leaned against, Flax was suffering a nightmare. The yelping of a hound pack filled his entire sleeping world, and each shadowy beast was far larger and swifter than he was. He was feeling scalding breath on the back of his neck when he woke—and realized that although the dream had ended, the sound had not. It was nowhere near so loud as it had seemed while Flax slept, but still it set his heart hammering as the dream had not, pounding and trying to fly free of his ribs.

When forever had passed—twice at least—the baying dwindled to a few excited yips. Flax sagged back into his bedding, just as the night air shivered with another sound.

Bright, sharp as winter stars and as ageless, the sound was quite unmistakably a death-cry. Flax's breath stopped as instantly as if the cry had been his own. But, though his lungs were still, there was nothing more for his straining ears to hear. The night and the world might have been frozen in their places. Flax lay wide-eyed, having no idea why he wanted so desperately to weep.

At dawn Flax arose, body sore from tension and mind aching with the twin terrors of dream and reality. The outside air was cool, soothing to his spirit and relaxing to his muscles after a bit. Blackberry brambles provided him with breakfast, but fruit was not his quest that day. Flax wandered slowly along the fringes of the cart-track that led to Ylowfort village, gathering the heads of purple thistles into the coarse-woven sack bound to his belt.

Not so many ripened here as he had hoped—and soon there'd be folk abroad on the road. Flax did not care much to meet with the villagers. The night had harrowed him, and he needed solitude to recover—as he needed it always, simply to live. He had heard goldfinches singing beyond the oak grove some days past, and had marked the spot in his memory, for the birds often chose to nest close by the thistles whose seeds they favored. Flax skirted a field of ripening barley and vanished into the forest, where twilight still held sway.

Coming to a stream, Flax knelt to drink, then altered his course to strike out for the far side of the wood by the easiest path. A patch of white drew his eye, and he moved through the sparse undergrowth toward it, curious to see what flower bloomed in the depth of the summer forest.

The triad of white petals confounded him, for trillium flowered ere Beltane, and that season was long past. The forest canopy was dense at midsummer, letting through little of the light that blossoms needed. And there beside the trillium—a bloodroot? That should have bloomed earlier still. Flax's fingers probed the loam, and his herb lore was confirmed when they found the root. Fingers and soil were stained with scarlet sap—it welled from the earth as if from a wound. Flax started. For an instant the terror of his dream was back with him, in the sight of the blood, the memory of the cry he'd heard as he woke.

Shaking his head, Flax started to rise—and saw something more under the trees. Something also white, but no flower. It was watching him.

At first he took it for a pony foal—its hooves still birth-soft, their cloven nature was not obvious. It was male. The body was finely made, white all over, coat soft as the thistledown Flax gathered. It was as like to a deer as a horse—the wild grace, the long-lashed eyes huge and dark. The nostrils were horselike, in a muzzle of soft velvet, not the wet button of a deer. There was a bump in the middle of the fawn's forehead, and Flax wondered if it had been injured.

Or . . . a unicorn? Flax extended his fingers, expecting the fawn to vanish like an errant bit of moonlit mist, left over from the night.

It had no fear of him. The fawn sucked at Flax's fingers, its mouth warm, soft, real. He felt milk teeth along its gums.

Just born—where then was its mother?

The night cry rang in Flax's ears again—he thought he might well hear it echoing all his days. His heart pained him as the blood coursed through it after a skipped beat.

He looked down at the fawn, still nursing strongly at his fingers. The birth sac lay over its hindquarters, fine as a spiderweb. It had not yet been on its feet, and whatever had kept its mother from returning had not found it. Perhaps it was scentless at birth, like a deer fawn. Perhaps the doe had led pursuit safely away. Perhaps the hounds would be satisfied with their kill, and seek no further prey. He hoped so. Flax desperately hoped so.

Flax's mother had come a stranger to Ylowfort, had remained one all her days. Witch, the villagers named her, and harlot—the latter lie told for spite when she'd have none of the village's eager young men. None knew where she dwelt, but summer nights did not find her under a roof. She roamed fields and forest in quest of herbs, and sold her gleanings for her livelihood by day. She was dark of hair, blue of eye, and silent as a stone.

Silent still, with only a nod for her assent before the priest, she wed Duke Lionel's swineherd on a winter's day when the wind's howl might have made a cottage and a warm fire seem precious beyond measure. The pig-keeper alone of the village's men had pointed no finger, poked no crude jests—indeed he was nigh as silent as his bride, and quite as much an outcast on account of his calling. Against all speculation, she made a good wife—and soon a mother.

They named their son Flax, perchance for the bleached color of his hair, which was as unlike his mother's as any changeling's. Otherwise he grew to be very like her—the more so after fever took his father. His mother took Flax, not yet walking steadily, on her resumed woodland rambles. The forest creatures were his only playmates, the trees and fields his schooling.

Witch, they called his mother again—mute as a snake, and her brat no better. They said she taught him no human speech, but only dark arts. They said she'd traded away his soul, or his wits, or both.

Witch or not, it was iron-shod hooves killed her, and as cold iron was known to slay witches, the matter was deemed proven. She was run down by recklessly galloping horsemen as she hastened homeward through a sudden thunderstorm. After that, Flax dwelt alone at the edge of the forest.

* * *

Flax sat back on his heels, regarding the unicorn. The white fawn nestled in the bed of bracken fern Flax had gathered for it, drowsing in the cottage's dim shelter. It slept a great deal, being very weak.

The fawn needed nourishment. Flax could number its ribs, trace the inner workings of hip and shoulder well enough to see that it was very horselike in those parts. He suspected the doe had not had time to suckle it ere she left it, and knew that if he couldn't coax it to take a substitute from him soon, the fawn would simply sink into the shadows, following at its mother's heels.

It had refused the cow's milk Flax had stolen—letting the notorious milk snakes take blame for a less than full udder when the cow returned to her byre at evening. Flax had warmed the milk to body heat, had stirred honey into it, and when the fawn would not lap, he had put the liquid into a leather bottle and tried to squirt it down the little creature's throat. It had resisted that with a surprising strength, and Flax knew enough to let be before it exhausted itself past recovery.

Come dark, he'd run a larger risk, visiting a villager's goat pen. The goats had been milked once, and were resentful of Flax's clandestine attentions. The unicorn refused the few drops he finally managed to collect. Yet it licked his fingers readily enough when they were not fresh-dipped in milk.

Flax coaxed milk from a plowhorse with a foal at heel. He gathered tender grasses, sweet herbs, cresses, apples. The fawn rejected all, and regarded Flax with increasingly dull gaze. He offered it the oatmeal gruel that was his own usual dinner, not surprised when the fawn merely sniffed the offering before resting its gray muzzle again upon the bracken. Flax stroked its soft coat, going gently over the bones so close under it, then ate his meal and heavy-heartedly began his evening's task.

Flax emptied out the sack of thistleheads, selected a plump specimen, and pulled the fluff from among the prickles. Seeds came out with the down—these he removed to an earthenware bowl. The evening was warm, the fire banked, but a saucer of pig-fat wicked with a twist of linen thread gave off all the light Flax required for his monotonous work. He could have done it in the dark, or his sleep.

After an hour he had the bowl half filled with seeds at his right hand and a large heap of thistledown on his left. The prickles kept it mostly anchored, but a few bits of fluff were stirred by breezes wafting down the chimney, and drifted across the floor.

One such silver wisp fetched up against the unicorn's muzzles, was held there by the fawn's faint breathing. The teardrop nostrils flared round, contracted, flared again. The fawn's lips moved, gathering in the puff of thistledown. Its ears flopped as it chewed.

Flax noticed only when it stretched after a second drifting bit of fluff. Barely hoping, he pulled the down from the seedhead he held, and ignoring fingers carelessly pricked, held the morsel out to the fawn. Velvet lips snatched it from his fingers so delicately that all Flax felt was a bit of warm breath.

For an hour, Flax fed the fawn as rapidly as he could part down from seed. Then—with fewer of the awkward preliminaries Flax had observed in horse-foal of calf—the unicorn struggled to its feet, took a few wobbling steps into the corner, and neatly relieved itself.

By morning the fawn was completely sure of its legs, and its fine bones were covered to much the same extent they would be when it matured. It would have followed Flax when he left on his day's gathering, but he shut it in the cot for its safety and went forth to cut as many thistleheads as he could carry.

The fawn was gifted with a name, if only in Flax's thoughts: Thistledown.

The moon waned to a delicate sickle, and waxed once more. The unicorn grew likewise daily, and nigh as visibly. He had discovered foods beyond his namesake and was especially fond of apples. Thistledown's energy, when Flax turned him out to play in the safety of the night, was boundless, and an arrow's flight was not swifter than his gallop across a clearing. No human-fletched arrow, howbeit, could have executed the turns that Thistledown did, as he veered from the woodshore and returned to Flax's side. Then off he went again, throwing his heels up to the moon in midstride, kicking and bucking in fierce joy of the movement, whirling like a leaf in the wind.

Flax was nowise near so fleet of foot, but he joined the game with a will, and afterward shared a dreamless sleep upon the bracken. Thistledown shed the silken wool of his baby coat, and his mane grew out to a fringe standing more than a handspan in height ere it began to lie more neatly upon his neck.

The single horn split through the bloodless skin that had covered it, showing pale pearly tints of all the rainbow's hues among its convolutions. Flax rubbed the base with his fingers and with wisps of dry grass, rewarded for the massage with sighs and gentle caresses of Thistledown's warm tongue.

"Lowise! *Lowise!* Plague take us, Dilys, where's the girl?"

Dilys set down her basket of washed wool, and dusted her skirts. "Not likely she'd be here, is it, Maude? Lowise well knows there's wool to be carded today—and my lady hates carding wool."

"Aye. As she despises the spinning, the dyeing, the weaving, the bread-baking, the ale-brewing, the sausage-making and the reviewing of the accounts! Show me a job of work that child would come to willingly! Why the Lord Lionel ever contracted for her as wife to our Master Lothair—"

"Our brother Lionel contracted for her—and a canny bit of dickering it was, too, as you'll remember—because Lowise is heiress to both her father's and her mother's-father's lands. She's a great catch for our Lothair, as well you know." Dilys settled herself upon a bench, and picked up her carding combs. Three small girls, who'd trailed the sisters into the hall, also lifted combs and settled to work under Dilys' careful eye.

Maude ranged the room, dealing whacks to a tapestry she suspected of harboring moths. "Ten years the girl's been here, fostered and raised by us till she's of age to wed—and has she learned one *single* thing she'll need to know when she's lady of this manor? She takes no interest in it at all—or anything else save those screechy birds of hers!"

"Perhaps Lothair will take her to live at court, Maude. Then her housekeeping skills won't matter. But there or here, Lowise will be Lady when she's wed, so best speak kindly of her songbirds—she loves them, and we shall be under her rule one day."

Maude snorted. "Not likely! Did you not hear her Tuesday-week? Told the priest *she's* not going to wed, and lose her life in childbed before she's twenty. What a notion for a girl of twelve! I should like to know how she thinks she'll slip out of the betrothal. It won't be as easy as dodging chores."

Dilys bent her head over the wool. "It must be hard for the child— she lost her own mother so young that she hardly knew her."

"Be harder still for her, does she not mend her lazy ways! Lothair will have scant patience with an idle wife without the wit to manage his estates. She'd do best to give him an heir the first year—if not, she'll see we were far kinder to her than she may think this day." Maude gave the tapestry another smack. "If she's not trained proper as she should be, there's none of us going to find living here so pleasant."

Dilys got to her feet. "I'll fetch her, Maude. Keep the girls at their carding."

She passed out of the hall with never a glance at the doorway arch— where a sad trophy hung. Primitively stuffed, the unicorn's head was greatly altered and far less magical than it had been long ago, in its life. The fluted horn was dim with dust, the mane lavishly festooned with cobwebs that had escaped notice from the floor. The beast's eyelids had been stitched closed with long decorative threads that counterfeited lashes lying on its cheeks, and it no longer seemed to weep.

* * *

The Lady Lowise posed in the center of a room lined tier upon tier with wicker cages, a lustily singing bird perched upon her slender forefinger, which she held before her face. The canary paid court to his mistress with trills, purls and ripples of sound; with bobbings of his body and enticing flutterings of his wings. The object of the performance was equally as enthralled by the bird as was he by her. Her unbound hair was dark as the feathers capping his elsewise yellow head, and their eyes were equally dark and bright, though Lowise's were much larger in her heart-shaped face.

From the cages, other males sang to counterpoint or compete with the favorite. Flax cocked his head, listening, and heard the canary hens calling more demurely to mates or chicks.

"How they do love the fresh thistleseed!" Lowise smiled brightly. "Flax always seeks out the fattest, sweetest seeds for you, my beauties. Have you brought any teasel?"

Flax was momentarily perplexed—when Lowise spoke "teasel," he sensed sheep's wool, and a task detested, and he could reconcile neither in any way with the birds. Finally he sifted out an image of the tall teasel plant before its dried prickles had been turned into carding combs, and got her proper meaning. He shook his head. Just yet the prickles were soft and green, ringed with lavender blossoms. No ripe seed so early.

"But you'll bring some when you can?"

Flax easily read the question on her face, and nodded solemnly.

"Then you shall have a bag of oats now, for bringing the thistleseed, and perhaps a bit of cheese, and—" Lowise turned her gaze back to the canary on her hand, as she rewarded it with a scrap of dandelion leaf. "And a bit of sausage! Do you want a sausage, Flax? Come along to the kitchens, and I'll see you get your pay."

She returned the canary to an empty cage, where the bird hopped excitedly from perch to perch. "Don't fret, pretty one. I'll be back directly. Sing for your other wives whilst I'm gone."

* * *

Flax collected his wage, astonished when he actually received the promised sausage. Cook would only allow Lowise a small sausage for him—one whose seasonings, poorly mixed, had allowed mold to nip it slightly—but it was better fare than Flax was accustomed to.

Laden, he walked to the gatehouse with Lowise chattering along at his side. Flax let her discourse on the merits of various seeds wash over him like birdsong, knowing that her questions now didn't require him to make answer, for which he'd have had to closely attend.

Still, her prattle masked other sounds, and it was Flax's feet, not his ears, warned him of horses approaching up the road. An instant later the courtyard was a confusion of horses, men, dust and pennons and dogs— marking Duke Lothair's unannounced homecoming from court.

It had been years, since last he so favored Ylowfort. Lothair was not often in residence, though his name was much invoked—a young man finding better ways to pleasure himself at court than buried on his country estates. Flax was not especially interested. He was mostly concerned with circling quietly past the milling horses and striking out for home before any of the Duke's dogs began to inspect him. He was far beneath a Duke's notice, but not so that of the coursing hounds. Flax began to edge to his left, away from the stables where horses and dogs would be directed.

Something bumped smartly against his right calf. Once. A second time. Flax felt—and heard—a loud sniffing. Glancing sidelong, he beheld a great wolfhound, its jaws dripping foam exactly as in his nightmares, as if his fear had conjured it. The dog prodded Flax's legs again with its muzzle, working hard to get a scent Flax absolutely knew—as if it had been written in fire on his brain—was not his own, nor that of the sausage.

In terror, he marked the stiff posture, the lowered head, the rising hackles. A beast bred to chase game, the wolfhound had no interest in a bit of old sausage. It had the scent of prey in its nostrils. A unicorn's scent. *Thistledown*'s.

As he could call rabbits and squirrels to him, and bespeak seeds to sprout rapidly, Flax could betimes cause animals to disremember seeing him. Such skill was useful when he came unexpectedly upon a pastured bull, or chose to pass untroubled by a villager's chained dog. Sometimes he could avoid the villagers by the same means.

This hunting dog proved another matter altogether. Fearsome of itself, it crystallized as well all of Flax's terrors, the nightmares and his true memories—his mind emptied, he could work no tiny magic upon it. Flax could scarcely force himself to stand still, though he knew his least move-ment would incite its attack. He read the set of its stiff tail, the lowered ears, the glowing yellow gaze. He did not need to hear the low rumble from the hound's throat to know what would happen should he stir.

Lowise saw him frozen in his tracks, and actually fell silent when she saw his face whiten and sweat bead it. Looking where Flax did, she saw the cause, and gasped.

"Stand still, Flax. It won't harm you." Lowise thought to reach for the hound's collar, but its size alarmed her, and she drew her hand back. "It's all right," she said less certainly.

Corlinn leaned closer to the scene shimmering within the cheval glass. The images were still, but far from static. A trembling boy, a bristling hound—neither in a posture likely to hold for long. The wizard frowned, trying to puzzle out their meaning. The boy—he'd seen that pale face before, surely.

"What's that?" A furry head, large-eared and long-nosed, thrust be-tween wizard and mirror. The remainder of the puppy's long-legged body could proceed no farther into the confined space between chair and wall, but her white-tipped tail brushed her master's back.

He reached out hastily to secure the framed glass. " 'That' is my scrying glass, and nothing your careless nose should be so near to! Off with you, now—I'm busy."

The dog's pale blue eyes fixed intently on the mirror. The hairs along

her spine rose slightly, but her ears and tail drooped—she was not sure of herself, as she watched the wolfhound.

"Lie down, lie down," she whined. "Quick! He means his threat!"

"Softly, Mai," the wizard said. "They can't hear you."

"Who is he?" the dog fretted.

"I'm not certain. The glass shows him from time to time. When last it did, he'd found an orphan unicorn fawn—and kept it alive."

The mirrored scene boiled with the beginning of motion. The blue-eyed dog yelped another desperate warning and batted at the glass with her paws, so swiftly that the wizard's reaching hands could not forestall her. The mirror swung in its frame.

Corlinn scarcely kept the glass's lower edge from striking the wall. He brought it carefully upright once more, sweating from the near-disaster, then turned a baleful look upon his young familiar. The mirror now reflected nothing save her cringing body and the tips of his own fingers, where they still gripped the frame.

"Well? Do you think he escaped?"

The blue-eyed dog crouched, tucked her tail to her belly more tightly and lowered her ears to their most miserable attitude. That sufficed for her answer.

The wizard sighed. "I suppose you'd know best. Pity. There was a promise about him—"

"Promise of what?" the dog asked, in a tiny voice that hoped to divert further rather than call attention to her misdeed.

"Oh, herbs and unicorns, passing across this glass unbidden—those are signs, and I thought they might mean something. Perhaps I was only wishful."

"Were you going to take an apprentice?"

"An *apprentice*?" Corlinn's brows raised. "When my familiar has barely shed her milk teeth and looks likely *never* to shed her puppy ways? Do you think me daft?"

The blue-eyed dog covered her nose with her paws. After a moment, her tail beat the floor hesitantly. A hand reached down to rub her ears.

Flax understood Lowise's reassurance, and read the tension in her tone. She was uneasy, but thought a moment's patience would save him. He had no means to tell her, no gesture to explain the hound's interest in him, the real danger. Flax began to tremble.

"I'll have someone call it off, Flax. Don't move. *Don't run. Stand still—*"

The hound's breath was furnace-hot upon him. Flax measured the distance to the gate, knowing his fear-scent and the unicorn's scent would push the dog to attack no matter what he did. Abruptly, he bolted. Flax ran for his life, the hound leaping after him.

Flax sprinted well, but in three long-legged bounds the hound had him, its fangs snaring the homespun cloth of his trousers, seizing the calf of his leg beneath. Flax hurtled forward, hard against the stone curb of the courtyard well. He didn't struggle to free himself from the hound's grip, and if he cried out in pain or fright, the sound was drowned by the hound's victorious snarling.

Travel-wearied as they were, the horses were mightily upset by the commotion. Lothair flung himself without dignity from his plunging gray, yanking savagely at the reins as he spun toward the trouble while his mount tried to flee. A girl was screaming, the shrill sound so bothersome that the young Duke was minded to spare a moment to slap her silent. A groom swung a whip at the hound, which nonetheless refused to relinquish its prey.

Lothair strode forward, grabbed the hound's wide collar, and dragged it off of Flax. Half-lifted, it reared upon its hind legs till dog and man were almost of a height. At last the Duke got the beast behind him, and a snarled command kept it a little distance away.

Panting, Lothair bent to assess the damage.

Flax's eyelids were pressed tightly closed, his brows drawn together till they nearly meshed. He shied away from Lothair's touch, beginning to twitch violently.

Lothair's mouth tightened, as did his grip on Flax's tunic.

"Here now! The beast but knocked you down, you're not so much hurt. He might as easily have torn your throat out—never run from a coursing hound!" He lifted the boy to his feet, waited for him to find his legs. Flax swayed, pressed a hand to his head, and made no sound.

The Duke caught his breath, and had leisure to inspect what he supported. Dirty, ragged—and evidently terrified out of whatever wits it possessed. Not wearing his livery, therefore probably a villager and not one of his servants—but in need of a bit of care. It bled from a gash at its temple that its fingers were doing little to staunch. Lothair swept his traveling cloak clear of the mess.

He turned to call for herbs and bandages, his thought straying already to his wolfhound—ruin a dog if you let it get onto hunting two-footed prey. The habit was worse than sheep-killing.

At the slight relaxation of grip and attention, Flax twisted free of his hold and fled the courtyard as if fiends were on his track.

The wolfhound tried to oblige him there, but the Duke forestalled it with a snapped command which he was heartened to see it obey instantly. The hound checked with a disconsolate whine, and Flax vanished into the trees.

"Lothair—my lord Duke—welcome home."

The Duke exaggeratedly swept half a bow.

"Aunts. May one inquire just what the devil goes on here? Who was that filthy mooncalf, that almost had me trampled by my own horse in my own courtyard?"

The Lady Maude was red-faced and likely to burst into tears on the instant. Dilys was hardly more coherent, as Lothair let his aunts fluster their way through apologies and incomprehensible explanations about herb-boys.

"The witch's brat? Still hanging about? Shouldn't he have starved by now?"

Dilys fingered a spot of blood on her nephew's sleeve. Soapwort, and quickly, before the stain set. She hoped Flax had brought them a recent supply. "The boy brings field herbs, and food for Lowise's birds. Was he much hurt?"

"And run like that, Aunt? He's in better fettle than I find myself in— I want wine, food, and a bath—at once!" The Duke turned, snapping orders at the servants his aunts and chamberlain should have been directing. "You—clear this mess up. Put those horses away, and see they're well rubbed down before you dare leave them! You—get that baggage inside. *Now!*"

The courtyard burst into motion, but orderly, not the addled milling that had so thoroughly irked the Duke. One figure remained motionless amid the bustle, and caught his eye.

"Well, girl? Surely you've *some* task to return to?"

Her glare took him aback. The expression on her tearstained face was unnervingly hostile and not the least servile.

"I was settling accounts with the herb-boy, till your ill-mannered dog tried to kill him at my feet." Her tone suggested that the dog was not the sole creature present lacking in manners.

Lothair's stare widened. *Lowise?* But she was a *child*. Could she possibly be twelve now, and marriageable? Had he been away at court so long? And had she grown so fair?

"My lady—"

He was already speaking to her back, and that not for long.

Flax might have ceased running once he'd reached the forest's safety, when he heard no sound of the dog's pursuit, or once the extremity of his terror left him. Yet he did not slow, for any reason. His lungs were afire, the pain in his head was blinding, but he paid neither the slightest heed.

When he staggered at last through the cot's doorway, erratically gasping, his legs continued to labor uselessly as he collapsed into darkness.

Fortunately, he landed partly across Thistledown's bed of bracken. The unicorn, who had retreated into the far corner at his hasty entrance, shied back again as Flax fell, then nickered a confused greeting.

Flax made no response. His ragged breathing gradually slowed to normalcy and finally was scarcely perceptible, but he knew nothing of that. He sprawled face down in the bracken, a trickle of blood pooling beside his averted face.

The unicorn stepped cautiously closer, nostrils flaring. He put his silver muzzle to Flax's shoulder, seeking to rouse him as he often did at morning's first light, or moonrise. The blood-scent was alarming, but curiosity was stronger. Thistledown sniffed the wound, then licked at it, laving the salty blood away. Flax did not stir, and the gash bled freshly.

Thistledown softly bleated his dismay. The blood welled up unceasingly. Flax's pale skin was cooler each moment, his shallow breaths drawn less and less frequently. The unicorn's sharp ears could plainly hear his heart beating, faltering like a weary horse that stumbles often.

Thistledown trembled. Instincts commanded him, but he knew not what to expect of them. Gently, as if dipping it into a drop of dew, he laid the tip of his tiny horn against Flax's cracked skull. The horn, barely through the skin of the bud, was stained crimson. Abruptly it blossomed salmon—a glow from within transforming the colors.

The unicorn cried out in pain as the colors changed, the shrill sound rising beyond any hearing save his own—yet the fawn would not break the contact by drawing back. Thistledown huddled in the bracken alongside Flax, his neck bent double to press the horn against the wound. Presently the angle grew easier for his neck—the glowing horn had lengthened, and grown more deeply fluted. The light playing about it was white, cream, then firefly yellow—feeble and flickering, then strengthening, brightening. After a time, it gradually dimmed once more.

The only sound, above the rustle of bracken and the mingled breathing, was a counterpoint of the night wind in the willow trees. If a dog howled at the Duke's manor, for once the sound did not carry across the night. The wind's sound dwindled with the light, and soon all that could be heard was the regular sigh of Flax's lungs filling and easily emptying—followed by the flower-scented exhalations of the unicorn.

Flax woke. Feeling relaxed and well. Somehow, that ease seemed false to him. He was curled beside Thistledown, as he had often slept while the fawn was small and needed his body's warmth to supplement its own. From the angle of the light, Flax knew he had slept overlong, and he marveled at that—he was rarely late abed.

Probably 'twas the sun had waked him—and not glimmering round the flap over the eastward-facing window, but finding entrance through a gap in the roof thatch so that a broad shaft struck him full in the face. Flax sat up, yawning and rubbing at his neck, where a bracken stem had pricked it.

Thistledown nickered a greeting, and nuzzled his chest. Flax absently scratched at the base of the fawn's horn, teasing off dry flakes of the skin that had covered the bud. The horn was as long as his hand now, growing so rapidly—it seemed he could almost watch it doing so.

What was amiss? Flax frowned. The day was quiet, Thistledown seemed healthy, and he felt well enough himself. He never noticed the blood dried brown upon the floor, blending with earth and bracken.

He remembered nothing now. A bad dream, faded save for a lingering sense of unease? Flax stretched—and as he did so, saw the torn cloth of his trousers, where the dog had grabbed his calf.

Memory flooded back, so strongly that Flax nearly lost his senses again, without aid of any blow to his head. His heart lurched wildly, his lungs turned traitor and refused to let him draw a proper breath. The bright sunlight faded and all but vanished.

Thistledown bleated anxiously. As if the sound released him from enchantment, Flax opened his eyes, and shivered. He put a hand gingerly to his head, probing for a tangible reminder of his terror.

There was no trace of any wound.

No bruise. No tenderness, no caked blood, no sudden pain—not even the ridge of a scar. Flax's fingers explored feverishly, doubting his memory, but there was nothing for the fingers to report. Yet he remembered hammerblows of pain, while he fled headlong through woods and fields with destruction at his heels. He remembered hot blood running down his face—and how, as he'd tried to staunch the flow, he'd felt bone shift like cracked eggshell. He remembered the world dimming around him, drawing away, until he fell into a greater darkness. How could there be no mark, no sign of any of that?

Flax's blue eyes looked deep into the brown pools of the unicorn's, their wide wonder eventually interrupted by a commonplace. Thistledown began to rub his horn against Flax's fingers, begging him to work harder at the itch. Flax obliged. The plainest plants were often the most useful herbs—so why should a miracle-working creature not be otherwise as any other beast?

Crops ripened, in the wild forest and in the manor's walled fields. The harvest proceeded. Flax kept close to home—out of sight by daylight, and even by night he and Thistledown did not venture far from their little cot. He did his own harvesting of crops no man's hand had sown, alert to the least sound or scent, and brought Thistledown out to graze only after the moon had set, or was dimmed by clouds. Otherwise Flax cut fodder and carried it home. Thistledown accepted the new restrictions with good grace but much puzzlement.

The oak leaves were bronze, and red hips fattened on the rosebushes in the hedgerows. Frost covered the medlar fruit Flax gathered to dry for winter keeping. Leaves dropped, save from the oaks, and Flax moved with special care through the crackling drifts of them, keeping as silent as he might.

Snow fell. It was easier to see at night, but there was danger too. A unicorn's cloven tracks differed from those a deer or sheep might leave—and there might be others than Flax knowledgeable about such matters, so he was careful to brush all of Thistledown's tracks away as he went, with a bit of pine branch serving him for a broom.

The winter deepened, and when the nights were colder and the wind raged wildly, Flax could let Thistledown roam more widely, taking the exercise his growing body and restless spirit craved—sure that none less wild than they would be abroad in such weather. The wind took care of the tracks, though close to home Flax assisted it.

Flax even strove to disguise the smoke from the small cookfire he permitted himself on the hearth. That worked well enough for the village folk, who'd seldom been certain till Beltane whether Flax had lived through a given winter—but there was another who could not be so misdirected.

Thrice, Lowise rode her dappled palfrey past the village to the cot's deserted dooryard, dismounted, and pleaded for Flax to come out—till her words and her voice both gave out. That the cottage appeared empty as a nest whose birds have flown deterred her never the slightest. That she never set eyes on Flax himself, and had not since he'd fled bleeding from the manor, did not stay her from returning.

Flax knew what she craved of him so desperately—but even the knowledge that her songbirds were forced to feed on wheat and roughly cracked corn could not force him to brave the manor again. His own fear he might perchance have mastered, but the cause of it would still remain, and Flax could not hazard Thistledown's life. He knew it would come to that, soon or late.

At Candlemas, when songbirds by custom begin their courtships, Lowise returned a fourth time. She called Flax's name, then howled it—and finally flung something at the doorplanks, whirled her horse, and galloped away through the crusty snow. Flax made no move to investigate—he knew, without need of sight, that Lowise's favorite bird lay dead on the snow, still-bright feathers cloaking its malnourished body. He felt her pain, shared the grief. He fully expected that all her birds would die.

Flax had hoped to wait out the winter, let spring bring out new green shoots among the sere grasses—but there was an urgency to the wind that hinted he dared not. Go, he and Thistledown must—and soon.

Lothair plucked the white pebble from his betrothed's fingers, less from interest in the object itself than to discover what she found more engrossing than their conversation before the hearth.

"Lowise? Where did you come by this?"

Her glance left him in no doubt as to how small a store she set by speech with him, but Lothair was too distracted to be easily withered.

"Outside the village," Lowise answered grudgingly, both annoyed and indifferent. She doubted Lothair would know where Flax's cottage was, but she was quite certain he'd object to her having gone there. The Duke objected to everything his pledged bride was, said, or did. The very sight of him infuriated her, especially since he had set himself to get to know her better, and spent more time at her side.

Lothair stepped away from the fire, calling his huntsman up from his place farther down the hall. The white pebble was presented for his expert examination.

"*Well?*"

"A unicorn fewmet, my lord. Fresh. Mark how the white's not yet darkened to rose."

"Yes. I thought it must be! I had heard that Gerard took one on his lands in the summer, but I took that for his usual empty boasting. I would not have thought to discover another of the beasts so near." The Duke glanced at the mounted head above the doorway. "They're such solitary creatures. And there's been none sighted on these lands since my father's day. *A unicorn.*" Lothair's voice all but trembled with his excitement.

"Shall I make ready a hunt, my lord? For Beltane, perhaps?"

"A hunt, aye, but let us try our luck as soon as may be. Beltane is too weary a while to wait! This winter has been tedious for us all—the dogs and we need the sport."

"Then I shall see to obtaining the . . . bait, m'lord."

Lothair's attention flickered briefly. "No need, Raimund. The Lady Lowise is yet a maid—she'd best be! So noble a quarry deserves a nobler lure than some peasant's daughter bought with silver."

A man, clad in forester's green from cap to boots, prowled the cottage dooryard. Flax had been aware of him since the huntsman's grain-fed horse had borne him to the outskirts of the village. He had sensed him for the past hour, creeping closer and closer until at last his examination of lane and field and copse had brought him to the cottage.

Flax had by then gone to ground, his already tiny cookfire banked till it was only a smothered ember which he might coax to life again if it became safe to do so. Despite the chill swiftly pervading the cottage's single room, Flax was sweating. He strove not to communicate his terror to Thistledown. They had burrowed beneath a pile of bracken and oak leaves, back where the cot met the hill it was built against—cold there, but dimmer than the rest of the cot, and therefore safest.

Flax was doubtful of their safety. The door was barred—but had he overlooked a single cloven track in the snow outside, perhaps where the hawthorn's low branches made it difficult for him to venture? He'd gathered all the droppings, and fed them to a nearby stream—but unicorn fewmets lack odor, and color till they age and grow rosy. Their whiteness could be one with the snow. He might, Flax feared, have missed the very signs the Duke's man now sought, for all his care.

Finally Raimund departed, but when Flax unbarred the door, the day's last light was fading. He was hung all about with bundles and covered overall with a length of coarse cloth that served him for a cloak. The ember of the cottage fire was left dying in its own time.

Overhead, the stars were sharp as huntsmen's knives. Flax did not regard them. He carried a pine bough in his left hand, and brushed away the tracks where he and Thistledown passed.

That same morn, Lowise had been informed by her betrothed that she would assist his unicorn hunt—in the capacity of bait—because it was his pleasure that she should do so. That moment, she saw mapped plain the road her life would thereafter take—for whatever space the rigors of estate-managing and childbearing left her.

The revelation left her so dumbstruck that Lothair never suspected she had not acquiesced. Lowise kept close to her chamber all day, so the Duke knew naught of the rebellion flaring in her heart—this once she'd spoken no least word of it. Lowise did not sup in the hall that night. As the mead and wine were going round, she was lying beneath her velvet coverlet, fully clad in her warmest clothing—which extra warmth would have lent credence to her excuse of being feverish, had anyone disputed it.

By the time Lothair was being lighted to his chamber, flushed with wine and cherishing close his dreams of a trophy such as few of the royal court had even a hope of glimpsing—Lowise was out upon the road, under the bright starlight. She had not dared risk encountering a groom, and she had never saddled a horse with her own white hands, so she was afoot—but free. For the moment, the joy of that was stronger than any dread of the dark, and well worth any pangs of cold.

Lowise had, of course, no destination, no plan—and no food beyond the nightbread she'd snatched from her room along with its companion flagon of wine. By the time she'd reached the village, Lowise was winded, her feet were cold and soaking, and she had begun to suspect a nasty difference between knightly romances and reality. She hurried past the dark shapes of the peasants' huts, anxious not to be discovered—but as the last was put behind her she lingered, looking with longing at the rim of light around its single, shuttered window. Ahead shone no welcoming yellow fire, but only the cold white glow of starlight on snowdrift.

Lifting her chin, Lowise marched on. To return meant Lothair, living his life, taking his orders, bearing his children till she died of it. What was a bit of cold, next to that?

There was one more hut, far past the point where the village street had dwindled to a mere thread of beaten snow. Lowise was startled to see hoofprints marking out the way—who save she had ridden to Flax's home? Ridden lately too, for snow had fallen since last *she'd* gone that way.

The tracks stopped at Flax's dooryard, but Lowise hesitated only a moment before plunging on. A more or less open path led into the trees before her, and the unbroken snow was not deep, only treacherous from hidden stones and fallen branches. She soon came out of the wood, into the stubbled drifts of an oatfield. Skirting the edge of it, Lowise made for the trees once more. Beyond, she thought, might lie a road. At least the walking should be easier, where trees had kept the snow from settling deeply.

As she reached the woodshore, a flicker among the trees brought a gasp of alarm to her cold lips. A moment till her heart's frantic hammering calmed—then she could see that the glow was neither glare from searching torches nor greenish witchlight either, and therefore no danger to her. The light *did* move, and Lowise began to follow it with her feet as well as her eyes. Some white beast—a deer, perchance—reflecting starlight and snowlight from its coat. It was slender, and lovely, and made her long to come close to it, to see it more clearly. . . .

From tree to tree Lowise darted, slipping down icy banks and scrambling over fallen logs, all as silently as she might. The light drew closer, ever closer, as she came closer to it.

All at once, she lost sight of it. Lowise stumbled to a halt, then began to circle, in tears without knowing their cause. Surely, surely, she would have seen the creature run. How had it fled her, abandoned her so suddenly and so silently? She put a trembling hand out to grasp a boulder as she passed it, wanting support in the slippery going.

The rock moved under her hand, rising up and lurching toward her. Lowise screamed.

She would have fled, but her legs would not obey the command. Lowise thought she would faint, or expire of fright on the spot—then she realized incredulously that she was looking into Flax's familiar face, and she saw that he looked quite as terrified as she felt! Lowise clutched him, to save herself toppling into the snow, and Flax was scarcely the support she anticipated—he staggered and swayed like a tree wracked by storm, and they both all but fell.

She babbled questions at him, pouring them out as she always did, while Flax made no more answer than he ever had. When Lowise ran out of snatched breath at last, a white owl with a heart-shaped face glided over, calling one final query at them both.

As if to answer, a snowdrift rose up on slender legs, stretched its neck, and tossed its silver mane about its ivory horn. Diamonds of frost flew sparkling under the stars.

"Ohhh!" Lowise breathed, nearly silenced by awe. After that, there was no question but that she was going with them.

The Lady Lowise's disappearance was not noted until late the following morning—matters would have gone otherwise had the day been the dawn of the proposed hunt—but the Aunts merely assumed she was avoiding the morning's weaving, and Lothair supposed she was avoiding him. It was a long while before anyone began to search in a serious way, and a longer while still before it was determined that she was nowhere about the manor. Her palfrey was still snug in its stable. No one countenanced the theory that the Lady Lowise might have gone out into the cold drifts afoot.

Raimund the huntsman was abroad early, seeking to more closely confirm the whereabouts of his fabulous quarry. He still found no very recent sign, and nervously searching far afield for some trace, was gone all the day. 'Twas long past nightfall ere he returned, frustrated and anxious on account of his master's temper. The search of the manor had just been completed, raising no more trace of the Lady Lowise than had his search for unicorn spoor.

The hall was in a ferment all that night. Not till morning did Raimund recall having seen tracks not his own, going past the village as he approached the area where the unicorn was thought to shelter. Tracks could belong to anyone, but Lothair demanded to be shown, and duly was.

The two men entered Flax's cottage. It was empty, but plainly had not been so for any great while. Lothair was surprised—having quite forgotten Flax's existence. He was further amazed when they unearthed a single white pebble beneath the scattered bracken that served the cottage for a bed, and discovered a cloven track in the hearth-ashes.

"He was keeping the beast *here*—like a milk-cow?"

"It would seem so, m'lord." The huntsman had never heard of such a thing, but his mind was open to the evidence of his eyes.

Lothair's frown deepened, as he made other connections. "She's run off with him, that addled toad-herd!"

The general opinion, however, was that the Lady Lowise might as easily have been abducted by Flax—the witch's spawn, capable of any evil. A rescue was noisily organized for her, and it set off in almost completely the wrong direction once it was past the oatfield.

In the tales the minstrels sang so sweetly, a maid might take to the greenwood as a chaste unselfish companion to some falsely accused knightly beloved, subsisting on nuts and venison and song, clad in a kirtle of rough homespun, sleeping boldly upon the cold ground with an unsheathed sword beside her. Lowise had always taken such tales for utter truth, and though Flax was no knight and bore no sword, she entered into their adventure with her whole heart. She uncaringly got her gown wet with snow, spattered with mud, torn by brambles as she marched along after the unicorn hour after hour. She happily shared Flax's meager supper of pease porridge and catnip tea. When Flax stretched out to sleep beneath a fir tree's sheltering branches, Lowise agreeably did likewise, and composed herself for slumber.

The dry fir needles had at first been a soft enough mattress, but they could not for long disguise the essential hardness of frozen ground. Lowise shifted restlessly, and comforted herself with thoughts of minstrels singing her name in angelic tones. Needles pricked through gown and cloak to tender skin. Lowise craftily rolled over to escape them. Now cold nipped rudely at her, despite her woolen clothing. Lowise irritably curled into a ball. That was warmer, and with her arms for a pillow, her cheeks were safe from needle-jabs. She closed her eyes.

An owl called, and Lowise sprang up, heart racing, her straining ears unable to hear anything over the rush of her blood through them. The fire was out, the woods were dark as a velvet bag, filled with unidentifiable, perilous noises. Lowise crouched beneath the fir until she trembled with exhaustion. Weariness tamed her fear, but when she dropped back to the needles at last, the ground seemed harder and colder than ever, and forgetting the minstrels and the brave maidens, she began to weep.

Not since she was very small and called inconsolably for her dead mother had such tears failed to produce the results the Lady Lowise desired. Yet now, when she was in such utter distress, weary and hungry, cold and uncomfortable and terrified, no remedy was offered her. In fact, Flax seemed to have instantly found the sleep she so vainly sought, and there was no one else to hear.

Warm breath touched the nape of Lowise's neck. *A wolf*, she thought, and, prepared to be devoured, too frightened to cry out, she tensed helplessly for the snap of teeth.

Instead, a cool velvet muzzle brushed her cheek, whiskers tickled her nose, and flower-scented breath mingled with her own. Lowise opened her eyes.

The unicorn knelt beside her, shining in the darkness. It had a little tuft of needles caught about the base of its horn, and Lowise lifted timid fingers to untangle them. The creature sighed, folded its legs, and lowered itself carefully between Lowise on the one side and Flax on the other. Lowise laid her cheek against its shoulder, which was softer than her satin pillow at the manor. Presently, she slept.

The Duke never for an instant suspected Flax of having forcibly abducted Lowise. Lothair knew nothing of Flax's character, but he had observed a great deal of his betrothed's during the winter's course, and had thought when first she was missed that she might have run off to spite him. Running away with the herb-boy simply meant that Lowise was unlikely to return the moment she missed a meal or blistered a pampered foot.

What he might have done to provoke her remained uncertain—the least word or deed of his was likely to set her off, Lothair had noted. Such was the marriage of advantage his father had devoted years to arranging for him!

To be just, his father could neither have desired nor predicted his present humiliation. Lowise had been a newborn when the negotiations had begun, a toddler when the betrothal contract was signed and she was conducted to what would become her home. His father had orchestrated the union of their landholdings, and ensured a golden future for his heir—and then had died, safely free of it all.

The hue and cry of the searchers annoyed the Duke. Not likely one could beat the woods for a maid as one would for a deer, and they'd seen no sign of a track for hours—not human, not unicorn. Not even Raimund's trained eye could conjure a trace.

The search spread wide, but had not progressed more than a league outward by dusk. It was decided to return to the manor and proceed afresh with the dawn.

Lothair accepted the plan, not voicing his reservations. Despite the chill he'd endured daylong, he touched his wine but lightly, as he silently chewed the food the servitors put before him. His people mistook his black mood for concern about his betrothed, and stayed tactfully at a distance—leaving the Duke alone with his thoughts in their gossiping midst.

Lowise had shamed him—as publicly as was possible short of walking away from him at the very altar. None suspected it yet, but when the search caught up with the Lady Lowise and her peasant, the unfortunate truth would be revealed. Lothair found that he shrank from forcing such a conclusion. It could serve no one's cause—least of all his own.

Dragged home like a criminal, put in her place as she'd have to be—Lowise would never, the Duke thought, forgive him that. Far better if he could manage matters quietly. It would save his pride, and would not savage hers publicly. Lowise might already be penitent of her hasty departure. Why punish her more than her offense warranted, when she might be right glad to come home with him if he took the trouble to spare her feelings? She was very young, her spirits were high. He could afford to be gentle with her, and they might hope to put this indescretion behind them.

And . . . there was the unicorn. A crowd could frighten it clean out of the kingdom. Or some other might take a lucky bowshot, and claim a trophy Lothair already thought of as his own. Without his retinue to interfere, he might be able to bring back the beast's head as well as his flighty betrothed.

The Duke had provisions packed, quietly, and the horse he threw his saddlebags across was not his swift courser, but a retired war-horse steady and used to the hardships of winter travel. It was not troubled by the brace of ash-shafted spears he hung at its side.

It proved in no way difficult to let himself be separated from the general mass of the hunt, next day. By midday he had gone his own way, unremarked, choosing for his direction the one no one else had tried.

Lowise knew less than nothing of the preparation of food. 'Twas brought to her when she was hungry, or when she ought to eat. Cookcraft was for servants. Should she express a desire to taste the red raspberries growing beneath her window, that fruit was plucked, washed, and served to her with cream in a silver dish. It would never have been permitted that she touch it otherwise—she was to be a duchess when she was wed. Lowise had only the barest notion of what was fit for her beloved song-birds to eat, with dire results.

Dawn had just broken. Her maid had never awakened her so early, but hunger was not so gentle with her. Lowise felt sore, stiff, and full of holes as a pincushion. She sat chasing fir needles out of her hair with a carved wooden comb.

Flax rekindled the fire, and tucked the mug among the embers. When the water in it bubbled, he dropped something into the cup, presently rising to offer Lowise a share of sour tea. The gloss of adventuring having somewhat worn off, Lowise hesitated to put her lips to the rough un-washed crockery, but presently thirst overruled fastidiousness. Her stom-ach rumbled rudely. The loaf of bread she had carried away from the manor seemed inadequate and dainty as they shared it.

The tea drunk, Flax reached into the cup and drew out red rose hips. Their flavor was pleasantly tart, like the rare lemons which Flax had prob-ably never tasted. Lowise fed breadcrumbs to the unicorn.

Flax cleaned and stowed the cup, put out the fire, shouldered his bun-dle and slipped from the fir tree's shelter. Lowise scrambled hastily after him. The winter morning's sky was overcast, promising more snow. That already on the ground was gray in the dim light.

Trotting so lightly that it seemed unlikely to leave tracks, the unicorn went to Flax and rubbed its head against him. By daylight, Lowise saw that it was scarcely half grown, a coltish awkwardness competing with its grace. It suffered her to stroke its mane, and she could have continued so, entranced most thoroughly, for days, or till her body starved and per-ished of thirst, and been uncaring of any of that. When the unicorn stepped away from her hands, Lowise blinked as one awakened from deep slumber.

She found she was walking alongside Flax, between trees whose trunks had not been there an instant before, by her reckoning. Their branches were bare, save for the occasional dark conifer or holly bush. Ahead, a little off to the left, she saw the unicorn's gently swaying hips, glowing white.

"Does it have a name, Flax? Of course, it would hardly need one—it's not as if there are dozens of them running about, and you wanted to call just this one. I've never seen one before this, except pictures in books, never at all—"

Flax bent down, and pulled the brown stem of a thistle from a tangle of weeds by his feet. He offered it to Lowise.

"You call it 'Thistle'? But Flax, thistles are so brown and ugly and prickly, and it's *nothing* like that, really! It deserves a proper name—"

Flax's nimble fingers found one bit of fluff caught among the dry prickles, and teased it free. The wind took it and sent it dancing away. Thin winter sunlight caught it too, and the down sparkled as it drifted, bright as a star.

"Oh!" Lowise stared. "Well, *that's* a different story. *Thistledown.* That suits it exactly, Flax. It's just as white, and as graceful as thistledown on the wind."

She was silent a bare instant after that.

"Flax, where is it going?"

Flax helpfully pointed out the direction in which Thistledown was plainly walking ahead of them. Lowise sighed.

"I *meant*, where are you taking it? Not that I blame you for running away—Lothair wants to hunt it, kill it. But where will you go? What will you do when you get there? Are there other unicorns there? How do you know?"

Whither were they bound? That was the true thing Lowise wanted to know.

Even had words come easy to his tongue, Flax could not have answered. *Away*, had been his sole intent. He knew nothing of whatever shape the world took beyond his own woods and fields. Thistledown, however, moved with obvious purpose, drawn onward by a call that, if not clear, was still far from the idle wandering and foraging of a grazing animal. Flax had noticed that as soon as they'd put the cottage behind them—that was the moment he stopped leading and had begun to follow.

Flax had no gesture to explain any of that, if Lowise could not see for herself, so he simply kept walking. Lowise seemed to have forgotten her question, commenting instead on how happy she was not to be carding wool.

"I'm running away too, you know. I'm supposed to be marrying Lothair, but I won't, and no one can make me."

Flax watched a crow wheeling overhead.

"I don't see the point to marrying anyway. First thing, you start in having babies, and then pretty soon you die. My mother did. And Lothair's—she died when he was born. Is that what happened to your mother, Flax?"

The crow took noisy roost in a shattered-looking pine, bare at its top. The bird was joining a pair already perching there. Flax understood more of the crow's speech than he did of Lowise's—but then he was paying more attention to it.

They walked all day through wooded land. The course Thistledown set was far from straight—ridges could be easier skirted than climbed, and sometimes a quicker-seeming path led only to streams too fast-flowing to have frozen and too treacherous to ford. The trees thinned. The ground leveled, and presently they were in grassland. There was less snow, which warned Flax of wind sternly scouring the ground, bending the heather stems flat to the cold earth.

A clump of boulders kept the worst of the wind from them. Flax built a tiny fire of dried brush and fed it carefully while his cup steamed at the edge of it.

Lowise chattered continually—till a jackdaw would have seemed silent by contrast. She viewed the tea with disappointment, which did not surprise Flax. They were at the cruel end of the year, and his tiny store of dried peas and gleaned oats had hardly made the pair of them one decent meal. Flax had not expected to have company on his flight. Woodland might have yielded a squirrel-cache of nuts, but on the moorland there was no food to be had—unless one could graze like a sheep, and even a sheep might have been close to starving. Flax dropped herbs into the cup, stirring first one way, three times, then back the other, also thrice.

Lowise's stomach complained bitterly at getting only tea—but when she had finished the drink, it quieted. She was surprised to find that she felt heartened and well satisfied—as if she had eaten a full meal, not merely a few dried rose hips.

The next nightfall did not see them to any shelter. Flax searched out the lowest spot he could find, burrowed into the heather, and helped Lowise to do the same. There was no safe place to build a fire, so they chewed slowly at a handful of dried currants, sharing with the unicorn, and they all went hungry to their night's rest.

Flax lay back against Thistledown's flank, troubled by Lowise's discomfort as he was not by his own. Eventually her eternal one-sided conversation dwindled to a mumble, lost in Thistledown's wind-braided mane.

Lowise dreamed that night of her dead mother—she dreamed that she held a child of her own for her mother's inspection. She desperately wanted to cast the swaddled thing away, and have her hands free to cling tight to the mother she'd thought lost to her—but she could not. Her arms were full of the child. Its weight was too heavy for her strength. It waxed heavier and heavier, and still she could not set it down, though her back bowed with its weight. It had Lothair's face, and when Lowise reluctantly tried to soothe its cries, the infant tore at her with teeth sharp as a fox's.

She gasped in disgust and fright, and tried to put it from her—panicking when it clung to her. Her mother was gone, as always she had

139

been, and Lowise was alone with a monster child that was murdering her. She was dying, growing so insubstantial that she could see straight through the flesh the babe was gnawing.

Lowise woke sobbing, clutching despairingly at Flax, at the heather, at the unicorn.

"I won't, I won't, *I won't!* I won't wed him! I'll die if I do—I know it. I know it!"

Her sobs were finally stifled against Thistledown's neck. Flax pulled stems of heather, twisting them together until his fingers made for dizzy watching to the one eye Lowise cautiously opened. When he laid the mat over her, Lowise found it warm and soft as the best blanket the manor boasted, and she was certain she was still dreaming. It actually draped over her, which was impossible. Lowise stared, for even she recognized that such work was not mere woodcraft.

"How . . . how did you *do* that?"

Flax was as puzzled as if she'd questioned how he knew to breathe the air. Her question was as clear in her mind as on her lips, he knew he did not mistake it—but its answer was utterly beyond him. No nod or head-shake would serve, no other gesture offer her anything. Flax gave Lowise the last sip from her flagon of wine, and settled her back to sleep.

They had reached forest again, when Lothair overtook them.

It was a place fitted for such a disaster—they had each been uneasy upon entering the wood, the unicorn restive, starting at the least untoward noise. Bare black branches twined overhead, joining like some ghastly charred lace, twisting in patterns that would look hardly more wholesome when the trees were in leaf. Quite unlike the pine forest, or the Ylowfort oak-wood.

The branches were black, but as Flax looked fitfully away from them he was convinced that their true color was red—first bright, then a de-cayed hue, like old bloodstains. He shivered, as part of his mind insisted that the color was only the sunlight, glinting on icy branches. Lowise for once fell silent. Thistledown tossed his head and quickened his pace.

A deer track took them down and across a slope, a dark ravine below on their left hand and the rest of the brown hillside rising sheer to their right. Single file, they descended.

A horse neighed, loud and very near.

Lowise, looking back, saw Lothair sitting his horse just above them on the slope, one hand resting on his sword-pommel and dire vengeance promised in every hard plane of his face. Flax saw too, and acted at once to thwart the most present danger he could anticipate. A hard slap to Thistledown's rump sent the startled unicorn galloping downhill, out of sight and to safety. Flax did not guess that the unicorn was not the Duke's primary quarry.

Lowise had never considered that he might be.

"*No!*" she screamed, all defiance and panic. "I *won't* go back! I won't go with you! *You can't make me!*"

Answering the Duke's spur, the war-horse slid on its haunches down the slope till its lathered flanks were interposed between Flax and Lowise. Lothair drew his sword, and saluted Lowise with the blade. His joy at seeing her safe astonished him, her wind-tangled hair distressed him—and the hatred on her face made the gentleness he had intended impossible.

"My lady." Lothair swung down, and the horse moved a few paces away, to stand waiting. "Well met. You also, witch's brat. What have you done with my unicorn?"

Flax made no reply.

"Call it back," Lothair ordered, deadly calm.

Flax shook his head. His knees were wobbly. He wanted to run, as he had from the wolfhound, but he remembered that outcome, and held his place.

The Duke's face darkened. "Then that's twice you've robbed me, peasant. You're going to pay for that."

"I'm not *yours*," Lowise interjected furiously.

Lothair raised a brow. "Ah, there you are mistaken, my lady. There's a contract. Very legal." He turned a little, and leveled his sword at Flax's throat.

"Lothair, no!" She could not quite believe what he intended.

"*Yes*, my lady. Witless he may well be, but you brought this on him when you chose to run away with him. You are my lawful betrothed, and I intend to be revenged for the shame you have visited upon me. Be glad I'll be content with this."

"It wasn't Flax's fault!" Lowise cried, horrified. "He didn't steal me! I only followed him—" Adventures didn't end this way. No minstrel would write such a thing.

Lothair advanced upon Flax, with a fencer's tiny careful steps, prepared for whatsoever move his quarry might make.

"Call the beast back, boy, and I'll let you off with half the beating you've earned."

Flax had a sense that the Duke did not intend killing him. Bloody him, assert his lawful authority which Lowise had challenged—there was something in it about a lesson for Lowise too, and a punishment—so snarled together that Flax could only feel it all, not understand it. He wouldn't be killed—he was property, even if he wasn't of especial value to the Duke. For Thistledown, Flax could hope for no such dubious mercy. The back of Lothair's mind burned with a bright image of himself lifting a bloody and precious trophy—the unicorn's severed head.

Shaking, Flax let his pack slip to the ground. He hefted a slender oak branch, which had been lying almost under his foot. It was a handsbreadth longer than Lothair's sword, thick as his forearm, and nearly straight.

The Duke smiled mirthlessly, to see him arm himself so.

"Even better, boy. Have at you, then!" He leaped into an attack. This little lesson taught, Lowise given precisely the awakening she'd been asking for—and the matter would be well-settled.

Flax jumped back by an equal measure, narrowly eluding the slash, and took a tighter grip on his stick. Was Thistledown safe? Surely he'd be far enough away soon, even a swift horse couldn't hope to catch him— not in woodland. The Duke had no dogs with him, Flax noted gratefully. He hadn't been sure at first. Whatever the combat's outcome, Thistledown would go free. That relief kept his own fear mostly in check.

Flax raised the oak branch to meet Lothair's next attack. Just for an instant, he felt a strength flowing between the branch and his arm—as, once laying palm to its trunk, he had felt the wind stirring a tree's upper branches. Blue-white sparks flew as wood met steel, and the Duke cried out in surprise. Flax staggered back, just as startled, and found himself in a tangle of wind-toppled trees. Instinctively he scrambled until he was teetering atop the pile, gaining what little advantage the height could offer him. A hopeful swing of the branch caught the Duke across the ribs. Flax retreated again, uncertainly.

"Witch's spawn!" Lothair cursed, and followed him, though less boldly. Not the easy lesson he'd anticipated—and did he let this mute peasant best him, not the lesson he wanted to present his bride with, either. His next cut was wary—but cold iron bit the oak solidly, and Flax felt no more strength flowing out from it. Whatever magic was in the branch was used up, and wood chips flew in place of sparks. Flax blocked a cut aimed at his head, and was suddenly left clutching a bare ell of branch as the remainder of his lopped weapon went spinning off into the forest.

His defenselessness brought neither respite nor pity. Flax jumped back desperately, sword-steel flashing just past his nose. The branches underfoot were heavily ice-glazed. Flax's feet shot out from under him, his leap of escape became a fall. He hit his head against a log and lay among the branches, stunned.

Lothair, panting, made his way over the treacherous tangle more cautiously, his swordpoint never wavering from Flax. His free hand rubbed

at his bruised ribs. Anger flared with the pain, and his blade twitched
eagerly.

A scream split the cold air. Lothair swiveled toward it instinctively.
Not surprising that Lowise should cry out—but his horse was bolting away
up the slope as if fiends were after it.

Lowise did not fear Flax's imminent murder. She had not even seen
him fall. Her gaze was fixed on a point just in front of her, as she screamed
once again. Almost under her feet, a heap of snow-covered leaves heaved
and shifted, rearing ultimately to a height half her own and spreading to
a bulk far greater. Everywhere among the black trees, similar drifts were
exploding upward and following the first toward the girl.

Fear replaced the heat of vengeance in Lothair's heart. Unlike Lowise,
he was able to move despite it. Abandoning Flax, he sprang to Lowise's
side, stumbling among the tangled deadfalls but still reaching her ahead
of the leaf-beast.

He swept his sword warningly at the thing—whatever it was—still
disbelieving his eyes. It did not retreat, did not seem to fear him—or even
heed him. Rustling, it crept closer while he was thrusting Lowise behind
him. Just as he managed to put himself firmly between her and the thing,
a pile burst into sight almost under his own boots.

Lothair swung a mighty stroke—and the leaf-beast simply flowed
around the blade and over him, choking off his sight and breath. The Duke
broke free at last, only to be struck from one side by another lump of
forest floor, while a third launched a rear assault. Leaves flew in every
direction as he rained blow after blow—no longer consciously attacking,
only seeking wildly to fend the things off. No stroke found a vital spot in
his enemies—or encountered anything solid at all.

The beasts swarmed ceaselessly up from the ground, whether dozens
or the same few repeatedly leaping, Lothair could not tell. Finally overcome, he went down and stayed down.

Lowise, upright only by virtue of the beech trunk she clung to, was suddenly past screaming. Having no idea how to faint, she watched with helpless, staring eyes as the beasts left the Duke to advance once more upon her. Lowise had no idea what they'd do to her. She didn't know what they'd done to Lothair, but he wasn't moving. She felt quite unable to move, herself, and was sure she couldn't escape them even had she been able to convince her hands to let go of the tree, her legs to bear her a few steps.

Flax, shaking his head dazedly, had found his feet but became worse entangled in the branches he had been lying among. By the time he floundered free, the leaf-beasts were ranged in a loose ring around Lowise. He stared at them, and at the Duke's body. The things seemed not to have noticed him yet.

Lowise saw that. "Flax, *run*," she pleaded. "Get away from here!"

Flax wanted very much to obey her. Terror poured from the heaps of leaves in waves and lapped ceaselessly at him. The evil he had sensed upon entering the wood had no more to it than the scent of salt air had to the sea, but he thought they were kin nonetheless. If he ran, he *might* just outrace them—they might be tied to their bit of forest, holding sway only within this cursed ravine, under its twisted trees.

That limitation made them no less dangerous. And once they sighted him, his best chance of escape was gone. How could he hope to fight them when the Duke had failed at it?

Flax's head swam, and the forest threatened to upend itself. When his sight cleared, he was still staring at Lowise's white face, though she no longer looked at him. A snared rabbit could not have looked more bereft of hope than she did. That look was the main reason Flax never trapped rabbits, though he could have called them merely by wishing and fresh meat was none so easy for peasants to come by . . .

The Duke's body sprawled just outside the circle, his sword lying nearby in the snow. Flax lunged toward the weapon, caught it up—and shrieked with pain as he flung the blade away. Something had bitten his hands like wildfire. He could not understand how lords could bear to fight with weapons that inflicted such pain on their wielders. The leaves where the sword had fallen were charred and smoking.

Flax almost reached for the blade again—then he snatched up a twisted branch instead and lifted it resolutely, if not hopefully. He stepped toward the nearest beast, and though it had neither face nor head that he could see, he knew somehow that it turned to face him. The sun had set, the last pink light was leaching rapidly from the sky. Despite the gloom, Flax saw a leaf-beast spring at him. A rustle of leaves further alerted him.

He swung the branch hard at it, repeating Lothair's futilities all unknowing. The beast crashed against his chest, and Flax's mouth filled with cold rotting leaves, while icy twigs stabbed for his eyes. He staggered, falling backward into a second heap of leaves. He struggled for air, tried to thrust the leaves away.

A shape white as frost hurtled through the wood, nimbly leaping the fallen trees. Lowise's heart leaped as well, then sank toward her toes in despair. Must the unicorn perish as well? Did the minstrel's song require that?

She cried out to it, urged it to flee, but Thistledown came gamely on, and as his hooves touched the clearing, he entered the battle with a slash of his gleaming horn.

Leaves flew in all directions—but this time the heaps did not instantly reform. Tatters sifted down to the forest floor, leaving a foul smell hanging behind them in the air. Flax rolled into view, choking as he got to his knees. Thistledown did not pause over him for a heartbeat, but charged the beast at Lowise's feet. His horn was so savagely bright, her eyes could not take it in save as an after-image, like a lightning bolt. There came a crack like thunder but louder, and Lowise fell to her knees, whimpering.

A pair of the leaf-beasts tried to overwhelm by strength of numbers, but the unicorn slashed left, pivoted, and attacked again to the right, fleeter than thought, its move an after-image as well. The horn was

146

everywhere at once, bright, terrible, flashing amid clouds of torn leaves, stabbing monsters. Lowise shut her eyes and waited for quiet.

When she looked again, Flax was on his feet, one arm flung over Thistledown's sweating neck, and the fearful light of the horn had dimmed to a glimmer no brighter than a firefly's. Sobbing her relief, Lowise stumbled to join them.

The sound stopped her in her tracks. Midway between groan and gasp, with a bubble in it like a kettle sluggishly at the boil, it tugged at her conscience. Much against her will, Lowise retraced her steps to the spot where her betrothed had fallen.

He lay on his face, and as Lowise tentatively touched him, she felt a stickiness on her hands. The bubbling sound continued irregularly.

Gradually, Lowise made out the cause as Flax helped her to turn the Duke onto his back. Lothair had been wounded in the chest, thrust through with a jagged branch whose end she could still see. Bubbles of air came with the blood. So *much* blood . . . He was striving to speak, and out of an utterly unforeseen pity, she bent closer to hear. His face was covered with white marks, like frostbite.

"They . . . saved you. More mercy than I have shown . . . them . . . or you."

Lowise felt tears between her lashes. Guilt held up a mirror to her conscience. It was *she* who had shown no mercy. She had ever been told that Lothair was not a patient man, but he had *been* patient with her. She had goaded him continually, and finally killed him, simply by refusing any order or instruction. No one could tell *her* what she must do! No matter what the order concerned, the mildest speaking of it enraged her blind, and she refused it furiously, absolutely. The mirror flashed, showing her the powerlessness feeding that anger. Abandoned by her mother, sold by her father into a life that led only to death at the end of her path, without the least glimmer of choice or hope.

She had never meant for it to end in Lothair's death as well. For the first time in her life, the Lady Lowise regretted an action.

Through tears, the light of Thistledown's horn was a bright dazzle. Lowise felt the unicorn's shoulder warm beside her on one side, the comforting pressure of Flax's hand on the other. She clung to them both, in turn. Facing her terror, she watched it dwindle, but the grief and the overwhelming guilt were not so easily mastered.

The Duke gazed at the beast standing over him, bemused. That a unicorn, a hunted thing, should come freely to the man who sought to slay it . . . Lothair was astounded. Hunt-lore said they came willingly only to the pure, and must be tricked within the hunter's reach. Yet, it had come to him. Even dying, the wonder of it caught his attention. He had not thought the beast would be so beautiful . . . white as the heart of a flame, a horn like moonbeams and rainbows. The shining horn dipped toward him, as if to offer him a caress.

Lothair gave a great cry, and Lowise knew that he was dead. Dead, and she had not even had the grace to offer him a parting word of kindness. She began to weep bitterly.

Lothair knew he loved her, though he could barely bring to mind the shape her face had, when it was not buried in her hands; or recall the precise color of her eyes. Her laughter, so rarely heard in his presence, so often from around corners, through doorways—that filled his memory, leaving a warm spot in his mind and in the center of his chest. It spread right out to his fingers, his toes. He loved her—and sorely regretted that he no longer felt he owned her, for free was free to choose—free to leave him.

Sitting up, the Duke saw astonishment on Lowise's face, apprehension on Flax's. His fingers curiously explored the smooth white scar where his wound had been, and at last he looked gratefully to the unicorn. Its horn seemed longer than he remembered, as long as a fine sword, and as brightly shining.

* * *

When Thistledown led them onward, Lothair went along with nary a word, save to insist that Flax take a portion of the bread and dried venison which the Duke had contributed to their store of provisions. Flax, chewing at some shriveled hazelnuts he'd robbed a squirrel of, accepted with wary courtesy.

Had Lothair questions as to their destination, they were left unvoiced. He might have proposed a return to Ylowfort, offered his protection to Flax and to the unicorn—but he was plainly aware that the unicorn was not being led, and that he was mightily privileged to be one that followed it. He felt strangely companionable with Flax, and though conversation never went beyond a word on his part and a nod on Flax's, a sort of friendship grew.

Between the Duke and Lowise, there was a most careful and distant courtesy, but the Duke seemed content to share even so little with her, and never pressed her for speech.

The forest thinned. There were meadows, and new green spears of grass among the old stems. Fragile pink flowers were thick at the edges of the trees. Lowise twined handfuls of them into Thistledown's mane, and her own dark hair.

"Master?" An inquiring paw left a smudge of dust on a finely woven sleeve.

"What is it, Mai? Oh—*not* the pot-herbs again! Can't you do your digging *out*side, now the weather's warmer?" He laid his book aside hastily.

The blue-eyed dog looked deeply offended. "Your mirror has a picture in it. Never mind. Maybe it will go away." She spoke as if the matter were one of utter indifference to her.

"A picture? Well, of course it does—Oh!" Corlinn rose quickly, and made his way to the glass. After a moment the blue-eyed dog overcame her hurt feelings and joined him.

The cheval glass no longer reflected any portion of the wizard's cottage. Trees filled it, side to side and top to bottom. It was a moment before Corlinn noticed the trio of figures moving between the trees.

Two men: one pale-haired and raggedly dressed, the other dark and travel-stained. A girl, who sometimes walked beside one of them and never beside the other.

Corlinn looked long at the ragged man—a boy, really, not yet come into his full growth. "So, you survived after all," he said wonderingly. "And you've come to my glass again. I wonder why?"

"Who's the other one? The hawk-face?"

"Duke Lothair of Ylowfort, and he'd hardly be complimented by your description."

The dog stared intently at the glass, unheeding of the rebuke.

"I saw Duke Lothair at Court, often. A young man of wealth and property—and unless I mistake, that girl there will bring him as much again, when they wed."

The blue-eyed dog sniffed skeptically.

"I quite agree. It doesn't look as if she's much taken with him."

"She doesn't even look at him!"

"Well—you were wrong about the wolfhound, too. We should have wagered."

The trio was coming closer, through the trees.

"Master? What place is that?"

"Those woods?" Corlinn leaned closer. "I believe I know them—about a day's travel from here, I should judge."

"Will they come here?"

"I would say so." Corlinn squinted a bit, trying to bring faces into sharper focus.

"Why?"

"Because this is where the trail they're walking finishes up."

"But why are they coming?" Large ears flicked.

"Unhappily, I am not omniscient."

The dog cocked her head. "If you don't know, just say so."

"I did, puppy. This glass shows me riddles, as often as truths. All the same—go out a little way into the wood tomorrow, and wait for them. It's important, I think."

The blue-eyed dog waved her tail eagerly, then bounced excitedly into the air, landing and at once leaping again, to rest forepaws upon her master's shoulders. He staggered as he caught her full weight.

"*Company!*"

"Yes, Mai, but not until tomorrow evening at the earliest. Contain yourself!"

The dog wiggled free of his grasp and ran to the window, where she stood, forepaws on sill, keeping watch.

The dog popped up from behind a clump of unfurling fern fronds, causing much starting and shying back among Thistledown's party. Its appearance was as unsettling as its arrival—it was tall and very narrow, with legs long as a colt's. Its honey-colored coat was splashed with white, as if it had gotten into a paint-pot, and both its eyes were the same pale blue the winter sky had lately been. One very large ear stood upright, while the mate flew rakishly out to one side.

"*Whoops!*" It spoke distinctly, tongue lolling. "Company for dinner, all right!"

The apparition vanished back among the trees, the bobbing of a white-tipped tail offering them their only hint of its route.

"Do we follow?" Lothair asked.

Thistledown snorted, tossed his head, and stepped lightly over the ferns.

There was a cottage among the trees, its back to the river's winding silver thread. A wisp of smoke issued from the river-stone chimney set into the river-rush thatching. The blue-eyed dog stood in the doorway, wriggling and wagging its tail excitedly.

"You see? You see? Told you, I did! *Company!* The ones you saw in the glass?"

"Yes," said the dog's master. "But neither the glass nor you mentioned a unicorn."

The dog's ears went down guiltily. "Haven't seen one before, have I?"

"No, I suppose not. There hasn't been a unicorn here since long before you were whelped. A rare guest, this. See you don't puddle the floor."

They were given warm water to wash themselves, benches to rest upon, a meal which caused them to recall that they owned bellies. Sweet mead after, smoky on the tongue and fiery going down.

The drink was heartening, as was their host's gentle manner. Else the combination of talking dog, a meal whose preparation must have been begun hours before even the dog could have known they were coming, and sundry articles appearing out of the air at a flick of their host's fingers would have locked fast even the Lady Lowise's nimble tongue. He had no need to announce to them that he was a wizard, as he did when he asked their names and said that his own was Corlinn.

Flax, nervous of the company and wary of the dog—though it seemed benign enough—had removed himself to the wide window ledge once he'd eaten his meal. Thistledown leaned against his legs, offering the untangling of his mane for a diversion. Fingers busy, head bent, Flax made no effort to follow the conversation at the table. He knew Lowise was reciting the tale of their journey. Since he'd lived the tale, its retelling didn't interest him.

His attention turned instead to the room. So many shelves attached to the whitewashed walls, and such a miscellany on them—herbs both potted and dried, chunks of colored crystal, bones, old birds' nests. On the shelves, and stacked on the floor as well, were a vast wealth of books. Flax knew what a book was, though he had never touched one and certainly could not have read one. Books were precious—the village priest had two, and their covers were kept safely closed with tiny silver fetterlocks.

He couldn't understand why Thistledown had led them to such a place. Surely not for shelter—they had been in worse need of it before the weather began to warm. Nor for food—they had been hungry, but not starving. Always, when they camped, Flax had understood an urge to move on, to be in motion. Now that had ebbed away. The unicorn seemed quite content, but Flax was baffled.

Was this journey's end? The wizard seemed kindly enough, maybe it was a place he could safely leave the unicorn to live out its life. Flax had heard tales of wizards, and magic, and knew unicorns belonged to such a world, far more than that of Ylowfort village.

Leaving Thistledown was far from his desire—but Flax had no hope that they both might be allowed to remain. His heart was heavy, but he knew he must be content to keep the unicorn safe. There was a book on the ledge beside him. Timidly, Flax lifted the coverboard.

"Unicorns by nature are solitary creatures," Corlinn said, lighting his pipe with two crackling words, whilst the blue-eyed dog rested her chin on the table and watched adoringly. "Even among their own kind. I am puzzled to see this one so content in company."

"I think Flax found it as a fawn," Lowise said, and her thoughtful gaze went suddenly wide. She swung toward Flax.

"*That's* what the hound was after, not you! The unicorn's scent! *That's* why you wouldn't come back, no matter what—"

Flax looked at her miserably, as if across the pile of starved birds. He nodded. Lothair looked from one of them to the other, perhaps understanding.

"Well," Lowise went on, very gently. "It wasn't your fault."

"Can't he speak?" the wizard asked.

Lowise tried to remember if she'd ever heard Flax make a sound, beyond the whistles he'd charmed her canaries with. She could not think of a single time—except for his scream when he'd touched Lothair's sword.

Flax had bravely opened his book wide enough actually to glimpse the pages. Under his fingers was a vivid painting of a foxglove plant, from its purple flower spire to its bared root.

"He's simple, sir," the Duke offered helpfully.

Lowise's dark eyes flashed. "So say they in the village! That he's half-witted, and cursed! I wouldn't speak either, if they told such lies about me!"

A smile touched Lothair's lips, at the thought of her silent for even an hour, but he was careful not to let her see.

Flax just watched them both, as if he expected something to come of the exchange but had no hope it would be pleasant for him. It seemed unlikely that, if asked, he would suddenly break silence to answer.

"What they say in the village . . . it may not be true, of course, but they do say his mother was a witch." The possible impropriety of repeating such a charge at a wizard's table made Lothair uneasy. "They said it had cost her her tongue, but I doubt she could hear, either."

"What happened to her?" Lowise asked apprehensively. "Did she die when Flax was born?"

"No," Lothair said, plainly surprised at her conclusion.

Corlinn gave the girl a sharp look. "Child, sometimes women die in childbed—but not all of them, by any means. I'm a seventh son, myself, and I have two sisters as well. My mother lived to see us all grown."

Lowise's eyes were very wide, and she unexpectedly had no more to say, though much to think upon.

"It was some while after," Lothair resumed. "I . . . was there, actually. I was riding with my father and his men, hunting. A storm came up, we turned for home. The sky was black as pitch, with rain falling, thunderbolts all around. She just stepped out into the track—no one was there, and then all at once *she* was—the huntsman was in front, and he rode her down. He had no chance to stop. All the noise-hounds, horses, the horns blowing—she didn't seem to hear. And she was killed. Trampled. It was . . . the worst thing I'd ever seen."

Lothair looked toward Flax, sure that it was the worst thing Flax had ever seen, as well. Flax was showing no distress, and seemed not to have followed the exchange. The matter might not have concerned him. The book was closed again, but he had a finger inside to mark his place. The other hand was resting on Thistledown's withers, idly drawing invisible patterns.

When the wizard rose to his feet, however, Flax did likewise, and it was plain he would have bolted if he'd had a clear path to the door.

"How did you find me?" Corlinn asked. "Why have you brought the unicorn to me?"

Flax shook his head emphatically. He also tried to step back, and his look became desperate when he met the wall. He rather obviously gauged the distance to the window.

"Gently," Corlinn soothed.

"Sir," Lowise said urgently, wondering what sort of trouble Flax was in. "Flax didn't bring the unicorn here. He—we, that is—we followed it. Thistledown brought *us* here—or at least to where we met your dog, and she led us to you."

A tail thumped the hearthrug in pleasure at the recognition.

"Yes, Mai did invite you to dinner. But 'twas no chance meeting—I sent her out to await the folk I saw in my scrying glass, yestereven. A most vexing vision—I did not perceive the unicorn, and I am at a loss to say which of you bears the wizardly gift this meal was planned to honor. Plainly even the one who carries it is similarly ignorant."

"Gift?" Lowise frowned. They'd brought no gift. Was one expected? How could they have known?

"That explains this welcome," Lothair said.

Corlinn chuckled. "Aye, my lord Duke. 'Tis ever wise to welcome fellow wizards—it may be most hazardous not to. But let me discover whether I have begun to surmise correctly."

Corlinn reached a hand toward Flax, who flinched away from the touch until he came up against Thistledown's shoulder. The unicorn did not yield to him, but pushed him back. They eyed each other sidelong, and finally Flax looked back to Corlinn, and held out his hand. Cool fingers brushed the inner side of his wrist.

It was as if the sky opened, spilling light in the wake of a storm—like instant daylight, full noon with no dawn preceding it. Every moment of Flax's life, every thought in his brain seemed to rush and swirl out of him, while others swept in, fighting the current. Questions, answers—no longer muffled, no more half-understood. It was wonderful, and it was utterly terrifying. Flax burst into tears, which rolled unheeded down his cheeks as his inner silence continued to shatter. Out of a desperately confused babble, at last a single amused voice.

So, that's the way of it? Poor lad, you must have nearly forgotten how it feels, to be bespoken. It won't always hurt so.

"What's happening?" Lowise wanted to know. Lothair stood beside her, and she did not step aside.

Softly, now. There's time. A world of time.

Flax broke the contact of their hands, flung both arms about Thistledown's neck, and buried his wet face in the unicorn's mane. Corlinn drew a deep breath, and let it slowly out again. He took a step that was closer to a stagger, and smiled ruefully as his familiar pressed close, concerned.

"A touch unsettling. No doubt a considerable shock for him, as well."

"Did he *speak* to you?" Lothair asked, not certain he understood, but feeling he might be close enough to risk the query. "*How?*"

"How? Rather like yon stream, when the snowmelt sends it tumbling over its banks." Corlinn chuckled again, and reached out to touch the unicorn, which nuzzled his hand, than turned its attention back to Flax.

"But . . . I heard nothing."

"Nor did I. Nor could this lad's mother. How could she teach him to speak, unable to hear his words? So, she taught him to converse mind to mind—a way wizard-folk have, and such she must have been. Most effective, except that she died, and left him alone among those who had no hope of understanding him."

156

Lowise had begun to pat Flax's shoulder.

"Will he learn to speak . . . normally, do you think?"

"Oh, most certainly, and perhaps rather quickly! There's naught amiss with his wits or his tongue. Anyway, it's the mind-speaking that tends to give apprentices fits. A cramp or two in his tongue, from the unaccustomed exercise, that will be the worst of it." Corlinn sat, relit his pipe. The blue-eyed dog caught the word "apprentice," and grinned knowingly.

Lothair reached for another sip of mead. "The unicorn will of course be safe on my lands," he said, playing with the cup. "Still, best not take chances. Can you shelter the beast here?"

"The unicorn? Well, of course it will stay here—or wherever Flax is. That's the way of familiars." A tail thumped the floor. "Though I will admit 'tis highly irregular for the familiar to select the wizard. It's supposed to work the other way 'round."

Familiar? Apprentice? Mind-speaking? Lothair set the cup down. "You aren't saying *Flax* is a wizard?" The stretch of perception, from half-wit to sorcerer, was too great—even if it was only to be sorcerer-in-training. Come to that, he'd never thought of wizards as having to learn. Didn't they appear fully-fledged?

Lowise, one hand on Flax's shoulder and the other playing with Thistledown's forelock, recalled warm blankets spun out of heather, herbal teas standing stead for meals. She remembered tracks vanishing at the touch of Flax's fingers in the snow, dream banished—and an oak branch standing up to sword-steel.

"Of course he is," she said.

Lothair set his pack down, and shifted awkwardly before he spoke.

"Had you given thought to what you'll do now? Will you stay here with them?"

"No," Lowise said, not looking at him. "There's no place for me here. I've no wizard's gift."

"I think they'd let you stay."

Lowise didn't answer. As Flax had begun gaining his speech, she seemed to have lost hers.

Lothair was silent a long while too, his face showing flickers of a struggle. At length he wet his lips and spoke again.

"I know that marriage to me was never . . . to your taste. You were at pains to make that clear to me even while you supposed you had no choice about it. But Lowise, I still want you to wife. *I* want *you*—myself, not to fulfill the contract my father signed with yours! We were each of us prepared once to settle and suffer—but it could be more than that! It could be a partnership between us. Would you agree to it? Will you wed me?"

Lowise studied the Duke's dark face. Pride was there still—he didn't like to let her see how her refusal would hurt him—but the arrogance that had been a second skin over him had been shed a long while before. She considered living a life with him, bearing his children, watching them grow. It suddenly seemed more like a future than a sentence.

"You hadn't *asked* me before," she said. "Now that you do, I will."

She put her hand into his.

THE OLD SOUL

WAYLAND DREW

L ISTEN!" SAID THE MERCHANT, raising his hand so that his jeweled rings glittered in the sun. "There it is again!"

The travelers stopped walking.

For the second time they heard the plaintive summons. It rose from the marshes to their right, where dusk was already spreading like a frayed garment. It chilled them like the brush of a bat's wing yet was so beguiling that they huddled together and reached for one another's arms.

The Merchant had a flickering vision of surf rolling forever on a vast shore.

The Doctor heard mountain winds.

The young Architect thought of the Child. "How near it is tonight!" he whispered when the last echoes had faded.

"We had best make camp and build a fire," the Doctor suggested quietly, and the others agreed at once.

They left the path and followed the Merchant through swaying sedges to the beach. To the west lay the iron-gray sea beside which they had traveled for two days, crossed by the path of the setting sun. To the north and the south the shore curved away like shimmering arms reaching into the mists. For as far as they could see there was no human habitation, no other living soul.

They gathered driftwood, and soon they were eating beside a cheerful blaze. Steam from their breaths and bowls swirled upward with the smoke.

Occasionally one of them stopped eating and looked at the crystalline heavens, looked at the frost glittering on the beach grasses. No one spoke.

Fate alone had brought these unlikely travelers together; for, had their original plans unfolded, they would never have met, or would have met only casually as passengers strolling the deck of the vessel bound for the capital, three-score leagues across the bay. However, each had been delayed only enough to miss the sailing. The Merchant, having sampled too much good claret the night before, had overslept and his chamberlain had failed to wake him; the Doctor had lost himself in esoteric studies; the Architect, betrayed by youth, had dallied too long in the company of a favorite lady.

So, as Fate would have it, they found themselves together on the quay watching the lanteen sails of their vessel billow as she warped out and set her course into the cold fog. She would not return for a week at least, and there was no other ship for hire. Each of them had urgent business in the capital. Each gave vent to his feelings: the Merchant cursed, the Doctor silently raised his arms heavenward, and the Architect sat and buried his face in his hands.

At length, the Merchant recovered himself and addressed the other two. He proposed that rather than face delay they join forces for an overland trek. At first, the others laughed incredulously. Anxious though they were to reach the city, the idea of going overland was preposterous. Such a journey was fraught with peril. Many travelers had vanished on the old road which twisted around the foot of the bay, and many tales were whispered of those leagues between sea and marsh. Indeed, it was said that to venture there was to go beyond the known and knowable.

The Merchant, however, claimed that in his youth he had traveled the route often with never a misadventure. He remembered the way well, he said, and standing on the wharf in the warm sun and soft sea breeze, he had scoffed at fear. To be sure, the region was a wilderness but what of that? Did not caravels and caravans venture from civilization every day into similar wildernesses and return safe and prosperous? Besides, were there not three of them, all robust men and sensible? Could they not go well-armed? Could they not rely on one another? Why, if they left immediately and rode hard, they might arrive at the capital even before the ship.

So persuasive was he, and so eager were they to reach the great city, that at length the Doctor and the Architect agreed. They returned home, ordered their best horses saddled and provisioned, and met again at midday. With high hopes and spirits they had followed the Merchant through the city gates and toward the somber bay that lay to the east.

An observer would have seen little to distinguish these three from other travelers, with the exception that each held his reins with only one hand. With the other he clasped to his breast some precious object. In the case of the Architect that object was a cluster of scrolls carefully rolled and wrapped; in the case of the Doctor it was a weighty bundle of manuscripts; and, in that of the Merchant, something buried deep in the folds of his clothing, something so valuable that he never withdrew it from its hiding place.

Until evening their journey was uneventful. For several leagues they rode single file through inhabited countryside where smoke from sod-roofed cottages gathered in damp hollows. They passed stubble fields, pastures where shaggy cattle grazed, and meadows sloping to the sea. Gradually the trail left farmland behind. It skirted the edge of the great forest which stretched forever to the east, and then curved northward into the brooding marshes around the end of the bay.

At sunset the Sound came for the first time. The horses heard it before their masters. They shied and shivered, eyes wide, nostrils flared, ears pricked up. Then the men heard it—a vibrant, persistent summons—and stopped breathing until the last echoes faded.

The Merchant licked his dry lips. "An elk," he said, glancing at the pale faces of his companions. "Surely an elk and nothing more."

"Or perhaps a bear," the Doctor suggested. "One of the Ur-bears of the North."

"Or perhaps the Forest People," said the Architect, "for I have heard they craft strange and hollow instruments to speak across vast distance."

They made camp at once and built a fire. They watered their horses at a nearby stream, fed them, and tethered them securely for the night. Then they cooked their evening meal. They spoke no further of the Sound, and it did not come again.

The Merchant ate hungrily. He was a large and florid man, no longer young, and the exertions of the day had whetted his appetite. When he had tossed his last bone into the fire he wiped his hands in the long grass and said: "My friends, since we shall be journeying together for several days, and in strange circumstances, it behooves us to know one another better. Therefore I propose that each tell something of himself and disclose the nature of the business that takes him abroad so urgently. What say you, gentlemen?"

His two companions readily agreed.

The Merchant laughed genially and continued. "I am a man of business who enjoys a wager. So, to add spice, let us decide when we have finished whose mission is the most urgent and important." He gestured toward the tethered horses and the darkness beyond. "Let us say we had but one mount; which of us would most deserve to claim it and ride ahead to the city?"

The others smiled. "An odd fancy," the Doctor said, "but an entertaining one for a long, cold night. Begin, sir."

And so, the Merchant settled himself, drew up his cloak against the chill, and began: "As I have said, I am a man of business and a successful one. My enterprises have brought prosperity to me and to our region. My cutters provide your wood; my miners, your metals. My mill workers turn materials into serviceable goods. But, my friends, it is no accident that commerce has gone well with me. I work hard, I take risks, and I have foresight." The Merchant emphasized his merits, each in turn, with a raised finger.

"It is the last, foresight, which takes me on this journey. For, although all is well at the moment, a time is fast approaching when we shall no longer have resources close at hand. Wood, metal, and perhaps even food will have to be found abroad. So I am making this journey, to commission a fleet from the shipyards in the capital for that purpose."

He smiled and gazed out at the sea—now more silver than red—as if he owned it and could already see his galleons plying its broad expanse. Then from deep inside the folds of his clothing he drew a chamois bag as large as two fists.

"But, you ask, what is the urgency? *This*, my friends. This bag of gold is the urgency. For the longer I travel the longer I shall be exposed to thieves, and if this small fortune should be lost, with it would go my dream of a fleet, and so your prosperity and comfort." He laughed confidently, secure in the strength of his argument. "Therefore, because the welfare of so many rests upon me and my resources, I am, I submit to you, most worthy of the horse.

"Now, sir," he said, turning to the Doctor, "tell us something of *your* affairs if you will, for it can be no ordinary business that tempts so distinguished a gentleman to brave this wilderness."

The Doctor, a tall and erect man with piercing blue eyes, smiled and shook his head. His white beard gleamed in the firelight and he touched the bundle of manuscripts beside him. "No, sir, no ordinary business. Far from it. In fact, at the risk of immodesty, I must say that the value of these manuscripts is immeasurable. From these instructions and formulae, my life's work, will come potions which will so reduce disease and extend life that you and I, sir, although we are no longer young, may meet a century hence as sound in body and mind as we are today."

He smiled at the Architect's astonishment and the Merchant's sudden interest in the bundle. "Do you believe I exaggerate? Permit me then to describe my studies and my successes. . . ." And so he outlined for them thirty years of meticulous inquiry into the mysteries of life, and described many miraculous cures his medicines had effected. It was an account which established beyond doubt the selflessness of his scholarship and dedication to humanity.

"So," he concluded, "even if we were not playing this game I am confident you would agree that my claim to the horse would be strongest. For I am on my way to the capital to disclose this work to my colleagues, and to publish my manuscript. And I ask you, what project could be more worthy than extending the lives of all people?"

The Doctor's blue eyes twinkled. He drew his long hands from the sleeves of his garment and spread them in an eloquent gesture which repeated this unanswerable question.

"As I suspected!" the Merchant exclaimed. "I knew yours was no ordinary mission, my friend, and I am happy for you. For though you will never be a wealthy man you will have great acclaim and the satisfaction that you have improved the lot of humankind. Indeed, your claim to the horse is a formidable one.

"And now, sir, what of *your* business in the capital?" The Merchant peered through drifting smoke at the Architect. "Tell us what takes you abroad, if you please. I have no doubt it concerns those scrolls which you guard so jealously and keep so carefully covered against the elements."

The young man laughed, patting the rolls beside him. "Indeed, and when you have heard what I shall tell you, gentlemen, if there were in fact only one horse you would urge me, nay, *beg* me to take it and ride ahead, for the enterprise I have in hand is by far the most deserving!"

He raised his hands to silence the amiable scoffing of his companions. "Ah, I see I must first build my foundation. Very well, then. Hear me: I grant you the importance of commerce and of medicine, but ask you to consider whether it is not art, of all endeavors of humankind, which is the most sublime. For only in art do we understand where we have been, share our dreams, imagine and select our futures. And what is true of all art is true also of architecture; but, mark you, it is architecture which is the most permanent, which most firmly stamps the human will and

presence upon the land. Architecture, gentlemen, embraces at once the humblest shelter and the loftiest human aspiration. Do you not agree?"

The young man paused, noting the thoughtful silence of the Doctor and the reluctant nod of the Merchant.

"Now, of all architects I am the most fortunate, for I have been selected to plan a new heart of our capital and our nation—the new seat of government, the new banking house, the new church." He paused again, gratified by fresh respect in the eyes of the older men. "These are my plans for that endeavor, the fruits of many years of labor. They are the only copies, and though I would most gladly spread them out for your perusal, I dare not lest some damage befall them. Instead, my masters, permit me to describe the magnificence which will stand in the center of the capital when my labors are complete. . . ."

So he began a fulsome description of the buildings of his dream. His hands and his words so vividly sculpted them out of air that they seemed to rise as he spoke—a gleaming assemblage of domes and parapets, sweeping walls and buttresses, cloistered walks and spacious avenues. There they were, crystalline in imagination. And inside! Who would not long to enter there as the young man spoke? Who would not stand in awe of those splendors—the soaring council chambers for noble debate, the gardens and the church for meditation, the stout vaults of bank and library where the nation's treasure would be kept secure forever? What a triumph this vision was! What a monument to human will!

"And so," the Architect concluded quietly, "I trust you will not think me presumptuous when I claim the horse, if indeed there were only one. For what, finally, are the achievements of commerce and science beside the glories I have described?"

His listeners sat in silence when he finished. The Doctor stroked his beard, regarding him thoughtfully. The Merchant took his turn in feeding the fire. "Indeed," he said at last, "I cannot quarrel with your claim, for if I were to be lost, and with me this little fortune, another would soon replace me. The money would be raised and the ships built. But if *you* met with misfortune (may the gods forbid!) how could this splendid vision be replaced? Never!"

"Very true," said the Doctor. "I too defer to you, my friend. Though it pains me to admit that I am not indispensable, all my work could be reconstructed by colleagues from notes in my laboratory, and in time these manuscripts could be rewritten syllable for syllable. Far more important is that there be a place to keep them safe, and such a place you have described to us. Therefore, it is your mission which must proceed, and I concur that you would be entitled to the horse."

They shook hands with the Architect and warmly congratulated him. Then, well pleased with an evening's entertainment which had distracted them from the cares and uncertainties of the journey, they retired to sleep.

By morning, all three horses had vanished.

The tethers were still securely tied, but the halters lay unbuckled at their ends. "How?" the travelers asked, staring numbly at each other. "How?"

They considered their only choices: they could return afoot to safety, and so forfeit their expectations; or, slower and more vulnerable than they had been, they could venture deeper into uncertainty. At length, pride led them to make the second choice.

In the cold dawn, by the light of a sun that was a pale disc in the swirling fog, they resumed the journey, each carrying only what he considered essential besides food and blankets—the Merchant his gold, the Doctor his manuscripts, and the Architect his plans.

The Architect, born with a painful abnormality of the foot, was the slowest of the three and so lagged slightly behind his companions. At first he thought only of their troubling misfortune, but as time passed he grew mesmerized by the rhythm of walking and beguiled by his surroundings. Listening to the gulls and to the crashing of waves upon the shore, soothed by soft fingers of fog caressing his face and neck, he became ever more serene, until at last, in the haze of midafternoon, it seemed to him that they had left the realms of space and entered Time itself, magically passing through those tranquil millennia when the shore had lain innocent of all human striving and all human need. . . .

In truth, when he first saw the Child, he could not have said how far they had come or even how long they had been walking. At first she was not a child. She was only a darker shape in the swirling mists, now moving along the great beach to their left, now vanishing in the thicker fogs shrouding the marshes to the right. But slowly the Architect realized he was watching a person, a thin girl of eight or nine years, whose long black hair trailed wraiths of vapor.

"See!"

"What is it? What?" His companions came close and looked where he was pointing.

"I see nothing," said the Merchant.

"Nor I," said the Doctor.

"But there! A child!"

"Impossible," the Doctor murmured. "A mere trick of fancy. This fog plays strange pranks."

"No sir, not impossible." The Merchant peered ahead. "These low-lands are the haunts of savage men as well as savage beasts. Therefore let us be watchful, for our companion may have sighted a wild child, and others of her kind may lurk close by."

They saw no one else however, and although the Architect kept looking the Child did not reappear. For the remainder of the day they traveled in silence. At dusk the sinking sun reddened tiers and blossoms of cloud to the peak of heaven, reflected off the tranquil sea, and reached out to enfold them.

Then it was that the Sound summoned them for the second time.

"How near it is tonight!" the Architect whispered as the last resonance faded.

"We had best make camp and build a fire," the Doctor suggested, and the others agreed at once. In single file they followed the Merchant down

169

off the path and onto the beach, where they cooked their supper in the dusk. As he ate the Architect kept searching, and in the last teasing flickers of light he suddenly stood, for he believed the Child had reappeared some distance down the beach. But he could not be sure. Perhaps it was a log, a boulder, a shadow in the dunes. He said nothing. *If it is she*, he thought, *she may seek food and warmth. She may come close to the fire.*

Indeed, shortly after they had finished eating, footsteps approached. The Doctor heard them first. "Hush!" he commanded, lifting his hand and peering with alarm into the shadows, for these were not the light footfalls of a child. All three rose slowly and reached for their weapons.

Soft, mocking laughter drifted out of the darkness. "Gentlemen, do you fear an old woman who asks only to share the heat of your fire?"

The crone who came into the light was not merely old, she was ancient, as twisted and bent as an antique cedar. Her clothes hung upon her in strips and ribbons, like shaggy bark. One eye gleamed fire-red; the other shone white as a wave-washed pebble. In one gnarled hand she carried a woven basket; in the other, a tangle of roots with which she gestured at the men across the fire. "Good masters, grant an old woman a bit of warmth, for the night is cold and my journey has been longer than your own." Again she laughed, and her laughter hissed like surf.

"Sit, Mother," the Doctor said, gesturing to a place across the fire. "There is warmth for all and food as well."

"A thousand thanks."

Slowly she lowered herself to the ground and drew her garments around her. And when she had settled she turned her palms to the fire and with a small gesture sent a cloud of sparks soaring aloft until they mingled with the stars. The three men felt a chill that was more than the chill of night. They drew up their collars and the cowls of their capes and inched closer to the fire.

"Who . . . who are you, Mother?" the Merchant asked. "And what is your business with us?"

"What I am you know," she said, turning the white eye upon him. "I am an old woman, one you would call a savage, perhaps. As for my business, why, I have come only to share your company and the warmth of your fire on this cold night, as I have said. And for that kindness, gentlemen, I shall repay you with—" she opened her hands and again the sparks clustered and circled them, spiraling upward, "—a tale."

"A tale!" the Doctor exclaimed.

"A child's tale. An innocent tale. One that may speed you on your separate journeys."

The Merchant laughed nervously. "Separate journeys? You are mistaken, Mother. We three are embarked on one journey, and share but one destination."

"So you say."

"However that may be," the Doctor said, "a child's tale. . . . What foolishness. . . ."

"Foolishness?" the old woman's eyes closed and she smiled. "Do not mock the tale, my friend, for it too partakes of life, as you will see, and it too has its powers."

"Begin," said the Architect, "for the night promises to be long and I for one would be glad of some amusement."

"You shall be amused," she promised. "You most of all."

Then she began:

This is the story of one who was very old and very wise, although for many years he did not know that he was either. He was a child the same as you once were, good gentlemen, the same as you might be again. . . .

His name was Eiver. His family were simple folk who lived deep in the forest and labored to draw a living from the land. Eiver was their only child, and he grew accustomed to hard work from infancy. He milked the cow, fed the pig, and tended the little garden near the river. What time was his own he spent deep in the forest, and so grew close to solitude and to the creatures of the forest. Deer and bear, fox and wolf, otter and rabbit—none feared him, for his silences were theirs, and with him they spent many afternoons in the forest glades, on quiet riverbanks.

Indeed, their soft language was all he learned to speak, for he was mute.

Like any child, he dreamed. He was curious about the world beyond. Sometimes in the evenings he followed the path to the hills, two leagues away. There he would climb to the highest crags to see, far in the distance, the walled and ancient city of Govrina. Sometimes it shone like gold in the rising sun. Sometimes it floated on cool and purple mists like the galleon of a queen. Sometimes haze drew it so magically close that Eiver believed he could really see pennants curling from its parapets in a lazy breeze, and the glint of leaded windows, and the elegant passage of ladies in fragrant gardens.

What a beautiful city was Govrina, and how its splendors multiplied in Eiver's imagination! How he longed to journey there just once! Often he had listened at his parents' hearth while travelers, their eyes wide, told tales of that legendary place. So he heard of the great caravans that brought the riches of the world to Govrina's markets—rare perfumes and silken fabrics, brooches of rubies and gold, necklaces of sapphires more radiant than stars in a purple night, statuary of purest ivory, and a thousand delicacies from the Eastern Sea to delight the palate and the eye. So he heard of the learning and wisdom of Govrina's scholars, of the treasures of their libraries and the eloquence of their discourse, the richest and noblest in all the kingdoms.

So too, from those same travelers, Eiver had heard of the sadness of Govrina's Prince, who had long ago lost his one true love. How? Ah, there was a mystery! No one knew. Some said she had been beguiled by river sprites and had swum with them to the Western Sea whose edge was the edge of the world. Some claimed the spirits of the forest had taken her while she slept, and that she slept still, in a hill known only to them. All agreed the Princess would not have departed willingly from Govrina, for why would she do so? Everyone agreed on her dutiful nature, her radiant person, her beautiful soul.

And all knew that the Prince had offered an astonishing reward to whoever found her: any wish within his power to grant. Had they not heard the offer ready every day at dawn in Govrina's central square, so hunters in the wilds and sojourners to distant lands would be watchful? Had they not all, each traveler, dreamed of what his request would be should he find the Prince's lost love?

Eiver knew the story well, and it kindled dreams in him, as it had in countless others. . . . But then, having dreamed, he returned to his milking, his hoeing, his wood-gathering, and to his long and quiet hours with gentle friends in the secret places of the forest.

One evening when he was nine, however, his dream of going to Govrina was fulfilled, and in a strange manner. He was hurrying home later than usual. It was just dusk, neither light nor dark, that gray span between the little world of knowledge and the shoreless realms of Mystery. When he rounded the last bend he crashed headlong into someone hurrying in the opposite direction. They both went tumbling. When Eiver shook his head clear and stood up, he heard a high-pitched wail, part pain, part outrage, coming from the bushes. He groped through the brambles and the darkness until he found the other traveler. With his hands he apologized and made small animal sounds of concern.

"Lout! Imbecile! Oaf! You broke my leg! Broke both legs! Broke my neck! Killed me!" A tiny man sprawled on the moss, eyes bulging. He was clad in the close-fitting skin of some soft animal. A cap of the same material lay nearby, decorated with colored beads in intricate patterns. His hands and face were dark and leathery; his eyes, sharp blue. A tangle of white hair swirled around his head and stretched to his knees.

Gently Eiver helped him into a sitting position.

"Can't walk!" the little man groaned. "Carry me! Take me home."

Impatiently he motioned for Eiver to turn around, and climbed nimbly onto his back. "Hurry! Getting dark! Can't be out after dark! Owls! Big eyes, wings, claws! Owls get you, you're gone for good! That way!"

Eiver started to trot in the direction the little man had indicated, back the way he had come, until they reached an inconspicuous path branching into the woods.

"Turn here!"

And so, bearing one of the Forest People, Eiver left the trail he knew well and entered the darkening woods.

Now, you must keep in mind that the world was different in those days. For one thing, it was wilder and safer for spirits and Forest People; so, they moved much more freely. For another, those who lived then understood that with them in the Great Mystery lived many strange creatures. Sometimes they called them spirits, sometimes gods, sometimes forces, sometimes Others, sometimes Forest People.

Although all knew that they existed, only a very few special humans had seen them. Eiver was one of those. Once at dawn he had discovered fresh, tiny footprints in the sand at the river's edge, and when he followed them into the forest he came upon a boy his own age but less than half his size. For a moment they gazed solemnly at one another; then the elf grinned, stamped his foot, and vanished. Another time, Eiver had seen at dusk the reflection of pale green light among the trees, and when he crept close he saw twelve fairies circling in an airborne dance. Once he had heard strange singing, and once laughter so high and fragile he thought at first it was the tinkling of distant bells. He longed to tell his parents about these events but of course he could not. He kept them in his heart, but he knew, even more acutely than others in those days, that the world was a place of magic, and Life was Mystery.

Full of excitement he carried his small burden through the darkness, suffering an occasional cuff on the ear or punch to the shoulder. "So big!" So clumsy!" the little man kept saying, "Turn here. Here!"

Before long they entered a magnificent stand of pines so old that at each step Eiver sank to his knees in centuries of moss and needles, and so thick that their canopies hid the stars.

"Stop! Wait here!" The little man slid agilely off his back and scampered into the darkness. "That boy's here!" Eiver heard him shouting. "I've brought him. Caught him on the path. Come out. . . ." His shrill voice echoed and faded among the trees and Eiver was left alone in profound silence. He heard only the thumping of his heart. But it was not long before he heard other sounds as well, small sounds—rustling, crotchety complaints, querulous demands echoing up through labyrinthine passageways in the earth. Green fairy light filled the glade and brightened as the sounds grew louder until Eiver saw that he was surrounded by a multitude of very small bodies and very large eyes all peering at him from behind trunks and above bushes. More small people crowded in, and still more, until those in the forefront were pushed to within a few feet of Eiver, protesting shrilly. Some scrambled up on the low branches of the pines. From the edge of the crowd Eiver heard shouts: "Move over! Can't see! Let me see him!"

There were scores, hundreds, all small and very hairy people regarding Eiver intently. "But he doesn't look like one," a child said before her mother hushed her, and several nearby nodded agreement. "Doesn't," they said. "Doesn't look like one!"

Warm orange light flowed from the dozens of tiny lanterns they held high, but its glow was pale compared to another light, a green fire that had gathered in the needles of the pine canopy and radiated over all below. Shading his eyes and squinting up, Eiver saw movement inside it— the sheen of sinuous tiny bodies, the shimmer of gossamer wings. He heard fluting laughter and an excited melody of conversation.

Then, suddenly, around and above him, all was still.

The crowd had pushed back to open a space in its center, and there, with feet apart and fists on his hips, stood a little old man in an oversized purple robe. He fixed Eiver with a baleful stare. "So!" he said. "So!" He was much whiter and bushier than the others, and much older. When he pointed at the boy his hand trembled. "You're the one, are you?"

Eiver shrugged and opened his hands.

"The one who goes lumbering through the forest stepping on plants, stepping on people! *Not watchful! Careless! Why do you think we've brought you here? Caught you! Brought you to trial!"*

"No, no, Granach! Wait! You've got the wrong one." The elf Eiver had carried scampered forward and whispered in the other's ear. Eiver heard Princess, *and* Govrina, *and* old soul.

"What? What? Well why didn't you say so?" Granach cleared his throat and rubbed his beard, looking at Eiver more respectfully. "We understand that you, uh, would travel to Govrina. Is that so?"

Eiver nodded eagerly.

"In fact we've heard you want *to go. Can that be true?"*

Eiver nodded again, and all through the glade small heads nodded also. "He does," they whispered to each other. "He really does!"

"Want to see the mighty walls and the splendid buildings, eh? See the rich in their silks and jewelry? Marshals at the head of their armies?" Granach stared at him with round eyes.

Eiver nodded again.

"Stroll at evening through the market, breathe the fragrances of sandalwood and myrrh, of incense and perfumed soap the caravans have brought from the East, of the flowering trees whose branches trail. . . ."

The crowd shuffled. "Get on with it, Granach!" someone muttered. "We haven't got all night, y'know. He's already said *he'll go. Besides, there's work to be done!"*

"Well then," Granach rubbed his hands and edged closer to Eiver. "We have a proposition for you. We will take *you to Govrina if you will bear our message . . . to the Prince."*

Eiver gaped in amazement. But then he shook his head, and shrugged sadly, pointing to his speechless mouth.

"Oh, that," Granach said. "That's no matter. That will be all right when the time comes. We'll see to it. The question is, will you do it?"

Eiver nodded eagerly and the whole assembly broke into cheers and lively applause. The green light swelled until it was almost as bright as day.

"Hear our message, then," Granach said. "Tell the Prince . . ."

"Let me, Granach." A young woman stepped into the glade, a woman so beautiful that Eiver knew at once she was the Princess.

"Your Highness," Granach said, bowing, "there's no need. . . ."

"No, I want to give our message to this emissary, and my personal one as well."

"As you wish, your Highness."

The Princess sat on a large mossy root and motioned for Eiver to sit beside her. The small people crowded closer, and the whispering ceased. "Eiver, we are glad you will be bearing our message to the Prince. You are a special person to us. We have known you all your life. We have watched over you, watched you grow. Is it not true, my friends?"

"Yes, your Highness," they whispered. "It's true, it's true. . . ."

"You see," the Princess went on, "you are one of us. Of all the humans for many leagues, you alone possess eyes to see the Forest People, and ears to hear what they would tell. You are an old soul, a very old soul. You are richer than the wealthiest men in Govrina, more powerful than the Prince himself, and wiser in your heart than all the scholars of the city."

She smiled at the boy's astonishment. "All your life you will laugh at things others cannot see, weep at tragedies they know nothing of. You are one who has not lost touch with Earth and its creatures, and so you have a great task to accomplish. It is, it will always be, to draw humankind back to the forests and the lakes, away from certainty, back to the Great Mystery. That is why we want you to carry our message to the Prince— because you will understand it and speak it eloquently. Yes, you will," she said, taking his hand when he began to protest silently. "When the time comes, you will speak.

"It is a simple message, Eiver. Say first that you speak for those who love the Prince well. He will remember them from childhood. Tell him they are fewer now because of Govrina and what he has permitted there. They cannot live in Govrina, nor within many leagues. For them it is a place of death, and he—" the Princess's voice faltered and she bit her lip, "—he has become a prince of death. So, tell him . . . ask him, please, to find the ways to honor Mystery again, so that all may live."

Eiver nodded, amazed and bewildered.

She smiled sadly. "As for me, tell my love that I am well, and that when he has freed himself, when he is powerless, I shall return to him. Will you tell him that?"

Again the boy nodded slowly.

"Give him this. You will understand its meaning. Please, teach my love to understand it also." So saying, the Princess reached into the folds of her dress and placed in Eiver's hand a small white stone, an ordinary pebble. "Say I shall meet him at the place where it was made." She leaned forward and kissed him on the forehead. "Farewell, Eiver."

"Farewell!" echoed the assembly of little people. "Bear our message well! Keep it safe! Keep it whole!"

Then Eiver was surrounded by the green light and the hum of tiny wings, and lifted above the treetops into the cool dawn. Higher and higher they rose, until the forest became a soft, green comforter. Far away, the golden towers of Govrina rose through the mists on the plain.

Effortlessly he began to cross those leagues he had so long yearned to cross, but he was troubled by many questions. How could he be what the Princess had called him, an "old soul"? Was he not a mere boy, and a voiceless boy at that? How could he deliver the message? What did it mean? What did the stone mean? How could the Prince be "a prince of death," and how could Govrina be anything but beautiful?

"You'll see," the fairies whispered, reading his thoughts. "Soon enough you'll see."

And, indeed, already the land below had begun to change. Woodcut-

ters had been busy for many leagues around the city. The great comforter of the forest grew patchier and more ragged until at last it was little more than a few gaunt trees beside the roads. Scarred earth replaced it, some plowed but most sun-baked and barren. The rivers also changed as they flowed near the city, growing browner and more sluggish. Even the air was sickly, bitter with the wind-borne char of a thousand chimneys and with dust from scores of travelers.

At first singly and then in little groups, his fairy-bearers sickened and fell away, turning back toward the forest. Eiver sank lower and lower. "You see?" said one of them, darting ahead to show him how her bright wings were spotted and smudged. "Do you understand why we cannot go on?"

"We're sorry," said another. "We'll die if we do."

"Go on alone, Eiver," said a third. "When I've rested I may . . . I'll try to . . ." But what she attempted to say was lost in a fit of coughing.

Gently they set him down in a little grove of bushes beside the road. "Thank you," they said, "Good luck. Speak our message well." Their voices were very frail and they rose slowly on faltering wings. Indeed, before they had gone far, one of them collapsed and sank, her body tumbling like a tiny spray of milkweed.

Hesitantly Eiver ventured onto the road. The air was full of shouts and raucous laughter, the squeals of cartwheels and the desolate calls of caged animals on their way to market. He joined the throng and was carried along by it, so that before long he passed through the ironbound oaken gates, under the looming turrets, and into the fabled city.

Govrina was not at all what he had dreamed. There was no joy there. From a distance the city had been clean and cool, but already, although the sun was scarcely above the horizon, it was oppressively hot and a thick coat of sour dust lay everywhere. Except for the stately avenue which led from marketplace to palace, the streets were narrow, dark and dirty, and the marketplace itself was foul and clamorous. People shouted and cursed, haggled and laughed bitterly. Ragged beggars tugged at Eiver's sleeve, whining for a coin or a scrap of food. Even children shouted and fought. All dwellings along the streets were shuttered and locked, and when Eiver glimpsed the elegant ladies about whom he had heard so much, they too seemed yearning to be elsewhere, for they gazed with sad eyes over their garden walls and across the plains, to the forest.

Bewildered and frightened, Eiver made his way through the confusion toward the palace which stood pristine on a hill in the center of the city, a gleaming villa surrounded by terraces and topped with fluttering pennants. As he climbed, the breeze drifting down through the royal orchards cooled him, and the clamor of the city fell away.

At the gates he was halted by a guard and by a very old man who came shuffling out of the shade. His white beard touched the ground as he bent to peer at Eiver's face, and his bony hands trembled when he touched his shoulders. "Yes!" he exclaimed, his bleary eyes suddenly widening. "This is he! This is the ambassador!"

"Ambassador!" the guard exclaimed. "But this is a child!"

"Nevertheless, he is the very person. Let us pass, for he must go to his Highness at once!" So saying the old man hurried Eiver around the guard, down a winding garden path, and through the colonnade which led to the throne room. Moments later they entered the presence of the Prince. "The emissary you have been expecting, your Highness," the old man said, bowing deeply. "He has just arrived."

All conversation stopped at once. The Prince left the group of venerable scholars with whom he had been talking and hurried across the room looking intently at Eiver. "Yes!" he said, smiling. "Yes, this is the emissary!"

The travelers' tales had described the Prince as a young man, gifted in wit despite his age, and shrewd in the crafts of government. So Eiver had always imagined him, never thinking that although a tale is ageless, the world of humans is the world of Time. They reap Time, and the weight of it bows them down. So, although the Princess had miraculously not aged, the Prince had. Wisps of gray curled through the black hair at his temples, and his face was deeply creased. But he was handsome still, and agile, and when Eiver looked into his eyes he saw compassion behind a clutter of worries.

"I dreamed," the Prince said, leading Eiver to a tall window. "In my dream an owl, a white owl, spoke to me and told me to expect you. He said a messenger would bring the news that I have awaited these many years. Then, you appeared in my dream just as you are. Tell me what you have to say, my friend, for I am eager beyond words to hear it."

Eiver tried to speak. Again he heard the Princess: When the time comes you will find the means. . . . *But the time had come and he had no voice, no words. He tried again. And again. He shook his head sadly and opened his hands.*

"Speak, boy!" said one of the three aged scholars with whom the Prince had been conversing. "When his Highness commands, speak!"

But the Prince raised his hand for silence, and waited.

Eiver looked away. He gazed down over the turmoil of Govrina's marketplace and through the haze of the barren plain. Beyond, far beyond, he could see the pale green of the forest. He longed to be there. He wished he were dipping a bucket into the cold stream, watching the mist rise through the trees, listening to birdsong. He was ashamed, for he had undertaken a mission he could not perform.

Again he shook his head.

Then, in the shadows of a little grove beneath the window, he saw a small light—pale, and shimmering, and green—the light of a single fairy who had struggled through the furnace heat of the plain and who now lay exhausted on a little branch. Try, *the light said.* Keep watching me, and try.

"Do you . . . have word of her? Of the Princess?"

Eiver nodded.

"Have you . . . seen her?"

Again Eiver nodded.

"Tell me about her," the Prince whispered. "Is she well? Where is she? What must I do to see her again?"

Then Eiver spoke.

His voice was faint at first, but it grew stronger as he continued. This is what he said:

"Your Highness, I want nothing for myself. I bring greetings from one who loves you well. She is at peace with subjects who dwell far beyond your borders, deep within your boundaries."

"What?" the three scholars muttered, shuffling close. "What riddling nonsense does the boy speak?"

"They dwell in the air and in the earth," Eiver went on, watching the tiny light, "in the depths of the lakes and rivers, and in the fires that warm both your palace and the camp of the poorest hunter. They are legion, your Highness. Once, long ago, you heard their voices in the thunder, and in the breeze at evening, and in the pools of the waterfalls. You saw them on the happiest of the afternoons of childhood. Do you remember? You saw them circling with the eagle, darting with the dragonfly, rising with the pickerel among the reeds."

The Prince nodded sadly. "Yes. Yes."

"They too remember. You understood then that their world was not yours, nor the smaller world, nor the world still smaller, nor any of those myriad worlds which circle endlessly in the dance of life. They remember that in those days long ago you understood, and joined in the song, and in the dance."

"Yes," the Prince said. "Before Time. Before I was busied with affairs of state. Before I sought the possible. . . ."

"They love you well, your Highness, and their greeting is warm. They have tried many years to share what lies deeper than meanings, beyond all truth, at the moving heart of life. But you have refused to hear them."

"Time, Time," The Prince frowned, shaking his head. "Why now, even a ride in the country. . . ."

"For many years they have been patient, waiting for the return of the wisdom you once had."

"Wisdom!" The Prince laughed bitterly. "But I was never wise, only innocent. Innocent of the real world, like any child."

The fairy light glowed bright.

"They ask me to say to you, your Highness, that the world—the real world—is not as you imagine it."

The advisers shuffled and grumbled. "Impudence!" one of them exclaimed, but the Prince silenced them with a glance. "I asked the boy to speak," he said quietly, "and he shall do so freely, for he speaks from the heart for the little people and my Princess, and what he says is true." He turned back to Eiver and nodded to him to continue.

"They say, your Highness, you have forgotten the real world and neglected it. They say that through ignorance, through inattention and oversight, you have violated its mysteries and so imperiled the lives on which all lives depend."

The Prince was very pale. "Does she say this? The Princess?"

"Yes," Eiver said. He then placed in the Prince's hand the small white stone, and spoke the exact words of the Princess. "She hopes that you will know why she has sent this, and she says that if you return to the place where it was made she will meet you there."

For several minutes the Prince sat silently with his head bowed, holding the pebble in cupped hands as if it were a precious diamond. At last he smiled and spoke to the scholars. "Gentlemen, all my life I have sought your advice and you have given it. All my reign I have relied upon your judgment and your wisdom. And yet, this emissary now comes from the Forest People to say that I have misused my power and so imperiled the lives on which all Life depends. Draw close, for once again I stand in need of your learning and your counsel. Tell me, what is the meaning of this stone?" He held the pebble out to the first scholar, who examined it closely, squinting.

"It is a common stone from any beach, your Highness. It has no meaning for it is untouched by human artistry."

"It has no meaning, your Highness," the second agreed, "for it has neither use nor worth."

"Indeed," said the third, "it is pointless even to speak of meaning in such an object, a thing devoid of sensibility."

While the scholars had inspected the stone Eiver had drawn back. Now the Prince motioned to him, "Do you know the meaning of this stone, my friend?"

The boy glanced outside toward the selfless fairy clinging to the branch. Briefly her light flashed out. Eiver turned back to the Prince and nodded.

"Speak."

"Sire," Eiver said softly. "It means you must find again the ways to honor Mystery."

At this, the three scholars could contain themselves no longer, and they broke into shouts of scorn and protest. The Prince smiled broadly. "You may question him," he said, "but one at a time."

They conferred briefly and the eldest turned toward Eiver. His head wobbled, shaking flabby jowls; his eyes bulged from watery sockets. "Honor what, boy? Honor what?"

"M-Mystery, Sire," Eiver stammered.

"What nonsense you are speaking! Honor mystery? Do you suggest we stop learning, cease our quest to know?"

Eiver was silent.

"End the holy search for truth? Eh? Eh? Speak up!"

Eiver sat silently, waiting until the small light flickered. Then he said, "Sire, I know only that we must learn to know like animals. We must learn what we must not learn. We must grow wise through ignorance."

The old man gasped and staggered back, hands fluttering at his beard and eyes rolling. The others watched him anxiously. "Ignorance?" he exclaimed when he had found his breath. "Why, this boy is an idiot, your Highness! He babbles foolishness and riddles!" He waved in disgust and hobbled to a window at the far side of the room, muttering.

The second scholar sidled close to Eiver, his eyes shrewd and his hands hidden in the crossed arms of his gown. "What else, boy? What else do you ask for?"

"Nothing, Sire."

"Ha! Nor should you, for already you have asked the impossible! Do you not know it is not in the nature of humankind, boy, to rid itself of knowledge hard won and long cherished? Do you not know that knowledge is power, and that in power is safety? Besides, how else shall we make progress? How else shall we improve the world?"

Eiver shook his head sadly. "I am a simple boy, Sire. I know little of the nature of humankind. But I have observed forest creatures living without care for knowledge or for power. As for improving the world, that we can never do; for we have had no part in the making of the wild, and what is more perfect than wilderness?"

The scholar laughed mockingly. "Nonsense! The boy is indeed a fool! Not improve the world?" He flung his arm in a sweeping gesture which included the elegant chamber, and the immaculate gardens beyond the window, and the thriving, turbulent city. "Rubbish! Look around you! Is this palace no improvement upon a smoke-filled hovel? Eh? Is this city no improvement over a savage camp?"

"No, Sire," Eiver said.

The scholar flushed. His hands fluttered like small birds inside his sleeves. "Balderdash!" he said, joining his colleague on the far side of the room. "Poppycock!"

The smallest of the scholars now approached. He was wizened and brown and crippled, but his blue eyes shone keenly on Eiver. "Honor Mystery, you say? Go back, you say? But, my young friend, what of our curiosity? *What of this questioning which dispels the clouded and uncertain? Surely you do not suggest that we dispense with* that, *for does it not lie at the heart of Life itself?"*

The fairy light had faded and was almost gone. "With respect, Sire," Eiver said, anxiously watching its last, dim glow, "it is not curiosity which lies at the heart of Life, but humility and courage."

The scholar flung up his hands, still holding Eiver in his intent gaze. "The child's head is full of nonsense, your Highness, fancies and nonsense! Give him to me for one year and I shall school reason into him!"

The Prince smiled and shook his head. He had been watching a small green light flicker in the shadows of his orchard. For several minutes he sat thoughtfully, turning the white pebble over in his palm.

"And so," he asked the scholars finally, "the stone is of no importance?"

"None!" they said.

"Does its existence, then, not matter to you?"

"Not in the slightest," the first scholar said, and the others agreed.

The Prince stood. He looked old and profoundly sad. "Is this, then, the sum of Govrina's wisdom? You cannot tell me the meaning of this simple thing and yet you would do away with it? Destroy it? I fear I have been sadly mistaken in you. I see that wisdom is not what I believed it to be, for surely it is better to do away with what destroys."

The scholars began to protest but he silenced them firmly.

"Hear me. Long ago I made a promise that whosoever should restore the Princess to me should have whatever he desired. Now this messenger comes with a token from my love, a token which shows me the way I must go. So, the time has come to grant the reward. Make your request, my friend, and it shall be filled."

"Your Highness, I wish only to return home, to the forest."

"Done," the Prince said, gripping Eiver's hand. "You shall go on my horse. Return, and tell the Princess that I have understood. Tell her that I shall indeed honor Mystery once again, and that when I have done so I shall meet her where this stone was made."

186

And so, when he had rested, when he had gathered up the ailing fairy from her refuge in the garden, Eiver mounted the Prince's own stallion and rode back across the plain, escorted to the edge of the forest by a troop of the royal guard. Deep in the forest, almost home, the fairy light descended around him, and the song of the wilderness surrounded him, and scores of soothing hands lifted away the fairy who had helped him.

On he went, alone and content. When he arrived home, his parents, miraculously, seemed not to have missed him at all. . . .

True to his word, the Prince found the means to do what he had promised. In the last use of his power, he issued commands which began to end Govrina. Woodcutting ceased. The rivers cleared. Caravans that had wound their dusty way across the plains went by other routes to other destinations. Market stalls fell silent; the gates stood open; the soldiers on the parapets laid down their arms. The citizens dispersed. Over time, as the exodus proceeded, abandoned goods and chattels lay strewn across the plain. Flowers took root and grew in the pathways, followed by bushes, then trees. Coolness and moisture, animals and shadows all returned to the place where Govrina had been, and with them, Mystery. . . .

The Prince was among the last to leave the dying city, the place being reborn. Alone, he mounted a white stallion at the palace gates and rode him at a trot down through the empty streets. On the plain, the charger broke into a gallop, and the Prince gave him his head. When they reached the edge of the woods he dismounted, removed the horse's bridle and saddle, and bade him farewell. He watched until the horse had become a white speck in the distance; then he opened his pack, discarded his royal robes, and changed into a peasant's rough blouse and trousers. In this garb, unarmed, alone and vulnerable, he entered the forest.

His Princess was waiting where the river curved and broadened into a shallow rapid, tumbling and sparkling across a bed of white pebbles. Here they embraced, here he left the stone, and from here they departed.

Where they went and what became of them only the Forest People know.

As for Eiver, he grew old in the place he loved, rich in the acclaim of the Forest People, with whom he communed daily in that language beyond words. He strolled with Granach, swam with water spirits, danced with fairies. Often he walked to the edge of the forest and climbed the hill from which Govrina had once appeared to him so golden and so wondrous. For many years the city changed little; then, as the vines crept through its mortar, as the gardens ran wild and seedlings took root among its cobblestones, it crumbled to become just another undulation in the great plain, slightly higher than the rest.

Eiver spoke again only once. When he was a very old man, he climbed one evening with a child to the top of the hill, and faced toward the ancient city, and said, "Tell me what you see, for my eyes are clouded."

The child replied, "There is the great plain, Grandfather, with animals moving on it. And the wind, and the eagles soaring."

Then Eiver was satisfied, for he knew the circle of Govrina was complete, like the circle which enclosed the Prince and Princess, and the circle of his own life. And from that time on, he spoke no more.

The fire had died low. Out of the cold silence of the night came the call again, the long and haunting call that struck strange turmoil into the hearts of the Merchant, the Doctor, and the Architect. The old woman laughed quietly, laughter like a sinking wave drawing beach stones back to the sea.

Brusquely the Merchant tossed more wood on the coals, scattering a cloud of sparks. "A childish tale," he said loudly, feigning a yawn, "but it has shortened the long night, at least."

"Truly," said the Doctor, shivering inside his sheepskin robe, "it is a senseless tale which tells us nothing of your business, old woman. And I have lost an hour of precious sleep because of it."

The Architect did not speak.

The old woman said nothing more. She sat motionless, smiling, until all three men had retired and were sleeping soundly, and until the fire had died to embers. Then she rose with difficulty, hobbled close to the coals and lifted her arms. The smoke reached out for her, enfolded her, rose through her clothing and streamed toward the stars from the tips of her raised fingers. She waited, waited. Then, as the low summons came again from the marshes, triumphant, she sighed contentedly and vanished, becoming one with the sound and the darkness, one with the rising smoke. . . .

At dawn the travelers journeyed on. All had slept fitfully and were irritable as they set out. At first they talked little. No one mentioned the old woman or her absence; but as the sun warmed them they began to speak of her mysterious appearance and even stranger departure.

"Mad, quite mad," the Doctor said more loudly than necessary. "These barrens are full of such crones, wild hags full of fancies. They wander and die, uncared for."

"A piteous creature," the Merchant agreed, frowning, "and yet I thought her tale . . ." He stroked his chin, glancing from one to the other. "It was a foolish tale of course, a child's tale. And yet . . . And yet I felt . . ." He flushed and fell silent under the Architect's glance and the Doctor's scrutiny.

At dusk there was no sign of their destination, no way of telling how far they had come. All their surroundings were exactly as they had been the previous day: the path wound ahead into the mists, the shrouded marshes lay on their right, and the sea stretched endlessly to their left. To make matters worse, the weird call came more frequently. Several times during the day it had floated out of the wilderness, each time more insistently.

This lack of progress, this timelessness, was troubling enough, but what was most unsettling for the Doctor and the Architect was that the Merchant had begun to behave strangely. He no longer seemed frightened by the Sound, nor concerned about their situation. Several times he had laughed aloud at some private joke, and twice they had heard him talking to himself.

"See here, my friend," the Architect said late in the afternoon, "I fear that we have missed a turning in the path and so have lost ourselves."

The Merchant gestured seaward. "How could that be? Are we not following the coast?"

"But surely we should have arrived by now. And did we not travel this stretch of road yesterday and the day before, and . . ."

"No," the Merchant said, "for there is a boat ahead, and we saw no boat yesterday."

"I see nothing," said the Architect.

"Fog," said the Doctor, squinting. "Only fog and water."

"Believe me," said the Merchant, "it is there, half a league ahead. And before we reach it I shall have time to bid you farewell, and to speak to you from the heart, which I have not yet done."

"Farewell?"

"Yes. I confess, my friends, that the old woman's story moved me deeply for it recalled an old adventure.

"Long ago, when I was a boy, I entered the service of a prosperous trader. I yearned to grow as rich as he. He placed me as a mariner aboard a vessel laden with rich goods—silks and spices, fragrant incense and rare woods—and we set sail westward. Our voyage began propitiously. The sun shone warm and for two weeks a fair wind filled our sails.

"But then the weather changed. Scudding clouds hid the stars so that we lost our bearings, and the storms which followed were more ferocious than any I have seen. They shredded our canvas and tore away our rigging. We knew that we were doomed. The others gave up their souls to the sea and their senses to hogsheads of their master's wine. I climbed high into the tattered rigging and fastened myself there despite the violent swaying of the vessel, which threatened to catapult me into the very teeth of the storm. So, when the ship struck and the splintered mast plunged into the sea, I was carried with it. I remember only the terrible cracking of the keel, the thundering of the breakers, and the shrieks of perishing shipmates.

"When my wits returned I found that I had been swept ashore. The storm had passed and the wreck-strewn beach steamed in the sun. I was sorely hurt but I disentangled myself from the mast before the rising tides reclaimed it, and I staggered into the forest where I again lost consciousness.

"When I awoke I found that my wounds had been dressed and that I was lying in cool shade. I was given sweet juices to drink and nourishing foods to eat. I had been rescued by islanders—savages, I would have called them before I was their guest. Savages indeed! They were the kindest, gentlest, and wisest people I have ever known, and I learned much from their simple ways in the months I spent among them—how to respect all of Life, how to take only what is needed, how to share, how—in a word—to live. Above all I learned to know the spirit world. . . .

"Ah, my young friend, I see doubt in your eye. You think that I am mad, perhaps? You believe that an insect has no spirit? That a flower or tree has no spirit? That spirits do not frolic in the sun, in the pools beneath the waterfalls? No, oh no. Listen to me: They are present in all that lives, in all the places where the power of Earth is consecrated. They have many shapes and names, nor is mankind apart from them, for we depend on them for Life itself. This I learned in that world before Time, that world of innocence, and although I may cover that truth with the brusque mask of commerce I have not forgotten it.

"For twenty months I stayed. Then, by chance, another of my master's vessels stopped at our island to reprovision. I know now how foolish I was to reveal my presence but I did so unthinkingly. I approached the crew, and told them my story. They were amazed, for they had long since given up for lost all on board our vessel, but they were even more astonished when I led them to the cave where the people had gathered the goods salvaged from our wreck. These they loaded into their ship without protest, for the islanders were quite indifferent to them.

"Then, my friends, I made the fateful choice to return. Why? I cannot tell you. Perhaps I was ambitious; perhaps I believed I could go back at will; perhaps I simply yearned for home.

"My master was generous, my reward handsome; in fact, it was the foundation of my fortune. From that time forward I have been a wealthy man, a renowned and respected citizen. Yet, in sleepless hours when I ponder the purpose of my life, it is neither honors nor wealth I contemplate. Rather, it is the beauty shown me on that island long ago, a life of laughter, and love, and wonder. A life in harmony with all Spirit. A life I had thought closed for good with the passage of the years.

"Now, after this strange journey, after the story of the old woman, I believe I can return. Like you I have heard the Sound, and like you I have feared the cost of answering. But now . . ."

"There is your boat, my friend," the Doctor said.

"Yes! Yes, you see?" Moving like a young man, the Merchant hurried through tall grasses to the shore where, indeed, a small sailboat lay waiting.

The Architect felt sudden panic, as if part of himself were falling away. "Stay!" he shouted, limping after the Merchant. "Don't be foolish! Such whims possess us when we are most vulnerable—overtired and anxious, or exposed to danger as we now are. In a day or two you shall be safe. You shall have left these phantoms far behind."

"Safety, ah yes," the Merchant laughed ruefully, stroking the smooth gunwale of the little boat. "That is what I have sought all my life. I have grown old in safety, always fearful I would not have enough. But now . . . ? No, good sir, I bequeath to you all my excess safety. Let this gentleman be witness." So saying, he drew the chamois bag of gold from inside his clothing and gave it to the Architect. Then he launched the little boat into the surf and manned the oars, calling back from the darkening sea, "May you have good fortune with it!"

"Should we prevent him?" the Architect asked. "Surely he is mad. Surely. . . ."

The Doctor shook his head. "No, we should not prevent him."

Together they watched the Merchant row beyond the surf and raise his sail.

"He will die," the Architect said.

"But he has re-entered Life." The Doctor smiled. "And that is what is important. For as long as his voyage lasts there will be no happier man than he. Come, sir. I shall build a fire and cook a meal. Now that you are rich I must treat you with proper courtesy!"

That night the Architect slept badly. When he rolled one way the parchment scrolls dug into him. When he rolled the other he encountered the hard bag of gold. All night he tossed and turned. He was haunted by deep foreboding, and beset by dream fragments which stabbed like slivers of glass. Whenever he roused from this fitful sleep he saw his companion staring into the fire, cowled in his heavy cloak. Twice he heard the Sound although he could not be sure which wilderness it came from, the one around him or the one within.

At dawn they resumed their journey. The Architect's restless night had left him stiff and troubled. Despite the Merchant's generous gift he felt betrayed, as if somehow the man had taken more than he had given. So the Doctor's sudden announcement came as a rude shock.

"I too will be leaving you," the Doctor said.

The Architect halted and stared in disbelief, clasping his plans and his bag of gold.

"I too have heard in the Sound and in the crone's tale a summons from long ago," the Doctor went on. "Also, I have had a dream. Soon we shall pass the mouth of a great river where, beside the ford, will stand a tree with three hawks. There I shall leave you."

"But . . ." the Architect stammered, "your position, sir! Your duties!"

The Doctor laughed, opening his fist to free an imaginary bird. "They will be taken up by dutiful men, no doubt," he said. "Responsible men. Like yourself, perhaps."

"But we are so *near*. When we must be . . . so very *close!*"

"Yes, and yet so far. . . . But come, my friend, let us walk on. The river is still some distance, and I have time to tell my story.

"Long ago, like our friend, I too journeyed to a distant land. But whereas his quest was in search of wealth, I sought wisdom. I longed to find those elixirs which would end all sufferings, or bring eternal life, or . . . Who knows what I dreamed? The fact was that I longed to perform some noble act in the service of humankind, and humankind alone.

"I joined a caravan to the East, for I had been told that there lay the most ancient and arcane repositories of knowledge. For many weeks and months we journeyed, and the lands we passed through and the peoples we met were strange indeed. To this day I could not swear to you that they were real as our science knows reality, for after weeks of thirst and blazing sun, after incessant desert winds and the constant bawling of the camels, certainties and fancies wove together in a single thread. Then I learned that just as imagination conjures lush oases and cool tents, fancies real to the mind which yearns profoundly for them, so other fantasies may claim the human soul. . . .

"Since then I have known many who drifted away from this world and into another, and so remained there, happy and uncaring. Poor afflicted souls we called them, and yet, who can say that they too were not voyagers as I was then, emissaries from us all, surveying for the first time some region beyond the boundaries of the known?

"Weeks passed. Months. Days swirled in desert storms, tropical torrents, sunless leagues of forest. I left one caravan and joined another, then a smaller, then one yet smaller, until at last I was alone, entering the foothills of the mountains.

"There I heard the Sound for the first time. I believed it was the call of a great horn far above, summoning monks to prayer, scholars to council, dreamers to their dreams, tying all together as it tied the crystalline peaks of Earth.

"In great hopes I began my climb.

"But I never arrived. At least, I never found what I had led myself to believe was awaiting me. Each day as I ascended the call grew fainter, and when at last I reached the peaks I found no colloquies of scholars, no eternal truths, but only the stark and windswept crags, the mountain creatures waiting, and myself . . . alone.

"Then, my friend, I discovered gulfs more awesome than any mountain valleys I had beheld, any canyons through which eagles plummeted. I was afraid. I am ashamed to say I fled.

"I fled back to my own land, to safety. I buttressed myself with sureties, honors, accomplishments, endless concerns which I claimed were for the welfare of my fellow man. But, always in my heart I have kept the memory of that moment when, had I not been weak, I might have discovered . . . I might have truly gone beyond. . . .

"But see, we have come to the place where we must part, for here is the ford, the tree, the three hawks. All is unfolding as was foretold in my dream." The Doctor turned and laid his hand on the shoulder of the younger man. "Will you come with me?"

"No!" the Architect exclaimed, pulling away. "I have obligations! I have a duty!"

"Of course, of course." The Doctor smiled. "You are an honorable man. Since that is the case, let me place all the fruits of my scholarship into your safekeeping. Do with them as you will." So saying, he handed over the bundle of parchment manuscripts and made his way through the brush to the riverbank. With never a backward glance he waded across the ford, climbed the far side, and vanished in the wraiths of mist that swirled down to receive him.

As one, the three hawks silently left their perch and followed him.

The Architect added the bundle of manuscripts to his load and hastened away from that place, urged on by fear and bitter disappointment. A needle of envy probed him too, for why had those revelations which had so profoundly moved the Merchant and the Doctor been denied to him?

Still, he reassured himself, the city must be very close—perhaps just beyond the hills which loomed ahead. Safely there, busy once again with human concerns, he could put all memory of this strange journey behind him. He would sleep again untroubled by dreams, and see his plans fulfilled.

Besides, was he not rich?

Limping more under the additional weight, he struggled on.

The hills, however, proved farther than they seemed. For three more days, suspended between marsh and sea, he toiled toward them.

At dusk the first day he abandoned the Doctor's manuscripts. He thought, *They are in a safe place. When I reach the city I shall send someone to retrieve them.* At noon the second day, he left behind—with great reluctance—the Merchant's bag of gold. He thought, *It is hidden where no one can find it. Later, I shall return for it.*

During the nights he huddled in his robe, keeping a bright fire and not daring to sleep. At sunrise on the fourth day of his solitary journey, the Child came to him again.

He had been climbing numbly, paying little attention to his surroundings, when he realized that already he was hundreds of feet above the sea. Gulls drifted far below, their cries thin and plaintive as the wails of lost beings. Shore and road had parted, and the coastline curved into the mist where sails moved like moths' wings. "The port," he said aloud. "I shall soon reach the capital! I shall soon be safe!"

The shadows stretched as he climbed. A green glow moved beside him through the forest. The dusk thickened with sounds. Far away, a wolf's howl was answered by the barking of its young, and owls' calls searched like soft questions. Again he heard the Sound, and this time, he knew, it came for him alone.

As it faded he saw the Child. She was sitting on a rock farther up the path, and when she saw him she slipped off her perch and ran ahead into the dusk. Then she turned and beckoned to him: come. Again she beck-oned, and when he hesitated she ran back and took his hand.

"Who are you?" he asked.

She shook her head.

"What is your name?"

She shook her head.

He allowed himself to be led. In silence they climbed the last half-league through the forest to the top of the hill from which he could see the capital. There it lay in the last of the light, a stern gray presence on the verdant land.

The Architect gazed in silence, his heart and mind in turmoil. He should have been relieved that his journey was at an end, but he was not. He should have been excited that his plans would soon be realized, but he was not. As he watched, the city wavered under a greenish light and a vision of another city rose through it and above it. The buildings of his dreams stood at the center of this city but the sight of them gave no plea-sure, for nothing else was as he had imagined it. Instead of lying somno-lent in the evening, that city blazed with cruel light as far as he could see, brighter than sun on the sea, banishing all the mystery of night. Instead of the quiet, human sounds to which he was accustomed, that city was filled with a rumbling that shook the very hill on which he stood. Worst of all, no orchard fragrances drifted from that place, but only a stench that hung like a pall of death above the plain.

Groaning in horror, the Architect covered his eyes. When he uncov-ered them again the vision had vanished and the familiar capital lay barely visible in the darkness.

He turned back toward the forest.

The Child had already gathered wood and tinder, and in silence they made a fire and ate a frugal meal. In silence they sat long afterward, waiting. He was not surprised when at last the Child rose and came to-ward him. He was not surprised when she took his hand in both of hers and, opening it, placed on his palm a pure white pebble.

197

"Yes," he said, laughing. "I understand."

Soft laughter answered his own. At first it was the innocent laughter of childhood; then it changed to that of a young woman, a sound rich with surprise and delight; and again it changed into the rueful, patient laughter of middle age; and then again into that of a matriarch, laughter of primordial wisdom, laughter ancient as Earth. And finally it became not mere human laughter but the laughter of all Nature, of Mystery forever beyond human comprehension.

"I understand," he said again.

He built the fire and fed into it his cherished plans, scroll by parchment scroll. The flames soared in a clean pyre, consuming the fruit of all his knowledge, all his pride and his ambition.

The Child changed. Where she had been a green aura wavered like the flush of Northern Lights. It strengthened and swirled as he gazed at it, drawing darkness into radiance, stillness into a shimmering and eternal dance. The spirits of all Life danced there, and watching them the Architect felt like a tired swimmer who touches shore and comes out into the warmth of beach and sun. Finally the light became the old woman who was the teller of Eiver's tale. One eye gleamed pale as a beach stone, the other red as fire. Gnarled roots wrapped her fingers. Her clothes hung shaggily as cedar bark. "Tell me," she said. "Tell me what you have learned."

He shook his head. "I cannot."

"Think it."

He thought, *I journey with many companions, friends I do not yet know. Each moment may be our destination.*

"Yes."

When I listen I hear harmony. I learn again that it is more than beauty. When I am still I remember that wisdom is more than knowledge, more than truth.

She nodded. "Yes."

The Architect sat quietly watching the fire. Then he thought, feeling himself open like a seed, *And my task, my great task, is to draw human-kind away from small fears and certainties, back to the Great Mystery.*

The old woman got to her feet slowly and painfully. "Now you are truly one of us," she said. "Go in peace." Reaching into the smoke, she drew it down and around herself, became one with it, and rose.

That night the Architect slept a dreamless sleep.

At sunrise, carrying only the white pebble and limping hardly at all, he descended toward the city along an ancient path. He was not sure how he would accomplish his mission. He knew only that a great task waited to be done.

CHANGELING

BARBARA HAMBLY

I T STARTED WITH THE DRAGON. Brown Michael had feared its coming since word had first reached him from Grildon Dan, the Marchlord to the immediate north, of the creature's arrival and its depredations upon the cold autumn countryside. He called together the farmers and herders of the White Marches at Corfach Castle, the people he had sworn to defend and rule as his father and grandfather had before him, and organized them as best he could against the possibility of an attack upon the village. But in his heart he knew that when it came down to it, he'd have to fight the thing himself.

As the Lord of the White Marches it was his responsibility, taken up seven years ago when his father had been killed by wolves in a bitter winter. Brown Michael had been eighteen at that time, and newly married, and the last dragon sighted in the wild Marchlands had been over thirty years before. But he'd thought about it, even then.

So when his wife's cousin Amaris came riding hell-for-leather from the village to Corfach Castle crying that the dragon had descended upon the herds, slaying three cows and the head herd-boy, Michael prepared himself to seek it out and slay it, alone.

Brown Michael had heard from Grildon Dan that when the older Marchlord and his men had tried to surprise the dragon in its lair, it had sensed their coming from far off and had taken wing, rising to attack them from above with claws and teeth and spitting streams of fire. Michael, an inveterate hunter when his duties gave him time, guessed that the dragon had heard or smelled one of Grildon Dan's men, or perhaps one of the horses, and had been ready for the attack.

Thus, when after a week's careful searching he located the dragon's new lair in the clammy deeps of Firbolg Glen, in addition to muffling every weapon he would carry with leather and rags he bathed himself all over to take away his own scent and spent the night in the castle kennels sleeping with the dogs, who were very pleased with his company. His wife Anne, in the iron-dark hour of his setting out before dawn, allowed wryly that his tactic should work but kissed him anyway, trying to smile.

Then he left, on foot, a journey of a day and most of a night, to meet the dragon the following dawn.

When a man fights a dragon the outcome is usually quick. Either the man sneaks up on the dragon in its lair, disables its wings and kills it, usually with poisoned spears or lances, or the dragon takes to the air before the man gets close enough to strike, and from there the end is only a matter of moments. Brown Michael slew the dragon in the mouth of Firbolg Glen, where the overhanging trees, though burned and rotted from the accumulated poisons of close proximity with the monster, prevented its taking off.

Half-asphyxiated from inhaled fumes, burned and blistered and bleeding from a dozen minor cuts from the dragon's knifelike scales, for a time Michael could only sit slumped on a fallen and discolored tree trunk, staring unbelievingly at the great green-bronze carcass of the thing he had killed. It was nearly thirty feet long from its narrow horned head to the spiked tip of its tail; blood leaking from its wounds soaked blackly into the ground and made garish swirls in the puddles of ochre poison that turned the mouth of the glen into a filthy swamp. The stream running out of the glen was fouled for miles, and looking back into what had once been a chilly pocket of shadowy trees, of frogs and whippoorwills, Michael could see through the thick drifts of fumes how many trees had died and fallen, how the vegetation had perished and the very stones were dyed with the unnatural chroma of the dragon's slime. There was a cave back there, he knew, carved by the spring. It was there he guessed the dragon had hidden its hoard.

The thought was a sickening one. Not much was known about dragons, but Michael did know from Anne's book that they were hoarders by nature, though the hoard, in this case, would probably not be treasure. Dragons will transport almost anything to their lairs, including crippled or dying victims to devour at their leisure. He knew that in the past week the miller's son, and a woman from Oakhill farm, had vanished, as had others from Grildon Dan's lands, plus assorted livestock. It was hardly likely anything taken living into the dragon's lair would survive, but nevertheless, he had to look. Aching all over from the battle and hating the thought of what he might find, he turned his stumbling steps up the glen.

It was difficult to breathe in the yellowish murk, and the fumes burned his eyes. He found the body of a woman, and bones of what might have been cattle and pigs. But ahead of him, in the cave in the glen's steep bank shadowed by the dead and poisoned trees, he heard a noise, a faint scrabbling, followed by a coo, a whimper, a warbling sweetness from the dark hole. Cautious, Michael drew his sword again, the leather of the pommel chafing his blistered hand.

Eyes flashed in the dark of the cave; behind them, a sudden soft glow of light.

Then out of the cave an animal came: neither a deer, nor the long-legged rangy hounds bred to hunt deer, though there was something in it of both. Soft down covered it, like a chick's, only the down was green as spring grass; the creature's eyes were golden as honey, huge and soft and puzzled with the world. Behind it floated a cloud of lights, tiny fireflies of red and blue flickering within a soft nimbus of white radiance, bobbing and shifting and somehow undoubtedly alive.

Last of all, from the dark of the dragon's cave, stumbled a child, a little girl of two, naked and scratched, with mud in her dark auburn hair. She held out her arms to Michael and sobbed soundlessly, and as he sprang to pick her up, forgetful of his own injuries, the green deer put its head gratefully against his thigh, and the sparkling cloud of lights hung close over his head, as if they, too, felt that he had saved their lives.

They named her Kyah. "She should at least know her own name, poor thing," said Anne softly, leaning across to stroke the feathery red-dark silk of the child's hair, where it lay upon Michael's shoulder. "Rosebud did, at her age."

"Rosebud was asking the midwife who delivered her what she was doing and how she was doing it," Michael pointed out with a grin and a glance at his daughter, who lay on the other side of the hearth with her elbows propped before one of Anne's big old books of beasts, looking in the firelight for some picture which resembled the green deer, or some reference to a creature whose form is entirely made up of lights.

Rosebud said reprovingly, "Daddy, that's silly. But why would she forget how to talk? Did the dragon's poison make her?"

"Fear can make that happen," said Anne gently, as her two children—fair-haired as she, and giving promise of growing, like her, big-boned and tall—got up from their book and came over to stand near her chair and regard the foundling with curious eyes.

"You mean if I scared Marcus real bad he'd forget how to talk?" Rosebud giggled nervously.

"Would not," asserted her brother.

"Bet you would . . ."

"Not just scared," said Michael softly, cradling the child Kyah against him, as he had cradled her all that long walk back to the castle. The green deer, whom they had named Tassels for the little tufts of white feathers on her ears and tail, raised her silken chin a little from Michael's foot where it rested, blinking sleepily at the sound of the voices. The haze of lights stirred and sparkled beneath the chair, like the embers of a rainbow fire.

"Afraid," Michael went on, looking from his nine-year-old daughter to his son, "which is different. So afraid you can't think, so afraid you

206

can't even stand to be alive. . . . That afraid." In the two pairs of wondering blue eyes he saw their uneasy comprehension, and in his daughter's,
pity and sorrow as well. "And she's just little, littler than either of you.
Of course it would make her forget."

Rosebud reached out to touch Kyah's round little hand, and the child
regarded her with an unsmiling gaze as dark as ebony. "Will she ever
remember?" Her voice was small.

"If we love her enough," said Anne.

So the child from the dragon's lair was accepted into the family at
Corfach Castle, and treated as one of their own. Better, in fact, because
Rosebud forebore to boss Kyah about as she bossed Marcus, and kept Mar-
cus from being rough with her, as all six-year-old boys can be in play.
Nevertheless, in spite of the young girl's care and Anne's gentle affection,
Kyah remained steadfast in her preference for Michael himself, following
him around whenever he was in the castle, and listening for the returning
hooves of his horse upon the drawbridge when he'd come in from his
patrols of the cold woods and swampy, wolf-infested acres of the wide
Marchlands that were his to protect. The first time he rode out on patrol
Anne had to restrain Kyah—and her two inseparable companions, Tassels
and Limmifer—from accompanying him, and after another occasion upon
which one of the herd-boys found the child trotting along the frost-barren
fields in the tracks of Michael's horse, the green deer at her heels and the
filtered, nebulous cloud of brightness floating over her head, Anne and
Rosebud made very sure they knew where Kyah was at the times when
Michael left.

At all times Kyah was affectionate with the others of the household,
playing with the other two children as they romped with the graceful,
skittering green deer and the swirling cloud of lights, or gravely following
Anne about the kitchens, stillrooms, and pantries on her daily tasks. But
she never smiled. Though it was clear she listened gravely when others
spoke, and when Rosebud gave her daily lessons in the names of things,
she never herself made a sound. She would listen in the same way to the

barking of the dogs and the calls of birds, or to the wide-ranging songs and trills produced by Tassels—coos, twitters, a sound that was almost like laughter. She learned that her name was Kyah, and would come to it, as Tassels would come leaping and fawning like an affectionate cat, and Limmifer would float, sparkling and blazing with anticipation, but what her other name had been, she gave no indication that she even recalled.

Autumn deepened to winter and cold snows swept from the moors. Michael hunted through the White Marches and in all the nearby realms, and out into the sparse settlements of the badlands, for word of a child missing, a child with brown eyes and hair the dark red of chestnut hulls, and even sending word through a trader to the savages in the Zaranian Hills. But there was no more word of her than if she had been a changeling child, abandoned by careless fairy-folk at his door.

"Could that be what she is?" asked Anne one night, as sleety wind groaned around the castle walls and made the lampflames shudder in their tiny bowls of red and golden glass. "It says in one of my books that fairy children do not speak."

As she said it she glanced swiftly through the door of the nursery, which opened off their own big bedroom, making certain that Rosebud and Marcus were safe in their bed, and sleeping. Two pale flags of silver-gilt hair swathed the fur of the blankets. In the little cot in the deep shadows of the opposite wall only a tiny hump under the quilts showed, but Tassels lay in a curled knot of green silk and feathers at the bed's foot, and a dimly pulsing aura of deep blue light at the end of one of the bedposts proclaimed where Limmifer hovered, deep in sleep.

"I don't know," said Michael slowly, drawing his wife down to sit with him in his great carved chair. Made for his huge grandfather's girth the chair accommodated them both, though Anne was tall—taller in fact than he by a good two inches—and both muscular and plump. Her blond hair, released in crinkled waves from its daytime braids, streamed like a river down the front of his leather shirt as she laid her head against his.

"I'd have thought the Fair Folk would have guarded one of their own children better than to let her be taken by a dragon."

"They're said to be careless," replied Anne, "and without hearts, taking things up and casting them away. Some say they create strange animals for their own amusement, and then let them wander off to die when they grow bored. . . ." She frowned, worry lines puckering between her brows, and her eyes turned again towards the shadows beyond the nursery door.

"Tassels is growing out her puppy coat, have you noticed?" said Michael, affection for them all in his deep brown eyes. And indeed, even curled into a sleeping ball they could see that the queer little animal's fur and feathers were longer and smoother than they had been, and changing from a bright emerald to a somber and dignified medley of dark-green, bronze, and gold. "And sometimes I think I can see something in the middle of Limmifer's lights, a shape of some kind, like a shining ghost."

"I wondered if you'd noticed that." His wife sighed. "It used to be only in certain lights—I thought it was just my imagination." She reached out and ran a lock of Michael's bronze-dark hair through her fingers, still looking at the oddly assorted young sleeping in the gloom. Her voice soft, she went on, "It also says, in one of my books, that fairy children fare ill in the mortal world, and don't live long. And more often than not, the children raised with changelings also suffer."

"I know," Michael replied. "Much as I love her—much as I love the three of them, and will miss having them follow me about as they do . . ." He shivered a little. "Believe me, I don't look forward to the prospect of trying to speak to the Fair Ones the next time they hold one of their revels on the Barren Isle. But I think I'll have to try."

The Barren Isle stood half a day's ride from Corfach Castle, an ancient, flattened mound rising from a pond, with five standing-stones upon its crest. The fairies were said to dance there at certain seasons. Certainly no human had dared go near the place in living memory, except one child from Grildon Village who had been found wandering witless three days later, and had been little better than a wondering-eyed idiot ever since. Still, Michael made plans to ride there the night of the next full moon, when according to Anne's books the fairies might be expected to dance. But on that night a snowstorm covered the lands, and the next full moon, in the thaw-season of icicles and mud, brought tidings that drove all thought of such an errand from Michael's mind.

The month between brought other things as well. Tassels was growing. With the loss of her chick-soft down she had become larger and more rangy, rambling far over the iron-hard fields and chasing down winter rabbits and foxes. Since in these seasons wolves sometimes prowled close to the village walls Anne was hard put to keep the venturesome creature penned within the castle, not out of fear that Tassels couldn't outrun any wolf ever whelped, but because Kyah and Limmifer would invariably try to accompany her, the little girl struggling along in Tassels' light tracks. Twice, to Anne's horror, Rosebud and Marcus went after the three truants without notifying either her or their father: "We didn't want you to spank her," explained Rosebud, as Michael handed her, Marcus, and Kyah down into Anne's arms from the saddle of his horse after he'd gone out to find them in the twilight woods. All three children were pink-faced with cold and flecked with snow from head to foot; snow had begun to fall, catching like huge feathers in the fur of their hoods, in Tassels' soft-fluffed plumage as she fawned happily around Michael as he dismounted, and in his horse's black mane. Beyond the walls, the distant crying of the wolves could be heard from the winter woods.

Anne, shaky with the fear she'd felt for them, reflected that spanking Kyah wouldn't do any good anyway—the little girl would simply not understand why she couldn't go with her playmates. She only said, "You did right to go after her, Rosie-child . . . but please, another time, tell one of the stablemen, or me, or *anyone*, and get them to go instead. I promise you I won't spank anyone." Behind Michael, where he held Kyah in his arms with Tassels frisking like a huge hound about him, Limmifer hung glittering in the air, and in the fading light Anne could definitely see that there was a shape now within the dancing aura of the lights, a sinuous twisting brightness, like a salamander wrought of clearest glass and water, with diamond eyes—though it was hard to tell how many eyes—sparkling like a pale halo of stars.

Limmifer, too, was growing larger. He liked to play over the snow, or over standing water if he could find it, and like Tassels, he ventured more and more frequently beyond the walls of the castle, generally when Michael was away on patrol. On such occasions, Tassels and Kyah would prowl from gate to window to battlement, seeking a way to follow under Anne's worried eye. Many long evenings, when Michael was absent, hunting the wolves that preyed on the outlying farms or making sure that justice was done in the courts of the two small marchfiefs who held serfs of their own but owed allegiance to him, Anne would pore over the books of her own small library, seeking in the ancient bestiaries, the crumbling natural histories and centuries-old collections of travelers' lore, any mention of creatures that bounded like deer over the snow in their long, fluttering tatters of fur and feathers, or who danced in an aura of sparkling light.

But she found nothing. And as the moon waxed toward its full she found her thoughts turning more and more toward the legends of the fairies, creatures who lived in a glitter of magic and illusion themselves . . . creatures who might well hold the answer to the riddle of Kyah and her two strange companions. She knew that it was perilous for a mortal to seek them out, but nevertheless, began to prepare the things that were supposed to keep humankind safe from their enchantments: a lump of salt, a sigil of iron worked with holy signs, a packet of certain powdered earths mixed with the dried petals of a winter rose. She took out the wooden box containing the teeth and claws of the dragon Brown Michael had slain, wondering if they would have any protective virtue in them, but even after these few short months they were becoming brittle, decayed almost to dust, as the bones of dragons do. It would be dangerous, she knew, for Michael to ride to the Barren Isle in quest of these beings, but her instincts told her that things could not go on as they were.

Then two days before the moon's full, tidings reached Corfach Castle of another dragon in the White Marches.

Word came to Michael when he was riding patrol out past Goffin Swamp, brought by one of the shepherds. He and the man rode through the night to reach Corfach by midmorning. In the low grazing lands near Corfach Village, within ten miles of the castle, he saw the evidence: the blood on the ground, the absence of tracks of any sort, but, in the woods a mile or so farther off, the slime-scorched tree where the thing had perched, with the torn remains of carcass and bones in a puddle of dripped blood and poison beneath.

That night Michael bathed in clear water, and slept in the kennels again, making arrangements to trade clothes with Sam the kennelman for good measure, to be sure that, even close upwind, he would smell of nothing but dog. "Are you going to fight the dragon, Daddy?" asked Rosebud, her blue eyes huge.

Brown Michael shook his head. "Tomorrow I'm just going to see if he's hiding where the other one was, in the cave at Firbolg Glen. And believe me, Rosie-child, I'm not getting any closer to him than I need to." And he ruffled her hair and his son's. But after they had been sent off to bed he drew Anne to him, in the courtyard outside the kennels where last week's snow was turning to trampled slush, and said softly, "Keep close watch on them while I'm gone. Make sure Rosie and Marcus stay indoors. . . ."

He broke off, seeing her face troubled, and said, "What is it?"

"Nothing," she said uncertainly. "Only . . . tomorrow night is the full of the moon."

He was silent, knowing what she meant.

After a time she said, "The thing is . . . Kyah's growing restless. It may just be the coming of the spring, but she's getting cleverer in slipping out of the castle, bolder. . . . I don't think she knows what fear is. Two days ago, while you were on patrol she tried to climb down the old ivy on the north wall, to go after Limmifer. . . ."

"And where was Limmifer?" asked Michael quietly.

Anne shrugged. "Gone somewhere, into the woods, I think. He's done that, more and more, with the coming of spring as well."

Michael sighed, and the lines that in the winter had begun to settle into his face seemed to get a little deeper. "Yes," he said softly. "Yes, I know."

Anne frowned, seeing him worried. But when he said nothing she went on, "I'm afraid for her, Michael. Afraid what another month will bring. If she *is* a fairy child, she may be trying to rejoin her people, like a baby bird trying to fly before its feathers are grown. If you can't go to the Barren Isle, I think I should try."

Michael put his arm around her waist, and looked past her, to where some of the castle bondsmen were closing the great gates for the night. Through the black square of the lintels the frozen moat shone palely in the light of an early-rising moon, and above the ice Limmifer was playing, a swirling sparkle of silver light. Within the lights the ghost-shape rippled and danced, a glint of glass and diamonds where the moonlight caught; looking back, he saw Kyah, tiny in her white nightdress, standing at the top of the steps leading up into the castle keep, one hand resting on Tassels' feathered neck.

"Yes," he said softly. "I think you should. But before you go . . . put Limmifer under lock and key."

"Limmifer?" Anne looked at him, startled, then back at the sinuous coil of light and stars above the ice of the moat. Though the shadows around them were deep, Michael saw her eyes change as she understood.

"I'm not certain," he said, his voice low as her gaze returned to his, filled with shock and grief. "But in none of your books, Anne, does it say what dragons look like when they are young. They are creatures of magic—who can say whether they have bodies at all when they are born? But it's only now, that he *is* developing a body—and needing food besides water and snow—that we start hearing of dragon killings again."

"I've watched him play." There was the catch of tears in her voice, grief for what it would mean. "He hovers around the children—not just Kyah and Tassels, but all of them—follows them . . . I swear he doesn't mean them harm."

"Nor does a lion cub," said Michael, "until it grows big enough to remember that it is a lion."

So it was that before the young Marchlord set forth next morning for Firbolg Glen, he led all three of his little foundlings down to the dungeon—a very small dungeon, dug out by his great-grandfather and seldom used—and into a windowless room there. Then he and Anne gently set Kyah and Tassels outside the door, and last of all he slipped out, bolting the door behind him. As he did so he glanced back, and in the light of his torch it seemed to him unmistakable, that the form that coiled within the glow of Limmifer's lights was that of a diamond dragon: claws, eyes, and the shimmer of membranous wings.

Through the day Anne watched and listened nervously, but no sound came from below. Kyah and Tassels haunted the door in the courtyard that led to the dungeon steps—as often as she carried the little girl away from it, a few hours later she'd find her there again, tears glistening in her dark eyes as she tugged at Anne's sleeves, soundlessly trying to get her to open the door and free her friend. As the early winter darkness approached Anne put on a man's britches and boots and a heavy sheepskin coat, and filled her pockets with the things she'd prepared for Michael—the iron sigil, the lump of salt—and took her bow and a short halberd to protect her from the more mundane dangers she might meet in the woods. She braided up her long blond hair and jammed a knitted cap down over it, and taking the children—Marcus, Rosebud, and Kyah—up behind her on her big brown mare, she rode with them as far as her cousin Amaris' house in the village, where they were to spend the night.

Then she rode out alone over the snow, heading for the Barren Isle.

The children had cost her a certain amount of worry, for if Michael's suspicions were correct, she did not want to leave them in the castle with a growing dragonet—even one they had been playing with all winter. Amaris and her husband were rich, as riches were reckoned in the White Marches, and their house was stoutly built of stone. Though it was not as strong as Corfach Castle, the children would be as safe there as anywhere. But all the way there Kyah had kept turning around, where she sat on Anne's saddlebow, trying to leap down and run back, and staring up at her, mutely pleading not to be separated from her friend. Tassels had run back and forth between the horse and the castle walls, cooing and whistling worriedly, but in the end had gone with Kyah; Anne only hoped the graceful creature wouldn't find some way to escape in the night and take Kyah with her. "I'm leaving her in your care," she'd told Rosebud, before she'd mounted again in Amaris' courtyard, and the little girl had nodded gravely, putting an arm around Kyah's tiny shoulders. "Don't leave her for a second." And, seeing her daughter's solemn eyes, had smiled, adding, "I'll be back for breakfast—see if I'm not."

Amaris, standing behind them in the bar of yellow light from the house's kitchen door, had given her an answering smile. "They'll be all right; we'll keep them safe."

And with that Anne had had to be content.

When she had reached the Barren Isle it was fully dark, the cold air feeling hard-edged as diamonds in her nose. The moon stood high in a sky like liquid ink, circled with a shining blue-white ring, its light bright enough that every black and naked tree trunk, every leafless shrub and weed stem, cast its own attenuated shadow on the bitter crust of snow. Yet looking ahead to the hill itself, Anne could see nothing clearly. A mist rose from the pool which surrounded it, and the tops of the five standing-stones seemed to move and shift in the shining vapor. It seemed to her there was other movement there as well, movement which ceased when she tried to focus her attention upon it. Her mare snorted uneasily, and fidgeted her hairy hooves. Anne drew rein, and, dismounting, tied her to the limb of a tree, hoping that the presence of the faes which discomfited the horse would also keep prowling wolves at bay.

The pool around the hill had not frozen. Standing at its edge, Anne could see even through the mist that no snow lay upon the smooth curve of the Isle. It seemed to her that she could hear voices, thin and cold as the chirping of insects, and see the movement of shadows among the stones; she thought there was music as well. Digging the salt from her pocket, she scraped a little from the lump and put it on her tongue, and, as the books had instructed, she held the lump in her left hand, the iron sigil in her right. Then walking to the edge of the mere, she called out, "Beautiful Ones! In the name of your Queen and of all the Princes of the Air, I desire speech with you!"

Through the mists it was difficult to see, but all music—if there ever had been music upon that hill—fell silent, and there was stillness among the shadows of the stones.

Anne called out again, "Beautiful Ones! I mean you no harm, asking only that you do no harm to me. But in the name of your Queen, please speak to me."

Again there was silence, like some vast thing of darkness holding its breath. In it she could hear her mare snort with fear, and from the corner of her eye saw a little swirl of snow, like a wind flurry, only there was no wind.

A third time she called, "Beautiful Ones! In your Queen's name, please speak to me, for I have found a child who may be one of yours, and without you she will surely die!"

Then it seemed to her that the mists all along the hem of the island shivered, and among them she could make out shapes: dwarfed and squat, or impossibly elongated and thin; flat heads covered with coarse brown hair, pricked animal ears, the red gleam of eyes. A long hand with fingers like a spider's legs extended to her out of the mists, and a thin voice said,

"Come over, then, mortal woman, and have speech with the Princes of the Air." But looking down, Anne could see that the bridge that had appeared at her feet out of the waters of the mere was no more than a few strands of weed, made to look like sturdy plank and carved railings by a trick of shadow, and what at first glance seemed to be lamps hung along its stout balustrades were no more than the flash of the moonlight on the pool.

Whether it was the iron she held which opened her eyes, or the salt beneath her tongue, or whether it was the books she had read of the fairies—or merely because she was Anne—she didn't know. But she said tactfully, "Oh, my lords of Air, I would not risk dishonoring your customs by coming among you, or putting foot on ground hallowed to your use."

At this they all laughed, a thin, cruel sound that sparkled with the perilous beauty of shattered glass. Then one of them stepped forth from the mists, crossing over the water where the bridge seemed to be—the bridge they had set as a trap to dunk her, sheerly from the sport of a winter's night, not caring that she would undoubtedly freeze or at least become very sick by morning, but only thinking, as was their way, of how amusing it would be to see a big, stout woman floundering and splashing in the pond. As it crossed toward her she felt the shimmer of the shape-changer's heat which enveloped it, and saw the water beneath its feet steam, and where a squat, stooped, and flat-faced beast had been, there stood a beautiful naked man, wreathed and draped in green-black ivy, with holly twined in his waist-length brown hair.

"You are clever, Lady of the White Marches." He smiled, and in his coal-dark eyes she saw the distant gleam of alien stars.

"Too clever to be deceived by a little weed and marshlight," she replied. Oddly enough she felt no anger at them, any more than she would have felt anger at a packrat for stealing one of her rings. They were what they were, and did what they did with an animal's brutal innocence. "Is that form you wear illusion too? Or was the illusion, the shape of a beast that you wore before?"

217

"All form is illusion," he said, and reaching out his hand, touched her face. His fingers were warm, strong and rough as a mortal man's. "But it is only we, and others like us, that know it. We are children of air and fire, where you are the sons and daughters of water and earth; you change slowly, both in your bodies and in your hearts, and sometimes your hearts never change. When we die, even our bones perish like frost before the sun, as the bones of all shape-changers do. Where did you find this child, to make you think she was a changeling, and one of ours?"

"My husband, Brown Michael of Corfach, found her in the den of the dragon he slew upon the threshold of winter," she replied. "She is beautiful, like the form you now wear; and she does not speak, as they say your children do not. If she is a changeling, we beg you to take her back, for there is no place for such children in the mortal world, and they mostly fare ill, and die."

The Prince of Air smiled. "If she is a changeling, she will come to us of her own accord, for all young things learn their own natures in time. Perhaps, if she is our child, her mother thought you would be a better nurse, or at least more willing to do the work, for you must admit it is a tedious thing, to raise a child." He laughed, white teeth glinting in the moonlight. "Have no fear, little mother—if she is a changeling she will make the choice to be what she is, and then you will know."

Anne stepped back from him, repelled, and with a thunderclap of laughter he flung up his arms, dissolving into a spray of white starlight and fire. As he did so Anne's horse gave a whinny of fear, and turning back, she saw that several of the Fair Folk had slipped across the pool behind her and untied the mare's reins, so that the horse, terrified, fled away into the winter woods. Anne swung back around, but saw that the mists that surrounded the Barren Isle were gone. The five stones stood stark in the clear moonlight, without movement of any kind. There was no sign that the fairies had been there, save for a few leaves of green-black ivy, lying in the snow at her feet.

She shouldered her bow and halberd again, shivering to think of the long walk home. If Kyah were of these people, she thought, it was probably better that she had been fostered, like a cuckoo chick, where she was, for at least Anne would give her love. But if she was of these people, the counter question inevitably arose within her mind, how much was she capable of understanding that love? The child's nature was affectionate and caring now, but if the Prince of Air was right, would she in time become like them: cruel, selfish, tricky? Truly, as it was said, the families that took in changelings would fare as ill as the fairy children did themselves, if one whom they loved as they loved Kyah turned from the fiercely devoted child who followed Michael wherever he went, into one such as they.

All young things learn their own natures in time, the Prince had said, and one day, Kyah would make the choice to become what she was.

But the thought of the pain that would bring was heavy in Anne's heart as she turned away from the enchanted isle. Behind her she seemed to hear from the darkness on the hill the mocking glitter of their laughter.

After sleeping the night in his dog-smelling blankets, Brown Michael reached Firbolg Glen in the gray cold of dawn the next day. He approached the place with care, circling cautiously through the heather and stones of the hillsides, trying to get a look down into the steep-sided, rocky gully from above. The air above it, where a few dead and discolored tree branches still poked stiffly up like skeleton hands, seemed clear. The stench of last autumn's dragon poison seemed to have sunk into the ground. Nonetheless Michael edged warily down to the mouth of the glen, where the burned and fallen trees, the stained rocks around the frozen spring, still marked the place of his battle. The dragon's bones were gone, decaying even more quickly than the claws and teeth which Anne had saved.

In the glen itself there were marks of fresh poison dribbled here and there on the rocks, renewing the vile stains of vermilion and green. Fresh claw scratches scored the fallen trees, showing that the dragon had been here. More poison spotted the ground outside the cave, and a few newly stripped bones lay among the turgid, foul-colored puddles.

In the cave he found more signs, for the dragon had already begun to hoard, dragging to the place whatever seemed good to it: a fresh sheep's skull, the rusted turnpost joint of a wagon, a couple of green rocks from a stream bed. A stained cloak embroidered with gold and a ripped saddlebag which proved to contain a glass goblet and some silver told Michael that it had claimed at least one traveling merchant. And at the back of the cave, it had clawed and dug into its predecessor's hoard for whatever it could find.

And in doing so, it had unearthed the thing which chilled Michael's heart to look at it, once he realized what it was.

There was almost nothing of it left, only a piece the size of his hand. Even a few brief months had rotted it nearly to dust. But looking at it in the half-darkness of the fume-drifted cave, Michael could tell that it was a fragment of the shell of an egg.

"Gone?" Anne gripped the bridle of Amaris' horse, staring horrified up at her cousin in the thin white coldness of the bare woods.

Amaris leaned down and caught her hands. "Dear God, I'm glad we found *you*! When the shepherds found your horse wandering loose we were afraid . . ."

"Never mind that," said Anne, pushing aside her irritation at the Fair Ones and their pranks. "You don't think they went looking for me . . . ?"

Amaris shook her head, her blond braids bouncing against her jacket's embroidered hides. "No—as far as we can tell they left in the middle of the night. The first we knew of it was when the bondsmen from the castle came running down to tell us that Limmifer had escaped. . . ."

Anne swore in a very unladylike manner.

"Broke down the door of the dungeon, they said," her cousin went on. "From the way the blankets and clothes in the children's room were lying, we think little Kyah and her pet Tassels got up first, and got out the window, though dear knows how they managed to get to the ground without breaking both their necks. It looks like your two woke up later, saw they were gone, and went after them. We've been hunting since sunup but they could be anywhere. . . ."

"Not anywhere," said Anne grimly. "Is your horse fresh?" She was already hooking the sling of her quiver over Amaris' saddlebow, holstering the halberd on behind. Amaris swung down from the saddle and let Anne mount, groaning a little—her legs were stiff from her all-night walk through the snow. "Thank you," said Anne, wheeling the horse around in the crusted mud of the path where she'd met her cousin. "Can you make it back to the village all right?"

"It's only a mile or so. Good luck."

"I'll need it." Anne nudged the horse's sides; they set off at a trot, which swiftly turned to a muddy, slogging gallop when they reached the open wastelands between Corfach Village and Firbolg Glen. And as she rode, scanning the dreary landscape of snow and mud for sign of Rosebud's scarlet coat, the words of the Prince of Air returned to her again and again: *All young things learn their own natures in time.* Limmifer had remembered his, and she only prayed to whatever gods she thought would listen that he would remember, also, the love and kindness shown him by Rosebud, and Marcus, and Kyah, too, in her fierce, silent way— and that the memory would prove stronger than the call of his dragon nature which said, Kill and eat.

It was well past noon, the sun small and white and heatless in a colorless sky, when Brown Michael saw the dragon. He heard the whistle of its wings, as he walked southward through the dreary badlands back to Corfach Castle. Looking swiftly up, though it looked nothing like the dancing creature of glass and light he had known, he knew instantly that it was Limmifer. It came swooping down at him in the narrow crease of a rocky vale, where a few bare trees clumped beside a frozen spring; thin and sinewy, it was no more than a dozen feet long, sparkling silver flecked on horn and claw and tufted mane with bright patterns of red and blue. It circled once, and opening its mouth, screeched shrill delight. Landing on the rocks beside the spring it turned toward him, regarding him with bright diamond eyes.

It was, Michael knew, his chance. Limmifer had obviously escaped from the dungeon where he had left him locked, quite possibly with the intention of coming to look for him. Though the dragonet's trust stabbed him to his soul he knew that if he did not kill him now, another time, older and more cautious, Limmifer would not let him come near. Feeling like a murderer he loosened his big knife in its sheath, and started, cautiously, toward Limmifer, who leaped a little, and pirouetted, as he did when he was trying to get Michael to come and play.

Then on the ridge of hills above him a flash of green caught his eye, and a flicker of coppery brown. Turning in horror he saw Kyah and Tassels come running down toward them, Kyah beaming, her arms outstretched, and Tassels whistling and cooing with joy. Michael waited, knife in hand and the black grief of loss in his heart, as they came running up, Kyah stumbling a little in the snow as she threw her arms first around Michael's thigh, then around Limmifer's scaled neck.

They had followed Limmifer, he thought—or the three of them had decided to follow him. This far from the castle they must have left sometime in the night, after Anne had gone to the Barren Isle in search of the fairies. . . . He felt in his belt for a rope, to put around the dragonet's neck, wondering if Limmifer would permit him to lead him back to the castle, or if he would have to kill him there, in front of the two whom he loved. Tears half-blinding him, Michael cursed, knowing that Kyah would never understand, never forgive him for what he had to do. But he remembered the children slain by the other dragon, and the hardship and starvation that befell a countryside where a dragon hunted. The things found in the hoard had told him that the creature was a killer already.

Even at the cost of what it would do to Kyah—or what it would do to him—he could not let that happen to his people.

But as he laid his hand upon the dragonet's head the sunlight above him was blotted, and turning, he saw against the pallid sky above the hill the shadow of giant wings.

It was another dragon, a mature male, huge and skeletal, with a mane of black-tipped crimson and scales hued like ancient blood. The sun shined through the membranes of its wings to show the webs of the veins, and as it dived for him, its claws glinted like scythes. Michael whipped his sword from its sheath and in the same movement shoved Kyah toward the scant protection of the barren trees, yelling, "RUN!" as he tried to gauge which way the dragon would strike at him, with claws or fire—which way he must dodge.

But with a shrill scream Limmifer hurled himself upward at the vast diving shape, like a spitting silver arrow. Realizing that the dragonet was trying to buy them time Michael reached to catch up Kyah in his arms. . . .

The girl stepped back from him, and uttered a thin, high, fierce shriek, the first sound he had heard from her throat since he had found her in the glen. Her brown eyes huge, riveted to the two dragons wheeling above her she spread out her arms . . .

And changed.

Where Kyah had been an instant before, there was only a scorch of heat-shimmer melting the patched and dirty snow, and, springing sky-ward, a second dragonet, brown-bright as a little copper dagger, spitting hot darts of poison as she lunged to help her brother defend one they loved. A second later Tassels joined her, shedding her own camouflaging shape to take on her true body, bronze-green as their mother's had been, who had hatched the three of them in the glen.

Though the great red dragon could have cut them all from the air with a few slashes of its claws it wheeled before their onslaught, rising higher and executing a soaring turn, striking back with neither fire, nor

223

claw, nor dagger-long tooth as the three dragonets nipped and slashed at its face and wings. It withdrew before them, but as they came flying back to where Michael stood, useless sword in hand, it remained circling, far off in the colorless sky.

And Michael understood. It had come south to seek them, from the northern wastes where the dragons lived; had come, when it knew that its mate, their mother, was dead.

The three dragonets settled before Michael in the snow, copper, silver, and bronze. But all three horned heads turned toward the silently circling shape in the sky, as if, even while they fought the threat to the one they believed to be their parent, they had realized the truth. For a time Michael looked again into Kyah's deep brown eyes, and Tassels' golden amber; Limmifer's had the diamond sparkle of familiar stars. But they looked back, turning their narrow, birdlike heads on their snaky necks, again and again, at the distant shape of the scarlet dragon which seemed no bigger than an eagle, for the first time since their hatching, feeling and understanding what they were.

Then Kyah trotted forward, and bending her armored head pressed it to Michael's shoulder, the sharp horns pricking through the leather of his coat. Tassels and Limmifer came close behind, and he stroked the soft, beaded skin of their muzzles and eyes, remembering those three infants who had instinctively taken on whatever forms they could to protect themselves . . . who had believed, for one winter, that he was somehow their parent because he showed them a parent's love.

One by one they turned from him, and launched themselves into the sky. Michael watched them as they winged their way northward, to where the great dragon circled, waiting for its daughters and its son. A voice behind Michael said softly, "So that is what they were," and looking back, he saw Anne, sitting on a weary, steaming horse who still fidgeted, in spite of its tiredness, at the sight of the dragons, with Rosebud and Marcus, muddied to the eyebrows, clinging to saddlebow and crupper.

"I found fragments of eggshell at the glen," he said softly. "But of course it decays so swiftly there could easily have been three eggs. . . ."

"They are shapecrafty, like the fairies," said Anne softly, "but it seems, kinder of heart, and truer in their souls. The Prince of Air said they would remember, in time, what they were. Their father will take them away now, back to the northlands where the dragons live, and that is for the best."

Michael nodded, knowing she was right. But he was still watching as they followed the crimson dragon northward, away from the lands of men. It was the last he saw of them, or of any dragon, in his lifetime, nor did the dragons ever again return to the White Marches to plague humankind.

The Tinkling of Fairybells

Katherine Kurtz

AT FIRST SHE WAS DRAWN BY the sound of tinkling bells, so like the voices of her own kind. She had not heard such voices for a very long time, and the peal of joy from the little stone structure at the edge of the forest spoke to her of happier times, when others like herself had flourished in this Kentish countryside.

Alas, humankind no longer believed in the fairy folk—or at least, most of them did not. The Whiterobes had brought the magic of a new god to these Blessed Isles. Belief in the old magic was passing away, and disbelief could be fatal to her kind.

Still, the sound called to her most poignantly, so she came. And something besides the very sound drew her—an inkling, perhaps, that someone inside did not disbelieve, even though the magic of the place was of another kind from hers. Unseen in the brightness of the early morning sunshine—for she owned no physical body, and could only manifest as light, hardly larger than a man's hand—she peeped through a narrow lancet window in the sun-drenched wall and saw the humans at their magic: a white-robed man bowing over a table of stone where a disk and cup of gold shimmered with a light not unlike her own. A half-grown boy knelt in a pool of sunlight beside the man, and it was he who shook a handful of silver bells as the man raised the golden cup—he whose soul soared to embrace an older, wilder magic than that contained within the walls of stone.

In the boy's hands, the bells spoke a language that she almost could understand, rippling a paean of joy and the celebration of mere *being* that somehow transcended the strictures of the new ways. Tempered by the boy's exuberance, the accompanying magic was a soothing glow, despite its alien form, and she basked in the warmth that spilled past the sill of the lancet window, drawing comfort and sustenance from its energy.

After that day, she began to visit the forest chapel with some regularity—but only to watch, never to enter. The boy, she sensed, might not have minded, but the man was like most Whiterobes and, indeed, most humans, afraid of the open places and the forest fastness and the old magic that once had flourished there. The silver bells still beckoned, giving promise that their magic was offered for all the world; but a doubt remained whether she was really included in that intention, not being wholly of the world as humans understood it. Better to endure the loneliness, and survive, than to risk obliteration. Benign though this new magic might seem, she knew that other such could kill—*had* killed others of her kind, who still sang praises of the old ways, under an open sky.

The man grew older, the boy became a man and also began to wield the new magic inside the walls of stone, and another boy came to shake the silver bells. Gradually, as the older man grew more infirm, the younger man took to weaving his magic outside as well as in the chapel, often choosing a favorite spot in a forest clearing, with only the animals for his congregation. To her bewilderment, the closer observation thus permitted led past curiosity to an attachment she had never felt before. Even though he remained totally unaware of her presence, she came to think of him as *her* human. She soon learned that his name among humans was Peter, and that the local people called his kind of magic-wielder priests. Usually the new boy came to attend him, and to shake the silver bells at the high point of his magic, but one bright autumn afternoon the boy did not come.

Curious, she watched from the shelter of a hollow tree stump near where the boy usually knelt, closer than she had ever dared to come before, wondering what the priest Peter would do when it was time for the bells to ring. The forest creatures had come, as they always did, from saucy, bush-tailed squirrels and fat gray rabbits down to sleek brown mice

and velvety voles, with a variety of brightly colored birds studding the autumn-bare branches around the clearing. Today the magic had even drawn a stately stag, treading silently on the carpet of leaves to stand almost invisibly at the edge of the clearing and observe, his great, branched antlers blending with the bare tree branches.

The moment approached. Chanting in the magical tongue, a different language from the one he used when speaking with his own kind, the priest Peter slowly raised the gently glowing sun-disk of the ritual's magic. Its warmth was glorious, and filled her with such a pleasure that she wanted to sing. She had never been bold enough to reveal herself to him before, for fear of being driven from the place of magic, but as he lowered the disk and bowed before his forest altar, she dared a soft, shimmering sound, very like the bells the boy usually rang, but also akin to the wind gently rustling in the trees.

Peter's bow went a little deeper than usual, but he did not falter as he resumed his chanting and raised the golden cup as he had the sun-disk. This close, and compounded by the sun-disk glowing on the altar, the taste of his magic was so sweet that she could not contain herself. This time she made the bell-sound unmistakable, still soft enough that he *might* mistake it for imagination, but silvery and joyous. Peter's hands were shaking as he set the cup down and bowed again, and he bent his head over clasped hands for a very long time, eyes closed and lips moving silently.

Afraid she had presumed too far, she made no further sign of her presence that afternoon, letting him finish in silence and pack his magic-things away to return to the stone buildings. She could sense him mulling what he thought he had heard, seeking some rational explanation, but she did not follow. If he told the other Whiterobe about it, the old man might suspect that what had happened was not entirely of the new magic. That one's wielding of the power already was too rigid, and hurt at too close a range. That was why she had never entered the little stone chapel. The old man was always there when the magic was made, even if not wielding it himself, keeping the power concentrated, so that only where it spilled from the lancet window did she dare to taste. He would never countenance her presence, even outside the little lancet window, much less in the sacred precincts where the magic dwelt.

The old priest was there the next morning, when Peter made the magic in the chapel as he usually did. So was the boy who rang the bells. She noticed, as the bells chimed, that Peter seemed to pause and listen for just an instant, cocking his head, shaking it, and then proceeding as usual. She thought the taste of the magic spilling through the lancet window was a little sad that day, and she wondered why. When he did not come outside at all that day, she became certain that she was the cause.

But he came to the forest clearing the next day. The boy who rang the bells was conspicuously absent, but Peter had brought the bells anyway. These he carefully placed where the boy usually knelt, not far from the tree stump that had been her vantage point. As the animals gathered round, he began his magic as he always did, speaking in the magic tongue. She kept her light damped throughout, for the day was dull and shadowy; but when he lifted the sun-disk at last, she hazarded a faint, tentative, shimmering bell-sound.

His hands shook a little as he set the sun-disk down and made his bow, pointedly *not* looking in the direction of the bells, and his voice was almost inaudible as he lifted the golden cup.

The smooth, pure crescendo of the magic was almost too much to endure, cascading over the rim of the golden cup to wash down over the hands of the one who had called it. Moved by the joy that fountained up and outward, and emboldened by the steadfastness of his faith, she sang a wordless paean of joy with the voice of the bells, short but unmistakable, and oh, so sweet! He froze with face alight until she had finished, the golden cup held aloft in trembling hands, then set the cup down and bowed long before his forest altar.

She contained herself from further intrusion until he had finished, for she did not wish to disturb his magic any further, or alarm him. But when he had drained the cup and closed his book, she dared to make the tinkling sound again—a faint, sweet, joyful ringing as he bowed his head in thanksgiving. And as he looked up in wonder, she timidly extended her voice to his mind, speaking with the faint, silvery shimmer of the bells.

I give thee greeting, Priest Peter.

Peter blanched and looked around surreptitiously, stark reason temporarily supplanting emotion. He might have fantasized the sound of bells, but now a voice out of nowhere had addressed him by name. Gathering his coarse, white robe more closely around him, he peered this way and that, frowning as his eyes darted from shadow to shadow and saw nothing save the animals—who did not seem at all alarmed by anything.

"Did someone call me? Is anyone there?"

Apprehension was beginning to mask curiosity, and she muted her light in the tree stump, lest he see it and his apprehension turn to fright.

I am here. I have been with you for a very long time, though you knew it not.

He did not seem to have expected an answer. And having received one, he apparently was not quite convinced that there was no one hiding in the underbrush somewhere, trying to play a trick on him.

"You stop that, now! Johannes, is that you? Come out and show yourself, boy. I warn you, this is no time for trickery!"

She loosed a gentle peal of laughter in a ripple of bells, letting her light flare brighter in the tree stump.

It is not the boy. Please do not be angry. I mean you no harm. Your magic drew me, so I came.

"My *magic*?" he whispered, turning and then freezing, wide-eyed, as he saw the light gleaming in the tree stump. "Oh, my God, it's a demon!"

A demon? She cringed as she caught the gist if not the essence of his meaning. *Darkness? Evil?*

Briefly her light shone red and orange as she considered the notion, and she floated out of the tree stump in a glowing sphere of color. Her inadvertent drift in his direction elicited an even more agitated reaction.

"No! Stay away from me! Don't touch me!"

He had begun to tremble violently at the sight of her, easing around behind his forest altar and making vague warding-off motions with his hands. She halted uncertainly as he was brought up short against a tree trunk and covered his eyes with both hands. Since she had no true physical aspect, there was no way she could really harm him, even had she wished to do so—and to *this* human, in particular, she wished no harm.

Please don't be afraid, she pleaded. *I am not what you think. And I most assuredly am not a demon. Why, I couldn't harm you if I chose. I have only the form you see before you. I can't even touch you.*

Peter lifted one shaking hand from over his eyes and hazarded a glance. She could sense him reasoning that perhaps he was not in danger after all. His strange visitant had come no closer, and it did indeed appear to be no more substantial than a sunbeam—if somewhat oddly colored. But if not a demon, then what?

"You—you're sure you're not a demon?" he ventured.

Certainly not, she answered promptly. *Can light come of the darkness? I was drawn by your magic, which is also of the Light. See—I embrace it!*

With the swiftness of thought she was nestling in the golden cup, damping her glow to a pure, silvery ball of light that barely spilled over the brim.

Could a creature of the darkness do this?

She would not have dared it if the old Whiterobe had woven the magic here in the clearing, but the residue from *his* magic was sweet and comforting, having as much to do with Peter himself as with the actual magic he had made. Could this be what the humans called love?

Peter drew back with a gasp and made a hurried crossing motion from forehead to breast. When the light in the cup did not disappear, he made the cross sign over the cup, too. She had hoped he would not, for she still was wary of the new magic, and the power it could hold against her kind; but at his hand the sign did not burn or harm. Heartened, she let her light swell slightly higher in a pale, reassuring gold.

"Saints preserve us," he whispered under his breath, "for surely no creature of darkness could withstand that sign, or remain in the sacred chalice. But if not a demon . . ." Peter's thoughts flicked erratically down the list of other possible things his visitor might be, and came at length to the only other possible conclusion.

"You're an angel!" he exclaimed. "Yes, of course, that has to be it. You heard me praying and you came. Praised be the Lord, I am in the presence of one of His angels. Most excellent being, I welcome you!"

Resisting an urge to ripple through all the colors of the rainbow, she confined her response to a pure white flare of radiance as Peter threw himself to his knees and raised his arms in a prayer of thanksgiving. She noted that he had shifted to the magical language again, usually reserved for discourse with and about the Creator, and she was faintly amused.

You are *a creature of extremes, aren't you?* she observed, reverting to a gentle gold again as she subsided back into the cup. *First you believe me a demon, now an angel. I am neither, Peter. I am of the f—*

"No, you are an angel," Peter insisted, shaking his head stubbornly. "I know. I have read books. What else could you be but an angel?"

She had tried to tell him, but he obviously was not yet ready to know— though he had accepted her presence, which was an auspicious start.

Very well, then, I am an angel, if it pleases you, she replied lightly. *The name you call me by is not important. If you wish to believe me an angel, then that name will do as well as any other.*

"You are an angel," Peter repeated. And then his face fell. "But if you *are* an angel, why have you come? Angels bring God's tidings to mortal men, but they also visit His wrath upon transgressors." He sank back on his haunches and looked up at her apprehensively. "Have I displeased Him?"

Her colors rippled back through the blue-greens and took on a turquoise hue for just an instant. *You speak of the Creator? I do not know how you please Him, Peter. Only you and He know that. I was drawn here by your magic.*

"But I work no magic," he began indignantly.

No? she replied. *Then, what is this?* She let her light well out of the cup and spill down its sides, to pool on the golden disk as well.

If this be not magic, Peter, then why do you sound the bells?

"Why, to draw the hearts of the faithful to the miracle at hand," he replied. "That is no magic."

Is it not? she said quietly. *How, then, does it bring you such great joy, Priest Peter, that even the creatures of the forest stand in awe before it? What purpose does it serve, if not to draw you closer to the One?*

And the bells herald this One-ing. It was the bells that drew me, *first to the building of stone, where you used to ring the bells the way the boy Johannes does for you now, and then to this place. The joy was in you from the beginning, Peter—for* all *the magic of the Creator, not just this new magic. These children of the forest feel it.*

She shimmered the bells, and the woodland creatures came a little nearer, a red squirrel wriggling under one of his hands for stroking, the stag bending its head in homage.

Peter slowly got to his knees, staring first at the squirrel and the stag, then at her light. "The—*bells* are magical?" he said after a moment, still not understanding.

No, the magic simply—IS. Oh, how can I explain, how the magic fills me and calls me to lift my voice with the bells in joy? How shall I make you know it, feel it, taste it?

"Perhaps," Peter began, after a long silence, "perhaps what you speak of is the love of God for all His creatures—a love so great that He sacrificed His only Son to redeem the world."

His words of sacrifice meant little to her, who had seen so many gods come and go over the millennia, and sacrifice themselves and others for their various purposes. But perhaps love *was* the key. Certainly, no other human word came close to expressing the flavor of his magic, and what she felt increasingly for him—unless, perhaps, it was sheer joy.

I do not presume to know the source of your magic, Peter, she answered carefully. *I merely accept that it exists. What I do know is that joy and love spill from the cup when you weave your magic, and it is joy and love that resound in the voices of the bells, whether or not they are actually there. This is a truth that transcends the magic itself, whether that magic be old or new. Do you understand?*

He was staring at her—or at the cup, she could not be sure. Hope and longing were upon his face, but also bewilderment as he slowly shook his head.

"I—I'm not sure. My heart wants to believe, but reason says—"

Forget reason, she pleaded. *This is a truth that belongs to the heart, to the spirit, that one may only* know. *Open your heart, Peter. You have but to lift the cup and drink from it, to taste of the depth and height and length and breadth of a joy that extends unto eternity!*

She was not sure he understood even then, but her words obviously had struck some chord deep within him. Daring to trust, he reached out his trembling hands and took the light-brimming cup, bringing it before him to gaze in awe for a moment before bending to touch it to his lips. The light was bright and heady, like quaffing from the purest spring, and joy exploded up through the top of his head and then to the tips of his toes in a tinkling of fairybells.

It was as well the cup was empty of physical substance, that first time, for he fainted dead away. He never felt the cup slip from nerveless fingertips, as he swooned in the embrace of his angelic lover. He woke to the warmth of sunlight streaming into his eyes from between the thinning leaves above, and the gentle prodding of the stag nuzzling insistently at his cheek, and the sweet, alluring memory of a silvery voice mingled with the bells.

Ah, how thy magic is sweet, the voice whispered in his mind. *But only let me be the voice of your joy when you weave your magic—let me be your bells, and I shall stay by you unto all eternity. . . .*

He did not return to the clearing for several days; and when he did, she did not dare to show herself to him, for fear she had gone too far. To her disappointment, he did not work his magic that day, and stayed away the next; but on the day following, he appeared on schedule, as he always had, and made the magic with exquisite care. The boy was with him, so she dared not speak to him directly, but she whispered her joy with the ringing of the bells and knew that he heard. After several days of this, he finally came alone again, though still bearing the bells. She did not show herself, but she sang with abandon—and felt the soaring flutter of his own joy echoing hers at last.

After that, when he came to the forest glade to work his magic, he ceased to bring the bells or the boy who rang them. He had no need of either, for she became the voice of the bells for him, there under the open sky. At first he was careful to maintain what he deemed a suitable decorum, always conducting himself as if in the presence of the angel he supposed her to be. But in time, he came to accept her presence as companion as well as angelic helper, and often to linger, after the magic had been made.

"I think you must be my Angel of the Bells," he murmured, one balmy spring afternoon as he sat beneath a tree when they had finished. "*Angelus Tintinnabulorum meus.* Or, no. I think it must be *Angela Tintinnabulorum.*" He glanced at her sidelong, where she hovered atop a holly bush beside him. "But you wouldn't understand the subtlety of the Latin endings, would you?"

Latin endings? she replied.

Smiling, he shook his head and glanced away. "I know. It makes little sense to me, either, but—" He sighed and was silent for a long moment, then continued.

"I know I am only a foolish mortal, but I have—given this much thought," he said haltingly. "The holy writings teach us that angels have no gender, that they have no bodies. However, *if* you had a physical body, I think that you would be a beautiful lady."

She felt her colors soften to a more silvery tone, and knew that he spoke the truth.

Would that please you, if I were? she said softly.

He looked away, twisting a broken twig between his fingers and prodding at the carpet of leaves beside him.

"If you *were* a beautiful lady, my vows would forbid us all contact. And yet—"

And yet?

Smiling bitterly, he shook his head. "No matter. Perhaps it is better this way. To have an angel attend me and sing the Divine praises—"

I am not an angel, Peter.

"I have come to know that," he said miserably, not daring to look up. "But you must *be* an angel, if our love—if what we have is to continue. Father Bernard would exorcize you, if he ever found out, and I would be excommunicated."

Exorcise? Excommunicated? she repeated, not daring to mention the love he had just affirmed.

He tossed his twig aside and sighed. "No matter, my angel. We'll not give him that chance. So long as he lives—and I would not hasten his end, for he is a good man in his own way—so long as he lives, I shall continue to be the dutiful priest he would have me be, and you shall be my bells, here in the forest." He cocked his head at her. "That's why you have never sung in the chapel, isn't it? For fear of him."

Not—fear, she said after a moment. *But the new magic is strong within those walls, and his is tainted by his rigidity. Your magic transcends old and new. When he is gone, I shall sing with you even in the chapel. Until then, I shall sing with you here. And if you desire it, I shall give you to taste again of the One-ness we shared once before. I have longed to do so, but I did not wish to presume.*

"Why, 'tis no presumption," he breathed, sitting forward expectantly. "Ah, sweet angel, if you could but taste my joy to have you near."

But she *could* taste it, and he hers. As he cupped trembling hands to receive her, she came to him in a sphere of golden light. His touch was a caress as he lifted her to his lips, and the union of their spirits was the

239

sweeter for both their knowing, this time. It was a communion that would be repeated often, with joy and rejoicing, over the years that followed.

From that day forward, she was with him almost constantly, sharing in his magic, inspiring his devotions, and even, once the old priest died, venturing into the stone chapel, where she took up a vantage point in the lamp that burned above the stone altar. There she sang with the silvery bells when the magic was at its height, celebrating her love for him as well as praise for the true Maker of the magic. Gradually, Peter's chapel at the edge of the forest came to be known as a place of great holiness. The faithful came from miles around to witness the magic and hear the sweet sound of the bells, never guessing at her presence. Peter's fervor at the altar was taken as a sign of his piety; and gradually the holiness of the place began to be associated with Peter himself.

Thus did her love for him grow, and his for her. And if, sometimes, he regretted her unlikeness, if at times he lapsed into agonized wrenchings of conscience at his presumption to love an angel (or some other entity too strange and wonderful even to think about), she forgave him both extremes. After all, she reminded him, in this world he was vowed to wield the new magic. She understood that men so vowed were not for mortal women—and rejoiced daily in the happenstance that had made her neither mortal nor woman. Only one such as she might presume to share his affections with his God and still remain with him in honor.

As for Peter, he never questioned her too closely on this matter. Perhaps he feared that closer scrutiny might destroy the bond between himself and this wondrous creature he still preferred to think of as an angel— though his readings had revealed no other accounts of angels resembling his. The thought of losing her, or being made to give her up, was so repugnant as to be unthinkable, always thrust quickly from mind and banished to occasional frightening dreams that, happily, never materialized. She was his shield against the mediocrity of the world, his bulwark against pettiness and temptation, his link with the Infinite (or so he dared hope). For such a taste of joy on Earth, such a one was worth risking the loss of Heaven in the hereafter.

The years passed quickly. Peter's angelic companion did not change, but Peter added age and wrinkles and weight to his person, becoming increasingly known and honored as a most holy man. He became a friend and colleague of Augustine of Canterbury, the first Bishop to the English, and in time was entrusted by Augustine to go on a mission to Rome with another priest. None of Peter's superiors guessed that an angel was also his companion; and Peter did not tell them. He returned with a papal commendation for his zeal in assisting Augustine to establish the Faith in England; and shortly after that, he was called by Augustine to be the first abbot of the new church and monastery of Saints Peter and Paul, east of Canterbury. The Crown, too, came to know and trust Peter; so that finally, one gray autumn day, came the royal appointment: Peter would go on a mission to Gaul as royal ambassador.

But ambassadors are by no means immune to danger—even priestly ambassadors with angelic companions. On the day Peter set sail from Dover, a storm was building in the North Sea. The wind howled, and the lightning flashed, and the waves were like mountains, battering the tiny ship and engulfing it in the full fury of an early winter storm before it could reach safe harbor. The crew battled bravely, but the elements were stronger. Just off the tiny port town of Ambleteuse, a few miles north of Boulogne, the ship foundered on jagged rocks and began to break up.

The ship was sinking, and all around Peter, men were slipping into the sea to drown or be dashed to bits on the rocks. Above the howl of the storm and the crash of thunder and waves, mere human screams could not be heard, much less the frightened ringing of fairybells. What lanterns the ship had carried were among the first casualties of the storm, so that between bright-searing bolts of lightning, the only respite from the darkness was the ghostly, blue-white flicker of what the sailors called St. Elmo's fire playing on the shattered rigging.

But it was not Saint Elmo to whom Peter called, as the wind screamed in his ears and the lightning crashed around him, punctuated by the boom of the waves against the rocks.

"My angel!" he cried.

The wind ripped the words from his lips before any but she could hear, but there was nothing she could do to keep the ship from disintegrating around him. She wailed as a wave snatched him from where he clung to the stump of a mast and dumped him into the water with the rest. She followed as he went under briefly and came up sputtering, gasping for air.

But there was nothing she could do. For the first time in her very long existence she longed for a body, so that she might keep his head above the waves, might cushion him from the rocks; but his fingers slipped through her insubstantial light, closing on nothing that might save him.

I will never leave you! she cried to him. *Do not leave me! Oh, do not abandon me! Can you not hear me calling you?*

But he could not hear her by then. She was losing him. All she could do, as he and his shipmates sank beneath the waves, was to hover anxiously, her silent voice and gentle glow unable to compete with the forces of lightning, wind, and rain.

He was washed ashore with the daybreak, in a bay of the sea called Amfleat. She had stayed near him through all the lonely night, trying futilely to buoy him up, to protect his fragile human form from the waves and the rocks. She hovered close above his head as the tide left him limp on the dawn-drenched sand.

But the sea had changed him. It had taken away his identity, had robbed him of the essence that had made him unique among mortals. The once-bright eyes stared dull and sightless at the morning sun; and they did not move even when the wind blew sand and tendrils of dried sea wrack across his face.

Villagers from nearby Ambleteuse found him later that day, and dragged his sea-logged body from the waves along with others. From his white robe, they guessed him to be a priest, but from what place or of what name, they could not tell—and she dared not tell them, for fear of the magic of the Whiterobes among them. Dulled by grief, unnoticed in the brightness of the day, she could only watch from the edge of sunlight as they eased his body into one of a dozen newly dug graves, with words of a magic that was his but not *theirs*—words which the wind quickly scattered.

Dusk came, and with it solitude and a flood of bittersweet memories. In a calm, dispassionate sense, she accepted that he was dead; but any true comprehension of what that meant was outside the experience of one for whom death would never come. He had tried to explain it once—and how, when he died, he hoped to go to the Heaven promised by his magic. Such a notion had held little meaning for her then, but eventually she had come to understand it as a separation—a going where she could not follow. Now she sensed that it also was a loneliness for those left behind—a loneliness such as she had never known before, in all her wanderings upon the wide earth.

But she had no remedy for it. All she could do was to keep returning to the last place he had been: to the battered body laid in the shallow grave, even though his essence was no longer there. It was all she had of him besides her memories; and to honor those memories, and their love, she vowed to keep watch above his grave.

Nor did her devotion go unnoticed. Others watched too, and noted how a strange and ghostly light returned each night to mark the grave of the unknown priest. Did it betoken God's special favor? Who *was* the man who lay buried in the simple grave, so obviously beloved of God? Whence came he? The villagers had done their best, but perhaps the heavenly light meant that God wished a different fate for the body of His servant.

Inquiries brought word at last from England, of a holy man lost at sea as he sailed to Gaul on a mission for the King of Kent: the Abbot Peter, a trusted associate of Archbishop Augustine of Canterbury. Soon a legate came from the abbey at Canterbury to investigate—and fell to his knees in wonder at seeing the heavenly light. Hurried consultations produced almost immediate results.

Early one winter morning, Whiterobes from the village and from the cathedral at Boulogne came and, with great ceremony, unearthed the body and laid it in a burnished coffin. In the rich December sunlight, no one noticed the pale glow that took up residence in a smoking censer and accompanied the procession back to Boulogne.

She followed them into the great cathedral there, amid clouds of sweet incense and the gleam of rich beeswax candles, taking up a vantage point in the lamp above the altar, as she had in the forest chapel so many times before. Unaware of her presence, and with chants and words befitting a man of God, the Whiterobes wove magic for laying the Abbot Peter to rest. Their magic did not harm her, for the site of the cathedral was ancient, still reeking of older magic, but the flavor of the magic was bland without *his* harmony to give it texture.

So she lifted her voice with the sacred bells to sing of his remembrance—of her love for him, of her former joy and her present grief— seeing in the boy who shook the bells of this place another boy and the man he had become, mourning her beloved. The ineffable sweetness of her song brought tears to many an eye, and in years to come, several folk present on that day would remark that they seemed to recall a pale, sad angelic presence hovering over the altar at the moment of consecration. After, when the magic was finished, the Whiterobes sealed the earthly remains of the Abbot Peter beneath a slab of snow-white marble in the cathedral floor.

She thought they would never go away. When they did at last, she came down at once, letting her light wash recklessly over the tomb slab. No rational impulse drove her to search for him again—except that at the ringing of the bells, at the height of her grief and longing, she thought she had sensed just a hint of *his* presence, for the first time since that awful night on the sea. As she quested outward, not daring to hope, it surrounded her again, like the lingering musk of incense or the faint, pure reverberation of a single bell-tone floating in the stillness.

And all at once *he* was there beside her, in a flaring, strengthening point of celestial light and shimmering bells very like her own. Joyously he burst into glorious, rapturous light, shifting through all the known colors of the spectrum and then into colors that had no name for mortal eyes, the bell-like tinkling of his laughter harmonizing with hers, merging, becoming one, no longer hampered by words or any physical limitation.

For a moment they embraced in a single sphere of golden light above his tomb, too bright for mortal eyes, sparkling and glorious. Then, in an ecstatic streak of rainbow color they were lifting upward and away, together at last, passing through the colored glass of the eastern window as if it had no substance at all, soaring off toward the woodlands and forests beyond. Left behind on the altar step, the bells that had rung at the height of the magic shimmered a faint farewell, but never again would their music sound as sweetly as it had that day.

THE QUEST
OF A
SENSIBLE MAN

ANNE MCCAFFREY

ONCE UPON A TIME, LONG AGO,
when young men went on quests to prove their initiative, bravery and
common sense (for they often didn't get back home without *that*), Prince
Bieregard of Mundesland had been four weeks searching for a mare worthy of his dapple-gray stallion, Vard of direct Pegasan lineage. As companions, Bieregard had brought his roan gazehound, Fasteye, who
occupied the saddle pad behind her master while his kestrel, Mixer, circled
on his own wings in the air around flying Pegasan Vard.

Suddenly, despite a clear blue sky before them, they were buffeted by
capricious winds that heralded a powerful storm. From the air, Bieregard
could see that clumps of the ruined dwellings and barns were roofless and
long abandoned to the elements. Sensibly Bieregard directed Vard to land
at the edge of a strangely dense and silent forest which seemed the only
sort of shelter in the extensive grassy plain. Black thunderclouds, scudding
across the skies on ever fiercer gusts of winds, cut deep swathes through
the plains above which they had traveled since morning.

"Such rich grazing land could not be totally unoccupied," Bieregard
murmured as much to himself as to his companions. He looked over his
shoulder at the fast approaching storm, the wind whipping his hair in his
face and ruffling Vard's gray pinions. A jag of lightning split the sky behind them. "The storm breaks soon with lightning that near."

He reined in when Vard's strong stride brought them to the next hill-
crest and, standing in his stirrups, the Prince peered in all directions across
the wildly waving long grasses. He was long-sighted but, apart from the

disquieting forest, he could see no habitation or the rudest of shelters. Mixer's aimless circles at the greater height gave no hope that the kestrel had spotted anything serviceable.

"Well, good friends, it looks like the forest for us," Bieregard said, stroking Vard's proud-held neck, sticky with sweat from his recent exertions. "Though its aspect is scarcely welcoming." Fasteye gave a supportive growl and trotted down the hill. Bieregard whistled Mixer back to him.

He lifted Vard into a canter, heading straight across the undulating grassland to the forest verge. But as they neared the forest, Bieregard realized that Vard had shortened his stride. Fasteye was also lagging behind her traveling companion and Mixer let out a shrill sound that was warning rather than comment.

Bieregard, who had a hearty respect for the intuitions of his companions, reined in. "What is it?"

Vard danced on the spot, snorting and tossing his head, his wings half-raised. Fasteye whined and circled around the stallion while Mixer hovered at the end of his jesses. The wind pushed at all four, stiff and compelling, great drops of rain splattering down with waterfall force, a stern prelude of the torrents to come.

"Danger?" Bieregard soothed Vard's powerful neck with a gentling hand. "We have no option," he added and pressed his heels firmly into Vard's sides. "But I admit the forest is the strangest I've ever seen."

In truth, the forest was apparently limited to only two species, with neither underbrush nor saplings augmenting its growth. The larger tree, similar to one that the Prince had seen in swamplands on another journey, was most peculiarly shaped. It appeared to have two separate trunks which were connected about a meter and a half off the ground in a section parallel to the ground before the larger joined trunk, its hairy bark ranging from dull grays to ruddy browns, grew perpendicular again. It had needles on the upper branches whereas the other sort with its creamy pale bark similar to a birch sprouted variegated leaves like five-fingered gloves.

The two different trees grew, as far as the Prince could see, in pairs—though some of the pale trunks were entangled with the mangrove-type in a way that increased their grotesqueness.

For one long moment, Vard still resisted moving forward. Then suddenly, his ears pricked forward, he lifted his head and gave such a bugle as a stallion will when he senses a mare in season. Despite an onward bound willingness, Vard picked a cautious way, twisting among the entwined trees, Fasteye followed nervously, her tail clapped between her legs while Mixer shrieked a protest, digging his talons into the pad on Bieregard's shoulder. The storm broke behind them with the most convincing peal of thunder and a splintered shaft of lightning. Only the sound of Vard's hooves broke the dense silence of the forest. It was as if the storm could not enter its enchanted precinct.

"Enchanted?" Bieregard spoke aloud. Vard nickered deep in his throat, Fasteye gave a little yip and Mixer clung more tightly. "Well, we don't seem to be taking any harm from it. And we are dry. I see no path to suggest humans have come this way but this couldn't be the worst place in the world to wait out that storm. I doubt the rain can penetrate such thick cover."

Lightning bolted again, hitting the plain just outside the forest verge, a close reminder of its tremendous force. Thunder rumbled and Vard minced a careful way deeper into the protection of the forest.

"There's a terrific storm coming," Alav cried, bursting into the kitchen where his sister Sendra was kneading dough for their evening meal. "A really stupendous one!"

In emphasis, the flames on the hearth flattened and leaped high again as wind gusted down the chimney. Sendra watched to see that no cinders rolled from the grate for she had placed her father's wheeled chair close enough for him to get the warmth of the fire. His hands and feet were always so cold.

"The mares should be safe enough in the garden," Sendra said. "Of course, you didn't find anything in the harness room?"

"Not yet," Alav said with a shrug that made his sister suspect that he might not have been looking as hard as he'd promised he would.

She turned on him, holding her floury hands up. "Alav, we have *got* to find Jessedra's Amulet."

"What makes you think we can? You've been through the place," and he jerked his chin toward the thick wooden door that led into the main rooms of Castle Barnacane, "how many times now? There wasn't a day that old Bessie and Maia weren't grubbing somewhere or other. Even Ferruk hunted." He lifted his shoulders in an eloquent shrug of helplessness.

"We can't get out of here until we do find it, Alav. The mares have been barren since Barnakka died and we *must*, above all other personal considerations, keep the Barnacane line alive. Or what was the reason for all this?"

"That's usually my complaint, Sister," Alav replied impudently. Distant thunder rolled and his expression changed to anxiety. He might scoff but the mares meant as much to him as to Sendra. "Maybe we'd better get the mares in. Especially if there's lightning."

Sendra tried to keep her voice calm but she had experienced more and more attacks of sheer panic since Ferruk, the last of the faithful castle retinue, died three months ago. He had come as a stableboy in her grandfather's time. After the Forest was born, he had not tried to leave as so many of the frightened servants had. The death of the last stallion of Barnacane had broken even his stout heart and he had survived the loss only a week, visibly declining. Willing himself to die, Alav had said gloomily. Sendra dare not think how alone they truly were now, with Ferruk gone. To calm herself, she resumed kneading the bread. After all, they still had to eat. And a full stomach gladdened the heart, as old Bessie used to say.

While the last of the loyal servitors of Castle Barnacane had been alive, Sendra had known she could not get them to *try* to leave the protected zone. Even Ferruk would have balked, despite his lifelong devotion to the Mares of Barnacane. Sendra often felt that because the servants were so certain they couldn't, they wouldn't. At seventeen, she was far too young to command their obedience as her father had. *He* was now her first priority, even over the mares. Someone must be able to help the paralyzed Master of Barnacane, reduced to the use of his right hand and the few distinguishable sounds that indicated his daily needs. While Ferruk still lived, her father had been properly tended. She had managed to keep food on their table and, with Alav's eager assistance, maintain the last of the magnificent Barnacane Mares.

"I'll just make the loaves," Sendra said, "and set them to raise." She began to cut and shape the bread. "I don't know what we're going to do for flour this winter. We've been coasting on the good harvest we had two years ago."

"You see, you're going to have to let me try to leave, Sendra," and Alav raised his hands in a protective gesture. "I've taken no harm in the Forest no matter where I've gone."

"Arrggh!" The strangled cry from their father brought their attention back to him.

"Only see what you have done, Alav," Sendra cried, for their father's eyes had flared with fear and anger and the bony cramped fingers of his right hand strained in Alav's direction. Sendra went to soothe her father and Alav slumped down on a stool, sighing in despair.

"How are we ever going to know if things have changed, if . . . HE . . . is dead, if we don't go beyond the Forest and look?" Alav demanded.

"There, Father, Alav won't *leave* us," she said soothingly to the distressed Bijor. Over her shoulder she shot her brother a fierce look. "Get his potion for me. You can be so callous at times, Brother dear!"

They were both startled when the catflap on the kitchen door burst inward and two huge black and white cats came streaking in, merrowing loudly.

"What's got into them?" Alav wondered as the two made straight for Sendra.

"Oh, by all the holies, be careful, Batter, Knock. I'm pouring Father's medicine." The larger of the two cats walked up Sendra's right leg while Knock, the female, wove around the other, loudly proclaiming some urgent message. "No, no. Not now, Batter." Carefully, for Sendra was not rough with any animal, she shook her leg to dislodge Batter. He sneezed in disgust, said something to his mate, and the pair of them were off again, through the catflap.

"As if He were after them," Alav murmured, with a guilty look lest his sister or father had heard him.

"Here, Father," Sendra said, having poured the correct dosage of Bessie's herbal remedy onto the spoon. It did quiet her father when he became agitated, as he so often did, struggling against his handicap to impart something vital.

She made herself listen patiently when he tried to speak for there was always the chance that he might have remembered a clue to the whereabouts of his mother's magical Amulet. Without that, they were immured here. Ceaselessly her father had searched, pried open panels, chiseled out stones, wracking his brain, to find the elusive pendant. There was no doubt that frustration had induced his collapse five years ago.

And that was another thing Sendra must find time to do—make more of Bessie's potion for this was the last bottle and she feared for her father's health if she had none to soothe him. She had to be quite firm with him for he had closed his lips against the spoon until she pinched his nostrils shut, then dipped the dose down.

"There are times, Alav, when you are completely wanting in sense," she said as she moved Bijor's wheeled chair back from the fire and tucked his rug about him. She ignored her father's pleading eyes though she was not a heartless child. "I'll just finish this," she told Alav and gave the last loaf a thump she would have preferred to administer to him. "Otherwise we'll have no bread for supper." She dried her floury hands quickly on her apron, tore it off. "We've to see to the mares, Father," she added. On the way out the door, she grabbed a scarf to cover her neat coronet of black braids and followed her brother.

Behind them rose the massive Castle Barnacane, its great windows shuttered, its towers and spires gilded by the crepuscular light of the on-coming storm. When she and Alav had been children, old Bessie and Maia had regaled them with tales of the great days when the Masters of Barnacane had held lavish hospitality in the now dusty deserted apartments; when the guest rooms had been filled with noblemen and women from every land eager to buy the fabled Barnacane steeds.

To the west, high above the flaring umbrella top of the Forest, she could see the boiling bilious billows of storm, roiling across the sky on the back of a strong gale. No wonder the mares were calling in alarm. Alav was ahead of her, fumbling in the growing darkness with the much mended catch of the heavy wrought iron gate. The graceful metallic lace had once moved with the touch of a finger when it had opened into the formal gardens that surrounded Castle Barnacane. Now the gardens pastured the six remaining mares of the once immense herd of the Barnacane Bloods.

Rarely smaller than sixteen and two hands of a full grown adult, laid knucklewise from the ground to the top of their powerful withers, the Steeds of Barnacane had been the preferred mounts of kings, queens, princes and other heads of state. They had been fierce as war steeds—clever in the hunt, sturdy in travel and loyal to their riders beyond that of less intelligent beasts. And the Masters of Barnacane had kept faith with such loyalty and never sold one of their fine Breed to someone who would abuse their great hearts and bodies, or the advantage of their wings.

When HE had first sent minions, offering overlarge sums for all the five-year-old animals then ready for sale, the Master had sent a courteous but firm refusal for he had not liked the emissaries nor the nervy behavior and poor condition of the mounts they rode. A second deputation—with lavish personal gifts for the Master, his Mistress and his newly wed son and daughter—was given scant courtesy and sent back with a firmer negative. The clandestine purse also offered to the trainer had been returned with a more basic, and unrepeatable, instruction.

Then HE himself had come and, warned of HIS duplicity, the Master of Barnacane had met the unwanted guest at the gates of the Castle, his knights and horsemen, ostlers and students lining the great walls to reinforce their Master's wishes. When HE in his own person had been rebuffed yet again, the Master had been relieved to see HIM disappear across the plains, retreating from the then fenced land where graced the mares and young stock.

That very night there had been a great uproar, of frightened young horses, of vigilant mares, until the stallions had broken out of their boxes, freed the geldings from their stalls and gone to assist their herds, followed by armed men roused from their beds to defend their property.

By morning the Barnacane horses had all reassembled in the fields surrounding the Castle. The stallions and the geldings had been girded, their riders equipped to do battle; even the older mares past bearing had been mustered, ridden by students, ostlers and those of the land who owed service to the Master. Who, magnificently attired, astride the seventeen hand Pride of Barnacane, had gone forth to repel the impudent and imprudent tyrant who refused to accept "No."

There had been a battle, though few escaped to tell of it and HIS men would not dare mention defeat. The Horses of Barnacane were brave, fearless, indefatigable, clever but even so some lost their riders to well-placed lance, arrow and sword slash. When the Master was injured, retreat was sounded and though the Master's great stallion bore his rider swiftly back to succor at the Castle, the rest of the defenders ringed the Castle in their thousands and faced the onslaught.

Furious at this defiance, his dark horde decimated, HE called upon outrageous powers. While heavens darkened, thunder boomed and winds blew an evil stench, HE worked a mighty revenge that felled every horse and rider as a hurricane might flatten trees. Mistress Jessedra, watching from the highest tower of the Castle, countered by turning the fallen flesh of faithful man and horse into a Forest as dense as once their army had been. And impenetrable! Neither man nor horse of HIS dark horde could pass the barrier, though for some long decades an encampment had existed, sending riders on an endless quest for a way through. But that had been a long time ago now.

No sooner had Sendra and Alav slipped past the lacy gate and into the formal garden than the mares galloped past, soaring over the ha-ha, banking the big dyke and splashing in the long lake. Sendra wished that they wouldn't scare the carp which made a welcome change from poultry now that all the park deer were dead.

"They've seen enough storms not to panic like this," Alav said with some asperity. They'd be the devil and all to catch now they'd got so agitated. He handed his sister one of the lead ropes he'd wrapped around his shoulder. "Well, I'll see if I can get close to Farlandra," who was his mare. "Or if you can catch Manarda—" who was Sendra's mount "—maybe the others will follow her."

They parted company, calling into the deepening storm gloom, *"Farlandra! Manarda! Borisa! Sheela! Shanna! Lorna!"* The mares neighed, but not, Sendra thought, surprised at it, to their owners.

As Bieregard and his companions proceeded deeper into the Forest, he noticed that Fasteye began to quarter in a wider arc. On his shoulder, however, Mixer huddled closer, his feather tickling Bieregard. The Prince had to keep alert as Vard's erratic path was never two steps in the same direction, and he held his wings tight to his back to save them being snagged on branches. Encouragingly, Bieregard stroked the massive curve of neck before him, amazed when he felt Vard trembling beneath his hand. There was agitation in the short crisp steps, as if the horse would have galloped had he not been constricted by the forestation.

"Easy now, lad, this Forest does not go on forever. And we are sheltered from the storm. Not even so much as a breath of free air gets past those treetops." Bieregard was also beginning to work up a sweat under his leather riding gear.

Suddenly Fasteye gave a yip of surprise. Bieregard peered through around tree trunk and branches for a glimpse of her pale roan hide. She yipped again, her fast "see what I've got" sequence.

"We're coming, Fasteye, we're coming." Under most circumstances, hearing that summons from his hound, Bieregard would have loosed Mixer to go to her assistance, impossible in this constricted space. Mixer rustled uneasy wings, aware he could not play his usual part.

Fasteye spoke again, more conversationally this time, which surprised Bieregard since he could see nothing at all ahead or to either side of him but more interlocking trees. Vard, however, was aware of something and gave a peculiar snort.

Then, just ahead of them, completely at ease, Fasteye sat in a space between trees, her nose slanting upward, ears cocked. Abruptly Vard halted, his head up. It was only when the stallion extended his neck and put his nose up to a sturdy branch that Bieregard saw the two black and white cat faces.

"Oh, good day to you," he said, for Bieregard had too much respect for all animals to be discourteous to strangers, especially of such size.

One of the cats approached him, taking a leisurely route around the trunk from one branch to another, halting only when the branch began to sway alarmingly. It lifted its tail, its large luminous penetrating green eyes fixed on Bieregard's. Turning its head slightly to one side to address its companion, it made a quiet remark.

Fasteye spoke deep in her throat, not quite a whine, certainly nothing as definite as a bark. The cat looked down and made a second remark. Fasteye stood up and wagged her tail. Mixer gave a muffled croak while Vard whickered deep in his throat and lifted his off fore as high as he would in a formal salute before he dropped it to the ground.

"Well, do we pass inspection?" Bieregard inquired of the cats.

He was not prepared, though apparently both Mixer and Vard were, when the interrogator cat jumped lightly to the stallion's broad rump. The second cat dropped to the ground by Fasteye who delicately exchanged sniffs with it. While Fasteye would not disturb a cat in house or castle, the rules outdoors were different, and so her behavior was most exceptional. Bieregard was fascinated. Instantly Vard moved forward again, Fasteye and her unlikely companion leading the way.

The first hint that they were coming to the edge of the Forest was the swirl of wind and the spatter of rain that slanted in sideways at them. He caught sight of something high and impenetrable and then saw the faint track running diagonally to his left. Fasteye and the cat were already trotting along it. Vard lengthened his stride, his ears forward. He began the high blowing of impatience—or the awareness of shelter. The wall they reached was thick and of great age. Suddenly Vard bugled again, his speech loud and imperious.

"Great Gods, this is not the time for that sort of thing, Vard," Bieregard said, easily recognizing the full speech of an interested stallion. He held up one arm to protect his face as the full brunt of the storm lashed at them. "Let's move," he added, for lightning had illuminated a distinct path wide enough for Vard to gallop—to wherever it was the cats were leading them.

But suddenly the stallion stopped, the two cats planted in his way. Fasteye ran for cover under him and Mixer screeched just as a bolt of lightning arrowed down, crackling through a portion of the stone wall, reducing it to steaming rubble.

"Good boy!" Bieregard made much of his stallion, overwhelmed at such a miraculous escape. Two more of Vard's long strides and they'd have been fried meat.

A shrill neigh came from beyond the ruined section of the wall. To which Vard responded in an action so swift that Bieregard was unable to prevent him. Vard bounded first to his left, swung right on his hindquarters and charged at the smoking rubble.

"Noooo!" Bieregard cried but the stallion launched himself up and over the formidable barrier without so much as opening his wings to give him height or balance. On either side, Fasteye and the two cats cleared the obstacle in three great bounds.

Vard had no sooner landed in his light and graceful way than he gathered himself to jump again or crash into a solid mass. Somewhat off balance from the first unexpected leap, Bieregard lost his seat and, realizing the inevitable, tucked himself so as not to receive injury in the fall. On the other side of a substantial fallen column, Vard wheeled, whinnying a question as Bieregard struggled to a sitting position. He was covered in moss and clinging weeds.

He looked up at Vard, or rather three Vards, and shook his head to clear his vision. And exclaimed when a young girl materialized beside him.

"A stallion! Alav, a stallion has jumped the wall!" she cried at the top of a healthy pair of lungs. "Are you all right?" The girl dropped to her knees beside him, her blue eyes clouded with an anxious expression. Bieregard, who was too sensible to pursue as many pretty girls as his brothers, found much to please him in her face and willowy form. Absently she tucked back into her coronet a loop of braid that had come free. Short curls had sprung free to frame most appealingly her elegant face. "That was the most magnificent leap. Manarda and Farlandra are impressed." Then she smiled the most tremulous and hopeful of smiles. "How did you manage?"

"I didn't. It was all Vard's idea," Bieregard replied, rising energetically to his feet. He bowed slightly to the girl, a bow which also included the two mares beyond the column. They were making coy overtures to Vard who was standing stock still, his eyes rolling from one to the other. "It's all right, Vard. I can appreciate your enthusiasm and haste."

The stallion snorted, tossing his head twice in relief at his rider's reassuring words. After all, a stallion of his experience ought not lose his rider over any sort of jump. In his turn, he bowed first to one mare, Manarda and then the other, Farlandra. Through the earth under his feet, he could feel the vibration of other hoofbeats and, snorting a challenge, turned to face the newcomers. As did Bieregard.

"By all the vested holies! More mares!"

"And my brother, Alav!" cried the girl delighted as she pointed to the horse bearing a rider. "He jumped the wall, Alav! And just look at his stallion!" Then her face crumbled in dismay and she jumped onto the column. "My bread! Oh, quickly, Manarda, take me home." She was astride the larger mare and away across the neglected gardens before Bieregard could stop her.

"Come on, then, sir," the boy said, his mare halting a few paces from the Prince, "we'd best follow her before the storm returns. There's plenty of stabling to accommodate your grand fellow. Up, Batter! Knock! I'll lead you!"

Bieregard mounted quickly and followed the boy while four mares eagerly followed them.

Shelter was far enough away across the extensive gardens so that the rain soaked them before the boy rode right into a massive stone barn that once had surely housed an army of horses.

"He'll be comfortable here, sir, and there's water in the trough and enough hay in the mangers for them all. None of the mares are in season, though with such a magnificent horse as yours, I can't vouch for how long that'll last. Do you need assistance with your tack?"

To his surprise, Bieregard found the straw underfoot was deep and smelled sweet enough to please the most exacting stable manager. Vard was all too eager to be rid of his accoutrements and make better acquaintance with such unexpectedly delightful company. With a pleased squeak, Mixer made for the rafters, dislodging other denizens.

"Your kestrel's welcome to any rodents he catches," the boy said, grinning. "Batter and Knock do as well as they can so they'll be glad of a hand. Will your hound come in with you?"

"If you please. I still don't believe all this," Bieregard murmured as he hauled saddle pad and bags off the restless stallion and unbuckled the bridle.

"I'm having a little trouble with that road myself, sir," Alav said and even in the gloom of the storm-darkened barn, Bieregard could see a mischievous grin on the boy's face.

Thunder boomed and lightning flared. In its brief light, Bieregard retained a retinal image of a vast building, with blank windows, skirted by wide stone verandas, with spires and towers.

"No point in standing here when there's warmth and a hot supper waiting us in the kitchen. If you will follow me, sir?" With a grace that many of the courtiers in Bieregard's kingdom would have envied, Alav gestured for his guest to precede him so that he could secure the heavy doors of the barn.

They were both soaking as they plunged into the kitchen and indeed the aroma of hot bread and something else equally savory greeted them.

"Your tack will fit there nicely, sir." Alav gestured to pegs and racks suitable for saddles, bridles and oddments but holding few. "A towel?" and he offered one as clean and sweetly scented as any housewife would be glad to supply. "The retiring room is two steps to the right down this hall." Alav opened a thick wooden door which led into a corridor lit as far as the necessary door.

Gratefully Bieregard retired, Fasteye contentedly following, and found in the neat and spotlessly clean chamber all that he required to refresh himself. He could not resist peering down the shadowy corridor, broad enough to be a major passageway to the reception apartments of the Castle he had seen so briefly in the lightning. A gust from somewhere beyond the light skittered dust and sand onto the swept portion before the room: a gust that brought with it moldy smells of decay and neglect. Fasteye sneezed.

Opening the kitchen door, Bieregard took good note of the scene, several large hanging lamps spread a welcoming glow on a homely room. The kitchen was long and wide, a table which probably had dominated

its center was now pushed against the inner wall and served several functions. The end nearest him was used as a desk for there were books, one an immense red leather tome opened and its page covered by a neat hand: a deer horn embellished with fine metalwork held pens and another was closed against its ink drying. A basket of darning, a jumble of linen spoke of distaff employments. The center of the table bore oddments of leather straps and such gear while at the hearth end, three places had been set. In the inglenook, where a low lamp sputtered, Bieregard could just make out in the shadows what looked to be an occupied bed.

Then the girl, who had been stirring whatever succulent stew the kettle contained, turned and alerted her brother to him.

"Be welcome to Castle Barnacane, or rather the kitchen of it, sir . . ." the girl said, with a wry grin.

"Bieregard of Mundesland."

She made a graceful curtsy and her brother bowed slightly. "I am Sendra, daughter of Bijor and Belisa, and this is my brother, Alav . . ." She was about to add more but the boy was too impatient with formalities.

"Your stallion, Sir Bieregard, what line of Barnacane is he descended from?" He strode to the desk end of the table and began to riffle the pages of the big tome. "I have memorized every major lineage . . ."

"By Fastor whose sire was Wheelock whose sire was Benefan whose sire was Genthor, then Pelmet, Lassiot . . ."

"Lassiot!" The boy leaped on the name and flipped back the pages so carelessly that his sister cautioned him. "Ah, here! Why, Lassiot was sold by my great-grandfather, Busseler, to . . . the King of Mundesland!" Alav's eyes were great with excitement.

"I am his great-grandson, young Alav," and Bieregard bowed.

"The line prospered?"

"Indeed it has as you can see by Vard!"

"But neither of you shall prosper," Sendra said tartly, "if you do not stop talking bloodlines and come eat your supper. Simple fare, Prince Bieregard . . ."

"My hunger is sauce enough to make it a veritable feast, my lady."

Sendra gave an amused snort at the title, hefting the soup kettle off its hook and bringing it to the table. "Come then and feast."

Bieregard signaled Fasteye to settle herself on a stable rug by the door and grinned at Alav who was bursting to ask more questions. As Bieregard sat in the seat Alav indicated, he was aware that there was indeed someone lying well wrapped in blankets in the inglenook.

"Our father," Sendra said with great dignity, noticing his glance, "sleeps. It would be unkind to wake him even to give him the welcome news that a man—and a mighty stallion—have reached us through the Forest."

"You did come *through* the Forest?" Alav was strangely jubilant.

"We certainly didn't fly in this storm," Bieregard replied.

"First things first, Alav. You've already established the line as Lassiot's," Sendra said, with a wry grin for her brother's enthusiasm. "He does indeed know the Studbook of Barnacane by heart."

"The Barnacane Blood is still well regarded?" Alav asked eagerly.

Bieregard nodded, his mouth full of the tasty bread with a crust as crunchy as he liked it. "Indeed, zealously guarded by those lucky enough to own a full-blooded animal. It is indeed why I am so far from Mundesland."

"You came to find Barnacane?" Alav's eyes widened in awe and surprise.

"Not actually," Bieregard felt uncomfortable. "To be candid, I knew of its horses but not that there still existed . . ." He hesitated, not quite knowing how to proceed without giving offense.

"The Forest?" Sendra asked, sensing his quandary.

He nodded. "My father sent me to find new mares, to improve our stables. I hardly dreamed I would find . . ."

"Us!" Alav finished for him. "But somehow you did. Maybe we won't need that thrice condemned Amulet after all."

"Alav!"

With a snort of disgust, Alav took command. "And have you never heard of the Battle of Barnacane? The Forest which defied the Black Horde of . . ."

"Don't speak HIS name . . ." Sendra cried in real alarm, shaking her brother fiercely by the shoulder and glancing apprehensively at the sleeping figure. "He might hear."

"Have you heard nothing about the Forest of Barnacane?" Alav asked, incredulous.

"I know the name only as a Bloodline of horses superior to all others ever bred in any of the many lands in the world."

"Well, then, I had better tell the tale," Alav said, pushing off his sister's hands. "I won't name *HIM*, Sendra, but not even the greatest sorcerer can escape death! Correct?"

Bieregard emphatically seconded the statement. He was as glad to let the boy talk for he was very hungry and the stew, made of ingredients which he could not quite place, was by far the best he had tasted on this journey and far exceeded the travel fare in his pack. By the time Bieregard had finished his third bowl (after he made certain there was plenty for all), Alav completed the unusual and thrilling tale. The Prince experienced some regret that sorcerers and wizards did not abound in his time. The unexpected always livened things up.

"Then why was I able to penetrate the Forest?" Bieregard asked, reaching for yet another slice of Sendra's bread.

"That is perplexing," Alav admitted. "Because we haven't found the Amulet."

"We also don't know if HE is still alive," Sendra added. Bieregard saw the lift to her chin and the proud light in her lovely blue eyes and decided her caution was a needed contrast to her brother's recklessness. She was really quite lovely, as well as considerate, thoughtful and a very good cook.

"Write me his name, then, and I will know if I have heard it spoken. Offhand, I know of no sorcerers living who could summon the awesome powers you speak of."

Alav leaned toward Bieregard and, with a quick glance at the corner, inscribed three letters with his index finger.

"No, never heard the name," Bieregard said with surety. "Not even a song, and we have minstrels and troubadours from every part of the world. Your horses are known. And men have stolen ransoms to buy a Barnacane Mare but him I've never heard of."

"You're absolutely positive?" Sendra asked in a small uncertain voice.

Bieregard smiled at her, reaching across the table to squeeze her hand in assurance. The skin was rougher than the hands of maidens introduced to him by friend and father but he liked the strength and usefulness of hers.

"Then we could leave?" Alav asked.

Sendra shot a glance at the inglenook. "How can we convince our father?"

"I'm here, am I not? Is that insufficient proof?" Bieregard spread his arms wide, smiling at them.

Sendra smiled back at him, shrugging her shoulders. "Indeed, it is proof of one kind."

"You riddle me, Lady Sendra?"

She gave a patient sigh. "Until today, Prince Bieregard, the Forest has prevented anyone from entering. It has also prevented us from leaving its protection. And that I know. And you do, too, don't you, Alav?"

The boy dropped, head lowered and shoulders defeated by her question. "I can only get so far . . ." He sighed in despair. "A circle only. I cannot penetrate the Forest." He jabbed a fist against an impenetrable barrier.

There was a clatter at the far end of the room, startling Fasteye from her doze. Two black and white bodies made for the hearth, shaking heavy drops of water from their fur that made the fire spit and hiss.

"Batter! Knock! You'll soak us," Sendra said reprovingly, but she caught up a cloth and, kneeling, rubbed both cats somewhat dry. "You'll be hungry, too, won't you?" To which the cats replied. "And your gaze-hound, Prince Bieregard?" Without waiting for an answer, she took down three plates and ladled stew into them.

Bieregard thanked her and called Fasteye to eat.

"A grand hound, sir," the boy said, rousing from his depression.

"A breed as clever, faithful, and long-lived as Vard and my kestrel, Mixer. I think the storm has eased," and he turned to Alav, "I'd like to check Vard."

Alav jumped to his feet. "And I the mares. They were careering around and I want to be certain they haven't done themselves any mischief."

"They have mischief among them already," Sendra said, surprising Bieregard with her dry humor.

"Which reminds me to ask, what lines have they, young Alav?"

When the boy would have rattled them off, Sendra stopped him. "Recite those while you're checking the mares, Alav! They like to hear."

"This is an amazing tome," Bieregard said, reverently examining the Barnacane Studbook in careful hands when they returned.

"It holds the lineage of the original unadulterated Line of Pegasan winged horses, sir," Alav said proudly. The same pride touched Sendra's lovely face as she brought a table lamp to illuminate the desk end of the table. "Of course, the Stud Master then was very careful which mares he chose for Pegasus."

"The care was eminently successful for the Line," Bieregard murmured but he was suddenly more struck by the Studbook. "What workmanship!" He ran experienced fingers down the heavy leather covers and their delicate gold embellishments. A magnificent jeweled clasp secured the heavy vellum pages, its tongue fitting neatly into the carved gold lock. Four jeweled bars ornamented the spine, the gemstones of an ancient cut, their facets no longer as sharply edged with their long usage.

"See, here is the founder of his Line." Alav was more eager to display the contents of the Book and turned to the picture on the first page of the book. "It is a bit faded now," he added ruefully, "but you can almost hear him bugle, can't you, Bieregard?" Amid the informal tasks of checking legs, picking out hooves, and bedding tired horses, titles had been dropped.

Bieregard's silent admiration was not feigned for the depicted animal was truly magnificent. Pegasus had been painted in a rearing position, his feather pinions extended up and back, the tip slightly flared for balance. Such magnificent quarters, the breadth of his barrel was immense, and the bone of him truly amazing. In conformation, the foundation stallion could not be faulted. Even his Vard, adjudged by so many to be the finest example of his type today, fell short of this classic specimen.

"Of course, he is the founder," Bieregard remarked with apologies to Vard.

"Your stallion is a better example of the breed than our last, old Bar-nakka," Alav said, generously.

Bieregard ran reverent fingers down the painting and shook his head. "Not such as he, not such as he!" He closed the book then, fitting tongue into clasp, admiring the craftsmanship once more. "If I passed the Forest warders, may I not pass out with you tomorrow?"

"We can try!" Alav said stoutly.

"Yes, we can," though Sendra sounded very doubtful.

"Well, we *can* try," Bieregard said, and gave her arm a little encour-aging shake.

She took a deep breath then, answering his smile, and Bieregard found that he liked her resilient spirit.

"And we won't tell Father until we've succeeded," Alav added with a warning frown at his sister.

She glanced over at her sleeping parent who was still oblivious to the arrival of the Prince and stallion. If he woke to a complete solution of their problem, would not his health improve tremendously?

* * *

Morning dawned as bright and clear as the day after a fierce storm often does. Bieregard woke, Fasteye's wet nose pushing under one hand to rouse him. A moment later there was a light rap on the door panel.

"Come!"

Alav appeared with a cup of a steaming beverage, his manner so bright and alert that Bieregard knew that excitement had had the boy up very early that morning.

"I've fed them." Then he giggled in a manner more consonant with his actual age. "Vard's laid down the law, even with Manarda."

Bieregard grinned back, taking a sip of the hot brew. He didn't know what it was but it certainly charged him with energy.

"Sendra has breakfast ready, but Father's still asleep." There was a worried frown on Alav's face as he closed the door behind him.

Bieregard dressed quickly, glad of the last clean shirt in his travel pack, paused briefly at the retiring room and then proceeded to the kitchen where, once again, tempting odors promised a hearty meal.

"Alav was all for dashing out at first light," Sendra said, a tolerant smile of her face. "You needed rest after such a long and arduous journey and the horses have to have time to digest their corn."

"You still have corn to give them?" Bieregard was surprised.

"We have managed very nicely, thank you," Sendra replied, a touch of endearing hauteur in her manner for the first time.

"My pardon, my lady," Bieregard said with a flourish and a bow.

"Oh, stop that, Bieregard. My present rank is cook and your eggs are ready."

She served them deftly, added goldenly fried potatoes and made sure bread, butter and jam were near his hand. She was becomingly dressed for riding today, Bieregard noted, remembering the brief glimpse of slender tanned legs as she had swung up on her mare the previous evening.

Nor would she let Alav rush their guest though the boy was flipping the lock of the Studbook in and out with impatience.

"That was excellent," Bieregard said, rising and bowing to her. Then he picked up his plate, utensils and mug and deposited all in the sink as if he had done such menial tasks all his life.

"Thank you, Prince Bieregard," she said with a bob and droll smile. Then she went to the side of the bed, touching the hand Bieregard could now see lying on the top of the quilt. For a long moment, she bent over the sleeping form before turning away, shaking her head slightly, a sad expression on her face. "He sleeps still. I cannot have given him too much potion for there isn't that much to give."

"He often sleeps a whole day, Sendra," her brother said. "And what news will we have to give him when we return!" He was on his feet now, and bouncing to the door.

"Batter, Knock, you stay here, and one of you come get me if Father wakes!"

With vocal remarks as disgusted as the expressions on the two black and white faces, the cats stalked back and forth in front of the hearth. They were still complaining when the three young people closed the kitchen door behind them.

Vard gave a loud welcome when he heard Bieregard's footsteps on the flagging, and other whickers were heard. Fasteye appeared from some independent quest in the garden, her tail wagging, her roan hair wet to the belly with morning dew.

As the three threw wide the barn doors, the horses were lined up. Bieregard whistled Mixer awake and the kestrel chirped his readiness. It took only moments to tack the three horses. But Alav put head collars on the other four mares.

"When one goes, they all do," he explained to Bieregard. "See how Manarda submits to Vard, and she's lead mare."

"I never thought she'd do that," Sendra remarked, a trifle put out. "She had little use for Barnakka."

"Well, he was no use to her after she foaled Sheela," Alav replied and urged Farlandra out of the barn. "Let's go!"

He led the troop out of the flagged stableyard, then through a ragged arch of privet where once a proper decorative gate had stood, down a bank well traveled by horses, across a sward, red and blue bright with the blooms of little wildflowers, through another hedge onto a bareswept paved expanse which Bieregard identified as the broad apron setting off the facade of Castle Barnacane. The early sun touched its stonework gold and glinted off what glass remained in the wide long windows. Sendra and Alav were oblivious to the scene but Bieregard felt a stab of regret for the once great house in such decay.

Farlandra flowed in one long jump down the three broad stairs, and cantered to the next set. Vard's ears pricked and he followed fluidly as Manarda did, stately mare though she was. There were seven such flights, and it was almost an exercise in equitation, Bieregard thought, for the younger mare led while Vard and Manarda moved side by side, pace by pace, as one, Sendra's stirrup to his. Bieregard smiled at her and saw the mischief in hers.

If the lightning flash had impressed Bieregard the night before with the immensity of the Castle, today's clarity showed off its magnificent gardens, totally enclosed by the thick high walls. He saw orchards, the lower walls of kitchen gardens, even a large field—probably once a sport ground—with early oats well sprouted. How diligent the young people had been! He admired them the more.

Then suddenly, past an unusually tall straggle of deep green hedge, they came upon the gigantic gates. To Bieregard it appeared ridiculous that the great bars had not been run across. Until he remembered the Forest.

It took the three of them, and a rope to Vard's saddle ring, to pull one of the great gates open, and that with metallic protests that sent Mixer wheeling upward. Catching his breath, Bieregard watched the kestrel circle. Nothing impeded or alarmed the bird.

Setting the gate ajar was about the only progress they made. They went along the track, circumnavigating the grounds, but they could go only so far into the Forest before the press of trunks made it impossible for them to proceed farther. Even afoot.

"I don't understand it. I made it through," Bieregard said when they had returned to the lightning blasted wall the second time. "I came upon the track not far from here."

"The cats led you?" Sendra asked.

"They did but I was well into the Forest when they accosted me." He grinned so she wouldn't take offense at his wording.

"They aren't the least bit magical," Sendra said. "My grandmother Jessedra wasn't fond of cats and they weren't allowed into the house. Their mother used to mouse in Barnakka's stable and then . . . well, I brought them in when she disappeared."

"That means we have to find the Amulet or we'll never get out!" cried Alav in a fit of aggravated despair.

"You have tried flying out?" Bieregard asked.

"Try it," Alav suggested, making a flourish with one hand. "You've enough of a take-off space up the main drive."

Bieregard glanced skyward where Mixer had been observing their efforts, turning lazy circles in the clear morning sky.

"We will," he said, determinedly and began to turn Vard on his fore. Sendra's hand caught him and he saw the anxiety in her face. "Oh, I'll have a care, my lady," he said and, lifting her hand to his lips, kissed it.

As Vard retraced his steps to the main gate at a canter, Bieregard could not forget the sensation of his lips on her hand and the way her fingers had tightened on his. Fool to be so warm to a maiden who's known only her father, her brother and some ancient groom.

By the time he had wheeled Vard at the second shallow stairs, the mares, ridden and free, had set themselves on either side of the gates.

"Up we go now, Vard," he said and sitting deep into the saddle, he raised his right arm high upward and pressed both legs, heels well behind the girth against the stallion's sides.

Vard needed only that command to leap forward, wings unfurling, their forward edge parallel to the ground, the tips angled out until he had achieved sufficient ground speed. From the top of the last flight of stairs, Vard launched himself from powerful hindquarters, lifting his wings in a high arc over the Prince, and swept them powerfully down. Up, up, over the astonished faces, equine and human, and over the thick wall. Just as Farlandra called a loud warning, Vard floundered in the air, his head pushed back to his chest from impact with an impenetrable barrier. He reared, and Bieregard felt, rather than heard, his hooves strike something hard. Vard fell away to the left, only his extreme agility preventing them from a disastrous tumble. Feathers fell in a soft cascade from his right wing as he dropped, and he beat fiercely with his left wing to right himself.

They landed hard and ungracefully just outside the wall, Vard losing more feathers and hairs from his tail on the branches in their ungainly descent.

"Oh, are you all right?" Sendra was there first, her mare whinnying in fright as she skidded to a stop, blowing anxiously at Vard who stood with head down, right wing flopping to the ground, the left in only slightly better shape. With one hand, Sendra clung to Bieregard's knee, with the other she soothed the heaving stallion, sparing more murmurs for the injured horse than for his rider. Except that he was equally worried, Bieregard would have been jealous of Vard.

"No, no, it can be only strain and lost feathers. Vard was quick to recover from whatever it was we bashed into." Bieregard was shocked at the anger he felt for that unseen force. He glanced up accusingly at Mixer who ought to have warned them but the kestrel was far across the Forest now, unaware of the accident. Why the bird and not the stallion?

"What was it you hit, Bieregard?" Alav inquired, jumping down from Farlandra to join the Prince in inspecting Vard's injuries. The other mares nickered consolation from a discreet distance, sharing the general concern.

"Nothing that I could *see*." Bieregard set his jaw grimly.

"Did it feel like . . . like a sheet of very heavy glass?" Alav asked and Bieregard knew that Alav wanted confirmation of his own experiences.

"That is how I would describe it. Vard came against a barrier, and he certainly struck hooves off something very solid! I could feel it."

Alav nodded slowly, his eyes filming with despair. Head and shoulders drooped again and he half-turned, stayed by Bieregard's hand on his shoulder.

"You tried?" he asked. And when Alav nodded again, not daring to look at his sister who gasped at his daring, "With the mares?"

"And once on old Barnakka when he could still fly."

"We won't tell Father that," Sendra said emphatically, and pointed to the cat loping down the track to them, her summons becoming more audible. "And we must tend Vard. I hope he hasn't lost too many flight feathers."

"Does it matter?" Alav asked, sunk in despair. "I was so sure that Bieregard and Vard, not being of the Castle, could get through!"

"So was I!"

Bieregard barely heard her dejected whisper.

So they mentioned only Bieregard's attempt when Master Bijor, comfortably propped in his wheeled chair, was informed of the recent developments. Sendra thought her father looked very well this morning, with more color in his cheeks and certainly a fierce sparkle in his eyes when she introduced their visitor and told him of Vard. There had been fear in Bijor's eyes and his mouth had dropped open when Bieregard took up the tale of his attempted flight. When the whole tale had been told, Bijor fixed his rheumy faded eyes on Bieregard's face, a stare that fortunately did not discomfit the Prince since he was accustomed to the trenchant glares of his regal father. Then, with a great sigh, Bijor raised his right hand and, managing at great effort to point with his index finger, he indicated the ground.

"Staaaaay!" The word was unmistakable but not an acceptable command to Bieregard or to Bijor's son.

"Sir, I hear you," Bieregard replied, rising and bowing with formal courtesy to the ailing man. His inner thoughts were scarcely compliant and he walked quickly out into the bright noonday weather.

"Bieregard," Alav called, racing after him. "You can't mean to obey."

Impatiently, Bieregard flicked his hand up. "I said I heard, I didn't say anything about obeying." He swung around, looking at the immense ruin on every side. "I can't stay here! I will be . . . where's Mixer?" He scanned the skies, shielding his eyes from the high sun, then whistled long and repeatedly until he saw the faint blob in the sky that was the returning kestrel.

"He went! He got through!" cried Alav.

"And he can carry a message for us. Your mares alone are worth an expedition, Alav," Bieregard cried. "We'll be out of here yet, my young friend."

They curbed their excitement as they made for the writing implements and did not disturb Sendra, who was feeding her father.

It was a matter of deft fingers and fine thread from the workbasket to attach the message to Mixer's leg. He was accustomed to this usage and when Bieregard caught his head and stroked his crest, telling him to seek Dracklin, at Mundesland, the kestrel blinked twice. When Bieregard launched him, he immediately took off to the west.

"How long?" Alav inquired, clearly eager for instant results.

"We came on a meandering way," Bieregard replied, doing rapid sums in his head, "but with good thermals and fair weather, Mixer should be home no later than tomorrow sunset."

"And return?"

Bieregard did other sums. "A week, ten days. My message made it urgent!"

"Ten days?" Alav was aghast.

"During which time we will all search for the Amulet," Sendra said, coming upon them in the courtyard. "HE once massed his hordes against the Forest and failed. How could any force, no matter how friendly, prevail when the spell holds?"

"You have a point," Bieregard admitted candidly though Alav swung away, muttering expletives and childish denials. "But first, there are many tasks that must be done to keep us fed and sheltered here. Command me, my lady Sendra!"

She gave him a wide-eyed look of dismay. "Command *you* to weed the vegetables, or wash the clothes, or peel potatoes?"

He bowed with a great flourish of a nonexistent hat. "Even feed the chickens and pigs, if you have them. And I must wash a shirt or two." He couldn't help but laugh thinking what his chamber groom might say if he knew the Prince had washed his own laundry. He reached out and hauled Alav to his side. "Command us both, my lady!" And he jerked Alav into executing a bow.

With three sets of willing hands, it did not take them long to accomplish the necessary tasks, though Bieregard's hands had to be scrubbed of potato patch dirt when he checked on Vard before his noonday bread and cheese. The stallion was certainly comfortable in the dark quiet stable, nestled in an immense bed of straw with plenty to support the injured wing he extended to ease its strain. The mares went in and out as they chose, but mainly they chose to remain close to Vard, a choice which made Bieregard grin.

"Tell me," Bieregard said, stretching his long legs under the kitchen table. He cast a judicious eye at Master Bijor dozing again in his chair. "Tell me, exactly what does this Amulet look like?"

Sendra looked at him, stunned. Alav looked at her and then at Bieregard and then they exchanged bemused glances.

"You know, I don't believe I know exactly what it looks like," Alav said. "Except it would be on a chain, and . . . old."

Bieregard turned to Sendra. "Have you ever seen it?"

She blinked and then gave a weak laugh. "No. But Bessie and Maia had. And Ferruk, too. They were young servants when Jessedra was queen."

"They knew what they were looking for but you never have? Did you think it would leap up when you got close and say 'you're warm, you're warm'?"

Alav snorted but Sendra looked offended and instantly Bieregard was repentant. It also gave him a good excuse to touch her.

"I had no right to say that, Sendra. Forgive me?"

"I think you had every right to say that, Prince," she replied so he knew she hadn't quite forgiven him, "but I do know how we can remedy that oversight." She rose, checking for the tinder pouch on her belt and reaching for the clean lantern on the mantelpiece. "Come!"

She led them past the retiring room and through a heavy door with creaking hinges, through a wide and shuttered gallery, and finally into the great reception hall at the front of the Castle. Bats stirred on the rafters and great festoons of cobwebs stirred at their passing. Fasteye, at Bieregard's heels, growled in her throat. She didn't like spiders, having been bitten as a young dog by a particularly virulent one.

Sendra led them up a grand staircase and down a shallow flight of steps into another gallery. They passed this and into what must have been one of the wings of the Castle but the darkness made it hard to keep one's bearings. Then Sendra was feeling along the wall for something, found it, and depressed a handle, pushing hard against the door.

"King Rattaclan's state apartments. There is a portrait of my grandmother," Sendra explained and Bieregard courteously took the lantern from her hand to let it shine from a higher point in his.

"That is, if it hasn't been eaten. Over the fireplace . . . there!"

A huge, full-length portrait there was, in a frame which retained some of its gilding, but the face was lost in the upper shadows. By rearranging tables and a chair, Bieregard managed to light the upper portion of Jessedra's portrait.

"She looks like you," Alav said, awed.

"Nonsense," Sendra replied, her voice tart. "The Queen was rated one of the most beautiful women of her day."

"You look like her," Bieregard said calmly, "and she is wearing a pendant." He peered closely at it. "Either I've seen one just like it . . . No, how could I? Here, Sendra, I'll give you a hand up." Which he had planned to do anyway, since he would have to put his arm around her to steady her on the chair, wouldn't he? And her face was close to his as she peered earnestly at the pendant and frowned.

"I have, too," she said, turning to face him, her breath sweet, her face smudged with dust just like the portrait's. "I can't imagine where," she added with asperity at the elusiveness of the memory.

The chair creaked and the table wobbled and they got down hurriedly.

"Bother, I'll risk it," Alav said and taking the lantern, popped up on table and chair to get his own look. "It is familiar, all right, but how many times did Bessie, Maia, Ferruk—and who knows how many others— look for it in here."

"It's strange though, that I have any recollection of it," Bieregard remarked, cudgeling his brain to respond.

"All we know," Sendra said in the patient tone of someone who has endlessly repeated the words, "is that Lady Jessedra put it in—and I quote—'the very safest place in all Castle Barnacane' immediately after she made the Forest."

"And Father said, over and over again," and Alav rolled his eyes expressively, "that she had not retrieved it before her death because HIS men were still searching for a way in."

Fasteye sneezed, Bieregard sneezed and then Sendra.

"Let's get out of here," Alav suggested just before he sneezed.

"We also tried the stables, the harness, the pulls of chandeliers. Father dismantled half the panels in these rooms and the treasury was gone through item by item, and every coffer tested for hidden drawers," Sendra reported as they retraced their steps.

"In the statuary in her favorite garden," Alav took up the recital, "the carp ponds, the fountains, the decorative friezes around the Castle, the columns, the hedges, even in the rose bed and among the bulbs."

"Grandmother was never seen in the back gardens, but Father said the gardeners also turned the soil there, too. The wine cellars, the dungeons—not that they were ever used much," Sendra added. "The hems of the brocaded curtains, the sofas, the pillows—for a while you couldn't go anywhere upstairs for the eider blowing every which way—every gown she ever wore."

They were out in the sunny courtyard, sitting on the well, tired and somewhat discouraged.

"At least we know what it looks like now," Bieregard said, wishing to raise spirits.

It was as well that there were daily chores to be done, and the horses to be tended. Bieregard really enjoyed Alav's company for the youth was keen to learn of the world outside the Forest, and Bieregard was tactful not to appear too eager for Sendra's presence as he informed the eager boy. Bieregard had even managed to exchange greetings with Bijor who seemed much more alert, a fact Bieregard ascribed more to the presence of his stallion than himself. Bijor had conveyed the urgent need to see this paragon and Alav had wheeled his father to the barn. Vard was now standing, though his right wing still drooped. Bijor had tried to get across some message but not even Sendra could translate the gargled sounds. Bijor had slept all afternoon from the effort.

They were admirably supplied in foods, though Bieregard had yearnings for red meat by the seventh day. King Rattaclan's gardeners had been clever. The gardens were fruitful and the remaining glasshouse supplied unseasonal fruits and vegetables. Sendra served marvelous meals improved with unusual sauces and savories, light cakes and breads. To honor their guest, Alav ventured into the wine cellar and brought out filthy bottles from which superb vintages poured, making gay their evening hours. And somewhat softening the fact that they could not find the Amulet.

By the eighth day, Alav could not contain his impatience and he patrolled the walls, coming always back to the gate, peering through the trees as if he could will Bieregard's relief to come.

"He's impossible!" Sendra said that evening, thoroughly annoyed by her brother's behavior.

"He's young. He sees release charging across the fields with banners and he wants with all his heart to go beyond Castle Barnacane and see The World!" He wrote a capital T and W in the air.

Sendra sighed and flicked at an imaginary thread on her sleeve. "And if they don't come?"

Bieregard tilted her chin up with a gentle finger and smiled down at her, a lump in his throat for her mute despair. "They will. I sent for them. We are a loyal family, we Mundes!"

She did not resist his touch. Her lips were very close and he was just bending his head to kiss her when an unholy scream came from the barn. Out charged Manarda, Vard only a stride behind her. To be sure, his right wing was not completely furled but with the view Bieregard had of her raised tail, that was not going to interfere with Vard's intent.

"Oh! Manarda!" Sendra cried, jumping to her feet. "Of them all! Why, the hussy!"

Bieregard was choking on his laughter. "Isn't she lead mare?"

"She's also the oldest!" Then Sendra's expression altered from indignation to query. "What exactly *is* a hussy, Bieregard?"

"You have led a sheltered life here, Sendra," Bieregard said and drew her into his arms. He kissed her and neither of them heard the stallion's triumphant call as he attended to his lady.

Sometime later when Vard and Manarda could be seen grazing placidly side by side, Bieregard and Sendra returned to the house for something cool to drink. As they entered the kitchen, Sendra saw the open Studbook and blushed furiously.

"You will have to give Alav the particulars of Vard's breeding again, so he can make the proper entry."

"If we can ever get him back from his sentry-go," Bieregard remarked and went to pick up a pen. "I can do it as easily . . ." She caught his hand, a startled expression in her eyes. "I presume too much," he added, deferring to her unspoken objection.

"It is always for the Master of Barnacane to keep the Studbook," she said solemnly. "It is their responsibility from the moment they become the Master. Alav assumed the duty when my father no longer could. I admit that we shouldn't keep the Book out on the table but there's only been us and it's never out of sight here."

"Of course," Bieregard said, deferentially closing the ornate latch and pushing it tight. Frowning, he picked it up again, running his fingers along the decorations.

Suddenly Batter exploded from sleep, spitting, all hair instantly bristling on backbone and tail. Knock came awake in the same condition and both cats, exclaiming loudly, sped through the open door and across the courtyard.

"What can have got into them?" Sendra cried, rushing to the door. "Oh, Bieregard, they're headed for the break in the wall! And Bieregard, there's a hawk in the sky! No, two!"

He grabbed her hand and they raced to the barn, caught up a mare apiece, vaulted astride and were able to overtake the cats before they had quite reached the break.

"Look!" Bieregard's long sight caught the flash of metal and the color of banners. Then he pointed to the sky. "And it's Mixer with my father's Arrow!"

"They can't be coming through the Forest!" cried Sendra.

"They're coming! They're coming!" Alav on Farlandra came charging down the outside path, arms waving so excitedly that his mare had her wings half extended. "Banners and people and horses and hawks and dogs! And Batter and Knock have gone to greet them!"

Alav turned Farlandra and set her down the path after the cats. The mare stopped, head down. She backed carefully.

"The barrier?" Sendra asked in what was nearly a wail.

Alav turned and the answer was clearly written on his face.

"I'll be right back," Bieregard said, touching her shoulder compassionately. "Wait here!"

"Where else could I go?" And Sendra's plaintive question followed him all the way to the kitchen until he picked up the Studbook. "I think I'm right!" He vaulted again to Sheela's back and recklessly set her retracing her steps to the barrier.

The visitors were visibly approaching, two black and white cats leaping and diving in their van.

"Don't mention the Forest to them," Bieregard said urgently to Alav. "Just lead them to the gates."

"What are you doing with the Studbook?" Alav demanded.

"I'll tell you at the gates. Come, Sendra, we must bring your father. Do you have a cart of any kind one of the mares would pull?"

"We do, but why are you clutching the Studbook?" she asked even as she wheeled Borisa and cantered beside him.

"What is the very safest place in Castle Barnacane, Sendra?" He tilted the book at her to show her the ornate clasp. "But that doesn't make any difference now."

"I don't understand."

"I'm not exactly sure I do, only I think I do," he said enigmatically as they clattered back into the courtyard. "Where's the cart? I'll get it while you bring your father out. It will do him good to see this, I think."

"It's a carriage, and in that shed, the harness with it. Sheela will pull it."

He had the willing mare harnessed and between the shafts of the dusty carriage by the time Sendra had wheeled her father out, well-rugged against the spring weather.

"With your permission, sir," Bieregard said and while he didn't wait for it, he was careful how he transferred the frail old body to the seat. He put the Studbook carefully on his lap, then gestured for Sendra to ride beside him as they proceeded down the winding carriageway to the gates.

They could hear the excited babble of men, the jingle of spur and bridle as they drew up in front of the gate. Then Alav appeared, Farlandra sidling underneath him from excitement for most of the horses were stallions and she was likely to follow her dam into season at any moment. Alav danced her right up to the carriage, his eyes wide as he saw his father in the equipage. Mixer whistled and landed on Bieregard's shoulder while Arrow circled above, also giving glad cries. Fasteye sat in the shade, panting from having followed her master on these mad chasings.

The first of the guests turned into the gate.

"Father!" Bieregard cried, standing up and waving. "Mickor!" his older brother rode to his father's right; "Davildon!" his younger brother to the left. Behind he could see the faces of many of the young noblemen of his father's court. "I didn't think you would all come!"

Bieregard felt intense gratification at such an array as the travelers filed in and halted in two lines on either side of the gates. The baggage master discreetly directed his men and animals to one side and toward the distant Castle. Then all attention was directed up the main aisle as Vard led Manarda, Shanna, and Lorna to come to a halt behind the carriage.

"Here, my lord Father," Bieregard said, "is Master Bijor, his daughter, Sendra and his son, Alav. And the six Mares of Barnacane."

"The Master of Barnacane? By all the great holies, sir, this is an unexpected honor when the name has been but legend for decades!" Plumed hat in hand, Dracklin made an elaborate bow, only then realizing that the Master could not respond. With smooth tact, he inclined his head to the two scions of the Castle. Courtesies observed, King Dracklin turned his attention to the reasons his son had sent for him. His smile was broad enough to dispel any doubt Bieregard might harbor at the wisdom of his summons. "Superb animals. Superb! Never have I seen mares with more bone and spirit, with such well-feathered pinions! Incredible! Your quest has been highly successful, Son."

"They are all of Pegasan lineage, my lord King!" Alav cried proudly and caused Farlandra to rear and extend her wings in full display.

"Your indulgence, Father, Alav," Bieregard said. "Brother," he went on, pointing to Davildon who was more apt to take orders from him than Mickor, "humor me in this but retrace your steps through the Forest a ways!"

"It's been a long journey, Bieregard, and at speed," Davildon said but even as he spoke he was maneuvering his great brown stallion, Bast. Davildon had to bend the horse to get past the initial trees but when he had gone some ten meters in, he turned again, "Far enough?" And returned. "And why?"

"Alav!" Bieregard directed the young Prince to imitate Davildon. He was aware that Sendra was staring at him, her eyes wide with fear and bewilderment. She held up one hand to restrain Alav, sent a frantic glance at her father whose eyes blazed in his pain-lined face, caught Bieregard's reassuring expression and, trusting him, allowed her resistance to abate. "Go, Alav!"

His face set despite the doubts Bieregard knew he must have, Alav set Farlandra at the Forest and once again met the impassable barrier. He yanked the mare around on her hindquarters and in two strides was at the carriage, his eyes blazing.

"What is this, Bieregard? That strangers pass through the Forest and we—" his thumb stabbed his chest "—of Barnacane cannot!"

"They do not know that the Forest is impenetrable," Bieregard replied gently. "Nor do the cats, nor Mixer here. My father, my brothers and their men have also never heard of the Forest of Barnacane so it has no power over their minds. But the remedy is nigh. Take the Studbook from your father's lap. Look, really look at the clasp. *See* the design and remember Jessedra's portrait."

Alav turned the Studbook over in his hands, cradling it against his waist and fingering the decorations he had known since a child. Then he let out a bark of laughter. "Of course, the very safest place in Barnacane would be the Studbook, always in sight, the most treasured possession we have. But how?" Alav stared down at his father. "How could he not *know*?"

"Perhaps he really didn't wish to," Bieregard replied with a rueful smile of apology to the startled Sendra. "Now, end Jessedra's spell, Alav."

"Tell me how!" Alav demanded.

"Say HIS name! Tell the Forest that HE is dead! Hold up the Book, and the Amulet, and tell the Forest that HE is dead! His horde is dead! His memory is dead." Bieregard jumped down from the carriage seat and vaulted to Vard's bare back. "Sendra! You, too!" He urged Vard forward, one booted foot touching Sendra's, his other Alav's. "Speak his name, Alav, Sendra, and end the enchantment of the Forest."

Unable to resist Bieregard's exhortation and certainly wanting very much to believe his theory, Alav held the Studbook up before him, high over his mare's neck and kneed her forward, his young face resolute. Sendra, with a single appealing glance at Bieregard, signaled Borisa to move as Alav filled his lungs to shout.

"Fir is dead! His horde is dead! Their memory is dead! Castle Barnacane is safe! The mares are safe! Fir is dead!" Farlandra hesitated for a fraction of a moment at the point where she had just encountered painful resistance.

"Fir is dead!" Sendra's voice rang out. Brother and sister gave voice in unison as first Farlandra, then Borisa and Vard passed into the Forest proper. "His horde is dead! Their memory is dead!" And Bieregard added his strong baritone to their chorus. "Fir is dead! His horde is dead! Their memory is dead!"

A great groan, like an immense wind playing over a thousand faulty flutes, swept across the Forest. Farlandra jumped aside as a tree, one of the cream barks, slowly fell down . . . as did every tree in the Forest. The groan became a sigh as the entire Forest collapsed and, touching the ground, instantly dissolved into dust, a dust blown away by a gentle wind which rose from the freed meadows of Barnacane.

Alav let out a yell, an ululation of sheer joy and release. Farlandra reared, her wings sweeping the dust up into the breeze, blowing it away. She executed an incredible pirouette on her hind legs before she vaulted forward chasing the poufs of dust that had once been a dedicated Forest.

Bieregard was extraordinarily relieved that his theory worked but it had seemed only sensible. He moved Vard closer to Borisa and saw that Sendra had tears in her eyes. He gripped her shoulder firmly, as sympathetic to her reaction to the end of their incarceration as to her brother's.

When the general jubilation abated sufficiently, King Dracklin reined his great stallion up to the carriage to congratulate the Master on his happy release. Immediately he shouted for Sendra and Alav.

"Your father, too, has passed away," he said and, leaning forward, closed the Master's sightless eyes. "Let us hope that he saw the Forest's end and knew you safe at long last."

With tears streaking down his cheeks, the new Master of Barnacane shook his head sadly. "He was always afraid the end of the Forest would be the death of him. I don't think he could have faced an open world. But it means life for me and my sister, and our mares." Alav straightened his shoulders, a brave smile lifting the corners of his sorrowful young face. "For all this is a momentous day, my lord King, and we are certainly much obligated to you for your assistance, Barnacane cannot display the hospitality your rank and courtesies deserve."

"What? With all these gracious parks in which to make our camp?" And Dracklin gestured expansively across the wild miles of garden and grassy lawn. "We shall do well enough indeed, young Master."

"There are plenty of vegetables in the garden," Bieregard said with a sly glance at Sendra, wishing also to ease her grieving.

Sendra lifted her chin. "Send your cooks to me, my lord King, and you shall eat well of Barnacane's humble bounty."

"We've some absolutely superb wines to wet your travel-dusty throats," Alav added, cheering up.

"Then by all means, let us proceed!" King Dracklin grinned broadly in anticipation for he was partial to a good vintage. He gestured for one of his aides to take up the reins of the carriage and for his noblemen to follow in respectful cortege. The carriageway was wide enough for the King, Master, Lady Sendra, and the three Princes to ride abreast behind Bijor's equipage.

"Indeed let us proceed," Mickor said under his breath, shifting in a saddle he longed to be out of after hard riding. "And do me a favor, Master Alav, though we've barely met, of keeping my brother here. For it is plain you two . . . you three," and he inclined himself courteously to Sendra, "are of a mind concerning horses. I hear enough about them from my lord Father."

Bieregard shot his brother a grateful look for trying to put Alav at ease.

"As to that, Bieregard," Alav said with expected poise, "you cannot have all the Barnacane Mares when you marry my sister."

"My quest was for one mare comparable to my Vard," Bieregard replied. "And her mistress only if she is willing."

"Manarda's two daughters are also part of my dower," Sendra said with equal aplomb, though her cheeks were flushed as she proudly rode Borisa beside Mickor's unwinged chestnut gelding.

"And I will ask my father's leave to guard that dower here," Bieregard replied, as unwilling as she to leave Alav with the staggering task of rebuilding Castle and Stud. He admired and liked the lad, and not just for this day's testing either. "The third son of any king must make his own way in life." Bieregard gave his sire a quick, hopeful glance.

"A very good thought, my Son," King Dracklin said, eyeing Bieregard with a mock stern look. He turned to Alav, as one seasoned ruler to another, "If she's willing, and I see by her blush that she is, there's plenty of room," and he swept his arms in both directions, "for several great houses now the Forest's gone. You could do worse, young Master Alav, for he's an accomplished rider and stallion man." The King cleared his throat hastily. "Yes, and Bieregard doesn't want for sense, you know. That's a good quality in a man these days!"

And so it was and so will it ever be!

PORTRAIT
OF A HERO

LAWRENCE WATT-EVANS

THE DRAGON ATOP THE MOUN-
tain loomed over the village like a tombstone over a grave, and Wuller
looked up at it in awe.

"Do you think it'll come any closer?" he whispered to his aunt.

Illuré shook her head.

"There's no telling, with dragons," she said. "Particularly not the really big ones. One that size must be as experienced and cunning as any
human that ever lived."

Something was odd about her voice. Wuller glanced at her face, which
was set in a rigid calm, and realized that his Aunt Illuré, who had faced
down a runaway boar with nothing but a turnspit, was terrified.

Even as he looked, her calm broke; her eyes went wide, her mouth
started to open.

Wuller whirled back in time to see the dragon rising from its perch,
its immense wings spread wide to catch the wind. It rose, wheeled about
once, and then swept down toward the village, claws outstretched, like a
hawk diving on its prey.

For a moment Wuller thought it was diving directly at *him*, and he
covered his face with his hands, as if he were still a child.

Then he remembered how high that mountaintop was, and his mind
adjusted the scale of what he had just seen—the dragon was larger and
farther away than he had assumed. Ashamed of his terror, he dropped his
hands and looked up again.

The dragon was hovering over the village, directly over his own head.

Wuller felt a tugging at one arm, and realized that Illuré was trying to pull him out from under the great beast.

He yielded, and a moment later the creature settled to the ground in the village common, the wind from its wings stirring up a cloud of gray dust and flattening the thin grass. The scent of its hot, sulfurous breath filled the town.

A swirl of dust reached Wuller, and he sneezed.

The dragon's long neck dipped down, and its monstrous head swung around to look Wuller directly in the eye from a mere six or seven feet away.

He stared back, frozen with fear.

Then the head swung away again, the neck lifted it up, and the mighty jaws opened.

The dragon spoke.

"Who speaks for this village?" it said, in a voice like an avalanche.

"It talks!" someone said, in tones of awe and wonder.

The dragon's head swept down to confront the speaker, and it spoke again.

"Yes, I talk," it rumbled. "Do you?"

Wuller looked to see who it was addressing, and saw a young man in blue—his cousin Pergren, just a few years older than himself, who had only recently started his own flock.

Pergren stammered, unable to answer coherently, and the dragon's jaws crept nearer and nearer to him. Wuller saw that they were beginning to open—not to speak, this time, but to bite.

Then a man stepped forward—Adar, the village smith, Wuller's father's cousin.

"I'll speak for the village, dragon," he called. "Leave that boy alone and say what you want of us."

Wuller had always admired Adar's strength and skill; now he found himself admiring the smith's courage, as well.

The dragon reared up slightly, and Wuller thought it looked rather

292

amused. "Well!" it said. "One among you with manners enough to speak when spoken to—though hardly in a civil tone!"

"Get on with it," Adar said.

"All right, if you're as impatient as all that," the dragon said. "I had intended to make a few polite introductions before getting down to business, but have it your way. I have chosen this village as my home. I have chosen you people as my servants. And I have come down here today to set the terms of your service. Is that clear and direct enough to suit you, man?"

Wuller tried to judge the dragon's tone, to judge whether it was speaking sarcastically, but the voice was simply too different from human for him to tell.

"We are not servants," Adar announced. "We are free people."

"Not anymore," the dragon said.

Wuller shuddered again at the memory of Adar's death, then turned his attention back to the meeting that huddled about the single lantern in his father's house.

"We can't go on like this," his father was saying. "At a sheep a day, even allowing for a better lambing season next spring than the one we just had, we'll have nothing left at all after three years, not even a breeding pair to start anew!"

"What would you have us do, then?" old Kirna snapped at him. "You heard what it said after it ate Adar. One sheep a day, or one person, and it doesn't care which!"

"We need to kill it," Wuller's father said.

"Go right ahead, Wulran," someone called from the darkness. "We won't mind a bit if you kill it!"

"I can't kill it, any more than you can," Wuller's father retorted. "But surely *somone* must be able to! Centuries ago, during the war, dragons were used in battle by both sides, and both sides killed great numbers of them. It can be done, and I'm sure the knowledge isn't lost . . ."

"*I'm* not sure of that!" Kirna interrupted.

"All right, then," Wulran shouted. "Maybe it *is* lost! But look at us here! The whole lot of us packed together in the dark because we don't dare light a proper council fire, for fear of that beast! Our livestock are taken one by one, day after day, and when the sheep run out it will start on *us*—it's said as much! Already we're left with no smith but a half-trained apprentice boy, because of that thing that lurks on the mountain. We're dying slowly, the whole lot of us—would it be that much worse to risk dying quickly?"

An embarrassed silence was the only reply.

"All right, Wulran," someone muttered at last. "What do you want us to *do*?"

Wuller looked at his father expectantly, and was disappointed to see the slumped shoulders and hear the admission, "I don't know."

"Maybe if we *all* attacked it . . ." Wuller suggested.

"Attacked it with *what*?" Pergren demanded. "Our bare hands?"

Wuller almost shouted back, "Yes," but he caught himself at the last moment and stayed silent.

"Is there any magic we could use?" little Salla, who was barely old enough to attend the meeting, asked hesitantly. "In the stories, the heroes who go to fight dragons always have magic swords, or enchanted armor."

"We have no magic swords," Illuré said.

"Wait a minute," Alasha the Fair said. "We don't have a sword, but we have magic, of a sort." Wuller could not be certain in the darkness, but thought she was looking at her sister Kirna as she spoke.

"Oh, now, wait a minute . . ." Kirna began.

"What's she talking about, Kirna?" Pergren demanded.

"Kirna?" Illuré asked, puzzled.

Kirna glanced at the faces that were visible in the lantern's glow, and at the dozens beyond, and gave in.

"All right," she said. "But it won't do any good. I'm not even sure it still works."

"Not sure *what* still works?" someone asked.

"The oracle," Kirna replied.

"*What* oracle?" another demanded, exasperated.

"I'll show you," she answered, rising. "It's at my house; I'll go fetch it."

"No," Wulran said, with authority. "We'll come with you. All of us. We'll move the meeting there."

Kirna started to protest, then glanced about and thought better of it.

"All right," she said.

The thing gleamed in the lanternlight, and Wuller stared, fascinated. He had never seen anything magical before.

The oracle was a block of polished white stone—or polished *something*, anyway; it wasn't any stone that Wuller was familiar with. A shallow dish of the smoothest, finest glass he had ever seen was set into the top of the stone, glass with only a faint tinge of green to it and without a single bubble or flaw.

Kirna handled it with extreme delicacy, holding it only by the sides of the block and placing it gently on the table.

"It's been in my family since the Great War," she said quietly. "One of my ancestors took it from the tent of a northern sorcerer when the Northern Empire fell and the victorious Ethsharites swept through these lands, driving the enemy before them."

"What is it?" someone whispered.

"It's an oracle," Kirna said. "A sorcerer's oracle."

"Do we need a sorcerer to work it, then?"

"No," Kirna said, staring at the glass dish and gently brushing her fingers down one side of the block. "My mother taught me how."

She stopped and looked up.

"And it's very old, and very delicate, and very precious, and we don't know how many more questions it can answer, if it can still answer any at all, so don't get your hopes up! We've been saving it for more than a hundred years!"

"Keeping it for yourselves, you mean!"

"And why not?" Alasha demanded, coming to her sister's defense. "It was our family's legacy, not the village's! We've brought it out now, when it's needed, haven't we?"

Nobody argued with that.

"Go on, Kirna," Wulran said quietly. "Ask it."

"Ask it what, exactly?" she replied.

"Ask it who will save us from the dragon," Pergren said. "None of us know how to kill it; ask it who can rid us of it."

Kirna looked around and saw several people nod. "All right," she said. She turned to the oracle, placed her hands firmly on either side of the block, and stared intently down into the glass dish.

Wuller was close enough to look over her left shoulder, while Illuré looked over her right, and Alasha and Wulran faced them on the other side of the oracle. All five watched the gleaming disk, while the rest of the crowd stood back, clearly more than a little nervous before this strange device. Wuller's mother Mereth, in particular, was pressed back against the wall of the room, busily fiddling with the fancywork on her blouse to work off her nervousness.

"*Pau'ron,*" Kirna said. "*Yz'raksis nyuyz'r, lai brinan allasis!*"

The glass dish suddenly began to glow with a pale, eerie light. Wuller heard someone gasp.

"It's ready," Kirna said, looking up.

"Ask it," Wulran told her.

Kirna looked about, shifted her knees to a more comfortable position, then stared into the dish again.

"We are beset by a dragon," she said loudly. "Who can rid us of it?"

Wuller held his breath and stared as faint bluish shapes appeared in the dish, shifting shapes like clouds on a windy day, or the smoke from a blown-out candle. Some of them seemed to form runes, but these broke apart before he could read them.

"I can't make it out," Kirna shouted. "Show us more clearly!"

The shapes suddenly coalesced into a single image, a pale oval set with two eyes and a mouth. Details emerged, until a face looked up out of the dish at them, the face of a young woman, not much older than Wuller himself, a delicate face surrounded by billows of soft brown hair. Her eyes were a rich green, as green as the moss that grew on the mountainside.

Wuller thought he had never seen anyone so beautiful.

Then the image vanished, the glow vanished, and the glass dish shattered into a dozen jagged fragments.

Kirna let out a long wail of grief at the oracle's destruction, while Illuré called, "Find me paper! I must draw the face before I forget it!"

Wuller stared at the portrait. Illuré had come very close, he thought, but she had not quite captured the true beauty of the face he had seen in the glass.

"Who is she?" Pergren asked. "It's no one in the village, certainly, nor anyone I ever saw before."

"Whoever she is, how can *she* possibly kill a hundred-foot dragon?" Pergren's brother Gennar demanded.

"Maybe she's a magician," Pergren suggested.

"There must be more powerful magicians in the World than her, though," Gennar objected. "If it just takes magic, why didn't the oracle say so? Why not show us some famous powerful wizard?"

"Maybe she *won't* kill it," Alasha said. "Kirna asked who could *rid* us of the dragon, not who could *slay* it."

Gennar snorted. "You think she'll *talk* it into going away?"

"Maybe," Alasha said. "Or maybe there's another way."

Pergren and Gennar turned to stare at her. Wuller was still looking at the picture.

Illuré certainly had a talent for drawing, he thought; the charcoal really looked like shadows and soft hair.

"What do you mean?" Pergren asked Alasha.

"I mean, that in some of the old stories, there are tales of sacrifices to dragons, where when a beautiful virgin willingly gave herself to the monster the beast was overcome by her purity, and either died or fled after devouring her."

Pergren glanced at the picture. "You think that's what she's to do, then? Sacrifice herself to the dragon?"

Gennar snorted. "That's silly," he said.

"No, it's magic," Alasha retorted.

"Why don't you sacrifice *yourself*, then, if you think it'll work?" Gennar demanded.

"I said a *virgin*," Alasha pointed out.

"She said beautiful, too," Pergren said, grinning. Alasha tossed a pebble at him.

"We have a couple of virgins here," Gennar said. "At least, I *think* we do."

"Virgins or not," Pergren said, "the oracle said that *she* would rid us of the dragon." He pointed to the picture Wuller held.

"No," said Alasha. "It said she *could* rid us of the dragon, not *would*."

That sobered all of them.

"So how do we find her?" Pergren asked. "Do we just sit here and wait for her to walk into the village, while that monster eats a sheep a day?"

"I'll go look for her," Wuller said.

The other three turned to him, startled.

"You?" Gennar asked.

"Why not?" Wuller replied. "I'm small enough to slip away without the dragon noticing me, and I'm not doing anything important around here anyway."

"How do you expect to find her, though?" Pergren asked. "It's a big world out there."

Wuller shrugged. "I don't know, for sure," he admitted. "But if we had that oracle here, then surely there will be ways to find her in the cities of the south."

Gennar squinted at him. "Are you sure you aren't just planning to slip away and forget all about us, once you're safely away?"

Wuller didn't bother to answer that; he just swung for Gennar's nose. Gennar ducked aside, and Wuller's fist grazed his cheek harmlessly.

"All right, all right!" Gennar said, raising his hands. "I apologize!"

Wuller glared at him for a moment, then turned back to the portrait.

"I think Wuller's right," Pergren said. "*Somebody* has to go find her, and I've heard enough tales about the wizards of Ethshar to think that he's right, finding a magician is the way to do it."

"Why him, though?" Gennar demanded.

"Because he volunteered first," Pergren said. "Besides, he's right, he *is* small and sneaky. Remember when he stole your laces, and hid in that bush, and you walked right past him, looking for him, half a dozen times?"

Gennar conceded the point with a wave of his hand.

"It's not up to us, though," he said. "It's up to the elders. You think old Wulran's going to let his only son go off by himself?"

Alasha whispered, looking at Wuller, "He just might."

In fact, Wulran was not enthusiastic about the idea when it was brought up at the meeting that night, and started to object.

His wife leaned over and whispered in his ear, cutting him off short.

He stopped, startled, and listened to her; then he looked at Wuller's face and read the solid determination there.

He shut his mouth and sat, silent and unhappy, as the others thrashed the matter out, and the next morning he embraced Wuller, then watched as the boy vanished among the trees.

It was really much easier than Wuller had expected; the dragon never gave any sign of noticing his departure at all. He just walked away, not even hiding—though he did stay under the trees, hidden from the sky.

At first, he simply walked, marking a tree branch with his knife every few yards and heading southwest—south, because that was where all the cities were, and west to get down out of the mountains. He didn't worry about a particular destination, or what he was going to do for food, water, or shelter. He knew that the supplies he carried with him would only last for two or three days, and that it would probably take much longer than that to find a magician, but he just couldn't bring himself to think about that in his excitement over actually leaving the village and the dragon behind.

He took the charcoal sketch out of his pack, unrolled it, and studied it as he ambled onward beneath the pines.

Whoever the girl was, she was certainly beautiful, he thought. He wondered how long it would take him to find her.

He never doubted that he would find her eventually; after all, he had the portrait, and magic was said to be capable of almost anything. If one ancient sorcerous device could provide her image, surely modern wizardry, or some other sort of magic, would be able to locate her!

An hour or so from home he stopped for a rest, sitting down on the thick carpet of pine needles between two big roots and leaning back against the trunk of the tree he had just marked.

He had worked up an appetite already, but he resisted the temptation to eat anything. He hadn't brought that much food, and would need to conserve it.

Of course, he would get some of his food from the countryside, or at least that was what he had planned. Perhaps he could find something right here where he sat.

Glancing around he saw a small patch of mushrooms, and he leaned over for a closer look—he knew most of the local varieties, and some of them were quite tasty, even raw.

This variety he recognized immediately, and he shuddered and didn't touch them. They might be tasty, but nobody had ever lived long enough to say after eating them. Illuré had told him that this particular sort, with the thin white stem and the little cup at the bottom, held the most powerful poison known to humanity.

He decided he wasn't quite so hungry after all, and instead he took a drink from his water flask; surely, finding drinking water would be easy enough! If he kept on heading downhill, sooner or later he would find a stream.

Far more important than food or water, he thought, was deciding where to go. He had talked about going all the way to Ethshar, but that was hundreds of miles away; no one from the village had *ever* been to Ethshar. Surely he wouldn't really need to go that far!

He looked about, considering.

His home, he knew, was in the region of Srigmor, which had once been claimed by the Baronies of Sardiron. The claim had been abandoned long ago; the North Mines weren't worth the trouble of working, when the mines of Tazmor and Aldagmor were so much richer and more accessible, and Srigmor had nothing else that a baron would consider worth the trouble of surviving a winter there.

Sardiron was still there to the south, though.

To the west lay unnamed, uninhabited forests; he did not want to go there. True, beyond them lay the seacoast, and there might be people there, but it would be a long, hard, dangerous journey, and he knew nothing about what he might find there.

To the southwest the forests were said to end after about three days' travel, opening out onto the Plain of Aala. If Srigmor were part of any nation now, it was part of Aala.

He had never heard of any magicians living in Aala, though. He tended to associate magicians with cities and castles, not with farms and villages, and Aala had no cities or castles.

The Baronies of Sardiron it would be, then.

His grandfather had visited Sardiron once, had made the long trip to the council city itself, Sardiron of the Waters. If his grandfather could do it, so could he.

He stood up, brushed off pine needles, and marched onward, now heading almost directly south.

Streams were harder to find than he had thought, and not all were as clean as he liked; after the first day he made it a point to fill his flask at every opportunity, and to drink enough at each clear stream to leave himself feeling uncomfortably bloated.

His food ran out at breakfast on the third day, and he discovered edible mushrooms weren't as common as he had expected—though the poisonous ones seemed plentiful enough—and that rabbits and squirrels and chipmunks were harder to catch than he had realized. Skinning and cooking them was also far more work than he had expected it to be; the hunters and cooks at home had made it look so easy!

He almost broke his belt knife when it slipped while he was holding a dead squirrel on a large rock as he tried to gut it; he felt the shock in his wrist as the blade slipped and then snagged hard on a seam in the rock, and he held his breath, afraid that he had snapped off the tip.

He hadn't, but from then on he was more careful. The knife was an absolutely essential item now. He wished he had had the sense to borrow another to have a spare.

He had made good time the first two days, but after that much of his effort went to hunting, cooking, eating, and finding someplace safe to sleep. He dropped from seven or eight leagues a day to about four.

He had expected to find villages, where he could ask for food and shelter. He didn't. He knew that there were villages within three or four leagues of his own, and assumed there were more scattered all through Srigmor, but somehow he never managed to come across any. He saw distant smoke several times, but never managed to find its source.

By the third night he was very tired indeed of sleeping on dead leaves or pine needles, wrapped in his one thin blanket. Even in the mild weather of late spring the nights could be chilly—so chilly that only utter exhaustion let him sleep.

Late on the afternoon of the fourth day, though, his luck finally changed. He saw a break in the forest cover ahead and turned toward it, since such openings were often made by fallen trees that rotted out and became home to various edible creatures.

This opening, however, was not made by just *one* fallen tree. Rather, an entire line had been cleared away, and the surface below was completely free of debris. It was a long ribbon of hard-packed dirt edged by grass, with two shallow ruts running parallel for its entire length, and Wuller realized with a start that he was looking at a highway.

His spirits soared; checking his bearings from the sun, he set out southward on the road, certain that he would find other people to talk to within minutes. In his eager confidence, he did not worry about finding supper.

The minutes passed, and added up into hours, as the sun vanished below the trees to his right, while he encountered no one at all.

At last, long after dark, he gave up. He found himself a clear spot by the roadside where he unpacked his blanket and curled up in it, still hungry.

Despite his hunger, he slept.

He was awakened by laughter. He sat up, startled and groggy, and looked about.

An ox-drawn wagon was passing him by. A man and a woman sat on its front bench, leaning against each other as the woman giggled.

"I like that, Okko!" she said. "Know any more?"

"Sure," the man replied. "Ever hear the one about the witch, the wainwright, and the Tazmorite? It seems that the three of them were on a raft floating down the river when the raft started to sink . . ."

Wuller shook his head to get the bits of grass and leaves out of his hair, stood up, and called out, *"Hai!* Over here!"

The man stopped his story and turned to see who had called, but did not stop his pair of oxen. The woman bent quickly down behind the bench, as if looking for something.

"Wait a minute!" Wuller called.

The man snorted. "Not likely!" he said. The wagon trundled on, heading north.

With a quick glance at his unpacked belongings and another down the highway to the south, Wuller ran after the wagon, easily catching up to it.

The driver still refused to stop, and the woman had sat up again, holding a cocked crossbow across her lap.

"Look," Wuller said as he walked alongside, "I'm lost and hungry and I need help. My village is being held hostage by a dragon, and I . . ."

"Don't tell me your troubles, boy," the driver said. "I've got my own problems."

"But couldn't you help me? I need to find a magician, so I can find this girl . . ." He realized he had left the sketch with his pack, back where he had slept. "If you could give me a ride to Sardiron . . ."

The driver snorted again. "Sardiron! Boy, take a look which way we're going! We're heading for Srigmor to trade with the natives, we aren't going back to Sardiron. And I'm no magician, and I don't know anything about any magicians. We can't help you, boy; sorry."

"But I just came down from Srigmor, and I don't know my way . . ."

The driver turned and stared at Wuller for a moment. The oxen plodded on.

"You just came from Srigmor?" he asked.

"Yes, I did, and . . ."

"There's a dragon there? Where? Which village?"

A sudden rush of hope made Wuller's feet light as he paced alongside. "It doesn't really have a name—it's not on the highway . . ."

"Oh!" the man said, clearly relieved. "One of the back country villages, up in the hills?"

"I guess so," Wuller admitted.

"Then it won't bother *me*," the driver said. "Sorry, it's not my problem. You go on south and find your magician." He turned his eyes back to the road, and said to the woman, "As I was saying, the raft starts to sink, and they're too far from shore to swim. So the witch goes into a trance and works a spell to keep it afloat, and the wainwright gets out his tools and starts trying to patch the leaks and caulk it all up, but the Tazmorite just sits there . . ."

Wuller stopped, and watched in dismay as the wagon rolled on northward.

He had not expected a reaction like that.

On the rare occasions when an outsider happened into his native village, he or she was invariably made to feel welcome, given the best food, drink, and shelter that the village could offer. He had expected to receive the same treatment in the outside world.

It appeared that he had misjudged.

Or perhaps, he told himself, that rather hostile pair was a fluke, an aberration. Surely, most people would be more generous!

He turned and headed back down the road, collected his belongings, and marched on southward toward Sardiron, certain that the pair in the wagon could not be typical.

The pair in the wagon had not been typical; most people either wouldn't talk to him at all, or shouted at him to go away.

It didn't help any that all the traffic he encountered was northbound.

By midafternoon he had met half a dozen such rejections, and gone a full day without food. He was debating with himself whether he should leave the road to hunt something when he glimpsed a building ahead, standing at the roadside.

He quickened his pace a little.

A moment later he spotted a second building, and a third—an entire village!

Fifteen minutes later he stood on the cobblestones of the village square, looking about in fascination.

Roads led off to north, south, and east; he had come in from the north, and to the south lay Sardiron of the Waters, but where did the eastern road go? The mountains lay to the east, and while they did not look as tall here as they did back home, surely that was just a matter of distance. Why would anyone want to go into the mountains?

The square itself amazed him. He had never seen cobblestones before; the only pavement back home was the slate floor of the smithy. Here, a broad circle, perhaps a hundred feet across, was completely cobbled. He marvelled at the work that must have gone into the job.

At the center of the circle was a fountain, and he marvelled at that, too. He wondered how they made the water spray up like that; was it magic? If it was magic, would it be safe to drink?

Houses and shops surrounded the square, and those, while less marvelous, were strange; they were built of wood, of course, but the end of each beam was carved into fantastic shapes, like flowers or ferns or faces. He recognized the smithy readily enough by its open walls and glowing forge, and the bakery was distinguished by the enticing aroma and the broad window display of breads and cakes, but some of the other shops puzzled him. The largest of all, adjoining a shed or barn of some sort, bore a signboard with no runes on it at all, but simply a picture of a lone pine tree surrounded by flames.

Curious, he took a few steps toward this peculiar establishment.

An unfamiliar animal thrust its head over the top of a pen in the adjoining shed, and suddenly something clicked into place in Wuller's mind.

That was a horse, he realized. The shed was a stable. And the building, surely, must be an inn!

He had never seen a horse, a stable, or an inn before, but he had no doubt of his guess. An inn would give him food and a place to sleep; he marched directly toward the door.

The proprietor of the Burning Pine blinked at the sight of the peasant lad. The boy looked perhaps fifteen, and most northern peasants kept their sons at home until they were eighteen; if one was out on the road at a younger age it usually meant a runaway or an orphan.

Neither runaways nor orphans had much money, as a rule. "What do *you* want?" the innkeeper demanded.

Startled, Wuller turned and saw a plump old man in an apron. "Ah . . . dinner, to start with," he said.

"You have the money to pay for it?"

Wuller had never used money in his life; his village made out quite well with barter, when communal sharing didn't suffice. All the same, his Uncle Regran had insisted that he bring along what few coins the village had.

Wuller dug them out and displayed them—a piece and three bits, in iron.

The proprietor snorted. "Damn peasants! Look, that'll buy you a heel of bread and let you sleep in the stable—anything more than that costs copper."

Old stories percolated in the back of his mind. "I could work," Wuller offered.

"I don't need any help, thank you," the innkeeper said. "You take your bread, get your water from the fountain, and you be out of here first thing in the morning."

Wuller nodded, unsure what to say. "Thank you" seemed more than the man deserved.

Then he remembered his mission. "Oh, wait!" he said, reaching back to pull out the sketch. "I'm looking for someone. Have you seen her?"

The innkeeper took the drawing and studied it, holding it up to the light.

"Pretty," he remarked. "And nicely drawn, too. Never saw her before, though—she certainly hasn't come through here *this* year." He handed the portrait back. "What happened, boy—your girl run away?"

"No," Wuller said, suddenly reluctant to explain. "It's a long story."

"Fine," the innkeeper said, turning away. "It's none of my business in any case."

Wuller was gone the next morning, heading south, but not before listening to the chatter in the inn's common room and asking a few discreet questions when the opportunity arose.

He knew now that he was well inside the borders of the Baronies of Sardiron, that this inn, the Burning Pine, was the last before the border on the road north to Srigmor. Each spring and summer traders would head north, bringing the Srigmorites salt, spices, tools, and other things; each summer and fall they would come back home to Sardiron with wool, furs, and amber.

To the east lay The Passes, where a person could safely cross the mountains into the Valley of Tazmor, that fabulous realm that Wuller had never entirely believed in before.

There was little magic to be found around here, save for the usual village herbalists and a few primitive sorcerers and witches—but a mere fifteen leagues to the south was Sardiron of the Waters, where any number of magicians dwelt.

None of the people who had visited the inn had recognized the girl in the picture, or had any useful suggestions about finding her.

He also knew now that a lump of stale bread was not enough to still the growling of his stomach or stop the pinching he felt there, but that he could buy no better unless he could acquire some money—*real* money, copper or silver or even gold, not the cheap iron coins the peasants used among themselves.

As he left the village he sighed, and decided he needed to catch another squirrel or two—which would probably be a great deal more difficult now that he was in inhabited country.

Even as he decided this, he looked down the road ahead, past the trees on either side, and saw what looked like a very large clearing. He sighed again; squirrels preferred trees.

He watched both sides of the road carefully, but had spotted no game when he emerged into the "clearing" and realized his mistake.

This was no clearing. This was the edge of the forest.

Before him lay a vast expanse of open land, such as he had never seen before, or even imagined. Rolling hills stretched to the horizon covered with brown plowed fields and green grass, and dotted with farmhouses and barns. The highway drew a long, gentle curve across this landscape, no longer hidden by the forest gloom.

A few trees grew on the farms and hills, to be sure—shade trees sheltered some of the houses, and small groves of fruit trees or nut trees added some variety. In some places, neat lines of young trees marked boundaries between farms.

Most of the land was treeless, however, like the mountains where the sheep grazed above his home village.

He would find no squirrels here, he was sure.

Even as he came to that conclusion a rabbit leaped from concealment and dashed across the road in front of him, and he smiled. Where there was one rabbit, there would be others.

Two hours later he knocked on the door of a farmhouse by the roadside, a freshly skinned rabbit in hand.

In exchange for half the rabbit and all of its fur, he was permitted to cook over the kitchen fire and eat sitting at the table, chatting with his hostess while two cats and three young children played underfoot. Water from the farmer's well washed the meal down nicely.

Thus refreshed, he set out southward again.

Not long after that he passed through a fair-sized town—to him, it seemed impossibly large and bustling, but he knew it couldn't be any place he had ever heard of, since he was still well to the north of Sardiron of the Waters. A large stone structure stood atop a hill to the east, brooding over the town and a highway, and Wuller realized with a shock that that big ugly thing was a castle.

Having no money, Wuller marched directly through without stopping.

An hour later he encountered another village, and another one an hour or so after that, though these had no castles. They had inns—but Wuller had no money.

At sunset, he found himself on the outskirts of another town. Like the village of the Burning Pine and the town with the castle, this one had three highways leaving it, rather than just two. Unlike the other towns, here the directions weren't north, south, and east, but north, south, and northeast; it wasn't a crossroads, but a fork.

There were no fewer than three inns on the town square; Wuller marvelled at that.

He was tired and hungry, so he did more than marvel—he went to each in turn and asked if he could work for a meal and a bed.

The proprietor of the Broken Sword said no, but was polite. The owner of the Golden Kettle threw him out. And at the Blue Swan the innkeeper's daughter took pity on him and let him clean the stables in exchange for bread, cheese, ale, and whatever he could pick off the bones when the paying customers were finished with their dinners.

She also found him a bed for the night—her own.

No one at the Blue Swan could identify the girl in the portrait, but the innkeeper's daughter suggested he contact Senesson the Mage when he reached Sardiron itself. Senesson was a wizard who was said to be good at this sort of work.

There were a good many magicians of various sorts in her town of Keron-Vir, but she doubted any of them could help—and certainly not for free.

Wuller hesitated over that, but in the end he took her advice. After all, Sardiron of the Waters was only one day's walk away now, and he wanted to see the capital after coming so close. Besides, Darcy surely knew her own townspeople well enough to judge such things.

He did, however, stop in at the Golden Kettle and the Broken Sword to show the portrait around.

As he had expected, nobody knew who the girl in the picture was.

He shrugged, gathered his things, and set out.

He glimpsed the castle towers by midafternoon, and he could see the city walls and hear the thunder of the falls before the sun had set, but it was full dark by the time he reached the gates, with neither moon in the sky, and he made his entrance into Sardiron of the Waters by torchlight.

Even in the dark, he was impressed by the place. All the streets were paved with brick, flags, or cobbles—not one was bare earth, anywhere inside the walls. Where the hillside was steep the streets were built in steps, like a gigantic staircase.

The buildings were built up against each other, with no gap at all between them in many cases, while others left only a narrow alley—and even these alleys were paved.

Torches blazed at every intersection, and despite the gloom the streets were not deserted at all—people were going about their business even in the dark of night!

The sound was also amazing. The roar of the river was a constant background to everything, and fountains splashed in a dozen little squares and plazas, as well, as the city lived up to its name. A steady wind moaned endlessly around the black stone towers. On top of this were the normal sounds of a big, busy town—creaking cartwheels, lowing oxen, and a myriad of human voices chattering away.

The great castle of the Council of Barons reared up above the city, high atop the hill, looming darkly over everything.

The place was really like another world entirely, Wuller thought, as he looked about in confusion, wondering where he could eat or sleep.

A torchlit signboard caught his eye. There were no runes, but a faded painting of a dragon hatching from an egg.

That, he knew, must be an inn. And perhaps the dragon emblem was an omen, of sorts.

There was no broad window displaying ale kegs and pewter tankards, nor open door spilling light into the street, as there had been at the village inns he had seen so far—in fact, the only window here was a small one with bars on it, high above the street, and heavily curtained with black velvet. The only door was painted in four triangular sections, red at top and bottom and blue at either side, and studded with short spikes of black iron. It was tightly closed.

However, most of the city's architecture was equally strange and forbidding. He had seen no open doors or large windows *anywhere* inside the gates. This *had* to be an inn. He gathered his courage and knocked on the heavy wooden door, between the protruding spikes.

One of the spikes twisted, then slid back into the door and vanished; startled, Wuller looked into the hole it had left and saw an eye staring back at him.

Then the spike was replaced and the door swung open.

"We've no beds left," the old woman who had opened it announced, before he could say a word. "But if you've money for drink, we have plenty on hand."

"I don't have any money," Wuller explained. "But I'd be glad to work for a drink, or a bite to eat, or to sleep in a corner—I don't need a bed." He looked past her, into the common room, where a crowd of people was laughing and eating at tables set around a blazing hearth.

"We don't need any," the old woman began.

Wuller's gasp of astonishment interrupted her.

"Wait!" he said. "Wait!" He slid his pack off his shoulder and began digging through it.

"Young man," the woman said, "I don't have time for any nonsense . . ."

Wuller waved a hand at her. "No, wait!" he said. "Let me show you!" He pulled out the charcoal portrait and unrolled it.

"Lady, I've come all the way from northern Srigmor," Wuller

explained. "On an errand for my village—there's a dragon, and . . . well, you don't care about that. But look!" He showed her the picture.

She took it and held it up to the light from the commons.

"Seldis of Aldagmor," she said. "Good likeness, too." She glanced into the room beyond, where the young woman Wuller sought was sitting alone at a table eating dinner, then looked at the picture again, and from the portrait back to Wuller. "What do you have to do with her?"

Wuller decided quickly that this was not the time for the complete and exact truth, but for something simpler.

"I must speak with her," he said. "The seer in our village knew her face, but not her name, and sent me to find her. I had thought I would have to search for sixnights yet, or months—but there she is in your dining hall! Please, let me come in and speak with her!"

The old woman looked at the portrait again, then turned to look at the young woman in the room beyond, sitting alone at a small table. Then she shrugged, and handed the picture back to Wuller.

"No business of mine," she said. "You behave yourself, though—any trouble and I'll have the guard in here."

"No trouble, lady," Wuller said. "I promise!"

He settled into the chair opposite her, still astonished at his incredible good fortune, and astonished as well at her beauty. Neither Illuré's charcoal sketch nor the image in the oracle had really captured it.

"Hello," he said. "My name's Wuller Wulran's son."

She looked up from her plate and stared at him, but said nothing. The face was unmistakably the one he had seen in Kirna's oracle, the one that Illuré had drawn, with the vivid green eyes and the soft curls of dark brown hair. It was somewhat eerie to see it there in front of him as a real face, a small smudge of grease on the chin, rather than as a mere image.

The reality was more beautiful than the image, grease spot notwithstanding.

313

"I've been looking for you," he said.

She turned her attention back to her plate, where a few fried potato slices remained. Wuller glanced at them, reminded how hungry he was, then returned his gaze to the top of her head.

"No, really. I've come all the way from northern Srigmor looking for you. My village elders sent me." He pulled out the portrait and unrolled it. "See?"

She raised her head, put a slice of potato in her mouth, and began chewing. She blinked. Then she put down her fork, reached out, and took the picture.

She stared at it for a moment, then looked at Wuller. "Did you do this, just now?" she asked. "It's pretty good."

"No," Wuller said. "My Aunt Illuré drew it, more than a sixnight ago."

"A sixnight ago I was home in Aldagmor," the girl said, her gaze wary.

"I know," Wuller said. "I mean, no, I didn't know at all, really, but I know that Illuré didn't see you. I mean, didn't *really* see you."

"Then how . . . all right, then who's this Illuré person? How did she draw this? I don't know anybody named Illuré that I can recall."

"You've never met her. She's my aunt, back home in Srigmor. She drew this because she's the best artist of the people who saw your face in the oracle."

"*What* oracle?"

"Kirna's family oracle."

"Who's Kirna?"

"She's one of the village elders. Her family got this sorcerer's oracle during the Great War, and it was passed down ever since, and when the dragon came . . ."

"What dragon? One of . . . I mean, what dragon?"

"The dragon that's captured my village."

The girl stared at Wuller for a moment, and then sighed. "I think

314

you'd better start at the beginning," she said. "And explain the whole thing."

Wuller nodded, and took a deep breath, and began.

He described the dragon, how it had arrived one day without warning. He told her how it had killed Adar the Smith and given the village an ultimatum. He explained about the meeting in Kirna's hut, and how the oracle had shattered after showing them her face.

"And they sent me to find you," he said. "And here I am, and I thought I'd have to find some way to hire a magician to find you, only I don't have any money, and then by sheer luck, here you are!"

"No money?" she asked.

"No," he said.

"Does *anyone* in your village have any money?"

"Not anymore," he said, a trifle worried by this line of questioning.

He considered what he might do if she proved reluctant to come to the aid of the village. Small as he was for his age, he was still slightly bigger and stronger than she was; if worst came to worst, perhaps he could kidnap her and carry her home by force.

He hoped it wouldn't come to that. "Will you help?" he asked.

She looked down at the portrait she still held.

"Well," she admitted. "Your oracle wasn't *completely* silly. I do know something about dragons. My family—well, my father's a dragon-hunter. That's been the family business for a long, long time now. That's why I come to this particular inn when I'm here, the Dragon's Egg, because of the connection with dragons. I was here in the city selling the blood from my father's latest kill to the local wizards; they use it in their spells. And some of my uncles will get rid of dragons when they cause trouble. But ordinarily . . ." She frowned. "Ordinarily, we don't work for free. This dragon of yours doesn't sound like one I've heard of before, so there's no question of family responsibility—I mean, this isn't one that we taught to talk, or anything. At least, I don't *think* it is."

Wuller suggested desperately, "We could pay in sheep, or wool."

She waved that away. "How would I get sheep from Srigmor to Aldagmor? Even if they made the trip alive, I'd do better just buying them at home. Same for wool. We don't raise as much in Aldagmor as you do up north, but we have enough."

"If you don't come, though," Wuller said, "my village will die. Even if the dragon doesn't eat us, we'll starve when the sheep are gone."

She drew a deep sigh. "I know," she said. She looked around the room, as if hoping that someone else would suggest a solution, but nobody else was listening.

"Well," she said, "I suppose I'll have to go."

Wuller couldn't repress his smile; he beamed at her.

"But I don't like it," she added.

When she realized that he was not merely poor but totally penniless she bought him dinner, and allowed him to stay the night in her room at the inn. Wuller slept on the floor, and she slept on the bed, and he dared not suggest otherwise, either by word or deed.

For one thing, he had noticed that she carried a good long dagger in her belt, under the long vest she wore. The hilt was worn, which implied that it had seen much use and was not there simply for show.

In the morning she bought them both breakfast, gave the innkeeper a message to be sent to her father when next someone was bound to Aldagmor, bundled up her belongings, and stood waiting impatiently by the door while Wuller finished his meal and got his own pack squared away.

That done, the two of them marched side by side down the sloping streets toward the city gates. It had rained heavily during the night, and the cobbles were still damp and slippery, so that they had to move carefully.

This was the first time Wuller had seen Sardiron of the Waters by daylight, and he was too busy marvelling at the strange buildings of dark stone, the fountains everywhere, the broad expanse of the river and the falls sparkling in the morning sun, to pay much attention to his beautiful companion.

Once they were out of the gate, though, he found his gaze coming back to her often. She was very beautiful indeed. He had never seen another girl or woman to equal her.

He guessed her to be a year or two older than his own sixteen winters. Her face was too perfect to be much older than that, he thought, but she had a poise and self-assurance that he had rarely seen in anyone, of any age.

Although her beauty had been obvious, she had seemed less impressive, somehow, the night before; perhaps the dim light had been responsible. After all, as the saying had it, candlelight hides many flaws. Could it not equally well conceal perfection?

By the time they were out of earshot of the falls, and the towers of the council castle were shrinking behind them, he worked up the nerve to speak to her again for the first time since they had left the inn.

"You're from Aldagmor?" he asked.

Immediately, he silently cursed himself for such a banality. Where else could someone named Seldis of Aldagmor be from?

She nodded.

"Do you come here often, then?"

She looked at him, startled. "*Here?*" she asked, waving at the muddy highway and the surrounding farms. "I've never been *here* in my life!"

"I meant Sardiron," he said.

"Aldagmor's part of Sardiron," she replied. "Our baron's vice-chairman of the council, in fact."

"I meant the *city*, Sardiron of the Waters," Wuller explained with a trace of desperation.

"Oh," she said. "Well, that's not *here*. We left the city hours ago." This was a gross exaggeration, but Wuller did not correct her. "And I come down to the city about twice a year—usually once in the spring and once in the fall. I'm the one they can best spare, since I'm female and not strong enough for most of the work around . . . at home, so I make the trip to sell blood and hide and scales and order any supplies we need."

"Lucky we were there at the same time, then," Wuller said, smiling.

"Lucky for *you*," she said.

Wuller's smile vanished, and the conversation languished for a time.

The clouds thickened, and by midday it was drizzling. They stopped at an inn for lunch, hoping it would clear while they ate. Seldis paid for them both.

"This could be expensive," she remarked.

Wuller groped for something to say.

"We'll do our best to find a way to repay you," he said at last.

She waved it away. "Don't worry about it; it was my decision to come."

Two hours later, when they were on the road again and the rain had worked itself up into a heavy spring downpour, she snapped at him, "I don't know why I let you talk me into this!"

He said nothing.

They stayed the first night at the Blue Swan, in the town of Keron-Vir, but this time Darcy the innkeeper's daughter was much less cooperative. She took one look at Seldis, and despite the dripping hair and soaked clothing saw that this was a beauty she could not possibly match; she refused to talk to either of them after that.

Seldis once again paid for meals and a small room, and once again she slept in the bed while Wuller slept on the floor.

He lay awake for half an hour or so, listening to the rain dripping from the eaves, before finally dozing off. He dared not even look at Seldis.

The rain had stopped by the time they left the next morning, and by noon Seldis was once again willing to treat Wuller as a human being. After a few polite remarks, he asked, "So how will you get rid of the dragon?"

"I don't know," she said, shrugging. "I'll need to see what the situation is."

"But . . ." he began.

She held up a hand. "No, really," she said. "I don't know yet, and even if I did, I might not want to tell you. Trade secrets, you know—family secrets."

Wuller did not press the matter, but he worried about it. The oracle had said that Seldis could rid the village of the dragon, and Seldis herself seemed confident of her abilities, but still, he worried.

He remembered Alasha's words, about virgins sacrificing themselves, and shifted his pack uneasily. Would Seldis sacrifice herself to the dragon?

The idea seemed silly at first thought—she hardly looked suicidal. On the other hand, she had agreed to make the journey in the first place, which certainly wasn't a selfish decision. Just how altruistic was she?

He stole a glance at her. She was striding along comfortably, watching a distant hawk circling on the wind—scarcely the image he would expect of someone who intended to fling herself into a dragon's jaws for the good of others.

He shook his head slightly. No, he told himself, that couldn't be what she intended.

A nagging thought still tugged at him, though—it might turn out to be what the *oracle* had intended.

They stayed that night at the Burning Pine, in the village of Laskros, and as Wuller lay on the floor of their room, staring at the plank ceiling, he wondered if he was doing the right thing by taking Seldis to his village.

Why should she risk going there?

Why should *he* risk going back?

Wouldn't it be better for both of them if they forgot about the dragon and the village and went off somewhere—Aldagmor, perhaps—together? He would court her, as best he could with no money and no prospects and no family. . . .

No family. That was the sticking point. His family was waiting for him back home, relying on him. He couldn't let them down without even *trying.* Here he had had the phenomenal good luck to find his quarry quickly, as if by magic, and now he was considering giving up?

No, he had to go home, and to take Seldis with him, and then to help in whatever it took to dispose of the dragon.

He looked at her, lying asleep on the bed, her skin pale as milk in the light of the two moons, and then he rolled over and forced himself to go to sleep.

"We won't be staying in inns after this," he told her the next morning. "We should leave the highway late today and go cross-country."

She turned to stare at him. "I thought you said it was another few days," she said.

"It is," he replied.

She glanced eastward, at the forests that now lined that side of the road.

"If you headed east for two days, anywhere along this road, you'd wind up in the mountains," she said. "Three days, and you'd be on bare stone, wouldn't you?"

"If you headed due east," he agreed. "But I didn't say that. We head north-northeast."

"For three or four days, you said?"

He nodded.

"Why not follow the road until we're ready to turn east, then? We'll be almost paralleling it!"

"Because," he said reluctantly, "I don't know the way if we do that. I can only find the way home by following the trail of peeled branches I marked coming south."

"Oh," she said.

A few paces later she asked, "What were you planning to eat, if we're leaving the road?"

He stopped dead in his tracks. "I hadn't thought of that," he admitted.

320

Seldis stared at him with an unreadable expression. "What did you eat on the way down?" she inquired.

"Squirrels, mostly," he said.

She sighed. "I think," she said, "that we had best go back to the Burning Pine and buy some provisions. With more of *my* money, of course."

Shamefaced, he agreed, and they retraced their steps.

When they reached Laskros again, Wuller pointed out a bakery and a smokeshop, so they did not in fact return to the Burning Pine for food. They did, however, buy three more blankets there. Wuller was proud of himself for thinking of that, and thought it partly compensated for his earlier foolishness.

There were no other delays, but the shopping expedition was enough to force them to sleep by the roadside that night, without having left the highway. Wuller refused to travel after the light began to fade, for fear of missing his trail, so the two of them settled down a dozen yards from the road, built a fire, and ate a leisurely dinner of sweet rolls and smoked mutton.

They chatted quietly about trivial matters—friends and family, favorite tales, and the like, never mentioning dragons or anything else unpleasant. When they were tired, they curled up in their separate blankets and went to sleep.

The next day they proceeded slowly, watching for marks, and at mid-morning or slightly thereafter Wuller spotted a pine branch with the bark curled back on the top—the mark he had used.

Standing under that branch he could see the next, and from that one the next.

Retracing his steps from tree to tree, they left the road and headed cross-country, back toward his home village.

They slept two more nights in the forest, but late the following afternoon Wuller recognized the landscape beyond any question, and a moment later Seldis spotted smoke from the village fires drifting above the trees.

They waited, and crept into the village under cover of darkness, making their way silently to Wuller's own home.

When Wuller swung the door inward he heard his father bellow, "Who the hell is it at this hour?"

He peered around the door and said, "It's me, Wuller. I'm back."

Wulran was speechless. He stared silently as Wuller stepped inside, and as Wuller then gave Seldis a helping hand up the stoop.

The two travelers dropped their packs to the floor. Wuller pointed out a chair to Seldis, who settled into it gracefully and then put her tired feet up on another.

"You can sleep in Aunt Illuré's room, I guess," Wuller told her. He turned back to his father for confirmation, and was astonished to see old Wulran weeping silently, tears dripping down his beard on either side.

Wuller and Seldis arose late and spent the morning resting, soaking their tired feet and generally recovering from their journey. Meanwhile, Wuller's family scurried about the village, passing the word of his return and his success in finding the girl the oracle had shown them. A council meeting was called for that evening to discuss the next step.

Shortly after lunch, while Illuré was showing Seldis around the village, Wulran gestured for Wuller to come sit by him.

The lad obeyed, a trifle warily.

"Wuller," the old man whispered. "You know what Alasha thinks, don't you?"

"About what?" Wuller asked.

"About this girl you brought back—about how she's to rid us of the dragon."

Wuller thought he knew what his father meant, but he hesitated before saying anything.

"She's to be a sacrifice," Wulran said. "That's what Alasha thinks. We may have to feed her to the dragon."

Wuller's thoughts were turbulent; he struggled to direct them enough to get words out, and failed.

"It's necessary," Wulran said. "Give up one life, and a foreigner at that, so that we all can live."

"We don't know that," Wuller protested. "We don't know if it's necessary or not!"

Wulran shrugged. "True," he said. "We don't know for sure, but can you think of any other way that fragile little thing could rid us of the dragon?"

Wuller didn't answer at first, because in truth, he could not. At last he managed, weakly, "She knows tricks, family secrets."

"She may know the ritual of sacrifice, I suppose," Wulran said.

Wuller could stand no more; he rose and marched off.

Wulran watched him go, and was satisfied when he saw that his son was not immediately heading off in search of the Aldagmorite girl, to warn her of her fate.

Wuller wanted to think before he did anything rash. He looked up at the mountaintop, where the dragon was sunning itself, and then around at the village, where his kin were all busily going about their everyday business. The sheep were out on the upslope meadows, and the smith's forge was quiet, the fires banked, but villagers were hauling water, or stacking firewood, or sitting on benches carding wool. To the west of the smithy, the downwind side, a hardwood rick was being burnt down for charcoal.

He pulled the rather battered charcoal portrait out of his sleeve and looked at it.

Seldis' face looked back at him.

He rolled the picture up and stuffed it back in his sleeve. Then he looked around.

Illuré and Seldis had been down to the stream, and were returning with buckets of water. Wuller thought about running over to them and snatching Seldis away, heading back south with her, away from the village—but he didn't move. He stood and watched as she and Illuré brought their pails to the cistern and dumped them in.

Seldis was not stupid enough to have come all this way just to die, he told himself. She surely knew what she was doing. She would have some way to kill the dragon, some magical trade secret her father had taught her.

At least, he hoped so.

As the villagers gathered in Wulran's main room, that worthy man pulled his son aside and whispered, "We'll listen to what the girl has to say, but then we may need to get her out of here for a while. You understand. If that happens, you take her out and make sure she can't overhear anything. Later on we'll let you know where to bring her."

Wuller nodded unhappily, then took a seat in the corner.

He understood perfectly. He was to be the traitor ram who would lead Seldis to the slaughter, if it came to that.

A few minutes later Wulran closed the door and announced, "I think everybody's here."

A sudden expectant silence fell as the quiet chatter died away.

"I think you all know what's happened," Wulran said. "My son Wuller went south to find the girl the oracle showed us, and damn me if he didn't find her and bring her back, all in less than a month. The gods must like us, to make it as easy as that!"

He smiled broadly, and several polite smiles appeared in response.

"She's here now," he continued, "so let's bring her on out and get down to business!" He waved to Illuré, who led Seldis to the center of the room.

A murmur ran through the gathering at the sight of her.

"I am Seldis of Aldagmor," the girl announced. Several people looked startled, as if, Wuller thought, they hadn't expected her to talk. They had

324

been thinking of her as a thing, rather than a person, he guessed—the easier to sacrifice her to the dragon.

Wuller suppressed a growl at the thought. What good would sacrificing anybody do?

"My family has fought and killed dragons since the days of the Great War," Seldis continued, "and I think I ought to be able to rid you of this one. First, though, I need to know everything about it, and what you've already tried. Wuller Wulran's son told me a little on the journey up here from Sardiron, but I need to know everything."

Several voices spoke up in reply, but after a moment's confusion matters straightened themselves out. Kirna told the tale of the dragon's arrival and the death of Adar the Smith, and of the ancient sorcerous oracle and the image it had shown them. Her sister Alasha corrected her on various details, and Wulran interjected commentary as he thought appropriate.

Seldis listened, and asked a question every so often—did the dragon seem to favor one side over the other when it ripped the smith apart, or did it use both foreclaws equally? Was its flight steady, like a hawk's, or did it bob slightly, like a crow?

"So we all agreed that Wuller should go, and the next morning he did," Kirna concluded, "while we all waited here. From there on, lady, you know better than we."

Seldis nodded. "And what did you do while you waited?" she asked.

The villagers looked at her and at one another in surprise.

"Nothing," Alasha said. "We just waited."

Seldis blinked. "You didn't try anything else?" she asked.

Several people shook their heads.

"And you hadn't tried anything else before you talked to this oracle?"

"No," Kirna said. "What could we try? We saw what it did to Adar!"

Seldis stared around at the gathered villagers, and Wuller knew that she was trying hard to conceal genuine astonishment.

What had she *expected* them to try, he wondered.

Seldis closed her lips into a thin line, and then said, "Well, you haven't been very much help, not having tried anything, but I certainly know what I'm going to try first. I can't believe none of you ever thought to try it. You feed the beast a sheep every day, don't you?"

Heads nodded, and Wulran said, "Yes."

"Then I'll need about two dozen little pouches," Seldis said. "Pigs' bladders would be perfect. I didn't see many pigs around, though, so sheep bladders would do. Sausage casing should work, or even leather purses, if they're sewn very tightly. They need to be small enough to stuff down a sheep's throat—but not too small, and it doesn't matter if it hurts the sheep."

A confused murmur ran through the room.

Wuller blinked, puzzled. He glanced at his father in time to see Wulran giving him a meaningful stare and making a wiggling gesture with one finger.

His father thought Seldis was mad, he realized.

He rebelled mentally at that. He had spent a sixnight with her, and he knew she was not mad. Whatever she intended to do had to be a dragon-hunter's trick, not a madwoman's folly.

And whatever it was, he would help her with it.

The meeting broke up quickly after that. Seldis refused to explain what she had in mind. Most of the people didn't seem to think she really had *anything* in mind, but everyone agreed to let her have a day to make her attempt.

Wulran managed another surreptitious chat with his son, and made it quite clear to Wuller that it was his duty to keep an eye on Seldis and make sure she didn't slip away.

Wuller agreed, unhappily, not to let her out of his sight.

After breakfast the next morning Seldis rose from the table, stretched, and said, "I'm going for a walk to gather some herbs. Could someone lend me a basket? A big one?"

Illuré produced one that Seldis found suitable, and the three of them, Seldis, Illuré, and Wuller, strolled out into the woods beyond the village.

They walked for several minutes in companionable silence, enjoying the warm spring weather. Wuller glanced at Illuré, and then at Seldis, and then back at his aunt.

He had no desire to play traitor ram. If he could get Seldis away from Illuré he would warn her what the elders had in mind, and give her a chance to slip away.

Just then Seldis said, "I don't see what I'm looking for anywhere. Illuré, where can I find wolfsbane or nightshade around here?"

"Find what?" Illuré said, startled. "I never heard of those; what are they?"

Seldis looked at Illuré, equally startled. "Why, they're plants, fairly common ones. Wolfsbane has little flowers with hoods on them; of the sort that would be blooming at this time of year, the blossoms are yellow and very small, but the other kinds can have blue or purple or white flowers."

"I never heard of it," Illuré said. "And I don't think I've ever seen it. Are you sure it grows around here?"

"Maybe not," Seldis said, her expression worried. "What about nightshade?"

"What is it?" Illuré asked.

Seldis said, "Well, it's got flowers like little bells, dark red ones, and little black berries."

Illuré stood and puzzled for a moment.

"I don't think we have that, either," she said at last. "If you want flowers, we have daisies."

"No, I don't want flowers!" Seldis snapped.

"Well, then, what *do* you want?" Illuré asked.

"Never mind. Let's just go back." She turned and headed toward the village.

Wuller and Illuré followed her, baffled.

Wuller glanced at Illuré, wondering if this might be the best chance they would have for Seldis to slip away, but then he decided to wait. The Aldagmorite seemed far more worried than she had earlier, but still not frightened; Wuller thought she must still have something in mind, even without her magical herbs.

In the village they found Wulran glowering at them from his doorstep, and Kirna sitting nearby with a basket full of sausage casings. Other villagers were watching from a safe distance.

"Will these do?" Kirna asked, displaying her basket.

Seldis shook her head. "Those would be perfect," she said, "but I'm afraid my idea won't work. I couldn't find what I needed. I guess I'll have to think of something else."

Wulran snorted. "Lady," he said, "I guess you will, and quickly. The oracle said you could save us from the dragon, but you won't do it by wandering the hills, and we can't risk your wandering off completely. From now on, you'll stay here, in the village, under guard."

"But . . ." Seldis began.

"No argument!" Wulran shouted. The other villagers murmured.

Seldis didn't argue. At Wulran's direction, she was led into the house and sent into Illuré's room, where new brackets were set on either side of the door, and a bar placed across.

The window, too, was barred, and Seldis was a prisoner.

Wuller, quite involuntarily, found himself appointed her jailer.

"She's mad, and the mad are dangerous," his father explained, out of her hearing. "But she trusts you. She'll stay if you guard her. And if she can tell us how to kill the dragon, all well and good, but if she can't then we'll put her out as tomorrow's sacrifice. That must be what the oracle intended in the first place."

Wuller didn't try to argue. He knew Seldis was not mad, but he had no idea what she had been planning, and also saw that his father was frightened and angry and would brook no discussion.

Something would have to be done, of course, but not with words.

Wuller settled down at the door to Seldis' improvised cell and waited.

Early in the afternoon, when everyone else had grown bored and left, he called in to her, "What's so special about those plants you wanted?"

"Am I allowed to speak now, then?" she asked sarcastically.

"Of course you are. Listen, I'm very sorry about all this; it's not *my* fault!"

"Oh, I know, but it's so *stupid*! There's nothing magical about dragon-killing; it's easy, if you put a little thought into it. Everyone around here is just too scared to *think*! What good does it do to lock me up like this?"

"It keeps you from running away," Wuller said, a bit hesitantly.

"But that's idiotic. After walking all the way up here, why would I run away now?"

"Because . . ." Wuller began, and then stopped.

If she didn't already know she was to be sacrificed, would it do any good to tell her?

Maybe not.

"Never mind that for now," he said instead. "What's so special about those plants?"

"They're poisonous. Wuller, what are you hiding? What are they . . . oh, no. They aren't really *that* stupid and superstitious, are they? A maiden sacrifice, is that what they're planning?"

Wuller didn't answer. Her answer to his question had brought sudden comprehension. He thought for a moment, and saw it all—not merely what Seldis had originally planned, but what they could do instead.

"Wuller? Are you there?" she called through the door.

"I'm here," he said. "And don't worry. Just wait until tonight. Trust me."

"*Trust* you?" She laughed bitterly.

When Wuller brought in her dinner Seldis refused to speak to him; she glared silently, and after a muttered apology he didn't press it.

Later, though, when the others were all asleep, he carefully unbarred the door, moving slowly to avoid making noise or bumping anything with the heavy bar.

"Come on," he whispered.

She stepped out quickly. "Where?" she asked. "Are you just letting me go?"

He shook his head. "No, no," he said. "We're going to kill the dragon, just as you planned. I've got a sheep tied outside, and Kirna left the basket of sausage casings; everything's ready."

"You found wolfsbane? Or nightshade?"

"No," he said. "Those don't grow around here."

Seldis started to protest.

"Hush! It's all right, really, I know what I'm doing. Come on, and don't make any more noise!"

She came.

In the morning Wulran found his son sound asleep, leaning against the barred door of Illuré's bedroom. Wuller looked rather dirtier and more rumpled than Wulran remembered him being the night before, and Wulran looked the lad over suspiciously.

He hoped that Wulran hadn't gone and done anything stupid.

He wondered if there was anything to the stories about dragons demanding virgins for sacrifice.

How could a dragon tell, though?

More magic at work, presumably.

Whatever magic was involved, Wulran hoped that the girl was still in there to be sacrificed, and hadn't slipped out in the night. What if the boy's dirt came from chasing through the woods after her?

He poked Wuller with a toe. "Wake up," he said.

Wuller blinked and woke up. "Good morning," he said. Then he yawned and stretched.

"Is the girl still in there?" Wulran demanded.

Wuller looked at the door, still closed and barred, and then up at his father. "I think so," he said. "She was last I saw."

"And she'll be there when we come to get her for the sacrifice?"

Wuller yawned again. "You can't sacrifice her," he said. "I already fed the dragon this morning, just before first light. It's probably dead by now."

"What's probably dead by now, a sheep? You fed it a sheep?"

Wuller nodded. "Yes, I fed it a sheep, and of course the *sheep* is dead, but what I meant was, the *dragon* is probably dead."

His father stared at him.

"What?" he asked.

Wuller got to his feet.

"I said, the dragon is probably dead by now."

"Have you gone mad, too, now?" Wulran asked. "I didn't know it was catching."

"I'm not mad," Wuller said. He didn't like his father's tone, though, and he suddenly decided not to say anymore.

"Step aside, boy," Wulran demanded. "I want to be sure she's in there."

Wuller stepped aside.

He said nothing as his father unbarred the door and found Seldis peacefully asleep in Illuré's bed.

He said nothing at all for the rest of the morning, not even when the men came later and found Seldis still sleeping, and picked her up and carried her off to the flat stone where the dragon took its meals.

Seldis awoke the moment they laid hands on her, but she didn't scream or struggle. She put up no resistance as the party carried her to the flat, bloodstained stone outcropping where the dragon accepted its tribute.

There she was lowered gently to the ground. One end of a rope was tied around her ankles, the other to the tall scorched stump beside the stone where, prior to this, only sheep had been tethered. Her hands, too, were tied.

Then she was placed on the stone, and the others stepped back, leaving her there.

She looked up at the villagers and addressed Wuller directly.

"You better be right about those mushrooms," she said.

He looked up at the mountainside above them, and smiled. "See for yourself," he said, pointing.

She looked where Wuller pointed, and saw the tip of the dragon's tail, hanging down from a ledge like an immense bloated vine. No one else had noticed; they had been paying attention to their captive.

The tail was utterly limp.

"See?" Wuller said. "It's dead, just as you said it would be."

The villagers looked, and then stared in openmouthed astonishment.

"We'd better go make sure," Seldis said. "I'm not familiar with those mushrooms. If it's just sick, we'd better go finish it off while it's still weak."

"Right," Wuller said. He knelt beside her and drew his knife, then began sawing at the ropes.

Wulran tore his gaze from that dangling, lifeless tail and looked down at the bound young woman. "What did you *do*?" he asked.

"We killed the dragon, Wuller and I," she said. "I told you I knew how." Her wrists were free, and she sat up.

"But *how*?" Wulran asked.

"It was easy. Wuller let me out last night, and we went out in the woods and gathered mushrooms, two baskets full—those thin ones with the white stems and the little cups at the bottom. You don't have wolfsbane and nightshade around here, but you had to have *something* poisonous, and Wuller told me about the mushrooms."

"But how . . ." someone began.

Seldis ignored him and kept right on speaking.

"We ground up the mushrooms and stuffed them into those sausage casings, and then we stuffed *those* down the throat of a sheep Wuller

332

brought, and then we tied the sheep here—oh, look, some of its blood got on my skirt! Didn't you people see it was still wet?"

Wuller grinned at her as the rope around her ankles parted.

"Anyway," Seldis continued, "we tied it up out here, and the dragon ate it, and that was that."

"Poison mushrooms?" someone asked. "That's all it took?"

"Of *course* that's all!" Seldis said, plainly offended. "Do you think I'm an amateur? I know how to kill dragons, I told you!"

"You're sure it's dead?" Wulran asked. "I mean, I know those mushrooms are deadly, but that's a *dragon* . . ."

Seldis shrugged. "A dragon's just a beast. A very special beast, a magical beast perhaps, but a beast, of mortal flesh and blood. Poison will kill it, sure as it will kill anything."

"We need to check," Wulran said gruffly. "We can't just take your word for it that it's dead."

"You're right," Seldis said. "If I got the dose wrong it might just be sick for a few days. We need to go see, and if it's still alive we need to finish it off while it's weak."

The villagers looked at one another.

"You don't all have to go," Seldis said. "Wuller and I will check."

"I'll come, too," Wulran said.

"If you like. There's one thing, though—could someone fetch me a wineskin, the biggest you can find?"

The villagers were puzzled, but none of them were inclined to argue with her any further.

Several minutes later, the three of them, Wulran, Wuller, and Seldis, set out up the mountainside to the ledge where the dragon's tail was draped. Seldis carried an immense empty wineskin, the sort that would be hung up on the village commons during Festival, and still no one had had the nerve to ask her why.

They crept up onto the ledge, past the thick tail, and down into the stony crevice where most of the dragon lay, motionless and silent.

"It *looks* dead," Wuller whispered as they came even with the great belly.

Seldis nodded. "Looks can be deceiving, though." She took out her long knife and crept forward, toward the head.

"What are you . . ." Wuller began.

"Stay back!" she hissed. "I'm going to make sure it's dead."

Wulran reached out and grabbed Wuller's arm, and pulled him back to the edge of the ledge, where they could both slide down out of sight in a hurry if the need arose.

They waited for what seemed hours to Wuller, but watching the sun he realized it was only a few minutes.

"It's all right," Seldis called at last. "It's dead!"

Wuller ran back down the crevice after her, calling, "How can you be sure?"

Then he saw what she had done. She had rammed her long knife up to the hilt into one of the dragon's eyes.

If there had been any life in it at all, it would surely have reacted to that!

After that, she had swung her wineskin into position and cut open a vein, allowing the dragon's blood to spill into the waiting receptacle. Wuller stared at the trickle of purplish ichor.

"This will cover my expenses," she said, almost apologizing. "Wizards can always use more dragon's blood."

"It's really dead," Wuller said. "We did it! Seldis, we all owe you more than we could ever pay you, and particularly after the treatment you got. I'm sure that everyone in the village will agree with me on that."

Wulran came up behind him and said, "If they don't at first, I'll make them agree, young lady."

Seldis shrugged. "It's nothing. This one was easy. Hell, you people should have thought of it yourselves! You knew about the mushrooms, and you saw it eat a sheep every day—why didn't you try *anything*?"

Wulran shrugged. "We had that prophecy, that oracle—that you would come save us." He smiled crookedly.

Seldis stared at him.

"So you were going to sacrifice me?" she asked. "You thought that would save you?"

Wulran opened his mouth to reply, and then closed it again.

"Did it occur to any of you that if sacrificing me was *not* what the oracle had meant, that you'd be killing the one person who you'd been told could save you?"

Wulran merely blinked at that; he didn't even try to respond.

Wuller said, "I wouldn't have let them."

"Ha! I didn't see you doing much to stop them this morning!"

"But we'd already poisoned the dragon by then!"

"And what if the poison hadn't worked?"

Wuller's mouth opened, like his father's, but nothing came out.

Then he closed his mouth firmly. "I wouldn't have let them, unless they killed *me* first," he said.

Seldis looked at him for a long moment, then at the dragon. The stream of blood had stopped; she capped the wineskin and hung it over one shoulder. Then she shoved her way past both the son and the father and marched out of the crevice.

Wulran and Wuller watched her go. Wulran threw his son an apologetic glance, but Wuller was in no mood to accept it. He ran after her.

When he caught up with her he could think of nothing to say, and so the two of them walked silently back down to the village side by side.

When they reached the village, Seldis announced, "I'm tired, Wuller; we were up all night. I'm going to get some sleep."

He nodded. "Good idea," he said.

After she had gone into Illuré's bedroom—leaving the door open and unbarred, this time—he headed for his own bed.

Wuller awoke that afternoon to find her up and dressed and checking her pack. The wineskin of dragon's blood was at her feet.

"I'll be going now," she said, without looking at him.

Wuller blinked at her from the doorway of his bedroom. He looked around at the familiar house—his mother's painted tiles on the walls, the iron skillets hung by the kitchen, the broad stone hearth. His parents and his Aunt Illuré were somewhere nearby. Around the house stood his village, all the world he had known until a few days ago, home to his entire extended family and everyone he had ever known.

All of it was safe now, with the dragon dead, and Seldis was no longer needed. She would be going back to her own home, in distant Aldagmor, out there in the hostile and unfamiliar world beyond the village, the world where Wuller knew no one and had nothing.

"Wait for me," he said, snatching up his clothes.

To his surprise, she did.

ABOUT THE AUTHORS

ISAAC ASIMOV was born in the Soviet Union to his great surprise. He moved quickly to correct the situation. When his parents emigrated to the United States, Isaac (three years old at the time) stowed away in their baggage. He has been an American citizen since the age of eight.

Brought up in Brooklyn, and educated in its public schools, he eventually found his way to Columbia University and, over the protests of the school administration, managed to annex a series of degrees in chemistry, up to and including a Ph.D. He then infiltrated Boston University and climbed the academic ladder, ignoring all cries of outrage, until he found himself professor of biochemistry.

Meanwhile, at the age of nine, he found the love of his life (in the inanimate sense) when he discovered his first science fiction magazine. By the time he was eleven, he began to write stories, and at eighteen, he actually worked up the nerve to submit one. It was rejected. After four long months of tribulation and suffering, he sold his first story and, thereafter, never looked back.

What was left except quantity? At the present time, he has published over 340 books, and shows no signs of slowing up. He is married to Janet Jeppson, psychiatrist and writer, has two children by a previous marriage, and lives in New York City.

TERRY BROOKS was born in Illinois in 1944. He received his undergraduate degree from Hamilton College, Clinton, New York, where he majored in English literature, and his graduate degree from the School of Law at Washington & Lee University, Lexington, Virginia. He was a practicing attorney until recently; he has now retired to become a full-time author.

A writer since high school, he published his first novel, *The Sword of Shannara*, in 1977 and the sequels *The Elfstones of Shannara* in 1982 and *The Wishsong of Shannara* in 1985. *Magic Kingdom for Sale—Sold!* began a bestselling new series for him in 1986. Brooks presently lives in the Northwest.

C. J. CHERRYH's first book, *Gate of Ivrel*, was published in 1976. Since then she has become a leading writer of science fiction and fantasy, known for extraordinary originality, versatility, and superb writing. She has won Hugo awards for her books *Downbelow Station* and *Cyteen*. She lives in Oklahoma.

LESTER DEL REY was born in a small farming community in Minnesota. In 1931, he moved to Washington, D.C., to attend college, but dropped out after two years to work at a series of assorted jobs.

At age twenty-two, he wrote his first story, and from then on devoted himself to writing, with some fifty books and numerous shorter works to his credit. He was editor, story doctor, agent, and expert in the science fiction and fantasy field.

Del Rey is now vice president of Ballantine Books and fantasy editor for Del Rey Books. He has been a full-time editor for Ballantine, specializing in fantasy for the last sixteen years. At the age of seventy-six, he is still editing the best writers in fantasy and finding new writers to swell the ranks.

SUSAN ELIZABETH DEXTER was born in July 1955 in western Pennsylvania. She has spent her entire life to date in that area, except for shopping trips to New York and side trips to World Fantasy Conventions. She had an uneventful education until high school, when she enrolled in a three-year commercial art course in a local vocational-technical school. She has been employed as a fashion illustrator, layout and freelance artist for the past eleven years.

An interest in illustration led her to adult fantasy, via its many award-winning cover designs, but the roots of her interest go far deeper. In childhood her main literary interests were fairy tales and horses, and as she grew up she moved into historical fiction and the occult. From there, the next step was logical.

Her interests include omnivorous reading, fencing, herbs, macramé, weaving, soft sculpturing, and fine arts.

WAYLAND DREW was born in Oshawa, Ontario, and received his early education there. He began to write seriously in high school and continued while studying English language and literature at the University of Toronto. Since graduation he has combined high school teaching and writing. He is the author of *The Erthring Cycle*, a trilogy published by Del Rey Books.

Mr. Drew and his wife Gwendolyn live in Bracebridge, where he has taught English for eleven years. They have four children.

BARBARA HAMBLY has been, at various times in her life, a high school teacher, a model, a waitress, a technical editor, a professional graduate student, an all-night clerk at a liquor store, and a karate instructor. Born in San Diego, she grew up in Southern California, with the exception of one high school semester spent in New South Wales, Australia. Her interest in fantasy began at an early age with reading *The Wizard of Oz* and has continued ever since.

She attended the University of California, Riverside, specializing in medieval history. In connection with this, she spent a year at the University of Bordeaux in the south of France and worked as a teaching and research assistant at UC Riverside, eventually earning a master's degree in the subject. At the university, she also became involved in karate, making Black Belt in 1978 and competing in several national-level tournaments. She now lives in Los Angeles.

KATHERINE KURTZ was born in Coral Gables, Florida, during a hurricane and has led a whirlwind existence ever since. She holds a bachelor of science degree from the University of Miami, Florida, and a master of arts degree in English history from UCLA. She studied medicine before deciding that she would rather write, and is an Ericksonian-trained hypnotist. Her scholarly background also includes extensive research in religious history, magical systems, and other esoteric subjects.

Katherine Kurtz's literary works include the well-known *Deryni*, *Camber* and *Kelson* trilogies of fantasy fiction, an occult thriller set in World War Two England, and a number of Deryni-related short stories. Ms. Kurtz lives in Ireland with her husband and son in a Victorian gothic-revival house that looks like Toad Hall.

ANNE MCCAFFREY was born on April 1, and has since tried to live up to such an auspicious natal day. Her first novel was created in Latin class and might have brought her instant fame, as well as an A, had she attempted to write in the language. Much chastened, she turned to the stage and became a character actress, appearing in the first successful summer music circus at Lambertville, New Jersey. She studied voice for nine years and, during that time, became intensely interested in the stage direction of opera and operetta, ending this phase of her life with the stage direction of the American premiere of Carl Orff's *Ludus De Nato Infante Mirificus*, in which she also played a witch.

By the time the three children of her marriage were comfortably at school most of the day, she had already achieved enough success with short stories to devote full time to writing.

Between her frequent appearances in the United States and England as a lecturer and guest-of-honor at science fiction conventions, Ms. McCaffrey lives at Dragonhold, in the hills of County Wicklow, Ireland, with two cats, two dogs, and assorted horses. Of herself, Ms. McCaffrey says, "I have green eyes, silver hair, and freckles; the rest changes without notice."

LAWRENCE WATT-EVANS was born and raised in eastern Massachusetts, the fourth of six children in a house full of books. Both parents were inveterate readers, and both enjoyed science fiction; he grew up reading anything handy, including a wide variety of speculative fiction. His first attempts at writing SF were made at the age of seven.

After surviving twelve years of public schooling, he followed in the footsteps of father and grandfather and attended Princeton University. Less successful than his ancestors, he left without a degree after two attempts.

Being qualified for no other enjoyable work, he began trying to sell his writing between halves of his college career, with a notable lack of success. After his final departure from Princeton, however, he produced *The Lure of the Basilisk*, which sold readily, beginning his career as a full-time writer. *Nightside City* was his twelfth novel; of the twelve, six are science fiction and six are fantasy.

He married in 1977, has two children, and lives in the Maryland suburbs of Washington, D.C.

ABOUT THE ARTIST

MICHAEL PANGRAZIO was born in Glendale, California. At the young age of twenty-one, he began his career as a matte and special effects painter, creating extraordinarily lifelike backgrounds and environments to be used in film. For many years, he was matte painting supervisor for Industrial Light & Magic, Lucasfilm's special effects division, and has won many awards for his work, including two Emmys.

He now has his own special effects company in Marin, California. So rare is his artistic expertise that only a handful of people in the world do what he does for a living.

Michael Pangrazio lives with his wife and his son and daughter in Marin.